Unintended Consequences

A Novel

By Brian Daneman

This is a work of fiction and, as such, it is a product of the author's creative imagination. All names of characters appearing in these pages are fictitious except for those of public figures. Any similarities of characters to real persons, whether living or dead, excepting public figures, is coincidental. Any resemblance of incidents portrayed in this book to actual events, other than public events, is likewise coincidental.

ISBN: 978-0-578-00809-7

Library of Congress Control Number: ***To be determined.***

Dedication

I would like to thank all of my friends and family who supported me along this long and arduous journey. There are so many of you who took the time to offer not only encouragement, but also advice and direction when I needed it, which was much of the time. I owe a special thanks to those of you who read and critiqued each and every chapter. Sometimes you told me things I didn't want to hear, but I listened, and this book is better for it.

Last but certainly not least, I dedicate this book to my wife, Gerri, and my two children, André and Lily. Without your ongoing support and encouragement I would never have fulfilled this little dream of my mine. This book is as much yours as it is mine. Without the three of you, there is no book. I love you with all of my heart for that.

Brian Daneman

Table of Contents

“The ‘**law of unintended consequences**’ (also called the ‘**law of unforeseen consequences**’) states that any purposeful action will produce some unintended consequences. Stated in other words, each cause has more than one effect, and these effects will invariably include at least one unforeseen side effect. The unintended side effect can potentially be more significant than any of the intended effects.”

Robert K. Merton

Prologue

The Emergency Room

Riverview Medical Center Emergency Room, Critical Care Unit
September 8th, Saturday 1:00 a.m.

"He's stopped breathing. His heart rate's plummeting and his pupils are fixed and dilated. Give me two CCs of epinephrine, one milligram of atropine and get the damn crash cart in here stat!"

Dr. Malcolm Foster hastily jammed the two syringes into his patient's chest and then rechecked his vital signs. "Get ready to bag and tube him!" yelled Foster as the nurse next to him wiped the sweat from his brow. Foster looked to his charge nurse. "Connie, what do we know about this kid? What the hell has he taken, who brought him in…anything?" As Foster labored to budge the cumbersome, unresponsive patient, he searched the kid's arms for needle marks or other telltale signs of trouble. Struggling, he said, "Jesus, Connie, this kid's huge; give me a hand over here."

Connie rushed around the gurney to assist the doctor. She spoke in a clipped and professional manner. "His girlfriend called for the ambulance about twenty minutes ago. The Middletown rescue squad found him unconscious and barely breathing at a high school house party. He was face down in a pool of vomit. They tried unsuccessfully to wake him so they put him on oxygen, started an IV and rushed him over."

Connie grunted when she tried to lift the lifeless patient's shoulder. "According to witnesses, he just collapsed and never regained consciousness. The girlfriend came in with the ambulance, but she's a mess. She's outside on a cell phone trying to reach the boy's parents. Maybe she can... Oh no...doctor...I think he's seizing!"

Suddenly the patient went from catatonic to thrashing about violently. Dr. Foster climbed up on the gurney, straddled the patient and pinned the full force of his six-foot, two-hundred-pound frame on top of the boy in an effort to control his flailing limbs. Even with the doctor's considerable bulk resting squarely on the patient's chest, the kid's back arched skyward at an inconceivable angle.

"Connie! Come on! Get me some straps and call for help. This kid's as strong as an ox. I can't hold him down much longer! If he keeps this up, he's going to crack a vertebra in his spine!"

Connie screamed out into the hallway for assistance and within seconds two passing orderlies raced into the room. Between the four of them they barely managed to restrain the racking spasms of the wildly convulsing patient.

Once Dr. Foster got help and had a chance to think, he realized that the epinephrine and the atropine were the problem. They had to be. "Goddamn it! We have to find out what this kid is on! Get his blood drawn and tell the lab I need his tox screen like yesterday! And, Connie, get the girlfriend in here now! I need to know what this kid's taken before I can treat him with anything else. Damn it...the epinephrine almost killed him."

No sooner than he gave the order, the patient seized again and a mixture of blood and mucous spewed violently forth from his mouth. "Move, Connie! Get his girlfriend in here now!"

Connie dashed out into the hall and scanned the crowded waiting room until she spied a petite blonde huddled all by herself in the far corner of the room. The girl was shaking and crying hysterically into her cell phone. Connie ran over and snatched the phone away. Then she grabbed the girl by the shoulders and calmly but urgently said, "Okay, honey, what's your name?"

"I…ah…ah…I'm Esprit Burke. What's happening to Casey? Is he okay? Please tell me he's going to be okay!"

"No…he's not okay. He's in really bad shape and we need your help. You've got to pull yourself together and come with me. You need to tell the doctor what happened to your friend Casey. Do you understand me?"

Esprit, like the classic deer caught in headlights, simply froze and didn't respond. Connie again shook her shoulder. "Esprit, we need to know what's in his system, drugs, alcohol, anything, before we can help him!"

"We…we…were at a party. Casey doesn't do drugs…he hates kids that do drugs. I…I don't know, I mean I'm not sure...I think he might have had a couple of beers. There was a keg at the party. I...don't know…I don't know…I don't know! Oh shit, I need to call my father!" She reached for her cell phone.

With no time to waste, Connie dropped the cell phone on the floor and kicked away, then she pinned Esprit's shoulders to the wall. "Listen, girl, now I know who you are, and I sure as hell know who your daddy is, but he can't help you or your boyfriend right now, so get yourself together and come with me!"

She grabbed Esprit and half-dragged her back through the emergency room door. When they re-entered the triage room all hell had broken loose. Supplies and medical instruments were scattered all around the room, and the gurney, with the patient still bucking and heaving, was rolling and rattling across the tile floor. Dr. Foster and the two orderlies were straining to their absolute physical limit, still trying to hold the patient down.

Suddenly one of the orderlies lost his footing and slipped on the splatters of blood and bodily fluids that covered the floor. He crashed to the floor, but was back up and helping in no more than a second. The seizure raged out of control. Connie and the girl watched in horror as the patient's eyes rolled back in his head and blood seeped freely from his mouth and nostrils. Under the harsh florescent lights his skin had turned a deep purple and the veins in his arms, legs and neck appeared ready to burst right through his taught glistening skin.

Dr. Foster looked up at Esprit. Frantically he screamed, “Young lady, this boy is in the midst of a massive seizure. His temperature has just climbed past hundred and four, and he’s in big trouble! If you want to save his life, you’d better tell me what the hell he’s on right now!”

Chapter One

Sports, Steroid injections, and a Family Feud

One Week Earlier
September 1st Saturday Morning, 7 a.m.

Casey Collins smacked the button on his alarm clock to kill the awful sound that had woken him from a deep and peaceful sleep. He opened his eyes to yet another gorgeous late summer day and brushed his fingers through a tangle of curly black hair. As the early morning sun streamed through the blinds of his bedroom window he rolled out of bed, dressed only in a pair of boxers, and hit the hardwood floor to begin his daily routine. Each morning he religiously did four sets of fifty push-ups and four sets of fifty crunches as soon as he got out of bed. His six-foot-three, two-hundred-and-thirty-five-pound frame sped through the exercise ritual without even breaking a sweat while his heart never rose above sixty beats per minute.

The extremely low heart rate wasn't just because of his superb physical condition. He'd trained himself to shut down his mind while exercising to everything but the soft cooing sounds of the two gray doves that nested in the branches of the willow tree just outside his open window. This morning as he ran through his sets nothing existed for him but the sound of their sweet repetitive calls. When he finished, Casey sat back against his bed and watched the doves for a while, smiling softly.

These two gray doves, who Casey affectionately called Romeo and Juliet, had come back each spring to that exact spot in the willow tree to nest and mate for as far back as Casey could remember, and their soft warbling had become an integral part of his morning mantra.

For Casey, an eighteen-year-old senior year at Middletown South High School, this was the start of the year when his exercise routine would finally pay off, the year when college recruiters would make their calls. Casey had already been approached by virtually every major division-one school in the country with a football team, but today was the first day that he was eligible to receive official scholarship notifications. He expected to receive dozens, but he only wanted one. He wanted to play for Penn State, Linebacker U., home of the 'Nittany Lions' and coached by none other than the legendary Joe Paterno.

Paterno was thought to be over the hill by most of the so-called experts in college athletics, but to Casey he was still a football god. Paterno had put more linebackers in the NFL than any other coach in history, and Penn State was just the next logical step on Casey's well-ordered path to playing in the National Football League.

Casey sprang from his bed as effortlessly as a ballet dancer. He walked over to his desk and clicked on his computer. First things first, he'd get last night's scores off the Net. Who needed to watch all that crap on *SportsCenter* when you had the Internet?

He scanned the overnight sports news and scores, and then checked his email account. There were three emails; two from recruiters not from Penn State – *delete, delete* – and one from his girlfriend, Esprit Burke.

Casey and Esprit had been dating exclusively since the middle of their sophomore year, but recently Casey and Esprit's relationship had hit some rocky territory. Just two nights earlier, Esprit had called Casey around midnight begging him to join her at a party on the beach out at Sandy Hook State Park. When she called that night, Casey wasn't sure if he was more pissed that she'd woken him up or because she was totally trashed again. He remembered listening to her blathering for as long as he could stand it and then realizing she was too fucked up to drive so he had no choice, he'd climbed out of bed and left to pick her up.

When he pulled up at the beach a short fifteen minutes later, Esprit's car was gone, and she was nowhere to be found. Casey searched up and down the beach for almost an hour, feeling like a fool. It was out of his way, but he drove by her house to see if she'd made it home safe. Sure enough, when he looked through the gates of her family's estate, he could see her car parked, half on the driveway and half on the grass, up the hill in front of her house. By then it was almost two a.m. and he was pretty pissed. They'd fought about it for hours yesterday. Casey felt Esprit was spending way too much time with her friend Jamie partying at the beach, while Esprit insisted that it was the end of the summer, and that's what summers were for. On this particular issue they couldn't find common ground.

Casey opened the email. As always it was short and to the point –

hi stud, hope you are not mad anymore. party next friday at stacie's. please don't forget. call me about tonight. love me ☺ xoxo

The email didn't resolve anything. The real problem was that while Casey was steadfastly focused on conditioning, football, grades, and Esprit, in that order, Esprit was focused on Casey, partying, acting, and getting as far away from her father as she could. It was the drinking and drugging that burned him the most. Since he'd dedicated himself to football back in eighth grade, his body had become his temple; watching her destroy hers with the booze and the drugs just tore him up.

He gazed out the window, savoring the doves for a little longer. Then he reached into his desk and pulled out a small, locked box from the very back of the bottom drawer. It was time to finish the rest of his morning routine. He unlocked the padlock and opened the box. It contained half a dozen syringes, some alcohol swabs, and two small glass vials containing Winstrol, an anabolic steroid, a drug intended for use on horses and cattle.

He took out one of the syringes, ripped off the plastic covering with his teeth, removed the safety cap, and effortlessly slid the needle into the rubber top of the vial. He'd been doing this for a while. Then he gently pulled back the plunger, filling the syringe with the clear liquid. He carefully nudged the plunger just a little so that a couple of drops of fluid spurted from the tip and plunged the needle into the back of his thigh just below his buttocks.

Casey pulled out the needle and swabbed the area with alcohol. Then he broke the tip, wrapped up the used needle in tissues and tucked it into the bottom of his gym bag. He put everything else back in the box, locked it up and stowed it back in the bottom drawer of his desk.

When he was sure everything was back in its proper place, he stood up and walked over to the full-length mirror on his closet door for this morning's appraisal. Slowly, Casey flexed each set of muscles, beginning first with his neck and shoulders and then gradually working his way right down to his toes. This part of his morning routine wasn't about vanity; rather it was a clinical evaluation of sorts to check which muscle group he felt he needed to work on with his personal trainer, Frank Giordano, later on that morning.

He stopped short when he flexed his pectorals – his chest, today he needed to work his chest. And with that he was done. He casually glanced down at the red welt below his hip and frowned. He walked over to his nightstand and picked up the phone. It was probably way too early to call Esprit, but what the hell. He had to get to the gym and then to football practice. She'd forgive him for waking her, she always did.

He speed-dialed her number. After four rings she picked up,

and in a very sleepy voice barely managed to say hello.

"Hey, baby, it's me."

After a couple of seconds she said in a scratchy voice, "Hey, stud, why are you calling me so early? I didn't even get to bed till around two."

"Sorry, Spree, but I've got a busy day, and I got your email this morning, so I thought I'd touch base with you about tonight."

She didn't answer.

"I thought maybe we'd hook up after practice and catch a movie."

A few seconds ticked by before Esprit answered him. "Casey, I thought we were going down to the Hook to party with Jamie and her friends tonight."

"Spree, you know I don't want to do that again. Hanging out at the beach watching Jamie and her asshole friends get stupid just doesn't work for me, Spree, sorry! Come on, not again tonight!"

There was a long silence.

"Esprit, you still there? Wake up!"

"Okay, Casey, that's cool. But stop calling Jamie and her friend's assholes. Just because they smoke a little weed and play a little music doesn't make them assholes. Does everybody have to be just like you or they suck?"

"No, but I'm worried about you. I spent half the night looking for you Thursday night…."

"Okay, okay, I know you're still pissed about that, but you've got to lighten up a bit, all right? We'll do the movie thing. Anything to get out of this house, my dad's driving me up a wall."

"Cool, got to run. You pick the movie, anything but the new Julia Roberts flick. I'll call you on your cell after practice. Love you, Spree, you know that, right?"

"Love you too! Don't get hurt today, big boy!"

"Very Funny…Later."

"Later, baby."

Casey hung up the phone, grabbed a pair of sweats and headed for the bathroom. As he walked down the hall, he yelled downstairs, "Mom, I'll be down in five. Is my shake ready?

Downstairs Lisa Collins was sitting down at the marble-topped counter of her recently remodeled kitchen with a steaming mug of Starbucks, and she was going through the mail. There were several letters from colleges trying to recruit Casey but none from Penn State, the one he wanted. The next letter she turned over was a wedding invitation from her sister. She opened it and learned that her oldest niece was getting married around Christmas. Lisa frowned and looked out the French doors of her beautiful new kitchen at the sylvan pool in the back yard for a bit. She then pushed the invitation off to the side. Lisa was the only one of her family to climb out of the dire poverty they had grown up with, and every time she attended a family gathering, one of her siblings would either ask her for money or insult her for being a 'rich snob'.

She quickly perused the rest of the letters, mostly bills, and then turned her attention to the magazines. She chuckled at the first one, *New Republic*. It was Casey's. She still found it hard to believe that her son was actually a devout Republican. Over the past couple of years he'd grown increasingly conservative. Lisa assumed it was probably fallout from dating a Republican congressman's daughter. She laughed when she thought about the heated debates that she and Steve had been having with him around the dinner table. He would sit there all red-faced and berate them for their liberal views, or spout off about what it was to be a real patriot in the twenty-first century.

At first she'd been worried, but then one of her friends told her that a lot of kids in this part of New Jersey around Casey's age were turning to the far right, possibly as a response to the high number of local families that had lost loved ones in the tragedy of the World Trade Center Attacks.

She tossed the *New Republic* aside and finally came to the one she had been looking for, *Sports Illustrated* – it was her favorite magazine. This week there was a picture of Tom Brady on the cover. Someday that would be Casey. Ever since Casey had a hit on his first at bat in T-ball, Lisa had known he was going to be something special. Over the years she'd taken the term 'soccer mom' to a new level. She knew from the start that Casey was special, that he had the potential to be a great athlete, and she was determined to help him get there. For ten years she'd traveled with him to summer football camps, sports clinics, and wrestling tournaments all around the country. There wasn't a match or a game where Lisa couldn't be found right on the edge of the field or mat screaming encouragement to her son. She started reading *Sports Illustrated* long ago as a kind of tutorial. Now it was her most essential reading material.

But before she could start the magazine she needed to make Casey's breakfast shake. Each morning she prepared him a shake made from milk and fresh fruit mixed with scoops of several different powdery substances that Casey left for her in measured Ziploc bags he stored in one of the kitchen cupboards. She called these shakes Casey's rocket fuel.

Lisa was only too happy to make his shake every morning because she believed that somehow God had given her the perfect son. He was not only a superior athlete but a great student as well, even if he was at times a bit too demanding and sometimes a tad too serious. Hell, she could have raised a kid like the Fitzgerald boy next door, suspended from school every other week, and always in trouble with the police. No thanks! She couldn't begin to fathom how Casey turned out to be the fine young man that he was. God knows he didn't get it from her or Steve's gene pool. She considered herself very fortunate to have a son like Casey because he was her only child. When he was born there had been complications surrounding her pregnancy, and she'd been forced to have an emergency hysterectomy.

Lisa put down the mail and walked to over to her brand-new Sub-Zero refrigerator. She absentmindedly began pulling out various ingredients. After carefully blending up Casey's shake in her oversized blender, she sat back down at the breakfast counter with coffee in hand and was about to start reading her magazine when she heard car tires crunching up the stone driveway.

She knew it had to be the car service dropping off her husband, Steve. He was just coming back on the red-eye Continental flight from a business trip in Palm Springs. Happy to see him, she stood up and left the kitchen, walking to the front door to greet him when he came in.

As soon as she opened the door, Steve stumbled into the house and dropped his tattered overnight bag and golf clubs right down on the well-polished marble floor of the foyer. He looked worse than usual after a business trip, and he smelled like he hadn't showered in a week as Lisa found out the second he tried to kiss her. She was overwhelmed by his body odor – a fetid reeking combination of sweat and alcohol. She winced and held her nose. "Hi, honey, nice trip…I think you need a shower…oh God!"

Steve, red-eyed and unshaven, looked as though he'd been on a three-day drinking binge, which he probably had. Unfortunately, it went with the job. Steve was a bond trader for Merrill Lynch, and most of his business trips were more about golf and partying than about business. This sometimes really ticked Lisa off, but he did earn a great living and the trips didn't occur all that often. Besides, he did work his ass off, and his job was exceedingly stressful. He was entitled to blow off a little steam now and then as long as it didn't get out of hand. His Thursday night get-togethers in the city and the occasional 'business' trips were a small price to pay for the wonderful life he'd given her.

Steve's job commanded a high six-figure income, and in years with a good bonus it sometimes even crossed the seven-figure line. His salary allowed for a lifestyle that neither of them would have ever imagined some twenty odd years ago.

"Hon, sorry I'm such a wreck, but it's good to be home. The guys from Deutsche Bank were boring as hell, but on the flight home Phil sat right next to me and wouldn't shut up for five solid hours. But, hell, he and I wrote some serious business on the trip, and, Lisa, you wouldn't believe how beautiful Palm Springs is; the palm trees, the gardens, and mountains, they're everywhere you look! You and I really should go out there some time. I think you'd absolutely love it. The weather's fucking incredible, it's seventy-five and sunny every goddamn day."

Lisa laughed and pushed him toward the kitchen. "You want a cup of coffee? I just made a pot, Starbucks French Roast."

"Sure. Where's the golden boy? Has he heard from Penn State yet? I thought Coach Paterno himself would've been at our doorstep at the stroke of midnight with Casey's letter."

Lisa handed Steve a mug of steaming coffee. "Actually, he called on Thursday, but Casey hasn't gotten a letter yet. I don't know, Steve, Casey seemed a bit worried last night that the boy from Baltimore was going to get the scholarship over him because of his connections to Paterno's assistant coach."

"That ain't happening. Casey's the best damn linebacker in the country, hands down. Paterno obviously wants him or he wouldn't keep calling. Besides, we both know how much Pete Carroll wants him, and as a fallback scenario, USC ain't a bad choice. Hey, I just thought of something, if Casey ends up playing at USC, you and I can stop over in Palm Springs once in a while when we go out to see him play. Maybe we should think about buying a condo out there. I'm telling you, you'll absolutely love the place."

Lisa just shook her head and gave her husband a nervous smile. "I guess we'll just have to wait and see."

Steve took off his jacket, tossed it carelessly on the kitchen table and sat at the breakfast counter directly across from his wife. He was in poor physical shape, and if truth be told, he'd never ever really been in good shape. Now his career, comfortable lifestyle, and lavish dining habits were taking their toll on him. He was easily twenty pounds over weight and most of that sat not so firmly around his midsection.

Steve sipped his coffee and looked up at Lisa with a sad but bemused smile. "So what kind of mood has he been in the last few days? I hope better than when I left."

Lisa just shrugged her shoulders.

"Isn't it ironic," he sighed. "Here I am at forty-three, never having played a day of football, or any other sport since the age of twelve when I was in little league. I spent my entire high school and college years drinking beer, smoking pot, and banging keystrokes on my old IBM laptop, never once thinking about sports or about exercise, and today I'm the father of a muscle-bound son right out of the *Stepford Wives* movie, a son who lives at the gym, barely speaks to me, and who's become the poster boy for the Young Republican's Club." Steve pointed to the sky and laughed. "Someone up there must have a damn good sense of humor."

Lisa came around the center island and rubbed her husband's shoulders. "Relax, hon, I know you two haven't been getting along lately, but once he gets his scholarship, maybe the pressure will be off and you two can spend some quality time together. Hey, look at the bright side. We could have done a lot worse, just look at the Fitzgerald boy."

Steve nodded half-heartedly.

"Steve, I mean it. Casey's a great kid, even if he does take football and life a little too seriously."

"A little too seriously? Are you kidding me? Honey, Casey's wound up tighter than a bedspring for Christ's sake!" Steve shrugged, "Man, I swore when he was born that I was going to raise him a whole lot better than I was. I had this idea that I was going to give him more freedom and more self-esteem than my goddamn father ever dreamed of giving me. And you know what? I did all that. I gave Casey everything he could ever want. I let him make his own choices, and I never once forced that kid to do a damn thing he didn't want to do. So what do I have to show for my efforts? A son who thinks I'm an asshole and a failure because I smoke a little pot, I drink too much, and because I don't live in the gym. Lisa, I love Casey with all my heart, you know that, but he can be a real a self-centered son of a bitch sometimes."

"Shush, he'll hear you! You're just overreacting because you're hung-over and tired. Give it a rest; he'll be down any minute."

Steve's bloodshot eyes widened. "What? It's my goddamn house for Christ's sake. I should pussyfoot around so I won't hurt the feelings of my goddamn self-centered, narrow-minded shit of a son? I don't think so!"

"Steve easy…he's a teenager. Teenagers rebel against their parents; it's what they do. You and I did. So he's rebelling against us by being a Republican, so what? I promise, once the scholarship thing is decided, he will be better. I'll have a talk with him, but for now please, please just give it a…Oh…here he comes now."

Casey strode into the kitchen wearing sneakers, sweat pants and a tight-fitting cropped T-shirt. His ipod was clipped at his hip, and his ear jacks dangled loosely around his neck. He dropped his gym bag on the floor with a resounding thud. "Hey, Mom, where's my shake?"

"Good morning to you too, Casey!" she said. "It's over on the counter next to the fridge, where it is every morning. How about saying hello to your father?"

Casey turned and glared directly at his disheveled and odious father. "Oh, hey, Dad, I didn't see you. Man, you really look like shit this morning…."

Casey took a healthy gulp of his shake, "You keep this up and you're going to be dead in five years, but hey, don't worry, by then I'll be in the NFL, and I'll be taking real good care of Mom after you're gone."

"Hey, bud, nice to see you too," Steve growled.

Lisa winced. She knew Casey hated seeing his father like this, but did he have to be so damn self-righteous? She would talk to him.

Casey continued his attack. "Come on, Dad, Look at you. You're forty-three years old and still drinking and smoking pot like a teenager. You know there's more to life than a big bank account and getting stoned all the time." Casey paused a moment for effect. "You wanna know something? When I see you all banged out like this, I am embarrassed to be your son!"

Steve could no longer hold back. "Yeah, well, there's more to life than fucking protein shakes, four hours a day in the gym, and waltzing around town with that asshole congressman's daughter! Casey, you're a piece of work! I've spent my whole life taking care of you and your mom, and I've always tried to do the right thing by you guys. So where the hell do you get off thinking that you can speak to me with so much disrespect? I deserve better from you, a lot better, you ungrateful little piece of shit!"

With that Steve grabbed his coffee mug and stormed from the room.

Lisa, with tears in her eyes, walked to the kitchen counter, picked up what was left of Casey's shake and, as she handed it to him, looked up into his angry dark eyes. "Casey, you just went so far over the line it's not even funny. Your father has never claimed to be perfect, nor has he ever expected you to be. He's a good father and a loving husband. He loves you more than anything in this world, and your words this morning are killing him."

"What! My words…it's the booze and the drugs…not me…."

"Your words, Casey! Not the booze, not the job, not anything else. He doesn't deserve all your judgmental bullshit! Now finish your shake and go upstairs and apologize to him."

Casey tossed down the rest of his shake and handed her the glass. "Listen, Mom, maybe I went a little too far, but look at him. He's a frigging mess. I love him too, that's why I'm not going to sit back and watch him kill himself. Anyway, he's way too pissed off right now. I'll talk to him when I get home from practice. I'm sorry that I upset you, but he needs to hear the truth from somebody. Besides, I need to get over to the gym before practice." Casey kissed his mom on the forehead, grabbed his car keys and ran for the front door.

She followed him and sadly watched him go, wondering how the relationship between her husband and her son, a relationship grounded in the best intentions and one that was unbelievably close until the last couple of years, had deteriorated so far so fast. She wiped her eyes and sighed before taking a last sip of coffee, then she walked back to the kitchen, wondering how she was going to un-ruffle her husband's very ruffled feathers.

Chapter Two

Citizen Burke & The Burke Family

High up on the rocky bluffs overlooking the Navesink River, Congressman Ethan Burke and his wife, Jordan, were just sitting down to breakfast out on the bluestone terrace of their palatial turn-of-the-century home. Perennial gardens, which bordered their beautiful riverfront estate, surrounded the terrace. Off in the distance, sailboats drifted past on the sparkling, cerulean river, their rainbow-colored sails billowing in the breeze.

As the maid came over to freshen up their coffee, Ethan turned to his lovely wife. "Jordan, we've been through this a hundred times. I don't really care what Esprit has planned for tomorrow. This is an election year, and the vice-president is attending the fundraiser. You know damn well how much I need his support for my campaign. I need Esprit to be there, that's it! I don't ask for much of her time, but tomorrow's potential press and photo opportunities are just too good to pass on. You talk to her, Jordan, and you get her to agree. God knows she won't listen to me. She hasn't spoken a civil word to me in months."

Jordan sighed. "I'll talk with her, but what makes you think she'll listen to me? Lately, every time I speak to her she looks right through me as though I'm not even in the same room. And, God, do I rue the day she decided she was going to be an actress. The drama, twenty-four-seven!"

"I know, dear. I just don't know what to make of her

anymore. One day she's as happy as can be, and the next she's a monster. Whatever are we going to do with her?"

"I don't know, Ethan. I still think we made a big mistake not sending her to Petty or Lawrenceville for high school. God only knows what she's been exposed to in that horrible public school."

Ethan rubbed at his temples. "Jordan, we've been over this before. A congressman doesn't send his child to a private school. A senator maybe, a governor, yeah, sure! Why not? I don't know about down in Georgia, but in New Jersey a congressman is expected to be a man of the people. Besides, if public school was good enough for me, it's damn sure good enough for my daughter. I somehow managed to survive twelve years of a public education."

The truth was that he barely survived public school with a B average before entering Princeton as a legacy. Ethan's father had hated prep schools. He believed that they were only for children of old-money snobs. From Ethan's own experience at Princeton, he too had come to believe that those children who attended private schools because of their parents' wealth usually grew up to be spoiled and lazy adults, adults with little or no understanding of what it took to be truly successful in the world.

Jordan smiled. "Whatever you say, dear. But remember, you did ask for my help."

"I know. It's just that my family legacy and money have been more of a hindrance than a help to my political career thus far. That's exactly why I need Esprit to be there tomorrow. If I'm ever going to get a run at the Senate seat next year, I'll need to win this election by a much bigger margin than last time. That's the only way I'll convince those party bastards in Washington who control the purse strings to back my campaign."

Jordan took a bite of her blueberry muffin and then suddenly put it down. "Honey, here's an idea. Why don't you invite her to bring Casey along? Then she won't put up such a fight, will she?"

Ethan set down his coffee and began ruminating out loud. "He's a great kid, he'll look good on camera, and you can bet he would jump at the chance to meet the vice-president. Jordan, ask her this morning, will you?"

"No, no. I'll wait, and we will ask her when he comes over later on to pick her up. I overheard them talking on the phone; he's coming over tonight after practice. I bet if we ask her again in front of him, she's bound to say yes for his sake."

Ethan clapped his hands together. "Jordan, you are brilliant! Not only are you beautiful, you're as sly as a fox." He reached over and kissed her on the cheek. "You are going to make one hell of a senator's wife one day. Find out what time he's coming so I can make sure to be here, and when he arrives I'll ask them myself. Oh, this is wonderful!" He looked at his Rolex. "Oh…but now I've got to get over to the club."

Jordan smiled. "So whose donation are you losing a round for today?"

He laughed. "Roger Thompson, the vice-president of marketing over at Lucent Technologies and a couple of fellows from Lucent's outside public-relations firm. And for the record, I never lose on purpose."

Jordan laughed. "Yeah right, and I'm twenty-five! Should I expect you for lunch?"

"I don't think so. I'll call you from the club. Got to run."

As Ethan walked across the terrace back toward the house, his daughter, Esprit, came out, shielding her eyes from the sun. She slowly ambled past him dressed only in a pair of baggy men's boxer shorts and a skimpy sleeveless T-shirt. As she rubbed the sleep from her eyes, she softly yet sarcastically whispered, "Good morning, Daddy. Off to the club to steal some poor unsuspecting slob's money?"

Ethan didn't take the bait. "Nice to see you too, Esprit. Have a nice day. I'll see you later."

As he walked away she said under her breath, "I hope not,

you pompous son of a bitch!"

Esprit joined her mother at the table and poured herself a healthy glass of orange juice. She was having a hard time shaking off the fatigue of sleep this morning. It must have been the early phone call from Casey.

Esprit shared her mother's petite stature and voluptuous figure. She was strikingly beautiful even though she'd just rolled out of bed. Her hair, though unbrushed and decidedly tangled, fell across the bronzed skin of her bare shoulders like spun corn silk, brilliant in the morning sun. Her eyes, though she was clearly exhausted, still managed to radiate a bright aquamarine blue that can only be found in the waters of the Caribbean.

"Good morning, honey," Jordan said in her syrupy, Southern-belle drawl. "What are you doing up so early? It must've been after two in the morning when you finally got home last night. Where were you, anyway?"

"Slow down, Mom, okay? I just woke up. First of all, I'm up because Casey called and woke me early this morning. Next, I told you where I was going yesterday afternoon: to see Jamie's friend who plays in a band. They were playing a set at the Internet Café over in Red Bank. Anything else?"

"Darling, I was only making conversation. You're eighteen years old; what you choose to do with your free time is up to you. You know that. The only thing your father and I ask is that you take care of yourself and not do anything to embarrass us socially. Is that really so difficult?"

Esprit ignored her mother and dreamily watched a couple of kids on jet skis slash back and forth across the wake of a large motor yacht steaming down the river. She knew she was coming across a little bitchy so she tried to make amends. "I'm sorry, Mom, you're right. I'm just a little tired, that's all."

"That's all right, honey. Do you want some breakfast?"

"No, I don't think so; my stomach's a little off. I think I might've had a bit too much to drink last night. Just a cup of tea, thanks."

Jordan signaled the maid to bring her daughter a fresh cup of tea and asked, "So, do you have any plans today? I need a dress for tomorrow night. Would you like to come shopping with me?"

"Sorry, I've got to study my lines for the play. Rehearsals start on Monday, and I haven't even looked at my part! Besides, Casey and I are going out later on. We'll probably catch a movie or something."

"Oh, what time is Casey coming over? I haven't seen him in a while, maybe you two could have dinner with your father and I before you go out. You know how much your father likes that boy."

Esprit hesitated. Her mother had asked that a little too fast. She usually didn't take this much interest in Esprit's everyday life. What was she up to?

"I'm not sure," Esprit said. "Probably around five. He said he'd call after practice. But, Mom, I don't think I can handle a dinner with Dad tonight. I'm so sick of his lectures, and I know if I give him the opportunity he's going to ask me again to attend that damn fundraiser tomorrow."

Her mother quickly changed the subject. "So did Casey hear from Coach What's His Name yet? He must be very excited with football season about to start."

"Paterno, Mom, Coach Paterno! Today's the first day colleges can officially notify him, and it's Saturday, so he probably hasn't heard anything yet. Anyway, he didn't mention anything this morning." Actually, now that Esprit was awake she wondered. Why hadn't Casey said anything on the phone? He'd been so sure that he was going to hear from the coach first thing. Oh well, it was only seven a.m. when he called.

"Well, I'm sure he will. That write-up in the *Asbury Park Press* last week was wonderful. I didn't realize that Casey was such a good student on top of all the sports. He is quite a catch, Esprit."

Casey had been the feature story in the special, back-to-school, high-school-football section of last Sunday's paper. Along with a large photo, the paper ran a three-page story touting Casey as one of the best football players to ever come out of New Jersey, and it listed all of his athletic accomplishments. The article speculated on where he would end up playing football in college. The sports reporter seemed to think he was a lock for Penn State.

Esprit gave a little sigh. "Yeah, he is. He and I are so different, but he's so sweet to me. I just wish he liked my friends a little more. It's either just the two of us or we're hanging out with his jock friends, who are pretty much just a bunch of macho idiots with way too much testosterone!"

"Honey, he's an athlete, and you and your friends are into music and acting; what did you expect? Take my advice. Don't push him too hard on this subject, or you'll end up chasing him away."

"I don't know, maybe you're right. I can't wait for this recruiting nonsense to be over. Then maybe he won't be so tense all the time. Well, I'm going up to take a shower. Thanks for the advice, Mom."

Esprit took her cup of tea and headed back to the house. But there was still something tickling around in the back of her head. Her mother was being awfully nice to her. What was she up to?

Chapter Three

Friends, Football & Fighting

As soon as Casey left his house, he'd already forgotten about the fight with his father. He had more important things to worry about. He had only one dose left of his current cycle of steroids, and he really wanted to start another cycle right away. Penn State hadn't called yet. No registered letter, nothing! They must still be deciding between him and the kid from Baltimore. His first game was Friday, and there would definitely be PU scouts there. A really good game would tip the scales. Casey's whole future was riding on how he played on Friday.

As he drove to the gym he worked feverishly on the finer points of the argument he'd give to his personal trainer and steroid supplier, Frank Giordano. The argument had to be good. His future was at stake, and this conversation was way too important to screw up. Frankie would be totally pissed if Casey asked for another cycle so soon. He'd warned Casey over and over that he needed to take at least a two-month break between cycles because of the side effects and also to never do them in season, but fuck the rules, this was way too important. He would take an extra long break after the next cycle. By then his scholarship would be settled and football season would be just about over. He turned on the radio and began tapping the steering wheel in rhythm to a new hip-hop tune by DMX. Casey didn't usually go for rap music, but this tune was stuck in his head for some odd reason.

He arrived at the gym around nine. He locked his car, jogged into the building and tossed his bag in a locker. Then he scanned the near-empty gym for Frankie, but his trainer was nowhere to be found, so Casey headed for the free-weight room to begin his grueling chest workout.

He went to the nearest bench and began loading the bar with about two hundred and fifty pounds of plates, all the while continuing to run through in his head what he was going to say to Frankie. When he finished he moved off to the side, sat down on a mat and began to stretch. Casey hated stretching. He thought it was a big waste of time, but Frankie insisted that he do it before and after every workout. As he began to relax and stretch out, his thoughts wandered back to the fateful day that he first met Frankie Giordano….

Giordano had come to one of Casey's practices early in his sophomore year, right after the first game of the season. He'd sat all by himself up in the stands for well over an hour until the practice was over. When Casey finally walked off the field, Giordano stood up and slowly meandered over to him. He introduced himself.

At the time Casey wasn't really sure who he was, but he knew that the big man was coming his way.

Giordano walked up and said, "Hi, so you're *the* Casey Collins. I've been looking forward to meeting you. My name is Frankie Giordano."

Casey smiled because he immediately recognized the name. Frankie Giordano was a legend at Casey's school. Ten years before he was the star running back when he'd led the Eagles to two State Championships. Casey also knew that Giordano had played his college ball at Boston College, and that he did a short stint in the NFL.

"Hello, Mr. Giordano, it's an honor to meet you, sir."

"First of all, knock of the 'sir' crap. Call me Frankie."

"Okay…Frankie."

"Casey, do you have a couple minutes. I've been watching you play. You've got huge potential. I came here today to introduce myself and talk to you about a few ideas I have to help you reach that potential."

Frankie caught Casey's interest. "Sure."

"Good, then let's grab a seat, this could take a few of minutes."

They walked back over to the bleachers, took a seat, and Giordano began his spiel. "So here's the deal. You've probably heard a little about me, and you probably know that I own a local gym, but let me give you the real story, at least the short version. After I graduated from here I went on to play at Boston College. I was pretty small for division one, but I managed to have a solid four-year career up there. After my senior season I thought my playing days were over. I'd never even considered the pros. I mean I was only five ten and a hundred and eighty pounds soaking wet. But out of nowhere the Patriots drafted me in the seventh round. I guess it was because I was from a local school. So I'm thinking it was probably more of a PR move than anything else. Right?"

Casey just nodded.

"Anyway, I go to training camp and surprise, surprise…I actually make the damn team and I hang on by a thread for the next two years, busting my butt, playing on special teams. But the truth was I really was just too small and too slow to play in the NFL. After my second full season they cut me."

Casey listened, wondering where the conversation was heading.

"Well, after those two seasons, I wasn't ready to give it up. I mean come on…this was the NFL! So I tried to catch on with a couple of other teams at the start of next season, but they all said the same thing – I was too small and too slow to play in the NFL, but I wouldn't take no for answer. I'm one stubborn Guinea."

Casey laughed.

"So there I was without a team, but I had my degree in strength training and physical therapy from BC, and I knew a thing or two about how to get bigger and stronger, so I made a plan. I went back to the gym and I started busting my butt. I worked seven days a week in the gym, pumping like a madman, and I started getting bigger, but still not big enough. So then I started stacking steroids. Now I don't know how much you know about roids, but that means mixing combinations of oral and injectable steroids. See, I contacted this guy I'd heard about out on the West Coast who was working with Olympic sprinters, and he turned me on to what he called 'performance cocktails', which was just a fancy name for steroids mixed with a bunch of other crap. Now, Casey, I knew all about the bad shit with steroids…I mean Lyle Alzado had just died because of them for Christ's sake, but I studied up on the shit, and I was real careful not to overdue it."

Casey's eyes narrowed and he frowned at the mention of steroids, but he still listened intently.

"So for the next six months I busted my butt and did these cocktails. By the start of the following year's training camp I was up to two-twenty-five from one-eighty and I'd shaved a full second of my forty."

"Holy shit, a full second?" exclaimed a surprised Casey.

Giordano smiled. "Damn right!"

He continued. "So I had a friend on the coaching staff with the Eagles, and I signed on to training camp as a free agent. Casey, I'm telling you…I had a great camp. I played real good in the first three pre-season games, and I'm right on the cusp of making the team when in the forth quarter of the final pre-season game against the Ravens I take a hand-off, and I cut wide to the outside. I'm just about to turn up field and pop! I felt this excruciating snap on the back of my left leg. I hit the ground screaming in pain. I ruptured my fucking ACL! Can you believe it? Two hours later the team doc told me that my playing days were over."

"I'm really sorry, Mr. Gior…er…Frankie."

"Casey, those are the breaks. It was just a freak accident. So what are you going to do, right? Hey, I had my two years…not bad for a guy that was too small and too slow, right? I spent the next six months rehabbing my leg, and then I came back here to Middletown, which leads me to the reason I'm here today. I don't know if you know this, but I own a gym called PowerHouse here in town that specializes in training high-level athletes. I train college-level athletes in a dozen sports; swimming, baseball, basketball, football…you name it. I only take on the best clients and then only if their serious about making it to the top. I've been watching you, and, kid, you've got the whole package to make it to the NFL – size, speed, strength, and most importantly, you've got brains."

"I don't understand. Are you telling me that you want to become my personal trainer?"

"Casey, what I am telling you is that you have the potential to go all the way to the NFL, and I want to be the guy that helps you get there. So what do you think?"

Casey thought about the conversation in its entirety and he loved the idea of training with someone who had been to the big show, but the steroid stuff scared the hell out of him. He didn't want anything to do with that shit.

"Frankie…I'm blown away that you want to train me…I really am…but I don't want nothing to do with steroids. So if that is part of your plan, then you can count me out."

"Whoa…slow down, partner. That was my story. Not yours. Casey you're what? About six-two and two hundred pounds already, and you're only a sophomore. With the right training program and diet, you could be well over two-thirty by the time you're ready for college. I'm not talking about steroids, pal, but I am talking about a shit load of hard work. Do you think you're up for it?"

Casey smiled. "Hell yes!"

"Good. Why don't I come by your house this weekend, and

we will sit down with your parents and go through the whole plan? Casey, you're making the right decision, I promise you, but you had better be ready to work if you're going to make it to the NFL."

Casey began training with Giordano the following week and less than twelve months later the two agreed that Casey would do his first cycle of steroids.

Casey finished his stretching and started his workout. About an hour later Frankie strolled into his gym and heard the loud clang of free weights. He knew his most prized client was already there and pumping. He walked into the weight room and saw his boy on a bench at a Smith machine, underneath about two hundred and seventy-five pounds of plates. He walked over and pushed lightly down on the bar as Casey struggled to raise it. "Hey, dog! What's the problem? My mother could bench this!" He laughed and then helped Casey set the bar back on the rack.

Casey, soaking in sweat, sat up on the bench and laughed with him while gasping for breath. "Hey, Frankie. Where the hell have you been? I'm almost done with my workout? Oh, by the way, I've seen your mother. I bet she can put up a lot more weight than you can!"

Frankie smiled. "Watch it, pal. Don't you be talking about my mother, that woman is a saint! And from the looks of your pecs, I sure hope you're not done with your workout."

Casey stood up, looked in the mirror and flexed his chest muscles up and down. "What are you talking about? I've been busting my ass in here for almost an hour."

Frankie mussed Casey's messy hair. "Relax, sport, I'm only goofing. Sorry I wasn't here this morning to work out with you, I had a few errands to run."

Casey picked up his towel and wiped his face. "No problem. But hey, I really need to talk to you about something. Can we go to your office?

Frankie looked at him and saw how serious he was. "Sure,

sport, let's go."

They walked across the gym to Frankie's office. Once inside Frankie sat down at his desk. He watched in silence as Casey closed the door and sat down nervously in front of him.

"So, what's up, sport? Why the secrecy?"

Casey hesitated, took a breath and then he began. "Look, Frankie, I want you to hear everything I have to say without interrupting me until I'm done, okay?"

"All right, Casey, what's on your mind?"

"Frankie, I'm just about finished with my cycle, and I know you always want me to take a couple months off the juice before I start the next one, but I don't want to wait. Man, I can see the strength coming, and I feel great. I need to keep up this pace because now that football season's started I'll be cutting back my time in the weight room, and I don't want to lose the muscle mass I've gained."

Frankie could only gape. "Dude, is this about the PU scholarship? Are you out of your fucking mind? This is your third cycle in a little over a year, and this shit isn't aspirin! There are some real nasty side effects and you know that! How fucking big do you want to get?"

"But, Frankie, I need...."

"No...no fucking way! Casey, we've been over this a hundred times, if you're going to train with me, you're going to do it my way." He grabbed Casey by the shirt and stood him up, walking him to the mirror on the back of his door. "Take off your shirt and look at the acne on your shoulders, or the veins popping out of your forearms and calves. You're over-juiced right now. If you think I'm going to start you on another cycle right away, you're crazy! Besides, you are two hundred and thirty-five pounds of sculpted muscle right now. That's plenty big enough to play football at any level."

"Frankie, I know, but...."

Frankie slammed his fist down on his desk. "Man, you're going over the top, and let me tell you, the other side ain't pretty.

You even think about asking me again before December, and you're out of here. I mean it! I love you, dude, but I won't be a party to you killing yourself. Sorry!"

Casey saw how pissed Frankie was and backed off. "Frankie, I'm sorry, man, I guess you're right. Maybe I am taking this a little too far. I apologize and I promise I won't bring it up again, okay?"

"Casey, you look great. You're about to get your call from Paterno; you're on your way, dog! Please listen to me and don't blow this thing. I told you what happens to guys that over-juice. Just look at all those freaks in professional wrestling. They're all half crazy, their livers are shot, and they'll all be dead in ten years. I'm not going to let that happen to you."

Casey desperately wanted to start another cycle, but he was sure now that Frankie wasn't going to give it to him, so a plan began to percolate in his mind. "No problem Frankie, you're right. It won't come up again. I'm really sorry and I get it, okay? Listen, I got to hit the shower so I won't be late for practice. I'll catch up with you tomorrow in the a.m."

Frankie smiled. "Okay, dude, Listen, I'm running back out to take care of some business anyway, but I'll be back in a couple of hours. If you hear anything from Paterno, give me a call, otherwise I'll see you tomorrow at ten."

Casey nodded and left for the locker room. The last piece of his plan fell into place as he watched Frankie leave the gym and head out the door to his car.

After a very quick shower, Casey dressed and peeked his head out of the locker room. He found what he'd been hoping for. The gym was practically empty except for one trainer running on a treadmill near the other end of the gym. Casey cautiously looked around one more time to be sure no one else was there, then he tiptoed back to Frankie's office door. He silently let himself in, closed the door, and then frantically searched Frankie's desk until he found Frankie's extra set of keys.

He took them, rushed over to the cabinet in the back of the office closet and tried each key until he found the one that unlocked the door. Stored inside the cabinet was an assortment of supplements and medical supplies, but at the bottom there was a small steel trunk secured with yet another lock. Casey was feeling a little panicky. He rushed to try the keys. He struggled at first, but then he found the right key and opened the trunk. He took out a box that contained a thirty-day cycle of steroids and quickly stashed it in his gym bag along with another box of disposable syringes. Then he relocked the locks and stowed the trunk in the exact position that he had found it. Finally, he put the keys back where he'd found them in Frankie's desk and cautiously scanned outside the door to make sure that no one had seen him. When he was totally sure he hadn't been seen by the lone trainer, he sneaked back out and closed Frankie's office door. Then he ran from the gym.

For Casey this was a first. He'd never stolen anything in his life – he'd never needed to. His parents gave him everything he could ever want and had raised him with a decent set of moral standards. However, his obsession with getting to the National Football League was consuming him, and though he felt terribly guilty for stealing the steroids, he rationalized that in the end he was doing the right thing. He would somehow find a way to make it up to Frankie.

Once he was out the door, Casey ran to his car and threw his gym bag in the back seat of the mustang GT. It landed on top of half a dozen dog-eared muscle and fitness magazines. He thought for just a moment about what he'd done and then flipped on the radio before driving off.

He sped down the highway on his way to go pick up his best friend and teammate, Kevin Hahn. He picked up Kevin every morning during football season and they'd go to practice together. Kevin lived in a sprawling, suburban development just around the corner from the high school.

Since it was still the last week of August and school hadn't started, the team was still going through painful double-session practices – the first from ten to twelve and then again from one to four. Double-session practices in the hot summer sun were no picnic for most of the boys, but for Casey they were a piece of cake. His routine during doubles was to pick up Kevin in the morning and then between practices the two of them would go back to Kevin's house, eat lunch and play *Madden 2008* on Kevin's PlayStation III video system before heading back in the afternoon.

Kevin, like Casey, was also a senior, and he was the team's star quarterback. He was a hell of an athlete in his own right, but not anywhere near the level of Casey. At five feet ten and just under one hundred and seventy-five pounds, he was way too small for a division-one scholarship. However, he had been contacted by several good division two schools, and he was hoping to land a full ride at Monmouth University, a local division AA program that was on the rise. MU had gone eight and one the last two years and their quarterback was set to graduate. Monmouth had called him the week before to notify him that they were sending scouts out to see him play on Friday night.

Casey pulled into Kevin's driveway and beeped the horn a couple of times. Less than a minute later Kevin bounced out the front door and down the steps, looking more like the surfer he was in the off-season than an all-conference quarterback, with his messy tangle of long blond hair, cut-off sweat pants, Vans, and tie-dyed, Phish T-shirt.

Kevin tossed his gym bag in the back seat as Casey stepped on the gas and screeched out of the driveway. "What's up, dog? You're late! If Coach makes me run extra laps because you made me late, I'm gonna kick your ass!"

Casey laughed and smacked Kevin on the back of the head as they drove out of Kevin's neighborhood and down the road right into the school parking lot. Casey parked his car, turned to his friend and said, "Dude, based on the lame-ass way you were throwing the ball yesterday, running laps might be the best thing for you this morning, it'll keep you out of trouble with the coach."

"Very funny." Kevin frowned as he reached for the door handle.

"Seriously, Kev, sorry I was late. I had to talk to Frankie after my workout."

"No problem, I was just busting. How's that muscle-head Frankie anyway? I haven't seen him in a while."

Casey was about to reply when he looked out across the parking lot and saw players already coming out of the locker room and making their way onto the field. "He's cool. Shit! The team's already coming out. We've got to run!"

They both leaped out of the car and sped across the parking lot to the locker room entrance. Just as the two boys rushed through the door, Coach Callahan appeared, standing at the entrance with his big freckled arms crossed tightly over his chest. "Nice of you two girls to make it. Surfer boy, get your ass dressed and run some laps until I get out there, and if I see you dogging it, you will pay dearly. Casey, I need to talk to you."

Kevin ran in to dress. As Casey and the coach walked into the locker room, Coach Callahan turned and said, "Hey, pal, I just wanted to know if you've heard from Coach Paterno yet. I got an email this morning from USC wanting to know where you stand."

"Sorry, Coach, I haven't heard anything yet. Actually, I was hoping that you might have heard something."

Coach Callahan scratched his chin. "Sorry, Casey, I haven't heard a thing. I'll check my messages again after the morning practice and let you know. Now get your ass out there and run some laps with your girlfriend. I don't want the rest of the team thinking that I'm going too easy on you."

"You bet, Coach." He sprinted back to his locker to get ready for practice.

Casey practiced hard at both the morning and afternoon sessions. In the afternoon he was the first player to hit the field. He led the team on the blocking sled and on tackling drills and was by far the hardest working player out on the field. But there was also something else ticking inside him because shortly into the second session he uncharacteristically made a vicious tackle on his own teammate during a controlled scrimmage, and then just a couple of plays later, he totally lost his shit after being kept out of the play by a solid block from one of the offensive linemen. He'd been so completely blocked out of the play that he grabbed the offending lineman, a rather large boy named Shawn Murphy, by the face mask and shoved him so hard that the Murphy fell right on his ass.

The poor kid was surprised and slow to get up after that. A couple of the other offensive linemen retaliated by pushing back at Casey, but then the coaches rushed in and broke up the skirmish. When the scrimmage resumed, so did Casey's belligerent attitude. At times he played like a wild animal even though it was against his own friends and teammates.

Finally, around four o'clock, Coach Callahan blew his whistle calling the end of practice. As the tired players slogged off the field and headed for the showers, Coach Callahan called his prize athlete over. Casey ran up to the coach with Kevin right on his heals as soon as he heard his name being called.

"Hey, Coach, what's up?"

Coach Callahan shooed Kevin away with a wave of his hand. "Hit the showers, surfer boy, I need to talk to Casey, and by the way, you threw the ball all right out there today."

"Thanks, Coach," said Kevin, and he took off like a rocket in the general direction of the locker room.

Once they were alone Callahan stopped and looked Casey in the eye. "Casey, what the hell was going on out there today? Son, you're the best athlete I've ever coached. Hell, you might be the best damn athlete I've ever seen for that matter, but you've got to keep your temper in check. I've never seen you like this before. You almost killed a couple of my boys on offense, and you could have seriously hurt Shawn Murphy. Casey, this is the first and only time I'm going to talk to you about this. This is only practice and I already know what kind of player you are. You've got to take it down a notch or one of these days you're really going to hurt someone. Do you understand what I'm saying? Save it for the game on Friday when it really counts!"

"Coach, I'm sorry. I don't know what got me going out there. I've been real wound up over the Penn State thing, and I guess I let it get to me. I'll go apologize to the guys, and I won't let it happen again."

Callahan accepted the apology and told his star player to hit the showers. As Casey ran off, Callahan's offensive coordinator, Bobby Martin, trotted over and with a pissed off look in Casey's direction he asked Callahan, "Cal, did you watch Casey today? I'm telling you, I think he might be juicing! I mean take a look at him! He must've put on twenty pounds since May, and he was as crazy as a rabid dog out there this afternoon. You've got to do something about this before it's too late. Casey's going to seriously hurt someone any day now. Maybe you ought to consider giving Frankie Giordano a call because your boy's heading for a big fall, and it's going to be on your shoulders."

Coach Callahan was visibly angry. "Bobby, you don't know what the hell you're talking about. Casey's just a tough kid with the will to win. I just talked to him and told him to tone it down at practice. Hear me loud and clear, whatever training he does on his own time is none of your or my goddamn business, and Frankie Giordano's got nothing to do with us. I'll speak to Casey again if I see another problem, but let me tell you something, in fifteen years of coaching I have never had a kid on this team caught using steroids, and I don't plan on having one now. So, Bobby, unless you got proof, just keep your opinions to yourself, you got that?"

Coach Martin looked at Callahan in disbelief. "Okay, Coach,

you're the boss, but this kid's whole future is about to blow up in his face, and there's still time to help him."

Callahan glared right back. "Bobby, you made your point. I said I'd speak to him and I will, so stop worrying about Casey and focus on your job, which is to get my offense ready for Friday."

"Fine, Cal, that's what I'll do, but for the record, if Casey crashes and burns, and he will, trust me, I've been there, don't come looking to me to help you cover your ass. We've got legal liability here and a moral responsibility to that kid, and you damn well know it!"

"Bobby, you've made your position quite clear, now let's get back to coaching, shall we?"

Both coaches headed for the locker room. Coach Callahan walked through the locker room without stopping. He went directly to his office and closed the door without even talking to the team. He knew Coach Martin was right, but he wasn't sure how to handle the situation. He could see that Casey was probably juicing. The kid showed all the signs, but if he acknowledged that he knew about it, he'd legally have to notify Casey's parents and suspend him from the team. That would all but destroy Casey's future in big-time football. Casey was the best damn kid he'd ever coached. He owed his player something, and he felt the need to help him, but he just wasn't sure how to go about it without putting his own neck on the line. If he confronted Casey or even called Frank Giordano, that would constitute suspicion, and the league rules were clear – if a coach suspected one of his athletes was taking steroids, the kid had to be tested. No ifs, ands, or buts. Coach Callahan rubbed his temples as he thought about the problem when he noticed the message light on his phone blinking.

There were two messages; the first was another call from Pete Carroll at USC. The second was from Penn State's director of recruiting, a fellow named Tom Williams. Williams and Callahan were old friends from college, and he'd called to give the coach a heads up on Casey's status. His message said that Coach Paterno was leaning towards the kid from Baltimore for two reasons: One, the kid was a nephew of an assistant coach, and two, he was from a poor black community and Paterno really enjoyed seeing that kind of kid make it. Williams went on to say that Coach Paterno still thought Casey was the better athlete, so he was sending a couple of scouts to film Friday's game. Williams then said that Paterno had still not made his final decision so he was planning on taking one last look at the films on Saturday before making the call. Williams closed the message with, "Cal, it doesn't look too good for your kid. Make sure he has a whale of a game next Friday."

"Great! Just great! What the hell am I going to do now?" Callahan said to no one in particular. He had a lot thinking to do so he decided to hold off on talking to Casey again until after Monday's practice.

Casey and Kevin finished dressing and bolted from the locker room. As soon as they were in the car, Kevin turned to Casey and grabbed his shoulder. "Dog, we really need to talk. I'm the only one besides Frankie that knows you're hitting the roids, but if you keep acting up at practice, the whole team's going to know. You hear what I'm saying? Jesus Christ, Casey, you almost fucking killed me out there today…and I'm your best friend. I don't know if you caught what was going on over on the sidelines, but Coach Martin was really pissed off at Callahan for not putting a leash on you in the afternoon scrimmage. I think he might be on to you and truth…I'm getting a little worried about you myself!"

Casey was silent for a little while, but then he finally said, "I hear you, bro! Coach already chewed my ass out. What the hell do you think he called me over for? Don't you think I realize I'm losing it out there? I know I've got to chill. I'm…I'm just so keyed up about this damn scholarship."

"Listen, dude, I'm with you all the way, but you better start being more careful. You don't want to blow this thing." Kevin patted his friend on the shoulder and then changed the subject. "So what are you doing later? I'm going down to Belmar to catch some waves. Do you want to come with?"

"I wish. I can't. I promised Esprit a movie tonight. She and I have been fighting a lot lately. Tonight I need to do the right thing and besides, I just feel like chilling."

"That's cool."

Casey let out a long deep breath and shook his head. "Goddamn it, I can't wait for all this stuff to be over! My head's spinning a mile a minute."

The two boys finished the drive in silence. Casey pulled into the driveway and Kevin hopped out of the car. He stuck his head back in through the open window. "Listen, Casey, try to take it easy, okay? If you need me, you know where I'll be, otherwise I'll see you Monday morning."

"Later."

Casey backed down the driveway and drove off for home. He picked up his cell phone and dialed Esprit. She picked up after the first ring. "Hey, Spree, it's me. I just finished practice, how are you doing?"

"I'm good. I've just been sitting here working on my lines for the play. I'm glad you called. I need a break. How was practice?"

"Same as it is every day, although Coach got on my ass about playing too rough at practice. What time do you want me to pick you up?"

"I don't know. Why don't we grab a bite first? Otherwise I'll have to eat dinner with my father, God forbid! How about you pick me up around six?"

"Cool, but why can't you ease up on your dad? He's not so bad. You don't know how lucky you are to have a father that gives a shit about something besides getting drunk every night. I know your father can be a pain in the ass, but his intentions are usually good, unlike my father who only thinks about himself."

"Casey, let's not go there, okay?"

"You should have seen my dad this morning. He got home from a business trip, and I swear he looked like a banged-out heroin addict. I don't know why my mother puts up with him."

"Whatever, Casey. Anyway, does six sound good?"

"Yah. I'm going home to get changed. I'll be over around six. See you then."

Casey hung up the phone and thought about calling his mom to see if she'd heard from Penn State, but for some reason he changed his mind and put on some tunes instead. He thought about his crazy day so far and wondered if and when Frankie would notice the missing steroids, but as quickly as the thought came, it went and he was once again dreaming of playing in the NFL.

Chapter Four

Secrets, Lies, and a Night on the Town

Saturday Afternoon

The morning had been a roller coaster ride for Lisa, beginning with the argument between Casey and Steve. After Casey left the house, Lisa couldn't seem to get on track. Her mind wouldn't stop searching for answers to her family's difficulties. The arguments were becoming a daily occurrence, and their intensity was mounting as well. After Casey left the house she really wanted to go for a run, but she knew that her head wasn't in the right place so instead she wandered out to the pool to try and calm herself. For a good ten minutes she stood on the patio with her eyes closed and breathed slowly, inhale then exhale, just like her yoga teacher taught her to do when she was stressed. This morning she was very stressed.

As she took in the fresh air she felt the tension leave her body, and she began to relax. Soon she was calm enough hear and savor the natural symphony of sound that was emanating from her back yard: the mellow warbling tones of the two doves by Casey's window, the staccato chirping of the crickets that made their home in the hedges, the high-pitched notes of the robin's circling above the Elm trees. Giving it all certain pleasing tempo was the accompanying rhythmic swoosh of the automatic sprinkler heads as they rotated back and forth, splashing cool fresh water over the multitude of flowers in the professionally manicured beds that surrounded the sylvan pool.

She'd found peace in those few minutes, and at the end of her private time she smiled a bittersweet smile, but her peace and serenity would only be short-lived. She had way too much to do.

She left the pool and went up to her bedroom to see about her angry husband. She walked in and spied Steve coming out from the shower. He was standing before her dressed in only a towel. She moved to him and without a word spoken, not even a whisper, kissed him deeply on the mouth while at the same time gently exploring with her hand what was behind the folds of his towel. As soon as she caressed him he started to protest, "Honey, I'm not in the mood. That kid is really…."

Lisa didn't give him a chance to finish. She kissed him harder and pushed him over to the edge of the bed. Gently forcing him to lie down, she slipped out of her clothes and softly whispered in a husky voice, "Steve, we have all day to talk. I haven't seen you in three days and I want you."

Steve got the message, as evidenced by the slow and steady rise at the center of his towel. Lisa stood before her husband proudly, confident of her supple yet firm body. She was totally unselfconscious and full of desire. Her long dark tresses fell about her shoulders and her lips formed a pouty smile as she removed his towel. She lay down beside him on the bed and massaged him, first with her hand and then with her mouth. She knew just how far to take him before he'd lose it. She teased him right to the edge of orgasm before abruptly stopping. She lifted her head and grinned like a Cheshire cat. She said, "Now doesn't that feel just a little better than talking about Casey?"

Steve managed a breathless, "Yes," before urgently grabbing his wife and turning her over on her back. He moved down between her finely tanned legs and reciprocated her playful teasing by way of several minutes of lovingly placed strokes with his tongue. Quite soon Lisa was writhing and pulling at his curly black locks of hair while moaning with pleasure. At this point he too was just about to reach his threshold; he inched forward so that they were face to face, and he kissed her on the mouth as he entered her.

After twenty years of lovemaking, there was a comfortable familiarity with each other's needs and an established rhythm that usually started out very slowly gradually increasing until neither could stand the pleasure for even one more second.

Their bodies, because of years of practice, melded and they moved as one, until together they found that blissful release they were so frantically seeking.

When their lovemaking was over, Lisa prodded her husband over to his stomach and spent the better part of the next hour massaging not only his back but also his sour mood. By the end of the hour she'd convinced him to join her for lunch at their beach club.

They cleaned up and left the house an hour later, spending the next several hours on the sundeck of their club overlooking the Atlantic Ocean, feasting on chilled Dungeness crab, succulent Chincoteague oysters and cold Heinekens.

All during lunch Lisa was careful to keep the conversation light and as far away from the subject of Casey as possible. She knew that a lazy lunch at the club was just the thing to calm her angry husband. This was just the place for him to unwind, and she was grateful that he'd agreed to join her.

They'd been members of the Water's Edge Beach Club for about ten years and spent most of their weekends at the club swimming and sunning with all of their Wall Street friends. They'd typically arrive around lunchtime and stay at the club well into the evening, but not today. Today they had to go home early because they had made plans to go out to dinner with their friends, the Kimballs. They left the beach around three. As soon as they got home they headed out to the pool to relax for a couple of hours before dinner. By the time Casey got home from practice in the afternoon they were both resting outside by the pool, sipping margaritas and listening to a Jimmy Buffet CD on the stereo.

As Casey walked into the house he was still a little frazzled from everything that had happened that day. He walked in and went directly to the kitchen. He glanced out the bay window and spied his parents in the back yard. With a look of disgust, he turned around and marched up the stairs to his bedroom without even saying hello. He locked his door and stowed the box of steroids and the package of syringes into his locked box in the bottom of his desk drawer. He looked around to check that everything was put away and ran back down to the kitchen to check the mail and phone messages. He found a stack of mail on the counter next to a large, half-empty bottle of Mezcal Tequila. As he riffled through the letters he briefly looked outside at his parents again with more than a little contempt, but then his attention returned to the mail and he was soon disappointed because there was nothing from Penn State. There were a bunch of letters from other schools, but they didn't matter. He left them unopened on the counter.

Outside at the pool Steve removed his sunglasses and rubbed his eyes. "Do you think Casey will be home soon? I really want to clear the air with him before we go out to dinner."

Lisa paused for a moment. "Steve, do you really think that's a good idea? Casey didn't get his letter from Penn State, not even a phone call. He's not going to be in any mood to have a heart to heart with you today, and besides, you've had a few drinks. Don't you think that maybe you should wait till tomorrow?"

"You're probably right, but I've got to be honest with you, Lisa, I'm getting real tired of feeling like an outcast in my own house."

"I know, honey. Just wait till tomorrow, okay? Do you want me to freshen up your drink? I'm going inside for a minute."

Steve slipped his glasses back down over his eyes. He lay back down and simply nodded. Lisa picked up both glasses and walked back into the kitchen where she ran right into Casey standing at the window and staring off into space.

He looked over at her. "Hey, Mom, did I get any calls today?"

"I'm sorry, buddy, Coach Paterno didn't call. You know I would've called you right away if he had." She saw his look of disappointment and patted him on the back. Then she walked over to the counter and began fixing the margaritas. "Your dad and I are going out to dinner with the Kimballs in a little while. Would you like me to fix you something to eat before we go?"

"No thanks, Mom, I'm picking up Esprit at six. We're going to grab a bite to eat at the diner and then catch a movie."

"Listen, Casey, I know that you're not in a good place right now, but you will hear something soon, I promise. Your father is really upset about you attacking him this morning. He wants to have a talk with you, but now is probably not a good time for either one of you. Could you at least go out there and say hello to him and be civil for the next hour until you go out?"

"Do I really have to? Jesus, how much has he had to drink? If I go out there and say hello, is he going to start in on me again?"

"How much your father has had to drink is none of your concern, and for the record, Casey, you're the one that started in on him this morning. But if you must know, he's only had a couple."

She looked up at him with imploring eyes. "Casey, your father is very sad about the two of you. Just be nice, okay?"

Casey nodded, kissed her on the forehead, then turned and walked outside to the pool. He slowly walked up to his father and said softly, "Hey, Dad…listen…I'm sorry about this morning. I was out of line. I'm a little messed up about not hearing from Paterno."

Steve sat up and took off his glasses again. His eyes were still bloodshot. "Hey buddy, that's okay. I was a little on edge myself because of the long flight. How about you and I going out to lunch tomorrow? I really think we need to talk this whole thing out."

Casey reluctantly agreed. "Sure, Dad. Why not? I'll be home around lunchtime after my workout. But now I've got to run. I have to go get changed and pick up Esprit by six. You and Mom have a nice dinner tonight."

"Thanks, Casey. I appreciate it. By the way, how's the team looking for the game against Red Bank on Friday?"

"We'll be ready. Coach Callahan's been working us real hard the last two weeks."

"I'm sure you will, Casey. I'll see you tomorrow. Tell Esprit's parents your mom and I said hello."

"Will do."

He left his father and walked back into the house. Lisa was watching the exchange through the window. She smiled. "See that wasn't so bad, was it?"

"Mom, give me a break!" Casey turned and walked back upstairs to get ready for his date.

Casey took great pride in his appearance, especially when going over to Esprit's. He was meticulous about his grooming because he wanted to look his best for her parents, especially her father. After his third shower of the day he slipped on a pair of freshly pressed Banana Republic khakis, a light blue Polo golf shirt and a pair of tan, Sperry Topsider loafers. As he buttoned his shirt he glanced over at a photograph on his mirror of Esprit with her parents. The photo made him think first about his father and then about the man he worshiped, Ethan Burke.

His numerous conversations with Ethan Burke over the past couple of years had a much to do with Casey's conservative political viewpoint. Casey thought that any man who was willing to put his money and his career on the line to selflessly serve his country was someone quite extraordinary. Ethan Burke's political career exemplified selfless commitment at its finest, and total commitment was the founding principle of Casey's core set of beliefs.

Casey loved to sit and talk politics with Ethan, but Esprit always seemed to be a fly in the ointment whenever he tried to do so. He hated the way she always rushed him out the door whenever he went over to pick her up. He'd listened to all her complaints, but he still couldn't understand why Esprit hated her father so much. From what he could see, both her parents seemed to give her a lot of latitude and didn't seem to put much pressure on her at all. They encouraged her acting and never gave her a hard time about her mediocre grades or her wacky friends, at least not in front of him. The thing that seemed to most set her off was that once in a while they asked her to attend political functions, but not very often. However, she'd shared with him dozens of ugly childhood fairytales and the stories were always the same. Her mother and father would bring her out like a trophy at parties and political functions and make her perform like a trained poodle, and then they'd somehow embarrass her and send her away. Casey had never seen them do it, and he thought that perhaps it may have happened once or twice when she was young, but now she was probably just exaggerating.

He just didn't get her sometimes. He accepted that Esprit was an aspiring actress and she selected her role models accordingly. She'd naturally aligned herself with all those Hollywood liberals like Susan Sarandon, Tim Robbins, and that bigmouth jerk-off Martin Sheen from the TV show *West Wing*. With Esprit, when you mixed her Hollywood sensibilities with the undeniable fact that both her parents were conservative Republicans, well, it just made for some really bad family chemistry.

Casey thought about his last big fight with Esprit over politics. Last year, at Ethan's urging, he had taken a political science course in school. He loved the class and the teacher because her views were surprisingly similar to his own. For his year-end project he prepared a paper and an oral presentation on a book entitled *Shut Up and Sing*, by conservative political analyst Laura Ingram. His teacher recommended the book and Casey, after reading it, was blown away by its cutting and honest take on the hypocrisy and naiveté of celebrities who tried to use their public platform to attack conservative administrations.

When Casey had shown Esprit his report she'd just tossed it aside, saying it was all bullshit, and of course they had a huge fight about it. Casey wished that just once, Esprit would see those celebrity assholes for what they really were: naive, idealistic, fools, who way overvalued their own self-worth and their ability to influence the American public.

Casey often fantasized on this very subject. One day it would be fun to watch one of the Hollywood idiots – maybe even the biggest bullshit artist of them all, one Michael Moore with his grimy sweatshirts, grungy baseball caps, and his so-called documentary films, films that in reality were nothing more than highly crafted propaganda pieces, chock full of lies and self-interested, unsupportable, interpretations of political reality – finally put his own career on the line and run for public office instead of just using fame and celebrity to criticize those that actually have.

It was so damn easy for people like them to go on the attack without any personal risk or commitment on the line. Someday when his pro football career was over, he, like Ethan, would put his name and his reputation on the line and enter the political arena.

Casey put the finishing touches to his hair and spritzed on some Polo Sport cologne. Someday Esprit would eventually grow tired of the Hollywood act and come to see the truth. In the meantime he'd try to be patient with her and take every opportunity he could get to talk with her father. He was hoping to get a chance to talk with him tonight.

After a quick and painless goodbye to his parents, Casey put the top down on his mustang and drove to Esprit's. He was praying for a nice easy night with her and hoping for a little sex. He pulled up to the entrance of the Burke estate at the bottom of the steep hill at six o'clock on the dot and buzzed the intercom beside the imposing cast-iron gate. A few seconds later the gate mysteriously slid open as if by magic. Casey marveled at the security technology as he drove up the steep and winding gravel driveway.

He rang the doorbell and to his pleasant surprise, a smiling Ethan Burke answered the door. "Casey, my boy, it's so good to see you. Where have you been? We haven't seen you in a while. Please come in."

Casey shook Ethan's hand. "Hello, sir, it's great to see you too. I've been real busy getting ready for the season. How are you and Mrs. Burke, sir?"

"We're both fine, Casey. Esprit should be down in a minute. Why don't you come in the living room and have a seat. I'll ask Jordan to get you something cold to drink. Would you like a beer?"

"An ice tea would be fine, sir. I'm not much of a beer drinker, especially during the season."

They walked through the front door. Behind Ethan Casey spied Mrs. Burke walking through the foyer into the living room carrying a rather large box. She placed it atop the burnished mahogany Steinway piano and returned to the foyer to say hello to Casey.

"Why hello, Casey."

"Hello, Mrs. Burke."

Ethan smiled and looked to his wife. "Jordan, my dear, could you get Casey here an ice tea?"

She smiled. "Certainly."

She left the foyer as swiftly as she entered. As Casey followed Ethan into the living room, his eyes, glowing with awe and admiration, meandered around the opulent room, soaking in the exquisite décor. He sat down with Ethan on one of the many overstuffed couches strategically placed throughout the imposing living space, but his eyes continued to wander. The living room had incredibly high ceilings, at least fourteen feet by Casey's reckoning. The walls were covered in a pale yellow damask patterned cloth and bordered with ornate, frieze moldings and trim. The room itself was adorned with at least a dozen eighteenth century French antique tables and scattered about the black and white marble tiled floor there must have been six different Persian carpets. Casey couldn't help but continue to gaze. He thought the room so overwhelming that you could probably take out the furniture and play a decent game of football in it.

His eye was drawn to the massive paintings around the room. On two of the interior walls were hung huge 'Hudson River School' paintings, and on the north wall above the immense marble fireplace there was a remarkable portrait of Ethan's grandfather, Frederick Burke, that had been painted by Andrew Wyeth. At the south end of the room the wall faced the river, and this was perhaps the most impressive of all in that it consisted of a set of floor to ceiling leaded glass doors, the biggest doors he'd ever seen with matching adjacent windows that were festooned with richly brocaded, wine-colored, floor-to-ceiling drapes. The huge set of doors opened up into a large, glass-enclosed solarium filled with hundreds of flowers and plants, many of them rare South American orchids. At the far end of the solarium, some eighty feet in the distance, the solarium opened up to the terrace and gardens, and from there the views of the Navesink River were simply breathtaking.

When he looked across the room, Casey could see through the solarium that the sun was beginning to set. The entire river was aglow with a soft light, and he thought it was perhaps the most beautiful sight in the world. Casey loved this room, he dreamed of this room. To Casey the Burke estate wasn't about ostentatious displays of wealth, it was symbol of obtaining a kind of power and a level of sophistication that his own parents would never have but that he would attain someday.

Ethan sat back and smiled, watching Casey soak up the ambiance. He knew how much Casey loved this room – he felt the same way. After a minute or so he said, "So, Casey, I read that very impressive article in *Asbury Park Press* last week. Tell me, what's happening with your football scholarship?"

"Well, sir, today is actually the first day I can be officially notified of a scholarship offer. I've already heard from Coach Carol at USC, but I'm still waiting to hear from Coach Paterno at Penn State. I hope to hear something tomorrow, but it might not happen till Monday. Before I forget, my parents said to say hello."

"Well, don't you worry, Casey, I'm sure you'll hear something soon. Please give your parents our regards as well. Is your dad still making a killing on the market?"

"He's doing well, sir. He just got home from a business trip to Palm Spring this morning."

Ethan's eyes lit up. "Palm Springs, you say. Jordan and I have a small villa in Palm Springs, right on the golf course. You must tell your father the next time he goes out there I insist that he stay at our home."

A moment later, before Casey could reply, he heard the clip-clop of heels coming down the grand stairs. It was Esprit slowly making her way down the floating staircase. She cautiously entered the living room. Casey watched her every step. She was wearing a pastel-colored silk dress that showed off her rich tan and her sumptuous flaxen hair. She looked absolutely radiant. As Esprit walked into the room, right behind her followed her mother, carrying Casey's ice tea.

"Here you go, Casey!" Jordan handed Casey the glass and turned back to her daughter. "Esprit, don't you look lovely tonight. I just love that dress. It's stunning. Oh, that reminds me, come over here with your father and see the dress I picked out for the fundraiser tomorrow."

Esprit frowned. Jordan grabbed her reluctant daughter by the hand and walked her over to the piano. Esprit was suspicious of the mention of the fundraiser, but she walked with her mother over to the box on the piano anyway.

"I just bought it at Stacy Gemma's boutique over in the Grove. God, I just love Stacy's shop. She has such wonderful taste." She opened the box and carefully displayed a dazzling, black chiffon cocktail dress. It was quite beautiful with a deep-cut back, and the bodice was studded with shimmering rhinestones. Esprit looked at the dress. "It's beautiful, Mom, but Casey and I have to get going. We're having dinner before the movie."

Jordan looked first at her daughter and then at Ethan. "Hey, I've got an idea. The movie isn't until eight. Would the two of you like to join us for dinner? I'm sure your father and Casey would like to sit and talk a while. They haven't seen each other in such a long time, and besides, it's just about ready."

Without even looking at Casey, Esprit said, "Thanks, Mom, but Casey and I haven't seen each other this week, and we're kind of looking forward to being alone, maybe another time."

Casey was disappointed, but he kept his mouth shut. However, Ethan seized the moment to make his play. "Hey, you two, I've got an even better idea. I know you've got plans for tonight, and I don't want to spoil them, so why don't the two of you join Jordan and me tomorrow evening at Arthur Annonberg's fundraiser. Casey, Vice-President Mitchell is going to be there. How would you like to meet him?"

Before Esprit had a chance to say no, Casey jumped up with a wide grin. "Sir, we would love to. I'd be honored to attend the fundraiser. Are you really serious about introducing me to Vice-President Mitchell?"

Esprit, standing behind Casey, shot her parents the devil's look, but she held back, not wanting to disappoint Casey.

Ethan laughed. "Of course I'm serious. He's an old friend of mine. It's black tie though. You'll need a tuxedo."

"No problem, sir, I'll rent one tomorrow morning first thing. Thank you so much! I'm really looking forward to this!" He turned to Esprit. "Well, I guess we should get going or we'll never make the movie."

Ethan walked over and put his arm around his wife. Smiling, he said, “You’re welcome, Casey. You know we are very fond of you. Please be here by seven. The car will take us over promptly at seven thirty.”

Jordan smiled. “You two kids get going. Have fun tonight, and, Casey, we’ll see you tomorrow.”

Casey took Esprit by the hand. “Thanks again, Mr. and Mrs. Burke, we’ll see you later.”

Esprit turned and glared back at her parents with murder in her eyes as the two of them stood at the door arm and arm, smiling and waving goodbye.

As soon as Casey and Esprit left the house, Ethan kissed his wife. “Jordan, putting that dress on the piano was pure genius. It was the perfect set-up! Remind me to make you the campaign strategist for my Senate run.”

Jordan coyly replied, “All in a day’s work, honey, now let’s go eat dinner. The cook prepared Dover sole and I’m starving.”

Outside, Esprit and Casey walked hand in hand down the fieldstone steps that led from the grand entrance of the house to the brick paved porte-cochere where Casey’s car was parked. Neither said a word until they reached the car. Casey could sense that Esprit was ticked off, but he didn’t care. The vice-president! He couldn’t pass that up, no way!

Casey came around and opened the door for her. As soon as she got in the car Esprit cursed her mother. “God, sometimes I hate her as much as I do my father. It was a set-up. She planned that whole thing, the dress on the piano and everything, just to get me to go to that fucking fundraiser. She knew if my father asked you, I wouldn’t say no. Damn it! She pisses me off!”

Casey was taken aback by her outburst of anger. “Take it easy, Spree. Jesus Christ, you always make your parents out to be monsters. Your mother was just showing you and your dad a dress for crying out loud. You’re acting like it was some major conspiracy. Aren’t you being a little paranoid?”

"Listen, Casey, the last thing I want is to fight over this. I haven't been alone with you for almost a week, but my mother showed my father that dress a half-hour ago. I overheard them talking about it across the hall when I was getting ready. My father was pissed about the two-thousand-dollar price tag. That whole scene in the living room was a complete fabrication, calculated to use you to get me to go to the fundraiser so that my asshole father can get his family photo with the vice-president in the fucking newspaper! I told them three times I didn't want to go. I even spoke to my mother about it this morning."

"I think you're reading way too much into it, besides, we'll have fun. It'll be like going to the prom, only the vice-president of the United States will be there. That reminds me, let me call and order a tux before I forget."

Ignoring her obvious anger, Casey picked up his cell phone and called directory assistance to get the number of the shop where he'd rented his tuxedo for the prom last spring. After a minute or so they connected him and he discussed with the shopkeeper his new measurements because he'd put on about twenty pounds since then. He spent the next few minutes on the phone finalizing the arrangements while Esprit sat silently beside him, arms tightly folded across her chest.

As soon as Casey got off the phone, Esprit started in on him. "Look, Casey, I love you and I want to have a nice night, and I'll even go to the damn fundraiser, but you need to hear me out once and for all. My father is not some kind of saint because he happens to be a congressman, all right? He's a manipulative egomaniac and a son of a bitch who's squandering my great-grandfather's fortune. Now there was a great man, a man who worked his ass off to make something of himself, and who didn't give a shit about seeing his picture in the *New York Times*."

"But, Spree…."

"If you think my father became a politician because of some altruistic need to serve the common man, you're not only dead wrong, you're as naïve as hell! My father doesn't give a shit about the common man. He only cares about satisfying his big ego. And my mother…she's an opportunistic snake in the grass hiding behind her phony Southern belle façade!"

"Whoa! Take it easy! I know your father can be a bit overbearing and manipulative, but that's the nature of politics. It's not him, it's the system. He's just playing the cards he's been dealt. And he's damn good at it."

"Bullshit!"

"You're wrong about your father. I know he has a big ego. Name one successful politician that doesn't. But you're wrong when you say he doesn't care about the people of this country. I've talked to him about his ideas many times, and I think he's right on the money."

"Casey, you don't know what the hell you're talking about."

"I don't? I look at your father and then I look at my parents. Esprit, my parents haven't even voted in the last two elections! How about this! Last weekend I asked them to come with me and some of the kids from the team and their parents to spend Sunday morning working down at the Habitat for Humanity housing project in Asbury Park. They just laughed at me like my request was the funniest thing they ever heard. Esprit, my father has never given a dime to charity, that is until it hit close to home when he lost a bunch of his friends in 9/11, and then suddenly he was a fucking philanthropist, at least to all the Wall Street widows and to the firemen's families. And my mom…oh…she's charitable all right; she's never missed a charity luncheon as long as there was a cocktail hour and a silent auction."

Esprit ripped at her hair in frustration. "You really don't get it, Casey. You're really blind when it comes to your parents, you know that? Okay, so they like to party and have a good time. So what? They love you…they really, really, love you! Their lives are centered totally around you and your success. They adore you and give you everything that you could ever want. Christ, Casey, do you think you'd be who you are today without everything they've done for you? What about the sports camps, the tournaments, the private trainers, the cars, the money…?" Esprit started to cry. "Jesus, Casey, they love and support you, they're always there for you! My parents only want me around when it suits them and their fucked-up, snobby lifestyle. They don't give a shit about me. My father can't wait till I leave for school next fall. His only concern with me is that I don't embarrass him, and he totally hates the idea that I want to be an actress. Answer me this, Casey Collins, when was the last time you saw my father at one of my shows?"

She'd struck a nerve. He didn't respond.

She wiped the tears from her eyes, put her hand on his thigh and squeezed. "Listen, this is getting us nowhere. Let's just forget about our parents for a while and have a nice night, okay?"

Casey was blown away. She'd never talked to him like that before, and her passion was palpable. She'd made some good points, but he still thought that his parents' lives were shallow and void of any meaning. At that moment he was very confused, but he knew one thing for sure. She was wrong about her father, and eventually she would see the truth. He placed his hand over hers. "You're right. Let's knock off this crap and go have some fun."

Esprit smiled for the first time that night, and it was a beautiful smile. She wrapped her arms around his neck and squeezed him. Then she leaned over and tried to kiss him squarely on the mouth, but she only managed to kiss half of it because he insisted on keeping his head straight and one eye on the road. The car swerved a little as she leaned in to kiss him. They both laughed, each thankful that the night hadn't been ruined by another stupid argument.

Before going to the movie theatre Casey and Esprit stopped at the Americana Diner for a bite to eat. The Americana was the quintessential Greek diner in all its burnished stainless steel glory. From the faux railcar design, to the miniature jukebox at each table, to its shimmering aluminum-clad façade, the Americana was the real deal. And of course it had had the obligatory, totally over-the-top, thirty-foot-high neon sign out front on the highway. The damn sign could be seen for a mile, and it lit up the surrounding sky like a Christmas tree. And like all authentic Jersey diners, the Americana served the best food money could buy twenty-four hours a day. Not to mention that it was conveniently located on the highway about halfway between Esprit's house and the movie theatre.

The young couple squeezed side by side into the bright red vinyl booth, and Casey put a few quarters in the jukebox. He ordered an egg-white omelet with spinach and Feta cheese, two sides of sausage and a large orange juice. She ordered a California cheeseburger, medium rare, with fries and lots of catsup. Esprit washed her meal down with a large diet Pepsi – go figure. As the tinny music piped out of the little speaker beneath the table, they quickly polished off their meal. They talked of football and of Esprit's upcoming play, Shakespeare's *The Taming of the Shrew*, and somehow they managed to keep their discussion clear of parents, parties, and any other dicey subject.

After the quick dinner, Casey drove the final couple of miles to the Sony Multiplex at Monmouth Mall. Though it was always crowded, this was their favorite theatre because it had sixteen screens and stadium seating. It was the kind of seating where you could sit high up above the screen and where the arms between the seats folded back so you could make three seats into a couch of sorts. The folding arms allowed for Casey's extra large frame to stretch out comfortably, and for Esprit to have the room to snuggle up against him.

Casey let Esprit pick the movie, and she selected a new Adam Sandler comedy. She figured it was a movie they'd both like, and it would help lighten the mood. The film, as expected, was really, really, funny. It didn't have much of a plot, but Sandler goofed around while contorting himself into hilarious positions for about an hour and a half, and the two of them cuddled and laughed right through to the credits.

As they were leaving the crowded theatre, Casey looked at his watch. It was still pretty early, only a little after ten. He grinned and said, "Hey, my parents are out with the Kimballs tonight, they won't be home till way after midnight. Why don't we go back to my house for a swim before I take you home?"

"Esprit looked up into Casey's big brown eyes, at first innocently, but then her smile evolved into a sexy smirk. In her best Scarlett O'Hara voice, she said, "Why, Casey…I do believe that I don't have a swimsuit. Whatever shall I wear?"

He looked down at her grin with a deadpan expression and said in a very poor Rhett Butler imitation, "Why, Scarlett, my dear, I don't give a damn. I am a Gentleman!" They broke up laughing and headed for the car.

By this point they were much more at ease with each other than they'd been earlier. They left the theatre laughing and sped all the way home with the top down. When they arrived about fifteen minutes later, as expected, his father's BMW sedan wasn't in the driveway. Casey reached for Esprit and stroked her hair. "It's all clear; let's just stop in the house and check for messages before we go out to the pool."

They walked in through the front door and down the hall into the kitchen. Casey's eyes were drawn directly to the phone, but the message light wasn't flashing. He was momentarily disappointed, but then he looked down at Esprit and imagined her soaking wet body naked and wriggling around beneath him, and he quickly forgot all about football.

They left the house through the kitchen and walked across the back yard to the pool cabana. The cabana had recently been redecorated, and in reality was less a cabana and more like a fancy clubroom, replete with plush white carpeting, a massive leather sectional sofa, home theatre system, stereo, wet bar, refrigerator, bathroom, and two changing rooms.

Casey dimmed the lights and turned to Esprit. "I love you,

Spree." He gently placed his rough hands on her face and kissed her deeply on the mouth. He broke the kiss and pointed to one of the changing rooms. "Why don't you put your things in there and grab yourself a beer or a glass of wine, then meet me out in the pool."

She smiled and looked up into his eyes. "You go on out, I'll be out in a minute, and don't forget to get me a towel."

Casey watched her keenly as she walked into the changing room. Once she closed the door he couldn't get out of his clothes fast enough. Within seconds he'd shed his shoes, kakis, shirt, and boxers. He left them lying on the carpet where they fell. He grabbed a pile of towels from the closet, threw them on a lounge chair near the cabana door and then leaped into the pool with a loud splash. He swam around for a bit, but suddenly he jumped out of the pool and ran over to the left of the cabana door; he'd forgotten to dim the patio lights. He quickly corrected his mistake so that the area surrounding the pool was quite dark except for the one submerged spotlight at the deep end of the pool. The underwater light cast a soft shimmering glow about halfway across the pool, and the shallow end, the end closet to the cabana, was left dark in shadow. He snuck back into the pool before Esprit came out.

Esprit and Casey had been having sex for well over a year, and Esprit was not one to be shy. She was proud of her body, and she loved to show it off to Casey. She walked straight out of the changing room without a stitch of clothing and sashayed over to the fridge. She grabbed a Corona, popped the top, took a sip and headed unselfconsciously out the door and over to the pool. She wanted to seduce and arouse him, so she slowly and seductively, one careful step at a time, entered the pool in the shadowy shallows of the shallow end while he floated, less than patiently, in the deep end by the steps.

He waited for her to come to him because he wanted to make love to her in the soft light. Nothing drove him to the peak of sexual madness more than watching Esprit's facial expressions when they made love.

Esprit slowly stepped into the pool. The slight chill in the air caused her nipples to rise to attention and goose bumps to rise on the flesh of her arms. Casey followed her every move. Between the dim light and shadows wafts of steam rose from the surface of the pool, making her shimmering nakedness seem even more erotic. He could barely see her, but what he could see he wanted, and he wanted it now. Neither spoke as she ever so slowly took a sip of her beer and carefully placed it on the edge of the pool. Esprit pulled back her hair and silently slipped beneath the water of the shallow end.

She swam slowly and steadily just beneath the surface until she was just below and directly in front of Casey. As she languished under the water before him she gathered all her remaining energy and burst up from the depths, falling into his strong, waiting arms. Even though every inch of Casey's body was rock hard, over time he'd worked hard to become a gentle and patient lover, and Esprit knew just what to expect. Casey hungrily kissed her on the mouth, his tongue searching for hers, all the while gently caressing any and every part of her body he could touch. Her back, her thighs, her ass, her breasts, it didn't matter. Every inch of her felt astonishing to him.

Esprit eagerly returned his kiss and reached down between his legs until she found what she was looking for. She gently rolled him back and fourth in her hand while frantically touching the rest of his body with her other hand in the very same way that he was touching her. Casey's breathing became labored and urgent as he gently moved her yielding body over to the deep-end steps. He gently pried her away from him and rested her arched back on the top two steps so that he could look at her, all of her.

Her firm and swelling breasts and tiny waist were glistening with little droplets of water in the moonlight. She dropped her head and arched her back even further when he parted her thighs and softly kissed his way northward from her knees to the small triangle of damp golden curls. Watching her reach an orgasm was for Casey almost as pleasurable as having his own. In a few moments she was desperately reaching for his head with one hand while supporting herself with the other. He eagerly nipped and kissed her until she couldn't stand it anymore. Between each gentle stroke Casey smiled as he watched Esprit's eyes roll back and her moist glistening body begin to writhe and buck with pleasure. Very soon thereafter she reached her climax, and her body shuddered with the intensity of the pleasure. When her writhing and spasms finally subsided, Casey smiled, enjoying the moment as she panted to catch her breath.

Esprit eventually regained her composure and she went to him. She turned Casey around and sat him down on the second step of the pool, right where she had been moments before. For several minutes she skillfully and playfully returned the favor. Her mouth, sometimes soft, sometimes rough, stroked and kissed him until he couldn't stand the feeling for one more second. She knew his threshold, so she backed off just before he was ready to explode. She lightly kissed him on the mouth and face as she climbed up and straddled him. Casey eased himself into her and for a brief moment they were both absolutely still as they stared into one another's eyes. He took her breasts, each in turn, to his mouth as they began to rock back and forth, first slowly, and then with an ever-increasing rhythm until both approached the edge of an incredible orgasm. They tried to withhold the moment for as long as possible, but when it came, they moaned in unison.

Casey arched his back and let out a stifled moan. Esprit rested her head on his shoulder. They were both physically spent, but only for the moment.

"Oh God, Casey, that was amazing. I really missed you!"

"Me too, this beats fighting!"

"You better believe it!" She laughed.

He picked her up in his arms and carried her off to the center of the pool. They swam together for a while, occasionally pausing to intertwine and luxuriate in each other's bodies. After a while they left the pool, wrapped themselves in the big fluffy towels and went into the cabana where they cuddled up together on the big sofa.

Esprit looked up at Casey and said, "I'm sorry that you didn't hear from Coach Paterno today. He'll call tomorrow."

"I hope so. All this waiting is making me a little crazy. I've had a really short temper with everybody the last couple of days."

"Really? I hadn't noticed." She laughed.

"Well, tomorrow's a pretty big day. First I'm having lunch with my dad to clear the air, and then tomorrow night I get to go with you to meet the vice-president at a fancy party, and somewhere in between I hope to hear from Coach Paterno."

"Well, let's not worry about all that now. I promise I'll try to behave and attempt to have a good time tomorrow night with you at the fundraiser."

"Thanks, that means a lot to me. I can't wait to meet Vice-President Mitchell."

Esprit punched him in the chest and laughed. "Okay, you big jerk! I think it's time to bring me home. I've got to be up early tomorrow. I'm going to the beach with Jamie in the morning, and then I suppose I'll have to go find a dress for tomorrow night, a very expensive one."

They kissed one more time and got up to dress. Casey got dressed right there in the cabana while Esprit walked back to the dressing room. Once inside she closed the door, but before getting dressed she went into her purse and searched for her birth control pills. Lately she'd been very careless with her pills, and she was a little worried because she and Casey had been together a lot in the last month. She smiled when she found the round plastic case in the bottom of her bag and absentmindedly swallowed her pill. She then dried her hair and got dressed.

Casey waited patiently. After about fifteen minutes she came out and they left Casey's house and drove the few short miles back to her home. They were both very quiet in the car, each caught up in their own thoughts. She secretly hoping Casey wouldn't get the call from Coach Paterno and thinking about ways to get even with her mother, and he about the great sex he'd just had, starting his next cycle of steroids, and meeting the vice-president.

They reached the Burke estate and Casey drove up her long drive. He parked in the circle in front of the house and held her for just a moment. Then he kissed her good night and whispered, "Sweet dreams," in her ear.

As she closed the car door she whispered back, "I'll call you tomorrow morning. I love you, Casey!"

Chapter Five

Sunday Morning in a Pirate Paradise

Sunday Morning, September 2nd

Casey woke up early on Sunday morning, even though it was his light workout day. He had no football practice and only planned a short workout at the gym. Like he did every morning, he hit the floor and sped through his warm-up routine. At first he was a bit groggy, but as he worked his way through his push-ups he began to feel better. He thought about the previous night with Esprit. Though they'd argued early in the night, the fight hadn't lasted long and the end of the night had been awesome! Casey couldn't imagine life without her. She was smart and beautiful, and damn, she was hot!

As he finished his push-ups and rolled over to do his crunches he heard someone walking down the hall, probably his mother, and his thoughts turned back to last night's quarrel with Esprit. He wondered if there was anything to what Esprit had said about his parents. It was true they gave him everything he wanted, and he knew they both loved him, but what about them? What about the way that they lived? Their lives seemed so shallow and insignificant to him.

Casey believed a good life was measured by personal achievement, by a sense of accomplishment, and by one's contribution to the world around him, and to that end he was totally committed to many things other than football and school. He often did work for Habitat for Humanity when he could find the time, and he spent two weeks at the beginning of each summer as a volunteer councilor at a Fresh-Air Fund football camp for inner-city kids.

What charitable work had his parents ever done? His father barely made it through college, and then he was lucky enough to fall into a high-paying Wall Street job simply because of a friendship with a frat brother who'd already made it big on the street. His father earned a great living, but what did he do with it? Not much.

His parents spent their whole summer either down at the beach club or throwing pool parties in the back yard every weekend, and this year his father's number one goal in life seemed to be going to as many Bruce Springsteen shows as he could get tickets for. He'd probably already seen him ten times this year so far. The rest of his free time he spent trying to relive his good old college days. He came home every Thursday night drunk as a skunk from some lame-ass strip club or bar in the city, and then he'd stay high for the rest of the weekend.

As for his mom, well, what Esprit said was true. She was always there for him. There was no doubt about that. But in reality she wasn't any better than his father. She'd spent the last five years of her life in a fog; summer's at the beach, cocktailing all day long and into the night with all the other rich, spoiled housewives, and then the rest of the year flitting from one social event to the next. She had a teaching degree, but she'd never spent a single day in a classroom. His father's money had allowed her a very cushy life, and in doing so it had anesthetized her to the real world.

The honest to goodness truth was that the rest of the world and all its problems had ceased to exist for his parents. They were content to wear blinders to everything happening outside their small circle of friends. This was the one fact that bothered Casey the most. They had all the ability and the financial means to make a difference in the world, but they couldn't give a shit. That was why Esprit was wrong about them, and wrong about her father. Ethan Burke might seem like a jerk to his naïve daughter, but he was a man who'd sacrificed a large part of his own wealth to serve his country. That was something to respect and admire, not ridicule. Esprit needed to grow up a little, only then would she understand her father.

Casey finished his last set of crunches and his mind snapped back to the present. He began to plan the rest of his day. A quick trip to the gym, then pick up the tux. Then, unfortunately the obligatory lunch with his father. That was definitely something he wasn't looking forward to. After lunch maybe he'd kick back for a few hours, maybe go for a run or something, and then cruise on over to Esprit's at seven. He was really jacked about meeting Vice-President Mitchell. Who knew, maybe he could even get in the family picture. That would be so very…very…cool.

Then, as he'd done almost every morning for the past twenty-nine days, he went to his desk, pulled out his lockbox and administered his last steroid injection of the current cycle. Today he didn't even wince; his mind was elsewhere. When he was finished, without a second thought, he put the box back in the drawer, grabbed his sweats and headed for the shower.

Lisa and Steve were just getting out of bed.

They'd been out late with their friends, the Kimballs. The two couples had started their night at Doris and Ed's Seafood Restaurant over in the Highlands. Doris and Ed's was a posh restaurant with a stellar reputation and a mind-boggling wine list. The owner, Jim DeFillip, closed the waterfront restaurant for all of January and February each year and traveled the globe in search of the finest bottles he could find for his cellar. His award-winning wine list was considered to be one of the most excellent in the entire Northeast.

Four bottles, four full bellies, and three well-spent hours later, the two couples left the restaurant and headed over the Oceanic Bridge into the town of Sea Bright, intent on spending the remainder of the evening dancing at Mcloone's Bar and Grill.

Sea Bright was a postage stamp of a town that divided the Shrewsbury and Navesink Rivers from the Atlantic Ocean and Mcloone's was a happening waterside restaurant and lounge where the affluent, north of thirty-something crowd went for cocktails, dancing and to watch Tim Mcloone, the club's owner and popular local crooner, sing and play piano with his band. The two couples danced and drank until almost two a.m. By the time Lisa and Steve finally returned home, quite intoxicated, it was well past two a.m.

As Lisa climbed out of bed she turned back to her groaning husband and said, "How are you feeling this morning, honey?"

Steve replied in a barely audible growl, "A little better than yesterday, but I still have a little jet lag. Could you get me some Tylenol?

Lisa was one of the fortunate few who never experienced bad hangovers, and she felt fine. She patted her husband on the head and left for the bathroom. A few minutes later she came back dressed in a workout outfit and handed him a couple of Tylenol and a small glass of water. "Here you go, I'm going down to make Casey's shake, and then I'm off to Blue Moon for a yoga class this morning. Can I make you some coffee or get you anything before I go?"

"Coffee would be great. I'll be down in a few minutes. I'm going to grab a quick shower first. Maybe it'll help clear my head."

"I'll probably be gone before you come down. Don't forget you're taking Casey to lunch."

"Oh, thanks for reminding me. I almost forgot. I'll take him over to Barnacle Bill's. He likes that place, and they make a great burger."

"That's great, Steve, but don't sit at the bar. Remember why you're going there in the first place."

"Come on, Lisa, I'm not stupid! What time are you going to

be back?"

"I'm not sure. I've got some shopping to do after the class. I'll call you later. I hope you feel better. Maybe a swim after breakfast will help." Lisa kissed him on the cheek and left the bedroom.

First she went to the front door and grabbed the paper. Then she headed for the kitchen. As soon she started the coffee and began assembling Casey's shake he ambled into the room. "Hey, Mom, is my shake ready?"

"Hi, honey, it's almost done. How was your night with Esprit? Did you guys come back here for a swim? I saw a pile of towels on the chair outside." She winked. "I hope there was no hanky panky going on here while we were out last night."

Casey's face reddened a bit. "Mom, give me a break. We went to a movie and came back here for a swim. I had her home by midnight."

"I'm just teasing. Don't forget about lunch with your father. He's taking you to Barnacle Bill's. I know you like that place."

"Lucky me. We'll sit at the bar while he drinks half a dozen mugs of Bass Ale and watches the Yankee game on TV. This should be some father-son talk."

"Casey, don't be like that. Your father is not going to sit at the bar, and you guys are going to have a great lunch, so knock it off." She handed him a glass. "Here's your shake."

Casey gulped down the shake and finished it without stopping. "By the way, I need a favor. Esprit's dad asked me to join them at the big Republican fundraiser over in Rumson tonight, and I need to rent a tux. I'm a little short on cash. Could you spot me a couple of hundred?"

"Is that the party with the vice-president? I read something about it in the paper yesterday. Though it saddens my heart to think of you as a Republican, sure, honey, just take it out of my purse. It's right over there on the table." She laughed. "So my son is going to the big Republican Party with the vice-president and all those stuffed-shirts and wind-bags, isn't that something?"

"Yup! That's the one. Congressman Burke is going to introduce me to him. How cool is that?"

"It sounds like you're going to have a lot of fun. Good for you, buddy! You deserve it. You've been working pretty hard the last few weeks. It'll be a nice break for you. I have to run to yoga, please be nice to your father at lunch!"

"I will, Mom. I promise. I'm right behind you. I'm going over to the gym.

Not long after they left, Steve made his way downstairs from the shower. He grabbed his cigarettes, a cup of coffee and the paper and went outside to the pool. The sun was shinning intensely, not a cloud in the sky, and it hurt his eyes so he trudged back into the kitchen to retrieve his sunglasses. When he came back out he felt a little better. The aromatic smell of fresh grass clippings and the aroma wafting from the flowers in the flowerbeds surrounding the patio drifted into his consciousness and the pleasant scents helped to ease his headache. He lay down on the lounge chair, set his coffee and cigarettes on the table and scanned the front page of the newspaper. However, try as he might he wasn't able to focus on what he was reading because his thoughts kept drifting to his problems with Casey.

What exactly had gone wrong? Three short years ago the kid had adored him. They did everything together. They camped, went to ball games, to the beach, skiing in Vermont. So what the hell had changed?

Steve began to wonder who had really changed. He was still the same guy and the same father that he was back then. If it wasn't him, it has to be Casey, so what was so different?

He was kidding himself. He knew damn well what was different. Casey was no longer a child, he was a young man, a gifted athlete, and like all young men he wanted to get out from under his parents' wings and change the world. It was possible Casey resented him so much because he wanted to do better than him. He knew how driven Casey was to be the best at everything.

He then considered that maybe this was the way it was supposed to be between a father and a son, even in a healthy relationship. However, he struggled with this notion because he had no road map to follow. His own relationship with his father had been a disaster. His father barely ever spoke to him beyond the age of twelve, and when he did it was only to criticize him for not being enough of a man. Steve's mind wandered back to an incident in his own senior year of high school.

It was right around Christmas time and he'd just been notified that he'd received a full academic scholarship from Columbia University. Steve had excelled at math, and he'd become obsessed with computers. This was before the rise of the Internet, and Steve, like many other computer visionaries of his age, saw the future of computing. But unlike the others, he didn't see the computer for its future communication or commercial potential; rather he was more interested in the speed with which a computer could do complex math calculations. Early in his senior year he'd begun to experiment with statistical programming and his efforts were somehow brought to the attention of a Professor of Mathematics at Columbia. A few months later he was offered a full scholarship from the Columbia math department, as there was no computer science department at the time.

He remembered being really excited and happy about the scholarship because without it he probably would not have had the chance to go to college, but at the same time he was also worried by the prospect of leaving his mother and his sisters alone and at the mercy of his abusive father.

When his father came home drunk that night and found out about Steve's scholarship he went berserk. He berated his son and struck him mercilessly, spewing his drunken venom, "You think you're better than me?" and, "College is only for spoiled sissies," and, "You can forget about college, buddy, you're coming to work with me at the plant to help pay some of these goddamn bills."

Steve couldn't believe that his father was so furious and crazy over this, and he became defiant. He angrily shouted, "I'm going to college, Dad, and there is nothing you can do about it!"

His father stared at him with his milky eyes in utter disbelief. His son had never defied him before. He grew even more enraged, if that was possible, and charged at Steve like an angry bull, but his motor skills and coordination had been slowed by the drink, and Steve saw him coming. He sidestepped out of his father's way and then shoved him with all his might as the old man passed harmlessly by. His father flew right past him and smashed into an old, glass-fronted, china cabinet. It was the one piece of furniture that his mother cherished. His father immediately crumbled to the floor. His head was split open in two places, and he appeared to have broken his arm.

Steve's mother came rushing in and stoically observed the carnage. Without a word to her son, she picked up her barely conscious husband and drove him off to the emergency room. Several hours later she brought him home, all bandaged up, and without a word to his son, Steve's father went directly to his bedroom. He didn't speak to his son for several weeks following the violent incident, but he never attempted to hit him again. Just a few short years later Steve's father died of complications from cirrhosis of the liver while he was away at college.

At the moment, sitting there quietly at the pool, try as he might, Steve couldn't recollect ever having had a single civil conversation with his father, so he was clearly in unfamiliar territory when considering what to do about his deteriorating relationship with Casey.

Then another thought began to creep into his head. What was really bothering Casey? Steve knew it was his drinking. He wondered how the hell he'd ended up with such a straight-laced kid, but at the same time he also wondered if his drinking really had gotten out of control. He was drinking a lot lately. Now that he thought about it he was drinking far more than he realized. But it wasn't as if he was a drunk like his father, swilling cheap vodka out of pints in paper bags for Christ's sake. There were Thursday nights of course, but that was a Wall Street tradition that went way back, and besides, it was good for business, but what about the weekends? When he thought about it, he realized he really was drinking pretty much all of the time, especially on the weekends. It dawned on him that maybe his drinking was in fact becoming a problem. Could he cut back? He didn't drink that much during the week, and he'd be damned if it had ever affected his work. It was something he would need to think about, but at least for today, he wouldn't drink at lunch. That would be a good way to get off on the right foot with Casey. And with that final thought, Steve lit up a cigarette, opened the paper and turned to the sports section.

Ethan and Jordan Burke had just returned from the nine o'clock mass at Holy Cross Church. Holy Cross was situated across the river in the prosperous, if pretentious, little hamlet of Rumson. It was one of those wealthy Catholic parishes so cherished by the Catholic Church hierarchy for its ability to generate ridiculous sums of money to fill the diocese coffers. The parish membership consisted mostly of those affluent families who resided on either side of the Navesink River.

The Burkes never missed Sunday mass when they were in town, and today was no exception. However, two hours earlier when they tried to get Esprit to join them she'd refused, pleading she was too tired. Her absence at church was still bothering Ethan when he and Jordan sat down for breakfast out on the terrace.

Ethan loosened his tie and aggressively buttered a piece of toast. "Jordan, It really burns my ass that the one thing I expect of Esprit, to attend Sunday mass, she continuously refuses to do. How do you think that looks to the rest of the parish? How can these people have confidence in me to effectively manage this district if they see firsthand every Sunday that I can't even manage my family?"

There was more than a little irony surrounding Ethan and Jordan's serious commitment to Sunday Mass because both of them had been raised in religious faiths other than Catholicism. Ethan had been brought up as a Protestant in accordance with his family history, and Lisa, a Southern Baptist. They both believed in God in some Christian form, but over the years they'd developed a pragmatic doctrine rather than a spiritual one. Ethan, ever the political animal, made the decision early on in his political career to switch to Catholicism because it was the leading religion in his chosen congressional district, and Jordan had quietly gone along with his wishes.

"Oh stop it, Ethan, nobody thinks anything of the kind. It's all in your head. Besides, she's going to the party tonight, isn't she? Don't push your luck."

"I guess you're right, but did you see the way that she glared at me this morning? She hates me! I wish that there was some way I could get through to her that I'm not the bad guy. I was young once you know, and I didn't particularly like my father very much either, nor did I trust politicians. Hell, that's why I got into this racket in the first place, I wanted to be better than them, I wanted to change the way things were done."

"Ethan, let it go. You're making yourself crazy."

"I know, honey, but remember when I first started out in Washington I naively thought that I could enter public service without getting my hands dirty. I thought with all my family's wealth I wouldn't have to grub here and there from every little interest group for a few thousand dollars."

"Honey, give it a rest."

"Little did I know how much money was actually involved in a campaign. And more importantly, how much more valuable than money was the power that came along with forming those dirty little friendships. Even still, I've managed to keep my integrity mostly intact, and that's not easy in Washington. But Esprit doesn't even try to understand. She looks at me like I'm Bill Clinton screwing an intern in the oval office for Christ's sake."

"Ethan, she's only eighteen years old, and on top of that she's totally embarrassed by our wealth. Remember, honey, her friends don't live like we do. And don't forget that she's an actress. Sometimes she just can't separate her drama from her real life. You should count your blessings that she's fallen for a levelheaded boy like Casey. God knows the rest of her friends are really out there."

Ethan heard shuffling behind him and turned towards the house. Esprit walked up to the table dressed only in a bathing suit, T-shirt, sunglasses, and sandals. He looked up at her and said, "Good morning, Esprit, I'm sorry we missed you at church this morning."

Esprit raised her dark glasses, completely ignoring him, and looked directly at her mother. "That was some kind of stunt you pulled yesterday! I can't believe you used my boyfriend to make me go to that stupid party. That's one of the lowest tricks you've ever pulled, Mother!"

Lisa put her hand to her chest. "Esprit, honey, please calm down. I haven't the foggiest idea what you are talking about."

"Bullshit! And you know what really sucks? When I told Casey what you did, he didn't believe me. He thinks the two of you are so wonderful!"

"Esprit, is that language really necessary?"

Esprit ignored her. "Well, Mother, I'll be there tonight, and I'll try not to embarrass the two of you, but let's get something straight right here, right now! I'm doing this for Casey, not for you, and if you ever try to pull this crap again, I'll be out of here so fast you won't know what happened." She turned to Ethan. "And, Daddy, you can go explain that to your goddamn constituents!" Esprit turned on her heels and began to walk away, but she stopped suddenly and turned back again. "Oh, by the way, I'm going to the beach for a few hours, and then I'm going down to the Grove to buy the most expensive dress I can find because I am sure you and Daddy want me looking my very best this evening."

Before they could respond, Esprit turned away and left the terrace. They looked at each other and Jordan said, "Maybe we weren't as subtle as we thought."

"I guess not. We'll have to be very careful with her tonight, or this whole plan may blow up in my face. Thank God Casey will be there to keep her in check, otherwise this could be a fiasco in the making."

"Don't worry, my darling, she'll be just fine. With a new dress and Casey on her arm, she wouldn't dream of acting up this evening."

Casey pulled into the gym parking lot at nine o'clock. When he walked in, Frankie was standing there waiting for him. Casey was startled to see him there. He poked Casey in the chest and said, "Hey, sport, did you decide to sleep in this morning?"

Casey looked relieved. He dropped his gym bag in the corner and said, "Give me a break, it's Sunday for Christ's sake, and besides, I went out with Esprit last night."

"Oh, you did, did you? Dude, give me the dirt. You know how I think she's a hottie!"

"Whoa, dog, don't even think of going there! That's my girlfriend you're talking about." He laughed.

"That's cool, partner, but she's still a hottie! Any word from Paterno?"

"Nothing yet."

"Don't sweat it. You look good and always remember what I told you: Looking good is just as important as feeling good! What do you want to work on this morning?"

"Legs, let's do legs."

"Legs it is! Let's start at the squat rack."

They walked over to the rack and Frankie started loading

plates. "Hey, Casey, I know I was kind of rough on you yesterday, and I'm sorry, but it's my job to train you, and what you asked me to do was crazy. Another cycle right now is just too dangerous. You've got to give your body a chance to recover. We're clear on this, right?"

Casey looked away. "Sure, Frankie, I told you. I was an idiot for even asking. No sweat, it's over and done with."

"All righty then! Let's get to work."

Frankie and Casey threw themselves into a two-hour grueling leg workout. They did at least four sets on virtually every machine, bench, and bar in the gym until they were both dripping with sweat and ready to drop from muscle fatigue. Neither spoke much during the workout to conserve their remaining energy. When it was finally over Frankie, panting for breath, looked at his protégé admiringly and said, "Kid, you're in the most unbelievable shape of anyone I've ever trained, you're an animal, now go hit the showers and have a nice afternoon. You've earned it."

As Casey walked away Frankie watched after him with both envy and pride. He saw in Casey an unparalleled physical specimen, and he had absolutely no doubt that Casey was going to go very far in the world of football.

Casey got home from the gym around twelve thirty and found his father sitting alone in the family room watching ESPN on his sixty-inch Sony plasma. Steve looked up and smiled at his son from his fancy oversized black leather recliner. A couple of years ago Steve saw the recliner in a Sharper Image catalogue and paid over four thousand dollars for it. If you asked him, he would tell you it was worth every penny.

"The Yankee's lost again last night, now they're five games back with twenty-five to play, and the Red Sox are coming in next week. I'm getting tickets for Thursday night, do you want to go?"

"I'd love to, Dad, but that's the night before my game, so I don't think I can make it. Besides, you'll be going with a bunch of guys from work, right?"

Casey thought about the last time he'd gone to a Yankee game with his dad and the guys from his office. They all got shit-faced and one of them had started a fight in the stands. They all ended up getting thrown out of the stadium after the fifth inning. He remembered his dad's friends in the parking lot on the way out afterwards, all stoked up and standing around their limo with a cooler full of beer, talking like it was the greatest night of their lives. The night had totally sucked.

"Yeah, but it would still be great if you came. Maybe I'll get tickets for you and me to a playoff game later on in September or October. Anyhow, you ready to go to lunch? I thought we'd head over to Barnacle Bill's."

"Sure let's go."

They left the house and climbed into Steve's pride and joy, his brand-new silver BMW 725 Sedan, and drove over to the restaurant. It was only a short drive. When they entered the waterfront restaurant the tables were almost full and the bar was already crowded and noisy. Barnacle Bill's, because of its location on the river and the adjacent marina, always drew a huge crowd on weekends. The entrance foyer to the restaurant was bursting with people swarming in and out of the rustic, nautically challenged dining room. Barnacle Bill's had a casual and noisy atmosphere and a reputation for its simple, yet well prepared seafood and its freshly ground sirloin burgers. However, its true claim to fame was the free baskets of warm roasted peanuts that were placed on every table along with the big copper bin full of nuts at the entrance for refills.

The owner, Todd Sherman, an affable bear of a man with a thick main of hair that hadn't fought a comb in years, a bushy mustache to match, and an irrepressible smile, had been a fixture at Barnacle Bill's forever. As always, he greeted them at the door with a big grin and after a few short pleasantries, he offered to seat them. Casey and Steve followed Todd to a small table for two right next to the window overlooking the marina. As they walked to the table their shoes crunched on the empty peanut shells that were scattered over the wood plank floor. It was long-standing tradition to just throw the empty peanut shells anywhere. The shells were part of the restaurant's charm and added to the fun and ambiance.

Because their table was right up against window it had an unobstructed view of all the boats cruising up and down the river, but unfortunately the table was also only a couple of feet away from the crowded bar where a raucous group of regulars was watching the US Open Tennis Tournament. In between chugs of draft beer the noisy bar patrons were arguing the merits of Venus Williams versus Maria Sharapova.

Once they were seated Todd moved on to other customers. Father and son were left with an uncomfortable silence because neither Casey nor Steve knew where to begin. They buried their heads in the menus and then scrutinized the specials board hanging above the bar while gathering their thoughts. After what seemed like an eternity, but in reality was only a minute or two, the waitress finally came over to the table to take their order. Steve ordered a mushroom cheddar burger and an ice tea. Casey did a double take when he heard his father's order and then ordered a chef salad and a mineral water for himself.

As soon as the waitress left Casey looked at his father skeptically and said, "Dad, was that for my benefit? We've been here a hundred times and you've always ordered a beer."

"Casey, I know my drinking has a lot to do with what has been bothering you lately, so I decided that for today I would respect your wishes. It's only a beer after all." Steve sat up a little straighter, "I wanted to have lunch with you today because you and I need to set things right. Up till a couple of years ago, you and I were best friends, but now…now I feel like you're a total stranger. But more than that, lately I've seen nothing but hatred in your eyes towards me, and I don't get it. I'd like to know just what I've done to become the target of all your anger."

Casey thought it wasn't starting well, so he'd throw his dad a softball. "Dad, I'm sorry, and you're right. I've been real stressed out about my scholarship, and I've been taking it out on you. That's all it is, really!"

"Casey, nice try but come on! Give me a break! I wish it were that easy. You and I both know that there's more going on here than just you being stressed out. Look, we're here. Let's take the time to talk this out. Sweeping our problems under the rug isn't going to solve anything, so if it's okay with you, I'll go first."

"Sure, Dad, whatever you say."

"All right, I've been thinking about some of the things you've said to me. Maybe I have been drinking too much, and we both know that I haven't been taking very good care of myself."

Casey nodded his assent.

"Starting today I'm going to seriously make an effort to cut back on the booze and also get my fat ass back to the gym, but, Casey, you need to understand something. I will never be an athlete or in top physical shape. I never was, and I never will be. But the thing I don't understand is why my partying and poor health upsets you so much! Some of the stuff coming out of your mouth lately is, well…quite frankly, it's bizarre!"

Casey shifted a little in his seat. He was heating up. "You just don't get it! It's not just the partying. Listen to me for once, really listen. I know you and Mom love me and would do anything for me, but what the hell else do the two of you really care about? I'll tell you what! Money! Parties! Vacations! Buying new toys for the house! With you and Mom it's always about the best car, the best TV, the best pool! Neither of you has a clue as to what is going on in the rest of the world out there unless it affects you and your wallet somehow."

"Casey, be careful."

"I've watched you; every morning as soon as you step on the

ferry you spend five minutes on the sports page and the rest of the time you read the financial section, and to hell with the rest of the world. At night when you come home you eat dinner, pop a cork on a bottle of wine, and then it's off to sitcom heaven or a baseball game. You want to know what's really pissing me off? I think you and Mom are spoiled and selfish!"

"Casey, are you out of your mind? Who the hell…."

Casey was on a roll and not to be stopped. "Dad, please don't interrupt me. I know you take great care of me; you and Mom would do anything for me, but why? I'll tell you why. Because I'm your pride and joy, and because you get to brag to all your friends about your wonderful son, that's the only reason. You wanted this to be an honest conversation, so let me be honest with you. I don't work as hard as I do in sports or in school to please you or Mom, I do it for myself because I want to make a difference in this world someday. I want to do more with my life than just make money. I often wonder if you and Mom would still treat me the same way if I had the same problems that Tim Fitzgerald does, or would you just pretend that I didn't exist like his parents do with him?"

Mercifully, the waitress came and interrupted Casey's venomous monologue. Steve's skin was crawling, and he tried but failed to keep his composure. After she departed he took a bite of his burger and said as softly but as firmly as he could, "Listen, you idealistic, self-centered, naïve little shit! When did you learn to read a crystal ball? How the fuck do you know what your mother and I are thinking or doing twenty-four-seven? And where do you get off with your holier-than-thou attitude? You, my spoiled son, whom I've given every opportunity in life, excuse the hell out of me! Shame on your mother and I! Instead of going out and saving the poor and the hungry of the world, your mother and I focused all of our energy and attention on you! Shame on us for being so selfish and uncaring! And as for our lifestyle, don't you dare condemn it until you've walked in our shoes! You think about that every time you hop in your mustang convertible, make a call on your cell phone, or email your friends on your damn two-thousand-dollar computer!"

Casey lowered his head and stared at the floor.

"Jesus, Casey, your mother gave you two hundred bucks just this morning so you could rent a fucking tuxedo for that idiot's fundraiser tonight. Listen, pal, your mom and I aren't perfect, but here's a fun fact! Neither are you! So if you choose to worship phony assholes like Ethan Burke, that's your business, but don't you dare condemn your mother and me because you don't know shit!"

Casey raised his hands. "Great! This is why I didn't want to have lunch with you in the first place. I knew it would go down exactly like this; the only thing missing is your beer. Don't do me any favors, Dad, go ahead and order one!"

"Casey, you are un-fucking-believable! If you only knew the life I had growing up and the asshole I had for a father, you'd consider yourself the luckiest kid on the planet." Steve looked away. "But you don't get it and maybe you never will. But I promise you this, sport, someday you are going to regret the stuff you're thinking and saying, and you're going to realize that your mother and I are really good people."

Casey began to squirm even more in his chair but instead of responding he lowered his head, kept quiet and picked at his salad. Finally after another lengthy period of uncomfortable silence he decided to try and make peace for the second time, not because he bought into his father's speech, but because he wanted to finish his lunch and get the hell out of there.

"Dad, listen, I'm sorry! I'm being a total jerk. Forgive me. You're right, okay? I'm the one being selfish and starting today I'm going to lighten up on you and Mom. I'm sorry about the beer comment, and I'm glad to hear that you're going to try and get your health in order, really!"

Steve's expression said it all. He didn't buy a word of it. Even so, he finished the last few bites of his sandwich and said, "I hope you mean that, Casey, and you aren't just trying to slip out of an uncomfortable situation here."

Casey was no longer picking over his salad so Steve said, "If you're done eating, why don't we head back to the house and see what your mother's up to?"

They both stood up and Casey silently followed his father out of the restaurant. When they arrived back home, Lisa was still not home from shopping and the house was painfully quiet. Not wanting to spend another minute alone with his dad, Casey immediately ran to check the answering machine, which was not flashing any new messages. Then he came back and said, "Dad, thanks for lunch. I think I'm going out for a run." Without waiting for a reply he left to change and was out the door in shorts and sneakers not more than two minutes later.

Steve was not particularly happy with the outcome of their lunch. He knew in his heart that Casey hadn't been sincere at the end of the conversation. He was so frustrated and confused by the whole thing. He kept thinking back to his own terrible relationship with his father, and he couldn't find an answer. It just wasn't there. What had he done wrong? What could he do to fix it? No answers were forthcoming, so he went to the refrigerator, grabbed a beer, headed back to his recliner in the family room and flipped on the baseball game.

Chapter Six

Fun & Frolicking at the Fundraiser

Sunday Evening, September 2nd

It was a warm, steamy late summer night on the Navesink River. It was the kind of sweltering night when most people lock themselves inside with the air-conditioning set on about sixty-two, and only the hearty venture outdoors in the advent of a dire emergency. It was the kind of night where the humidity was so stifling that wearing clothing at all other than a pair of shorts or a bathing suit was next to unbearable. Regardless of the heat, the fundraiser was set to begin at seven thirty p.m. sharp, the expected temperature, eighty-six degrees, the humidity hovering somewhere around ninety percent.

The party was to be held on the great lawn of the riverfront Rumson estate of one Arthur Annenberg. Annenberg's magnificent home was situated out on the east end of the Navesink River, where it joined the Shrewsbury River and then together the two rivers swept out first into the Raritan Bay and then beyond into the Atlantic. Just across the river, opposite the estate, lay the long spit of land known as the Sandy Hook Peninsula.

The centerpiece of Arthur's impressive estate, aptly named 'East of Eden', was a thirty-room, twenty-eight-thousand-square-foot, French provincial manor house. It had been built in the late nineteenth century. East of Eden's façade was clad in pure white Vermont granite, and the front veranda was surrounded by at least a dozen thirty-foot-high, Corinthian columns. The stately home was situated on twelve private acres of sloping lawns and meticulously manicured gardens that fronted some of the most spectacular riverfront acreage in the Northeast.

Both the main house and the surrounding formal gardens had been meticulously designed by none other than the renowned architect Stanford White in 1886. The estate had been a wedding gift from a New York City railroad magnate to his eldest daughter.

Earlier in the day three circus-sized white tents had been pitched for the evening's event, and hundreds of workers were still scurrying across the grounds of the estate placing flower arrangements, setting up portable bars, and setting tables with fresh linens and silver.

Arthur Annenberg was one of the top entertainment lawyers in the country and the managing partner at Annenberg, Coffee, and Kellogg, a large New York law firm. He also happened to be an avid sports enthusiast and held minority interests in both the New York Giants and the New York Yankees.

At fifty-two he was also quite active in behind-the-scenes politics. A founding father and icon for the budding centrist wing of the Republican Party, he well represented those ever-expanding members that were fiscally conservative yet socially moderate. He vehemently opposed the far right wing, especially their position on gun control, and he was distinctly uncomfortable with the religious-right power base that until recently had controlled the party purse strings. As this year's chairman of the Republican National Committee, he was perhaps the most influential man in the party, and he wielded his power carefully, but always forcefully. His summer fundraiser this year was the hottest ticket of the political season short of the Presidential Inaugural Ball, and a must-attend for anyone with political aspirations beyond a congressional seat.

However, the event was first and foremost a fundraiser, so

invitations went first to those with the deepest pockets and only afterwards to the few politicians who were hot at the moment or running in tightly contested campaign battles where the party was at risk of losing a seat. If truth be told, Ethan Burke fit neither of those two categories, but since the man lived just across the river he'd been invited out of respect for local social decorum.

Annenberg dreamed of leading his party in a new direction, as far away as possible from those conservative bible thumping right-to-lifers and gun-toting cowboys. He was using every bit of his considerable wealth and clout to make that dream into a reality. Arthur's greatest strength had always been his stoicism and his ability to observe and digest everything going on around him. So along that vein for tonight's affair, he'd taken a page out of the local Democratic Party's fundraising textbook.

The geographical area often referred to as the 'Peninsula' in Monmouth County, New Jersey was not only an extremely affluent area, but because of its close proximity to New York City, it was also a hotbed of powerful Democrats. The local Democratic committee was well organized, and each year they threw at least a half-dozen of their own fundraisers; ones that traditionally did extraordinarily well – consistently far better than their Republican counterparts. This was because the Democratic organizers had figured out how to tap into the local celebrity market. They learned how to entice the well-known liberal celebs like Jon Bon Jovi, Bruce Springsteen, Maury Povitch and Geraldo Rivera, who happened to live in the area, to support their cause and act as lures to reel in the big fish donors. Nothing caused the wealthy corporate types in the community to salivate and open their wallets more than attending a local celebrity auction, or even better, to rub elbows with or perhaps even have a picture taken with a bona fide *People Magazine* star.

In a traditional well-heeled community, one's social status was usually displayed with big houses, fancy cars, jewelry, and club memberships, but between the two rivers, 'on the

Peninsula', a master of the universe reached the pinnacle of the social ladder only when he had secured a signed Springsteen or Bon Jovi guitar and hung it over his fireplace. And if by chance there was an accompanying photo with the celebrity, well, that was the absolute bomb. There were probably more signed guitars in wealthy Monmouth County homes than the two famous rock stars could have possibly played in three life times.

For this evening's event, Annenberg had tapped into his own entertainment treasure trove and pulled out two pretty big celebrity fish of his own, Rob Cronin, the conservative, slick-talking megastar of action films, who just happened to be native son of New Jersey, and James Switzer, former box-office superstar and current Republican governor of California. Annenberg represented both of them. He handled mostly their film-related legal affairs, but a few years back he'd negotiated a sweet deal for both of the stars with the owners of a budding Hollywood-themed restaurant chain, one that had an unusual marketing strategy and aggressive plans for a future public offering.

Annenberg had structured the deal so that each of his stars was paid a huge sum in the form of future stock options for what amounted to a just few personal appearances a year. When the restaurant chain finally went public both Cronin and Switzer were able to immediately exercise their options, worth millions at the time, and each walked away from the deal with a considerable amount of cash. Fortunately for them, they did so early on because less than a year after the public offering the company fell upon some very hard times and the stock became virtually worthless.

Cronin and Switzer remained grateful to Arthur for his past efforts and were more than happy to appear at his event. Enticing them to come all the way from California with the use of his private Gulfstream 5 Jet didn't hurt the cause either.

As Annenberg surveyed the frenzy of last-minute activity from his second-floor balcony, he knew that tonight's event was all set to go. Four hundred guests were expected at five thousand dollars a head. His accountant had projected that the event would clear a cool three million for the party coffers after the dinner and silent auction, and Arthur was pleased. Not bad for a night's work. At this late hour the event was in the confident hands of his crack executive staff and a highly qualified New York caterer. As he looked out across his lawn his one remaining concern was the stifling heat and humidity. Unfortunately, the heat was something he had little control over other than to order his staff to strategically place large outdoor fans and electric atomizers to waft cool mist around the grounds of the estate. So they'd sweat a little he thought, hell, it was for a good cause.

Across the river Ethan and Jordan were dressing for the party, and Ethan was more than a bit surly. He wasn't usually one to worry about sweating; politicians with a propensity for excessive perspiration didn't typically last long in such a public arena. However, this evening he was quite agitated by the heat and humidity because of its potential for spoiling his anticipated photo opportunities.

"Jordan, I'm just out of the shower, and I'm already sweating like a pig. Do you have a stronger antiperspirant anywhere in the house? I'm going to look like hell if this keeps up."

Jordan stood up from her dressing table, where she'd been putting on her jewelry, and went to a drawer in her closet. "Calm down, honey, I've got just what you need. You damn Yankees just wilt and fall to pieces every time it gets a little warm." She went to him and handed him a jar of some very expensive Estée Lauder antiperspirant cream. "Just rub that in all over, but not too much, even your face. It'll make your skin feel a little tight, but if you rub it in good, no one will ever notice and you'll stay dry."

"You're a life saver." He began to vigorously apply the cream to his entire body. As he did so he asked his wife, "Have you talked to Esprit since this morning? I hope she's in a better mood, and did you happen to see the dress she bought? God only knows what she picked out."

"I spoke to her while you were in the shower. She was a bit frosty with me, but she'll be fine. As for the dress, it's a stunning, lemony-colored, cocktail dress with spaghetti straps and a pretty, but not too daring neckline. In fact, it's quite elegant, and it only cost you fifteen hundred dollars." She chuckled softly.

"Fifteen hundred dollars? You're kidding me, for a dress she'll only wear one night?"

"You wanted her to be here, darling. It's the price you had to pay, so stop whining and get dressed. I'll help you with your tie in a few minutes."

Ethan grumbled some more and then began putting on his tuxedo.

Back at the Collins' residence Casey had just returned from picking up his tuxedo, and he'd gone up to his room to get ready for the party.

Downstairs, Lisa was moving back and forth between the kitchen and the patio, setting the table and preparing a special dinner. She was preparing grilled filet mignon with a buffalo mozzarella and tomato salad, and an expensive bottle of Chianti, Steve's favorite meal. She'd been out for the better part of the day, and when she returned around four she'd found Steve fast asleep in his favorite chair with a ballgame on the TV. At the time she'd decided not to wake him because she knew that he was probably still exhausted from his trip and also from partying so late the night before. At first she'd wanted to because she was more than a little curious how lunch had gone with Casey, but seeing him there so peaceful, she just didn't have the heart to wake him. She'd get him up just before dinner was ready, and then she'd find out what happened over a nice quiet meal with just the two of them.

Casey finished putting on his tuxedo and appraised himself in the mirror. He'd rented a black, single-breasted Hugo Boss suit with an athletic cut that fit him like a glove. Damn he looked good. He was going to have to buy himself one these monkey suits pretty soon. He was definitely going to need one.

He looked at his watch and noticed that it was almost six thirty, so he put the finishing touches of gel on his curly black hair and trotted downstairs. Lisa was in the kitchen preparing the salad when she heard his heavy footfalls coming down. She called after him to come into the kitchen before he left. He obediently complied and entered the kitchen with a big grin on his face.

"Well, look at you, Casey Collins! Don't you look fabulous! You clean up pretty good for a dumb jock!"

Casey's grin turned into a frown, but just for a moment as Lisa laughed and said she was only kidding. She came around the counter and gave him a hug. Then she held him away at arm's length and said, "You really look great, buddy! I hope you and Esprit have a wonderful time tonight!"

"Thanks, Mom, I hope so too."

He was about to turn and leave when Lisa asked him, "So, Casey, how did things go with your father at lunch today?"

Casey thought about the question for a moment. "To tell you the truth, Mom, it started out pretty bad, but we both had our say, and I think we made peace by the end of lunch."

Lisa did a double take. "Casey, what's that supposed to mean? You think you made peace. I don't understand what that means."

"Mom, I don't have time to give you the blow-by-blow details right now. I've got to get over to the Burkes. Why don't you ask Dad? He'll tell you all about it. Don't wait up for me. I'll probably be home late."

Before Lisa had a chance to react he was out the door.

Lisa was now more curious than ever because of Casey's cryptic response. Well, dinner was almost ready. It was time to wake the old bear up.

She walked into the family room and gently nudged her husband until he drowsily woke from a deep slumber. “Hey, big guy, dinner will be ready in about twenty minutes out on the patio, I’m making you a nice steak.”

“Oh…hi…honey…what time is it? How long was I napping?”

“I don’t know, I got home around four and you were out cold, so I let you sleep. The steaks are on the grill. Why don’t you freshen up and come out in about twenty minutes.

“Sure, Lisa, I’ll be right out.”

Casey showed up at the Burkes’ gate precisely at seven o’clock. Two minutes later Ethan personally opened the door to welcome him in. The very first thing Casey noticed as he walked past Ethan into the house was that the congressman’s face under the bright incandescent lights of the foyer chandelier seemed awfully shiny. It appeared as though he had a thin layer of plastic wrap tightly drawn over his skin. Casey didn’t think it was appropriate to mention it, so he kept the observation to himself.

Soon both Jordan and Esprit drew Casey’s attention away from Ethan’s bizarre skin condition when they made their way down the long spiral staircase. They looked like royalty, a queen and a princess. Jordan came first in her elegant black cocktail dress, followed by her beautiful daughter. He looked first at Esprit’s face and then at her dress, and she took his breath away. She looked simply dazzling in that soft yellow dress. He was in awe of the way that it clung to her gorgeous figure, yet it wasn’t the least bit sleazy. The contrasts of her golden hair, bronze skin and the lemon-yellow dress caused Casey’s heart to skip a beat.

The color of her dress spoke to him of innocence, but the cut gave him another message entirely, and Casey’s only thought was what it would be like to watch her take the dress off later on. He wasn’t able to savor the thought for long because barely did he have a chance to say hello before Ethan rudely interrupted, ushering them all to the door and out into the waiting stretch limousine that would ferry them to the party.

A short five minutes later the car crossed the river and arrived at the open gates of the Annenberg Estate. Once the driver turned into the drive the car slowed considerably and began creeping along the crushed seashell covered roadway that led to the main house. They were stuck behind a long line of other cars. Up ahead in the distance Ethan pointed out the two black Chevy Suburbans used by the secret service to transport the vice-president. When Ethan pointed them out, Casey craned his neck to the window, hoping to get his first glance of the vice-president of the United States. Casey looked around and was overwhelmed by not only the dozens of limousines parked on the lawn but also by the huge number of police and private security people roaming the huge property.

They had gone about three quarters of the way up the drive when suddenly out of nowhere they heard a dreadfully loud swooshing sound coming from directly above the car. The noise startled Casey until he realized what it was, a landing helicopter. By the time the car reached the designated drop off area in front of the house the deafening helicopter had landed not fifty yards away.

As the group exited the car, the cabin door of the helicopter folded down and out walked Governor James Switzer and his wife, followed by Rob Cronin and his date for the evening, the beautiful young actress and rising star, Cathy Cassidy.

The celebrities were ushered into the house by a gaggle of Arthur Annenberg's people to avoid the rush of popping flashbulbs and scrambling photographers. They passed by quickly just in front of the Burkes and Casey, who were stepping away from their car. Esprit ogled both Cronin and the beautiful Cathy Cassidy. She discretely pointed in their direction and whispered, "You guys can all go drool over the vice-president if you want, but I'm going to party with her and Rob Cronin."

Ethan, miffed by her comment, replied, "Please don't forget why we're here, young lady."

She just smiled at him. "Oh, don't you worry, Daddy. I know exactly why I'm here."

The two couples walked arm and arm up the steps to the house. They entered through a grand set of fifteen-foot, solid mahogany doors and found themselves in the crowded receiving hall. The opulent, white marble foyer was decorated with four massive flower arrangements in each corner. The arrangements were composed of hundreds of peonies, roses and lilies in every color of the rainbow. Beside each of the glorious arrangements stood the tuxedoed service staff, stiffly and professionally waiting to usher the entering guests through the large home and out into to the awaiting party on the back lawn.

Arthur Annenberg had been up in his bedroom suite attending to some last-minute business and was finally making his way down the stairs to the party when he spied Ethan Burke and his wife crossing the hall. He considered making make a swift detour so he wouldn't have to entertain yet another tedious conversation with Ethan about his plans for a possible Senate run. Arthur respected Ethan's political drive but found him to be a bit narrow-minded and extraordinarily long-winded. He knew that Ethan, if given the opportunity to start a conversation, would babble on forever and make it all but impossible for him to politely break away. He started to turn away, but when he looked down again he noticed a tall, handsome young man standing just behind the Burkes. Arthur said to his assistant, "I know that face, isn't he the blue-chip linebacker from Middletown South High School? Every major college in the country is trying to recruit that boy. I just read a story about him last week in the press."

Arthur then changed his mind and decided it would be worthwhile to put up with Ethan Burke for a just little while so that he could meet this boy. Who knew? Four years from now this young man with everything being written about him just might be the next Lawrence Taylor, and there was always the possibility that he could end up playing for Arthur's beloved New York Giants. He turned again to his assistant. "I think I'd like to meet that young man, and besides, Burke's wife Jordan isn't bad to look at." As they approached the group he whispered, "It appears that with her daughter, the apple hasn't fallen far from the tree."

Arthur angled through the crowd and made his way up to the Burkes. He warmly greeted Ethan and Jordan. Ethan turned to Esprit and Casey and said, "Arthur, may I introduce you to my daughter, Esprit, and her date for the evening, Casey Collins."

Arthur kissed Esprit lightly on the back of the hand, then turned to Casey and assertively shook his hand. "Ethan, my old friend, you don't need to introduce me to this fine young man. I know all about Casey. I've been following his football career for two years." He looked directly at Casey and said, "So, Casey, is it going to be Penn State or USC? I hear both schools are in the running for you."

Casey, a little taken aback by the surprising attention, replied, "Well, sir, I want to play for Penn State, but I haven't received my letter yet. I'm hoping it comes this week."

"Coach Paterno would be a fool to pass on you, but either way, you will be in good hands. I know Pete Carroll personally, and he's a hell of a coach. I don't know if you're aware of this, but I'm a minority owner of the Giants, and I'd love to see a homegrown athlete like you playing for the Big Blue in a few years."

"Thank you, sir, playing right here for the Giants would be a dream come true!"

"Son, remember those words four years from now when your agent is telling you to hell with your dreams, go for the money!" Everyone laughed.

Ethan saw his chance to interrupt. "Arthur, do you think you could spare a few minutes this evening to talk about my Senate campaign? I'd like to get it rolling right after the upcoming election."

Arthur paused for a moment, seemingly in deep thought. Then he turned and took in Ethan's apprehensive expression. He'd been considering what to do about Ethan for quite some time. Because there was no other worthwhile local candidate on the horizon, he'd already pretty much decided that he was going to back Ethan's campaign for the Senate seat next year, but he'd been planning on making him sweat a little longer, at least until after November. Quite frankly, Ethan Burke had earned the right to run with his hard work over the years, and though it was unfortunate that there wasn't a better candidate, Arthur was already prepared to back Ethan. But more importantly, right now he wanted to spend some more time with this Collins boy, so he threw Ethan Burke the biggest political bone of his life.

"Ethan, my friend, why don't you relax and enjoy the party with your lovely wife, there's really nothing to discuss. If you win your upcoming re-election by at least a twenty-point margin, which according to the recent poles you should do quite easily, I promise you right here and now that I'll back your Senate campaign next year with the full force of the national committee behind you."

Ethan couldn't believe what he'd just heard. He'd been waiting for eighteen months for a commitment from Arthur, and now he had it! He kissed his wife and grabbed Arthur's hand. "Thank you, Arthur, thank you so much! I promise you'll not regret this decision."

Arthur returned his smile. "I hope not, Ethan, but would you mind if I took your daughter and Casey for a while and introduced them around to a few friends? I think I know where there are a few people they just might like to meet, and Ethan, in a little while I'd like to get some press shots of you and your family with the vice-president."

Ethan couldn't believe his fantastic luck. "Sure, Arthur! That would be great! Jordan and I will be outside mingling with your other guests."

As Arthur took both Casey and Esprit by the hand and walked them away, Ethan beamed at his wife and said, “Jordan, I’m starting to believe that boy is my lucky charm. Let’s go get a drink.” They strolled off into the crowded party.

Esprit broke away from their little group early on when Arthur introduced her to Rob Cronin and Cathy Cassidy. She’d been pleasantly surprised to find that they were both really cool and totally down to earth, especially Rob Cronin, who was not only a hottie, he was actually funny. She decided to hang out with them for a while so she could learn as much as she could about the movie business. She politely begged off Arthur and Casey and stayed at their table for the rest of the hour, enjoying several glasses of chilled Krug champagne while Casey continued on the grand tour with Arthur.

Over the next hour Arthur introduced Casey to all his important guests. Senators, CEOs, and celebrities, it was all a blur. He bragged to each and every one that Casey was the best high school athlete in the country, and Casey, though embarrassed by the barrage of accolades, enjoyed every moment. They talked mostly of football. Arthur gave Casey the full court press on the merits of playing for the Giants, even though both of them knew that it would be the luck of the draft that determined where Casey would play his pro football, if he even made it that far. Casey, when he was introduced to ‘Big Jim’ Switzer, was surprised to find that he was considerably bigger than the former action star and present governor. He always seemed so damn big on the screen, and he had been Mr. Universe a long time ago. It must be true what they say – the camera does make you appear much larger than life.

At the end of the hour, one of Arthur’s aids came up to him and whispered something in his ear. Arthur turned to Casey and said, “Casey, the vice-president is getting ready to leave, and I promised Ethan that photo. I’m sure that you would like to meet him too, so could you go find your date and meet us all over by the fountain?”

Casey ran back to the Esprit's table. She was deep in conversation with Rob Cronin, so he politely waited for a break in the conversation. Finally, he saw an opening and said, "Sorry to break this up, but your father needs you for a photo with the vice-president."

Esprit wasn't ready to leave just yet and she slurred her words just a little. "All…right...Casey, I'll be there in a few minutes."

"Spree, I think the vice-president is preparing to leave, please come now."

Cronin watched the rising tension between the two and helped Casey out. "It's cool, Esprit, go take some pictures with the VP. He's actually a pretty righteous dude, just come back when you're done."

Esprit had no choice but to gracefully yield, and she left the table with Casey. As they made their way over to the fountain for pictures she grabbed another glass of champagne from a passing tray.

Casey frowned. "Hey, why don't you take it easy with champagne? I think you're getting a little tipsy."

"I'm fine, Casey, really. Let's just go get this over with."

Eventually they made their way through the crowd and over to the fountain, where Arthur introduced them both to Vice-President Mitchell. Casey was in his glory, but there was only time for a couple of minutes of small talk while the photographers were setting up. They talked of football and politics. Casey was blown away that Mitchell showed a real interest in the discussion. He was in awe just being in the vice-president's presence, and even more impressed with Ethan after witnessing firsthand his cordial relationship with the VP. He watched in admiration as the two men chatted so easily with one another.

Finally one of Arthur's staff began organizing everyone for the photos, including Cronin and Switzer, who just moments before were escorted by Arthur's people up to the fountain.

There must have been at least fifteen photographers and four TV news cameras down in front of the assembled group of dignitaries.

The crews were just about to begin shooting, but everyone froze when a young woman rushed in front of the cameras and asked Ethan to step outside of the shot for a moment. The woman was one of Arthur's people, a make-up artist. She pulled Ethan away to the side and patted his glistening forehead with a hand towel to remove the shine. Ethan, obviously embarrassed, shooed the woman away and stepped back into the shot. Esprit chuckled as the photographers began shooting. Casey, beset by the spectacle of it all just stood there like a wooden soldier, grinning from ear to ear, while the camera bulbs flashed and popped in his eyes.

Surprisingly, as quickly as the shoot had started it was over, and the vice-president was summarily escorted away by his Secret Service detail. After a few short one-on-one interviews with Arthur, Ethan and the two movie stars, the press crews left and everyone made their way back the party.

Ethan walked over to Esprit and Casey and said, "Before I forget, I want to thank the both of you for your support this evening, especially you, Casey. Arthur is obviously quite impressed with you. I can't tell you how much this night means to me!"

Casey smiled. "You're welcome, sir."

Esprit, already bored, tugged on his arm and said, "Sure, Daddy, we'll see you later."

As the party was hitting its stride, just a few short miles away Steve and Lisa were settling in at home for a nice quiet dinner. She'd set a lovely table on the patio. The steaks were a perfect medium rare, the salad nicely chilled and served with raspberry vinaigrette, and the Chianti had been opened to breathe a half-hour before and at room temperature. Lisa lit some soft candles and placed them around the table and then she put on the new Nora Jones CD on the pool house stereo. Jones's sultry voice was gently wafting out from the four speakers surrounding the pool. Lisa was hoping for a nice romantic evening with her husband and had done her best to set the mood.

She was already seated at the table when Steve finally strolled out of the house. He'd taken a shower to help him wake up, and his curly dark hair was still damp and messy. He came out wearing only a pair of shorts. Lisa watched him as he walked over to the table. He had really put on some weight around the waist, but other than that he still looked pretty good to her. His face was still the same as it always had been except for a few character lines around the eyes and the small patches of gray hair at his temples. He still had those big brown eyes, the strong chin and that impish smile that could melt her heart.

"Hey, how are you feeling? I hope you're hungry."

"I'm feeling much better now. I guess I was more tired than I thought. I must have slept for about three hours. The last thing I remember I put on the Yankee game, and I guess I just passed out cold. I feel a lot better now that I've had a shower. Dinner looks great." He reached across the table, selected a steak and put some salad on his plate.

Lisa filled both their glasses with wine and served herself a steak and some salad as well. "Honey, you should have seen Casey in his tux. He looked so grown up. I can't believe he'll be leaving for college in just a few short months."

"Speaking of college, did he hear from Penn State today?"

"No. Do you think there might be problem?"

"No, I just think Coach Paterno is having a tough time making up his mind. From what I've heard, the Baltimore kid could be every bit as good as Casey. You know it's funny, you'd never think it, but the college recruiting game is probably tougher on the blue-chip kids than it is for all the other D-1 prospects. The pressure on kids like Casey to play at the very best school is unbelievable. Unfortunately, these kids all watch ESPN twenty-four hours a day, and then they make up their minds by their junior year to limit their choices to only one or two of the top schools. And then God forbid if they don't get the one scholarship they want, because then they think themselves failures even though they've already reached the pinnacle of high school athletics. Look at Casey, he's either the best or second best high school linebacker in the country depending on who you talk to, and if he doesn't get the Penn State scholarship, it will absolutely crush him."

"You're right about that. Hopefully this waiting game will be over soon. By the way, how did your talk go with him today? When I asked him, he said it started out badly but in the end the two of you had made peace. What did he mean by that?"

"He said we made peace? That's how he described today? Well, he was right about the first part. It went very badly."

Steve spent the next ten minutes recapping for Lisa the details of their lunch. He left nothing out, beginning with Casey's feeble attempt to avoid the confrontation and closing with his son's half-baked apology. When he finished filling her in on all the disturbing details, Lisa found herself shocked and a little disturbed by some of Casey's comments, especially the ones about her. She couldn't even begin to comprehend the recent changes in his behavior.

"Oh my God, Steve, you're kidding me! What that hell is the matter with him? He's been acting so strange lately. You must have wanted to kill him!"

"To tell you the truth, after he ripped us both apart I almost lost it for a minute. By the end of the conversation I found myself yelling at him about how good we were and how rotten my father was. I told him that he was the one being spoiled and selfish. The truth is I really got angry, but I don't think I got through to him. In fact, I'm sure that I didn't. Once he realized that I was upset, he backpedaled and made another attempt at a half-assed apology. The second time I accepted it because the alternative was getting us nowhere. After that we finished our lunch in silence and left the restaurant. If he thinks that was making peace, then I guess we made peace. I really don't know, but I'll tell you this, nothing's changed and nothing's going to change until he grows up a little and gets to experience a little life for himself."

Lisa felt awful for Steve, and she was angry at her son. Steve didn't deserve any of this. She was going to set Casey straight once and for all in the morning. She got up, came around the table and gave Steve a hug.

"I'm sorry I suggested you go to lunch. I honestly thought it would help, but I guess I was wrong. Why don't you we finish dinner, grab a big bowl of Ben and Jerry's and go upstairs? I'll give you a nice backrub." She winked. "It's the least I can do to make it up to you."

Back at Arthur's estate the party was in full swing. Casey and Esprit were having a ball, dancing to the orchestra and hanging out with the movie stars. In between the dancing Esprit was drinking up a storm. Somewhere around eleven-thirty Ethan and Jordan walked over and Ethan informed them that they would all be leaving shortly, in about ten minutes. Esprit was now seriously drunk, and she had no desire to leave. She fuzzily looked up at her parents from the table and rudely said, "What's your hurry, Pops? This party's just getting started. Why don't you and mother leave us alone…go have another Cosmopolitan…or whatever it is you two are drinking these days…just leave us alone for a while?"

Ethan's face reddened, and he was just about to confront his obviously drunk daughter when once again the perceptive and diplomatic Cronin smoothly handled the tense situation before it got ugly.

He said to no one in particular, "Hey, you know what? I've got to get rolling myself. I've got to be up at six for a film shoot. Come on, Cathy, let's go fetch the Switzers and say goodnight."

Cronin kissed Esprit on the cheek, gracefully took his date by the hand and said good night to the rest of the group. As soon as they left, Ethan looked at his daughter, who was still pouting at the table. She was obviously tipsy, so he said, "Honey, I think you've had a little too much to drink. Why don't we just leave without an argument so no one embarrasses themselves? This has been a wonderful evening. I'd hate to see it spoiled by a silly fight."

Esprit glared up at him with a look of hatred and disgust, but then she turned and looked into Casey's pleading eyes and thought better of continuing the assault. When she tried to stand she faltered a little, but Casey took her by the hand and the four of them walked across the lawn. They made their way slowly across the crowded party until they reached the main house. Esprit tripped twice going through the house, but they eventually made it to the entrance foyer without incident. The group walked out the front door and down the steps to the waiting limousine with Casey carefully steering his date when Esprit turned and looked over to her left and spied the helicopter, not fifty yards away. Big Jim Switzer and his wife had already boarded and Cathy Cassidy was just stepping through the cabin door, but Rob Cronin remained standing on the ground, speaking to Arthur. Cronin looked up and noticed Casey and Esprit in the distance. He smiled and waved a goodbye across the lawn.

Suddenly, to the surprise of everyone, Esprit broke from Casey's hand and ran off like a newborn colt, wobbly legs and all, directly towards the helicopter. As she ran she lost both her shoes and haphazardly dropped her clutch bag in the grass. As soon as she reached the helicopter she shoved Arthur out of the way. She jumped up into Rob Cronin's arms and attempted to smother him with a sloppy kiss. Surprised, he pulled away from her and began to laugh at the absurdity of the situation, but unfortunately not nearly in time because two press photographers were hidden in the nearby trees and they quickly snapped up the 'money shot'.

Cronin spied the photographers out of the corner of his eye. He gently pushed the girl away and said, "Esprit, it was nice meeting you, but you'll probably regret that kiss in the morning." He laughed, said his final goodnight to Arthur and boarded the helicopter.

Ethan, Jordan, and Casey stood there watching the surreal episode unfold from across the lawn. Ethan was mortified, Jordan amused, and Casey bewildered. Casey knew Esprit was drunk and the kiss had meant nothing, but somehow that silly stunt had just ruined the most perfect evening of his life.

Once the helicopter was airborne, Arthur helped Esprit back to the car. She was already half-asleep on her feet. He looked to the silent group and said, "Ethan, I think you ought to get this one home, she's had a little too much champagne I fear." Then he turned to Casey. "Don't be too upset with her, she's a wee bit inebriated, and Casey, I will most definitely be speaking with you down the road. Good luck with your scholarship." With that Arthur turned and walked back into his home.

Casey helped Esprit into the car. Before the limousine even reached the end of the driveway, she was sound asleep, her head resting on Casey's lap.

Chapter Seven

Photos & Phone Calls

Monday Morning, September 3rd

Casey woke up right at seven o'clock even though he'd been out late the night before. He just couldn't help himself. As soon as he shut off the alarm he thought of Esprit and her loathsome behavior last night. What the hell was she thinking? He hoped she had one hell of a hangover – she deserved it. He was still really pissed over the fact that she'd ruined his perfect evening.

He looked out his bedroom window, hoping to see the doves. For some reason he needed them today. As soon as he spied Romeo and Juliet and heard their soft rhythmic song he smiled, rolled out of bed and once again started his routine. As he labored through the push-ups and crunches he momentarily forgot about Esprit and wondered if his picture with the vice-president made the morning paper.

After Casey finished his sets he tiptoed over to his desk. This morning he would start the new cycle of steroids. He was feeling somewhat anxious about it because the first few doses of the cycle were the strongest and with his past cycles during the first week he sometimes suffered a nasty headache that lasted for several days. He gave himself the injection and placed everything but the used needle back in the drawer. The needle he wrapped in tissue and put in his gym bag because he always disposed of them in the commercial dumpster behind the gym.

He threw them in the dumpster because it was the only commercial garbage receptacle he knew of away from his house, and he thought it was safe.

Casey didn't spend much time worrying about getting caught because he really didn't think he was doing anything wrong. He'd been doing steroids for so long that he rarely ever contemplated the illegality or the immorality of the act. When it was done he simply picked up his bag and ran off to the shower in preparation for a long day of working out and football practice.

Downstairs, Lisa had just sat down at the breakfast counter. She sipped her coffee and scanned the front page of the morning paper. She gasped; right there staring back at her in a large photo above the fold was Casey, standing tall, between Ethan Burke and Vice-President Mitchell. Her baby boy was right there beaming from ear to ear! Lisa smiled because he looked so handsome. "Imagine, my son in the paper with the vice-president of the United States." She'd heard Casey get in the shower a minute ago and couldn't wait for him to finish and come down so she could show him the picture.

Lisa shook her head. Seeing her son on the front page of the newspaper made her pause. On the one hand, she was proud of him, but on the other, she wanted to wring his neck because of his selfish and snotty attitude towards his father. As she struggled with these opposing thoughts the phone rang. She looked at the caller ID. It was Steve calling from work.

"Hey, hon, have you seen the paper yet?"

"I was just looking at it. I guess you saw that Casey made the front page. Doesn't he look so handsome? I'm just now reading the article about Ethan Burke's upcoming Senate run. Now we'll never hear the end of Casey's idol worshiping over that man."

"Don't be so sure, sit down, hold on to your coffee, and open the paper to page nine. Take a look at the color photo in the center of the entertainment section."

He waited patiently as Lisa turned the pages. When she finally got to page nine her jaw dropped. She stared wide-eyed at the photo in utter disbelief.

"Oh my God!"

There, smack dab at the center of the page was a large photo of a very drunk Esprit smothering Rob Cronin, the movie star, with a very sloppy kiss in front of a helicopter. The underlying caption leaped off the page in twenty point bold type. It read:

'Congressman's Daughter Goes Wild for Cronin at GOP Fundraiser'

The headline was followed by a brief story that described Esprit's mad dash for Cronin as he left the party. It contained very few facts, but offered many colorful adjectives describing Esprit's less than stellar behavior at the end of the evening.

"Oh…my…God, this is awful! Poor Casey, he must be absolutely furious with her. Oh my God, wait till he sees this photo!"

"I know."

"I was going to let him have it this morning, but maybe I should wait…."

Lisa was surprised to hear Steve chuckling over the phone. "It serves him right. Remember what I said last night. Welcome to the real world, son!"

"Steve, don't say that! He's your son for God's sake. How can you laugh at this? This is terrible. The poor kid is going to be so embarrassed when all of his friends get a hold of that photo."

"I'm not laughing, but you have to admit, there is a sort of poetic justice to this whole thing considering all the crap I heard coming from him at lunch yesterday. Besides, this is just the kind of thing he needed. Christ, Lisa, Casey needs to grow up, and if this helps him to understand a little better what it's like in the real world, so be it."

Lisa's eyes remained drawn to the photo. "Steve, how am I going to break this to him? I don't know what to say. Maybe I shouldn't show it to him at all. Maybe I should let him find out on his own. It's bound to be all over the place by now. Ohhh…."

"No, Lisa, you have to show him as soon as he comes down. It would be cruel to let him walk into this cold at football practice, or anywhere else for that matter. I know you think I'm a jerk for laughing before, but he has to be told about it. Do you want me to tell him?" She didn't respond. "Call him downstairs and put him on the phone."

She thought about her husband's offer but said, "No, that's all right. I think he'll take it better coming from me. I'll talk to him as soon as he comes down. He just got out of the shower, so I'm sure he'll be down any minute."

"Are you sure you want to do this?"

"Yes, Steve. Let me get off the phone. I'll call you later on to tell you how it went, all right?"

"Okay, but don't chicken out of this. You need to tell him. If there's a problem, just call me. I'll talk to you later."

After Steve hung up the phone Lisa stood there dumbfounded. Part of her agreed with him that this was just what Casey needed to get him off his high horse, but part of her also understood the fragility of the teenage psyche. This would be a painful experience for her son. She put down the phone and thought about what she was going to say. Should she just come right out with it or should she wait to see if he brings it up himself? Her thoughts were soon interrupted when she heard him coming down the stairs. She decided to just play it by ear and see how the conversation played out.

As Casey walked in the kitchen Lisa watched him for any telltale signs. At first glance he didn't appear to look all that upset. There was no frown or scowl. Maybe he was mature enough to deal with this kind of thing.

Casey saw his shake in the blender, went over to the counter and poured himself a glass. Lisa closed the paper and said, "Good morning, Casey. How was the party last night?"

"Well, it was great till the end of the night when Esprit pulled the bonehead move of all time. Mom, you won't believe what she did. Rob Cronin, the actor, was there. We were hanging out with him and his girlfriend for most of the night. We were all having a great time. Rob Cronin was cool as hell, and I even got a chance to talk to Vice-President Mitchell. There's probably a picture of us in the paper. Anyway, Esprit was drinking tons of champagne because she was pissed off at her father and, Mom, you would not believe, she…."

Lisa looked to her son with pleading eyes and interrupted him. "Unfortunately, Casey, I would…because I already know what she did. I'm sorry to be the one to tell you, honey, but there's a photo of Esprit the paper. Honey, I'm so sorry. You must feel dreadful, but there's also a great picture of you on the front page with Ethan Burke and Vice-President Mitchell."

"What?"

She reached out to hand him the front page. Casey dropped his shake on the counter and ran around next to his mother to look at the photo. He barely glanced at his own picture on the front page as he furiously turned to page nine. When he saw the photo he slammed his fist down on the table, scaring his mother half to death.

"Casey! Please! Take it easy!"

Casey flew into a rage. He picked up his half-empty glass and threw it into the sink, where it smashed to pieces and splattered the counter. Lisa was frightened by the violent outburst. She jumped back.

"That's it! It's over! I'm going to be the joke of my whole school. I'm gonna kill her! Damn it, how could she do this to me?"

Lisa watched helplessly as her son's face turned a dark shade of crimson. She really didn't know whether he was going to cry or explode. "Honey, I'm sorry this happened, but you need to calm down! Getting angry and making stupid threats isn't going to make anything better."

The phone rang, causing them both to jump. Lisa picked it up.

"Hello?"

"Good morning, Mrs. Collins?"

"Yes."

"This is Tom Williams, Penn State's director of recruitment. I'm sorry to call so early, but I need to speak with Casey. I have a meeting at eight and I wanted to speak with him before then. Is he awake?"

"Ah…hold on…just a minute." She looked at Casey with encouraging eyes as she held the phone to her chest and mouthed the words, "It's Penn State!"

When Casey realized who it was he almost choked, but then he took the phone.

"Hello."

"Good morning, Casey, Tom Williams over at Penn State. I'm an old friend of Coach Callahan. He and I spoke late Saturday afternoon. He asked me to give you a call to let you know what's happening, but I've only got a couple of minutes so try and hold your questions till the end."

"Sure, Coach."

"Casey, I want to be right up front with you. Coach Paterno thinks the world of both you and Tony Roberts from Baltimore, but quite frankly he is leaning towards offering Roberts the scholarship, and here's why…."

Casey felt sick. In the back of his mind he'd been dreaming about this call for the past year, and it was definitely not going the way he'd envisioned.

Williams continued. "…Coach Paterno's been following the Roberts boy for a number of years. You see Roberts comes from a broken home in a rough Baltimore neighborhood. His mother's a good woman, and she's tried her best to raise him on her own, and in truth, she's done a pretty decent job so far. But here's the thing; for his whole life this kid's been surrounded by a bunch of thugs and hoodlums, including a few of his own relatives. So far his mom's managed to keep those bad elements at a safe distance, but they've never been too far off. The two of you are great athletes, and both of you deserve a shot to play here, but we've only got one full ride for the middle-linebacker position. We've already got two middle linebackers on the squad right now, a junior and a sophomore, and it wouldn't be fair to any of you to carry four. There just wouldn't be enough playing time. Anyway, the situation looks like this. One of you is going to get the full ride from us and the other will, more than likely head to USC. Coach Paterno has mentioned to me in confidence that he is afraid that if he picks you, then the Roberts boy will go out to USC, where he'll once again be placed in an area where he's surrounded by thugs and hoods. USC's a great school, but it's only a few blocks away from some pretty bad neighborhoods. Casey, you're a real smart kid and you're going to be a great player wherever you go. The Roberts boy doesn't have that advantage. You can thank your parents for that. The bottom line is that Coach Paterno is leaning towards Tony Roberts because he wants to see the both of you make it, and he thinks this might be the best way."

"But, sir, I have dreamed my whole life of playing for Penn State. I don't know what to say!"

"Casey, don't say anything yet. Paterno's promised his coaches, who, by the way, are split right down the middle on this, he'd wait till Saturday so he can review both of your upcoming game films before making his final decision. I called this morning because I didn't want to leave you hanging all week, and I wanted you to get the straight dope from me and not secondhand through someone on our staff."

Casey was stunned. "Er…thank you, sir. I…I…appreciate it."

"You're welcome, Casey, remember, play hard on Friday and whatever happens on Saturday, you're still one hell of an athlete and a fine young man with a great future in football. Goodbye, Casey."

"Goodbye, sir."

Stunned, Casey hung up the phone and sat down at the kitchen table. He put his head in his hands and began to sob uncontrollably. Then he banged his fists on the table again and screamed at the top of his lungs. "This is the worst fucking day of my life!" And it was. Casey had never seriously considered USC as an option. Now it looked like it might be his only choice. For almost three years his every waking moment had been spent working towards one goal, playing for Penn State, and that opportunity had just been callously stolen from him.

Lisa, frozen with indecision, stood there like a ghost. She'd picked up on the gist of the phone conversation by listening to Casey's side of the call, but she had no way of knowing the final outcome. She watched his suffering, and it dawned on her that for the first time in her life she didn't know how to console him, so she let him sob and vent while she tried to figure out what to do next.

Casey looked up at her with tears streaming. "Mom, Esprit made a complete ass out of me, and Coach Williams just told me I'm probably not getting the scholarship. I…I don't know what to do." He chocked up a little before he went on, "I…I need to be alone right now. Call the gym and tell Frankie I won't be coming in today. I'm going out for a run to clear my head."

Lisa was desperate for some answers; she needed to find a way to help him. "Casey, what did Coach Williams say? Did he say Penn State is not offering you the scholarship?"

"He said that Paterno was more than likely going to offer the scholarship to the Roberts kid from Baltimore because I'm a good kid from a good family and the other kid's from the ghetto."

"What? I don't understand. Tell me everything he said."

"That's it! That's the whole story. The last thing he said was that Coach Paterno was going to look at our game films on

Saturday before he makes his final decision, but it sounded to me like the decision's already been made, and it sucks!"

Crying right alongside her son, Lisa finally went to him and gave him a hug. She held him tightly and wouldn't let go. "Casey…I'm so sorry! Maybe there's still a little hope. It sounds like the door's not totally closed…you never know."

Casey looked down at Lisa with tears flowing, no longer the hulking and angry monster, and now just a sad teenage boy struggling to control his emotions. "Thanks, Mom, I know you're trying to help, but I know. I could tell by his tone." Casey exhaled deeply, trying to regain his composure. "Man, what a morning." He wiped his eyes, and pulled away from Lisa's embrace. "I've got to get out of here. I'm acting like a damn baby. If Esprit calls, tell her I'm gone for the day. I don't want to talk to her."

"Okay, honey, I'm so sorry! If you need anything, call me, okay?"

Without saying goodbye, Casey walked out and went upstairs to change for his run. Not more than a minute later Lisa despondently watched him run back down the stairs and silently leave the house. As soon as he left Lisa went right to the phone and dialed Frankie at home. He picked up after the third ring.

"Frankie, it's Lisa Collins. I hope I haven't called too early, but I really need to talk to you about Casey."

"Hey, what's up? I was just leaving for the gym."

"Have you had a chance to look at the paper yet?"

"No. It's right here in my bag. I was going to read it when I got to the office. Why, what's up? You sound upset."

"If you've got a minute take it out and turn to page nine."

"Okay."

Frankie sat down and pulled out the paper. He opened it up to page nine and stared at the photo for a couple of seconds, then he whistled.

"Ouch…Casey must be nuts over this! Do you want me to talk to him?"

"I wish…he already left the house. Frankie, there's more. Right after he saw the picture he got a call from Penn State. This Coach Williams called and told him he probably wasn't getting the scholarship. He said Paterno wants to give it to the boy from Baltimore instead."

"You're fucking kidding me?"

"Frankie, I'm worried, Casey went ballistic! I've never seen him so irate. He was slamming his fists down on the table and screaming at the top of his lungs. I have to be honest here, I feel terrible for him, but he scared the hell out of me. I've never seen him like this, and frankly I'm worried. He's been angry a lot lately. I know he's under a lot of pressure, but he's always been such a calm kid…I just don't know what to think."

"Lisa, I'm so sorry. You and Steve must be devastated by all this. Where's Casey now? I'll try and call him; maybe we can have a talk."

"That's why I called. He asked me to tell you he won't be in today. He went out for a run, and then he is supposed to go to Kevin's before practice, but who knows? When he runs he usually goes out to the tip of Sandy Hook and back…" Lisa paused for a moment and then continued, "Frankie, have you noticed any changes in his behavior lately? I'm really starting to worry about him."

Frankie took some time to respond. "Lisa, I honestly believe that it's mostly just the pressure from the scholarship thing, and unfortunately, it's been compounded by this God-awful picture in the paper. Let's face it, Casey's been so successful because he's a proud and driven young man, and with that comes a large dose of ego. He's not used to this kind of bashing. I think it's taking its toll."

"You're probably right."

"Lisa, you, Steve, and Casey are like family to me. I promise you I'll track him down and talk to him right away."

"Thank you."

"And, Lisa, there just may be a silver lining in all this.

Remember, I've always told you and Steve in confidence that I'd rather see him play at USC anyway, so try and take it easy. I'll go find him, and if I think there's a problem, I'll call you back. But knowing Casey like I do, I'll bet once he's given time to digest all of this shit, he'll work through it on his own and he'll be fine."

Lisa sighed. "I hope you're right. Thanks for your help. Don't forget to call me once you've had a chance to talk to him."

"I won't. But, Lisa, stop worrying, he's going to be fine, trust me. Just give him a little time."

"Okay, bye."

Lisa clicked off the call and dialed Steve at work. She filled him in on the both the sordid story from last night and the phone call from Penn State. Steve's first reaction was anger. He had a hundred questions but Lisa had no answers. By the end of the call he didn't know what to think. When Lisa finally got off the phone her head was spinning. Her once seemingly perfect life was starting to unravel.

Over at the Burke estate, Ethan was sitting at his desk in his second-floor library. It was a decidedly masculine room, filled with leather-bound legal texts and hundreds of first addition classics from both the nineteenth and the twentieth centuries, many of them hand-signed by the author. The books were neatly organized by subject and placed along the dark walnut bookshelves that lined the two interior walls from floor to ceiling. Behind the desk to his back was a set of French doors that opened to a private balcony overlooking the river. On the wall opposite his desk, above a hand-carved Italian marble fireplace mantel, was Ethan's most prized possession – a large and ornately framed portrait of Ethan standing with President Bush, senior, not junior.

Surprisingly, Ethan wasn't much of a reader. In fact, it had been at least couple of years since he'd last read a novel, and more than a dozen since he'd picked up a law journal, but even so he thought it important to keep a quality library. For a dozen years now, most if not all of his reading focused on either the half-dozen newspapers he read each morning, or on his daily congressional brief that was prepared for him each night by his staff.

This morning's reading material was no exception. Spread across his two-hundred-year-old, birdseye maple desk, were at least a dozen morning papers. He'd sent the maid out earlier to the Daily News Shop to purchase papers from all the major cities around the country, and now each one was opened to the ghastly photo of Esprit.

Just moments before he'd finished a lengthy phone conversation with his campaign manager, Blaine Caswell, in Washington, and surprisingly, he was grinning from ear to ear.

Though he had expected it, when he first saw the photo he was furious, but then around seven Blaine called and sounded more than a little chipper over the phone.

When Ethan heard the congratulatory tone in Caswell's voice he was dumbfounded. Ethan thought he was either drunk or crazy. But then Caswell proceeded to offer up a detailed and plausible rationalization as to just why the photos were a Godsend.

It took almost an hour, but Caswell eventually made clear to Ethan why this was actually good. It seemed that a few years back during the Clinton presidency Caswell and a couple other Republican political strategists had accidentally stumbled across a very strange voting anomaly. Through very extensive historical research and with some extensive polling and demographic studies, they eventually discovered the political oddity that a campaigning politician (especially a Republican) with a petulant and publicly misbehaving teen would more than likely be viewed by potential voters in a surprisingly positive light, and with sympathy.

According to the astonishing findings of their collected data, it seemed that in the good old U.S. of A, middle-American voters, regardless of party affiliation, identified with and held empathy for elected officials with troubled teens. In fact, According to Caswell, the exploits of the likes of Chelsea Clinton, the Bush twins and even Jeb Bush's rehab-skipping, cocaine-sniffing daughter not only didn't damage their father's campaign efforts, the children's exploits in each and every case actually boosted their father's polling numbers by several points.

Blaine then clued in a flabbergasted Ethan that the tawdry photo of Esprit was perhaps even more powerful than the one of him with the vice-president. And even better, that the two photos when viewed in the same paper together on the same day, well that was pure dynamite. Ethan was incredulous, but the rational was simple. In the first photo with the vice-president Ethan came off as a credible political force, one to be reckoned with in Washington, but with the second photo, the one of Esprit slobbering over the Hollywood star, the public was also able to perceive Ethan as simply a man and a father. This gained sympathy for him by highlighting the difficult task of raising a willful child. You couldn't buy this kind of positive coverage at any price. Caswell had finished the call by promising to fax Ethan a set of the new polling numbers as soon they came in along with some ideas on how to further capitalize on his Esprit's little faux pas.

As Ethan looked over the photos and ruminated on his extreme good fortune, Jordan walked in with a cup of coffee. Ever the astute political strategist, she immediately picked up on her husband's grin.

"Ha! I told you that the picture was gonna be a good thing! You just spoke with Blaine and found out for yourself, didn't you? Thank the lord. You would've been an unbearable ass all day."

"Okay, so you were right once again. I feel wonderful."

"That's great, but remember when you see your daughter this morning to go easy on her. I'll bet she's really hung-over and feeling pretty bad about what happened right about now. I bet Casey's none too happy about it either."

"Don't worry; I'll do what I can to make her feel better. I just hope Casey doesn't break up with her over this. He's such a fine young man and damn if he doesn't bring me good luck! Maybe I should call him."

"One thing at a time, sport, let's just hold on and see how this whole thing plays itself out, okay?"

"What do you mean?"

"I mean, let's not get carried away. Esprit won't be expecting any sympathy coming from you. If all of the sudden you become her knight in shining amour, she'll know you're up to something. Just start by trying to be sympathetic, okay?"

Three doors down the hall Esprit was waking up, and she felt like total shit. The inside of her mouth and her tongue were parched and crumbly sweet and sour. The nasty taste in her mouth reminded her of eating day-old cotton candy. Her normally bright blue eyes were bloodshot and swollen, and her head pounding like a mile-long freight train steaming and thumping down a set of worn-out tracks. It shook the very core of her brain. Her alarm clock had just gone off. She was supposed to pick up her friend Jamie and be at school for play rehearsal by ten o'clock. She tried to crawl out of bed but was overcome by a wave of nausea. Right then and there she decided she wasn't moving. There was just no way she could possibly make it. No fucking way! She struggled to pick up her phone and then she dialed Jamie's number.

"Jamie, it's me. I'm so sick. I really screwed up big time last night! My father's gonna kill me, and I think Casey might break up with me too. Please get over here right now...please!"

Jamie replied, "Spree...what the hell did you do?"

"Just get over as soon as you can. I'll tell you everything when you get here. I think I'm going to be sick!"

"Okay, I'll borrow my mom's car and be there in twenty minutes."

"Esprit hung up the phone and ran for the bathroom. She made it to the bowl just in time. For the next several minutes she gagged and wretched until finally the bout of nausea passed. She stood up slowly, fearful that the feeling would come back at any moment. It didn't. She braced both arms on the sides of her sink and slowly looked into the mirror. What she saw made her cry. "Oh God, I look awful! What did I do? What the hell was I thinking? Casey must hate me!"

She shivered at the thought of the reactions that would certainly be coming from the two men in her life. Her father was likely to kill her, or at least try to ground her and take her car away, but that was small potatoes compared to what she imagined Casey might do.

She gagged again as she tried to swallow a couple of Advil with a small sip of water, and then she crawled back into bed. She needed to call Casey. She knew she needed to apologize and do it fast. He was already on a short fuse, and this could be just the thing to send him running. No matter what, she couldn't let that happen. The thought of the two of them splitting up was simply unbearable. She reached for the phone and tried both his house and his cell, but each time she got an answering machine. She hung up the phone, lay back down in between her pillows and began to cry once more.

Not long after, Ethan walked by her bedroom door and overheard her sobbing. This was his chance to do the right thing. He knew she'd be totally blown away by any show of sympathy or support. This simple act of kindness could go along way towards healing their estranged relationship. Whatever happened, his intentions were honorable and this time he intended to be there for her. He knocked softly on the door and whispered gently, "Esprit, it's Daddy. Can I come in?"

Esprit froze and thought, *Oh Christ, here it comes! Wait a minute; did he just use the word Daddy? Daddy...is he kidding?*

In a barely audible voice she said, "Come in."

When Ethan entered the room he was shaken by his daughter's fragile appearance. Her beautiful strands of golden hair were now a mess of tangles and knots. Her sparkling blue eyes were puffy and swollen, and her make-up and mascara were smeared all over her pale, ashen cheeks. It appeared she'd been doing a lot of crying. Ethan's chest ached and his eyes welled at the sight of Esprit, her prone body, so still and so pale, just lying there in her disheveled bed. The stale odor of alcohol permeated the room. He'd never seen her like this, and it was shocking and painful.

Esprit, half under her duvet cover, was still wearing her wrinkled dress from the party. She barely acknowledged her father's presence. As soon he entered she turned away from him and stared out the window.

Ethan was momentarily speechless so Esprit took the opportunity to fend off his expected attack. "Dad, I feel really sick right now, so if you're going to scream at me, could it please wait a little while. I know what I did last night was awful, and I'm sorry, but please don't yell. I think…I think I might throw up again."

Ethan moved over to the edge of her bed. He sat down lightly beside her and gently touched her forehead with his hand. He stroked her hair a few times as she continued to look away.

"Honey, I'm not angry with you about last night, and I promise I'm not going to yell. You made a mistake. We all make mistakes. Hell, your mother and I made a big mistake using Casey to get you to come last night. It was just so important to me, and I thought that it was the only way to get you there. I'm sorry for what we did to you, and I promise it won't ever happen again. I hope you can forgive us."

Esprit turned and stared up at him in shock. He continued, "Esprit, I know you think I'm a jerk, and that I only care about politics. But, honey, I really do love you and seeing you like this hurts me too. I only want to help you."

Esprit had expected yelling, screaming, ranting, and a long

list of punishments, but instead she was getting sympathy. And the bastard actually sounded sincere. She reached up for him and broke down. With tears in her eyes she cried. "Oh, Daddy, I am so…so…sorry!" Then she buried her face in his chest.

Surprisingly, his warm embrace comforted her. It had been along time since he'd made her feel this way. She looked up at him with a small smile and said, "At least I waited till the end of the night to embarrass you so the vice-president wasn't there to see it. I'm sure Casey is going to want to kill me today."

Ethan wasn't sure how to tell her about the photo in the paper, so he hugged her a little tighter and just came out with it. "Baby, I've got something to tell you that won't make you feel any better, but you need to know the truth and then together you and I will deal with it."

Esprit's stomach immediately began to churn and she was walloped by an overwhelming sense of dread. "What…Daddy…what are you talking about?"

"Esprit, last night there was a press photographer hidden in the trees by the helicopter pad. This morning there's a picture of you kissing Rob Cronin in the paper, and it's not very flattering. Unfortunately, I'd imagine that by now the photo's been picked up by the Associated Press and has probably run in a hundred papers across the country." Ethan felt her body tense. She let out a drawn-out, shuddering moan.

"Oh no…you're lying! Tell me you're lying to punish me! Please! Oh God! Casey's going to dump me for sure! That's why he wouldn't pick up the phone. Oh Christ, what am I going to do now?"

Ethan sat her up and looked her straight in the eye. "Esprit, I promise you that I'll personally call Casey today and straighten out this whole mess. He's a smart kid, he'll understand. I'll take full responsibility for what happened. I'll tell him about the pressure that your mother and I put on you. I'll tell him the only reason you screwed up was to get back at your mom and me. He'll listen to me, Esprit. I know he will, and then I'll make this right between you."

"You'd really do that for me…talk to Casey? I…I don't get it. Won't that picture in the paper really mess up your campaign?"

"Esprit, when I see you like this, I can't worry about what some silly photo may or may not do to my campaign. That problem can wait. Right now I'm worried about you." Esprit hugged her father tighter than she'd ever done before. As they embraced, Jamie bounced in through the door with newspaper in hand. "Girl, you really fucked up this time…uh…oh! Er...Mr. Burke, sir…sorry about the language."

Ethan was none too fond of Jamie, but now was not the time so he simply said, "That's all right, Jamie. I think our girl here could use a good friend right now. Why don't I leave the two of you alone?"

He got up and began to leave the room, but he then turned back and said, "Honey, when you are up to it, bring me Casey's phone number and I'll call him later this morning." Then he left the room.

As soon as Ethan closed the door Jamie ran over and leaped up onto Esprit's bed. She held up the picture in front of Esprit and said, "Bitch, we need to talk, and who the fuck was that because it sure wasn't your dad!"

Chapter Eight

Drugs, Daddy, and Drama

Jamie Heist was Esprit's best friend. The two had been inseparable ever since the eighth grade when they met while doing a play in the junior-high school drama club. Before long they were the best of friends and had been joined at the hip ever since. Two years ago on a cold winter night when they had nothing better to do they rented the movie, *Thelma and Louise.* The two girls were mesmerized by the film, and of course they were drawn to the two female characters. Since then they'd watched it at least a half-dozen times, and now they likened themselves to the two female leads. Esprit fancied herself the pretty if a bit flighty Thelma, while Jamie thought of herself as the tough and calculating Louise.

This was actually a pretty fair description because Jamie was indeed the polar opposite of Esprit in almost every way. Where Esprit was often described as being beautiful and sexy, Jamie was more the cute type, with her long legs, shoulder-length jet-black hair, freckles, and devilish smile. And while Esprit had been raised with every possible advantage, growing up in affluent Locust Point, Jamie lived much more modestly, literally on the other side of the tracks in the working class town of River-Plaza.

On one point Jamie was very much like Esprit, she was never short on admirers of the opposite sex. However, there was never competition between the two as their tastes in boys ran very different. Jamie didn't like jocks. It was that simple. She couldn't stand being in the same room with them. She thought they were stupid and only wanted one thing, to get in her pants and then brag about it. However, there was one jock at school that she did have a thing for – she had a huge crush on Kevin.

She thought of Kevin as an enigma of sorts. She considered him a freak in jock's clothing because even though he was a star athlete, he was cool and sensitive, and he didn't act like a total shit. They had double-dated with Esprit and Casey a couple of times, but to her chagrin nothing had ever come of it.

Where Esprit was usually cautious and reserved, Jamie was always daring and wild, and that was what drew Esprit to her. Jamie had been the one to introduce Esprit to alcohol and recreational drugs. It wasn't like Jamie was an addict or even a heavy user, she was just the type of kid who liked to party. She'd been offered harder drugs like coke and even heroin in the past, but she'd always passed on the opportunity. And it wasn't like she used drugs every day, far from it, but she partied a lot over the summer and on weekends during the school year. Drugs were readily available in her circle of friends, who were the bohemian types, mostly wannabe musicians and artists.

Jamie's drug of choice was ecstasy or 'X' as it was called on the street. She loved the wild and uninhibited feeling that it brought her, but on X she never lost control. When she used, she could party all night, and she swore that it lessoned her hangovers in the morning. Several months ago she'd given Esprit her first taste of X at a party, and Esprit loved it. According to Esprit, the best thing about it was that it made her feel so strangely alive. No one, not even Casey, knew she had done it. If he ever found out, he would kill her.

As soon as Ethan walked out of the bedroom and closed the door, Jamie leaped off the bed, pulled back the drapes, and opened the French doors to let in some fresh air.

"God, Esprit, it stinks in here!"

Esprit didn't move so Jamie pulled down the fluffy down

comforter that Esprit was hiding under and tossed the throw pillows scattered about the king-sized, four-poster bed onto the plush lavender carpet. Then she ran across the room, jumped up on the bed and sat cross-legged, directly in front of her friend.

"Okay, bitch, spill it! I want the whole story, every gruesome detail!"

And so began her interrogation. It took a while, but eventually she forced Esprit to cough up all the dirty details from last night's disaster. Esprit had been reluctant, but Jamie's excitement and enthusiasm slowly wore her down. After a good half-hour of prodding and probing for every last morsel, Jamie finally had the whole sordid story.

"Spree, what's the big deal? You fucked up! So you got drunk and kissed some big-time celebrity hunk and a sleazy photographer took your picture! So what? At least your father's not pissed at you! Stop worrying about Casey; he's crazy about you. And besides, your father said he'd talk to him. Casey worships your dad. I'll bet you this all blows over in a day or two. No harm no foul, you didn't fuck the guy, right?"

Esprit didn't quite see it that way, but she said, "Maybe you're right, but how weird is this whole thing with my father? I thought for sure he'd come storming in here ready to kill me for ruining his campaign, but he goes and does just the opposite. Go figure!"

"Yah, that part's got me a little mystified. But hey, shit happens! Even good shit! Maybe your dad isn't the jerk-off you always thought he was! Who knew?"

Esprit perked up a bit. "I don't know, but one thing's for sure, if I'm going to set things right with Casey, I'm going to need my dad's help. I wonder if Casey has even seen the photo yet."

Jamie laughed and said, "I don't have a clue, kiddo, but I'll tell ya this, he's gonna take a whole lot of shit for it from his friends."

This thought caused Esprit to drift back into a funk. "Jamie, my timing really sucks. He's been so wound up about his football scholarship. I guess I'll keep trying to reach him on his cell." She reached for the phone.

Jamie grabbed the phone and put it back on the night table. "Why don't you go shower and get dressed instead? We can still make rehearsal if you hurry. We're only doing the stage blocking for the first act today, so it should be a piece of cake."

Esprit dragged herself out of bed. Jamie patted her on the back and said, "That's my girl…oh wait a minute, I've got a little surprise for you."

Jamie reached into her purse and pulled out a small vial of pills. She opened up the bottle and shook one of the pills into the palm of her hand. "Here take this; it will help get you out of your funk."

She handed Esprit a hit of X, and Esprit swallowed it without a second thought. Then she took a sip of water and said, "Thanks, Jamie, you're the best."

Esprit grabbed some clothes from her closet and left the bedroom for the bathroom to take a shower. Twenty minutes later she emerged looking a whole lot better. Jamie offered her a hug and said, "There's my girl."

Two minutes later the girls left the house without even saying goodbye. They were in too much of a hurry, hoping to still make it to rehearsal on time.

When Casey left the house for his run his head was in a really fucked-up place. He often went for a run when he was chewing on a problem. It usually helped to clear his head. This morning he ran all the way from his house in Monmouth Hills to the northern tip of Sandy Hook State Park and back. It was ten grueling miles of hills, beaches and highways, but it was also a beautiful place to run because most of the five-mile stretch had the Atlantic Ocean to one side and scenic views of the many tiny bays and harbors on the other. An hour and a half later when he finally returned home he was barely even out of breath. The run had calmed him somewhat, but he was still angry, and now he had a throbbing headache.

When he got back to the house his mother wasn't home. He walked into the kitchen to grab a bottle of water and saw the light flashing on the phone. There were four new messages. He ignored them because he knew two things, one, they weren't from Penn. State calling back with a change of heart, and two, if they were from Esprit, he wasn't ready to talk to her. He still needed time to think the whole thing through. He had to get his head on straight first; only then could he deal with her shit. Instead, he finished the bottle of water, grabbed his football gear and left the house for Kevin's to pick him up for football practice.

At about nine forty-five he pulled into Kevin's driveway and beeped the horn. A few seconds later, Kevin limped out the front door, favoring one foot and struggling with his gym bag. He was also sporting a seriously swollen black eye. Kevin dragged himself to the car, got in and gingerly sat down in the front seat. He moaned, "Hey, dog. I bet that just about now you're feeling worse than I look." He reached into his gym bag, pulled out the paper and hit Casey with it. "What the fuck is up with your psycho girlfriend?"

Casey just gaped at his damaged best friend. "Dude, we need to talk, but first, what's up with your face? You get your ass kicked in a fight?"

"I wish! Truth, yesterday I was catching my last waves of the summer down at the surfing beach in Long Branch, and I caught on to this really nasty wave. I didn't read the break right, and it threw me like a rag doll right up on the jetty!"

"Holy shit!"

"Dude, I'm telling you, it fucking knocked me senseless. I ended up on the rocks and split my long board right in half. Good way to finish the season, right?" Kevin laughed. "It was totally awesome. A couple other dudes fished me out of the break and took me over to Monmouth Medical Center. No concussion and no stitches, but my parents freaked when they saw me and my entire body feels like ass!"

"Holy shit! You really look like ass. How the hell are you going to play on Friday? Does Callahan even know yet?"

"Relax, dude, I'll be fine, my muscles are a little sore. It's no big deal, really. So forget about me for a second and tell me what the fuck is up. What's the deal with Esprit? I saw the paper. Man, how could she pull that bogus shit? I mean…with you standing right there?"

"Kevin, she was so drunk she didn't know what the hell she was doing. But you haven't even heard the worst part. About two minutes after my mom shows me the damn photo I get a call from this guy, Coach Williams, at Penn State. He called to tell me that Paterno is probably going to pick the kid from Baltimore instead of me. He then tells me that Coach Paterno is going to take one final look at both our game films on Saturday, but, dude, I could tell by the tone of his voice. They've already made up their mind and I'm totally fucked!" Casey slammed his fist on the steering wheel.

"Whoa, calm down, boyo! This is fucking absurd! You mean to tell me you're really out at Penn State? You don't even have a chance? No fucking way! I don't believe it! Maybe if you have a monster game on Friday, it will change his mind."

"Kev, I seriously doubt it, but that's what I intend to do. But first I've got to make it through the rest of this week without killing anybody, starting with my girlfriend. Kevin, you're my best friend, you have to help me keep my shit together. I'm probably going to take a lot of crap this morning over that damn picture, and I'll end up popping someone. I can feel it!"

Kevin looked at his friend with worry. "Hey, Casey, I'm there for you. Just take it easy, and we'll get through this together, okay? Have you talked to Esprit yet?"

"No, she's already tried to call me a bunch of times, but I'm not ready to deal with her yet."

They pulled into the school parking lot and parked the car

near the locker room entrance. When they walked in there were already dozens of players getting dressed and there was a pulsating hum going around the room that unexpectedly dissolved into thin air the moment the two boys walked in. Kevin picked up on the silence right away, but Casey seemed oblivious to it all.

Kevin and Casey's lockers were side by side at the opposite side of the locker room near the showers. They made their way across the crowded room with Kevin a couple of steps ahead of Casey. As they came up on their lockers Kevin saw something taped on the outside of Casey's door. He looked at the two photos and whispered softly to himself, "Oh shit! This is not good!"

The two newspaper photos were taped side by side on Casey's locker. The first photo, the one of Esprit, was taped at the top and written in black magic marker across the bottom it read "Cronin's Babe!" The second photo, the one of Casey standing next to the vice-president, was taped right beside it, and its handwritten caption read 'Cronin's Bitch', with an arrow pointing right at Casey.

Kevin rushed to pull them down, but he was too late. Casey leaped by him and pushed him out of the way. He crossed his arms and glared at the photos. His head was still pounding so when he turned around to face the other players, his rage had turned his entire face a dark shade of purple and a large vein rapidly pulsed just above his eye on the left side of his forehead.

As Casey looked angrily out across the crowded room, his mind leaped back in time to another locker room incident that had taken place almost three years ago to the day when he was just a freshman starting his first year of high school football.

It had been a hot summer day, a day so hot that you could smell the pungent stench of melting asphalt wafting in the air, the type of day that when you looked out across the school parking lot and down the street, the whole world seemed to shift and shimmer under the burning August sun.

On this particular day, Casey had just finished his first week of practice as a freshman. He and Kevin had just entered the locker room with more than a little apprehension. This was supposed to be hazing day. He'd heard the rumors and stories over the summer about the things that happened to freshman, especially to the really good freshman players, in the locker room during the first week of practice, but he hoped that the stories were just urban legends used to scare the new kids. He was already a pretty big kid, but he was still just a freshman and some of the upperclassmen were pretty intimidating.

He and Kevin were peeling off their dirty practice uniforms in the back corner of the locker room when they were unexpectedly surrounded by more than a dozen of the biggest upperclassmen. The group surrounded them and one of the boys ordered the two of them to strip and stand back to back. Kevin and Casey were isolated from the others and so frightened that they meekly complied without further argument. A couple of the biggest boys began to tie them together with a long piece of rope. Once this was done, the rest began shoving them towards the showers and taunting them while one of the smaller boys kept watch for the coaches, but that wasn't necessary because none of them were around because they were all meeting in the coaches' office at the other end of the locker room, some one hundred feet away and around the corner.

The upperclassmen eventually pushed and shoved Kevin and Casey all the way into the shower room, and then they made them sit, back to back, in the center the floor. Casey and Kevin were shivering with fear, but they knew that if they called out for help, whatever punishment they were about to given would only get worse. The group of older boys could smell their fear and quickly became agitated. All at once they began to mercilessly punch and kick at the two boys, who were completely helpless to defend themselves.

One of the older boys, a tall skinny senior, came up and

stood directly in front of Casey. He reached down and slapped him hard across the face several times. "How do you like that, you piece of shit!" The boy hawked up a mouthful of spit and let it fly right into Casey's face. At that moment Casey wanted nothing more than to get loose and kill the kid. He struggled mightily, but the rope was too tight. Directly behind him, the same torture was being exacted on Kevin, who had started to cry. Kevin's sobbing and crying inflamed the older boys like an accelerant. All at once a horde mentality took over and they all began dancing around, hooting and hollering, and spitting all over the two helpless boys.

This continued for several minutes until the skinny kid, the one that had been working on Casey just moments before, approached him again and said in a menacing tone, "Hey, boys, these faggots got awful dirty at practice today, don't you think they need a golden shower?" He then began to urinate all over Casey. The others soon followed suit and urinated all over both boys. Casey and Kevin were quickly doused from head to toe with urine.

One by one, the boys finished, and laughing, they left the showers to go get dressed, leaving Casey and Kevin still tied together and sitting there by themselves, drenched in urine and spit. The last kid to leave was the skinny kid. He had been unsuccessfully trying to piss directly into Casey's mouth, but Casey had steadfastly refused to open it. When the boy finished, he kicked Casey in the ribs and said, "Welcome to Eagle Country you freshman fuck!" and then he too left the showers.

A few minutes later, a couple of the other freshmen sneaked back into the showers and untied them. Once they were free of the binding rope, Kevin collapsed on the floor, sobbing in pain and shame, but not Casey. Casey was crazed with anger and humiliation. He'd never experienced a feeling like this before and he couldn't control his rage.

He stalked out of the shower like a madman, stark naked, dripping with urine, and with a faraway look in his eyes. He stormed through the aisles, methodically searching each row of lockers until he found the skinny boy who'd tormented him. As he approached the boy Casey never said a word. He simply attacked the boy and savagely beat him with every ounce of physical energy he had left.

When the coaches heard the commotion and finally came and pulled him off the other boy, the kid was splayed out on the floor, barely conscious, with a broken collarbone, two cracked ribs, a broken nose and a face beaten to a bloody pulp. Casey stood up, backed away, and silently walked back to the showers. He reached down and picked up Kevin, still prone and sobbing on the shower room floor, and together they scrubbed their bodies clean of the humiliation they'd just received.

The battered boy was taken to the hospital by the coaching staff, and when he was able, he was made to confess to what had taken place in the showers. His parents never pressed charges and the boy never again stepped foot in the football team locker room. Over the next several weeks the coaches repeatedly tried to talk to Casey about what happened, but he wouldn't speak a word about the incident, not even to Kevin.

The coaches didn't want any more trouble, so Casey's parents were never even told about what happened. It was simply swept under the rug. Casey had never been able to put his feelings into words about the incident, and the rest of the team was forbidden to speak of it. Since that day, Casey had never once spoken of the incident to anyone, but he thought of it often and he made damn sure that no hazing had ever taken place in the locker room again, not on his watch.

Casey's mind snapped back to the present. He looked out at the players around the room and said in a soft but menacing voice, "Who did this? What motherfucker had the balls to put this shit on my locker?"

Most of the players' heads either bowed or turned away in fear of Casey's rage. However, one player, an offensive lineman named Shawn Murphy, the same boy that Casey had knocked on his ass last Friday for making a good block, let out a small laugh. Whether he giggled out of fear or out of shear stupidity no one knew, but right then and there he became the object of Casey's wrath. Casey leaped over the bench and grabbed Murphy by the neck. Holding his throat with one fist he backed the boy hard up against a locker and began to squeeze. With bloodlust in his eyes he screamed, "Did you put the pictures up there, you motherfucker? Answer me or I'm gonna snap your fucking neck like a twig!"

Kevin and several other boys jumped over the bench and tried in vane to pull Casey off the boy, but he was too damn strong. He wouldn't budge an inch. Murphy's face turned bright red, and he began to suffocate, his arms flailing at his sides.

Most of the team were yelling and screaming at Casey to stop when suddenly Coach Martin rushed through the door and witnessed the spectacle. Martin, a rather large man himself, charged onto Casey's back and slowly pried his fingers from around Murphy's neck.

"Casey! Stop it! Are you out of your mind?" shouted Martin as he labored to break Casey's grip.

Finally Casey relented and released his hands from Murphy's neck. The boy collapsed to the floor, sputtering and gasping for air. Confused, Casey looked at Coach Martin for help, but he was so full of emotion and anger that no words would come out. Coach Martin, adrenalin still pumping and still breathing heavily, attended to the boy on the floor. He saw Casey just standing there above him.

He looked up and yelled, "Casey, get you're damn gym bag and get your ass to the coach's office right now!"

Casey, in a daze, looked around for Kevin and found him sitting a few feet away. Kevin was visibly shaken by his friend's uncontrolled violence. Kevin stared right back into Casey's pleading eyes, but he didn't know what to say so he lowered his head and said nothing. Casey, feeling totally alone, turned and looked away. There was no one else to help him, so he slowly walked back to his locker, ripped down the photos, picked up his bag and left for Coach Callahan's office. When he reached the coaches' office, Callahan wasn't there. He was still out at a meeting, so Casey slumped down on the chair outside his door with his head in his hands and waited.

A few minutes later Coach Callahan walked into the locker room and saw Coach Martin on the floor tending to a hurt player. Martin was still steaming and out of breath. He stood up and grabbed Coach Callahan by the arm, walking with him back outside.

"I warned you something like this was gonna happen. Casey Collins just almost killed that boy!"

"Coach Martin, calm down, all right? Is Shawn okay? And where the hell is Casey right now?"

"Shawn's going to be fine, but he's going to have one hell of a bruise around his neck. You can explain that to his parents. Casey's back in your office waiting for you." Martin glared at Coach Callahan. "If Casey steps one foot on that practice field this morning, you'll have my resignation!"

"Okay, Bobby. I get it! I'll go talk to him, then I'll send him home, but could you please do me the favor of getting your shit together before you go back in there in front of the team, and then could you please talk to Kevin and some of the other seniors and find out what the hell happened here?"

Not waiting for Martin's response, Callahan stormed back through the locker room and went straight to his office, where he found Casey sitting outside the door with his head in his hands.

As he walked past he looked down at Casey and couldn't help but have sympathy for the kid. Casey's three years of football flashed before his eyes. He thought about what had happened to him as a freshman, he thought about the steroid allegation, and finally about the message from his friend Tom Williams. He knew Casey was in big trouble, and he wanted to help him not send him packing. But for the sake of the team, and so he could settle the unrest from his coaching staff, he had no choice but to play this out the hard way.

"Casey, get your ass in my office now!"

Casey stood up and followed the coach inside. Coach Callahan sat down behind his desk and took a moment to gather his thoughts. Then he said, "Would you like to explain why my best offensive lineman is laying out there on the locker room floor struggling to breathe and sporting a nasty bruise around his neck, a bruise that's suspiciously shaped just like your right hand? Goddamn it, Casey, what the hell's the matter with you?"

Casey, unable to speak, handed the coach the two crumpled photographs. Callahan looked at them and rubbed his eyes. "Jesus, kid, you can't catch a break!"

Casey regained a little of his composure and said, "Coach, I heard from Penn State this morning." He sobbed, and then he proceeded to tell Callahan the entire conversation. Callahan listened carefully but he already knew the story.

"Casey, I talked with Tom Williams on Saturday. I'm sorry, son, but you know what? Your world ain't coming to an end. Hell, the USC Trojans were national champions two years ago, and Pete Carroll's sending just as many players to the pros as Joe 'Fucking' Paterno. Son, right now you're in jeopardy of blowing your whole future, and I can only protect you so far. You really screwed up today. You're really lucky Shawn's going to be okay. And, Casey, if he wants you thrown off the team, I don't know if I can stop it."

Casey continued to stare at the floor.

"Listen, I don't know what to say about the photos other than I understand why you're pissed off, but it doesn't excuse what you did. I'm suspending you from practice this morning. I want you to go home and think about your future. If you want to play football here again, you come back after lunch and apologize to Shawn. Then you ask him if he still wants you to play on this team. If he says no, you're done. If by chance he lets you back, then as captain you are going to speak to the rest of the team and ask them. And Casey, make no mistake here, it's up to him. If he says you're gone, you're gone! I'm sorry, but that's the only way this is going to work. You're supposed to be the captain of this team, and if you're lucky enough to still be here tomorrow, you better start acting like it! Now get the hell out of my office and don't let me see you again until after lunch."

"Yes, sir."

Casey kept his head down and quietly left the office. Instead of leaving through the locker room, he left through an inside entrance at the rear of the locker room to avoid seeing the team. He walked bowed in shame down the empty corridors of the school until he came to the front of the building that opened up onto the main parking lot. He wasn't ready to face the other players, so this was the only way out. As he walked out through the front doors he spied Esprit and Jamie arriving for their rehearsal in the school auditorium, "Great, just great!" They were heading right for him from across the lot.

Jamie saw him first and said, "Oh my God…Spree…there's Casey!" Esprit looked up at him, his eyes were puffy as if he'd been crying, and he looked really, really pissed. As Casey neared them Esprit froze with fear. He walked directly up to her without even looking in Jamie's direction and said, "Jamie, could you go inside for a minute? I need to talk to Esprit alone."

Jamie bailed on her friend at once, but as she walked towards the front doors she yelled back, "Spree, I'll be just inside waiting for you." Esprit didn't respond.

Casey and Esprit had been through some rough spots before, but nothing like this. Casey towered over her menacingly. He kept the distance between them and with clenched teeth and barely controlled anger, he began. "Esprit, let's see, so far this morning I've lost my scholarship to Penn State, I was laughed at by the whole team in the locker room because of a picture of you sucking face with fucking movie star, I beat the shit out of one of my teammates. And oh yah, I almost forgot, I'm probably getting thrown off the team, and it's your fault. I HOPE YOU'RE HAPPY!"

Esprit's head was swimming with the hangover and the oncoming effects of the ecstasy. "Casey…I…I don't know what to say…I'm sorry…please forgive me!" She tried to step forward and touch his face, but he backed away.

"No, no way! This is all your fault! How could you do this to me?"

"Casey! I made a mistake, I was drunk. What do you want me to do? What do you want me to say? Please…listen to me. I love you and I am so sorry!"

"That doesn't change a thing! Don't you see? My whole life, everything I've worked for, it's all fucked!"

"No, Casey, you're just really upset, and that's okay! I promise I'll never do anything to hurt you again. God, Casey, I screwed up big time, but I never meant to hurt you. Please believe me!"

He swallowed and backed up another step.

"I have to go."

Casey turned and walked away in the direction his car, wondering if he could ever pull his life back together, and leaving Esprit standing there crying.

Chapter Nine

Love's Labor's Lost

Casey left the school parking lot and drove around for a while before eventually ending up at the only place he had left to go to. He pulled into the gym and spied Frankie's car out front.

Thank God he's here, Casey thought. *At least now I've got someone to talk to, someone I can trust. Kevin's my best friend, but he is way too close to the situation, and besides, he's dealing with a lot of his own stuff. Frankie's been through this kind of thing before. He's dealt with scholarships and with rejection. He'll understand how bad I'm feeling. He'll know what to do….* All of these thoughts played through Casey's mind as he ran for the front door.

Casey walked in and looked around for his mentor. Already he felt a little better, just hearing the comfortingly familiar sounds: the clang of metal plates banging together, the thunderous grunts of sharply expelled breath, and the hollow thud of heavy barbells hitting the thick rubber floor. His ears pricked up as he heard the comforting whirr of the large floor fans that re-circulated the warm stale air around the gym.

Even the normally unpleasant gym odors were familiar and soothing: the smell of sweat mixed with the strong citrus and ammonia-based disinfectant used by the trainers to wipe down the mirrors and equipment, and the odious stink of workout clothes being worn way past their washing date. At the gym Casey was in his element. This was his last refuge, the only place left where he felt safe. He'd spent the better part of the last year and a half in this place, and just being there brought him a small sense of calm.

As soon as Frankie spied his protégé skulking across the entrance, he got up and came out of his office. He walked right over and delivered a crushing bear hug. Over the last eighteen months Frankie had not only nurtured a very tight bond with Casey, he'd also developed a close relationship with Casey's parents. He thought of them all as family, and because he'd spoken to Lisa earlier he knew that Casey was in a bad way. He took Casey by the arm and led him back to his office.

Casey wasted no time spilling his guts to his mentor. He unloaded everything on Frankie: the fight with his father, Esprit's stunt at the party, the call from Penn State and lastly his violent outburst at practice. It took him the better part of half an hour to get everything off his chest. Guilt, shame and disappointment came flooding out as if deep down inside his chest a dam had broken apart.

Frankie never interrupted him, not once. He could see how much Casey was hurting so he let him get it all out.

When Casey finished he was emotionally spent, but somehow a great weight had been lifted from his shoulders. Even so he was left feeling bone weary. His body was more fatigued than he could ever remember. Every muscle ached as if he'd been working out in the weight room all morning, but this was a different kind of fatigue, one he was unfamiliar with, and one that a little rest and relaxation probably wouldn't cure.

When Casey finished telling his story, Frankie paused for a moment, considering his next words very carefully. He was painfully aware of the fragile state of his young friend. The poor kid had been blindsided from almost every direction and didn't seem to know up from down at this point. Frankie had to help Casey get through this, but to help him he knew he needed to be honest, and he'd have to tell Casey some things that maybe Casey didn't want to hear. After speaking with Lisa, Frankie was sure that Casey had gone way over the line with his parents, and this morning he'd been totally out of control because of Esprit and losing the Penn State scholarship. There wasn't much he could say about Esprit, he hardly knew her, but he was one of those people who believed Coach Paterno was long past his prime. He'd already tried to convince Casey that USC was the better place to play. Frankie had played for Pete Carroll a few years ago up at New England and knew he was one hell of a coach.

He was concerned by everything that had happened to Casey, but his biggest worry was Casey's aggressive behavior at school. He was pretty sure Casey's violent outburst was probably brought on by the steroids, or at least exacerbated by them. He felt personally responsible, and he was only marginally reassured by the fact that he knew Casey had just finished his current cycle and was going to be off them for a while. The effects could linger long after a cycle was done.

At the very least he would talk to Casey and offer him some sound advice without broaching that prickly subject. It wasn't that Frankie was concerned about his legal liability; he knew Casey would never tell a soul where he got the steroids from; it was that he felt a degree of guilt and culpability for Casey's rage, and he didn't like that feeling one bit.

"Casey, I know you're feeing like dog shit right now, and I don't want to make you feel worse, but if you want me to help you, I've got to tell it to you straight. I'm here for you, but I'm about to tell you some shit maybe you don't want to hear. Are you okay with that?"

"Yeah…sure…why not? What's the difference? I've screwed everything already. What do I have to lose?"

Frankie shook his head. "See, that's what I'm talking about, Casey. Your head is all fucked up. You haven't lost anything! First of all, I told you this before and now I'm saying it again, maybe you'll hear it this time, you are better off playing for Pete Carroll at USC. He's a better coach at this stage of the game, and he's way more connected to the NFL." Frankie paused to gauge Casey's reaction, but there was none so he continued, "As for Esprit, so she did something stupid, she made a mistake. Granted, a pretty fucking major one, but still, it was just a really dumb thing to do and you know damn well she's sorry about it. If you really care about her, then you should use this whole thing to your advantage, you idiot. That girl will be putty in your hands for months to come if you accept her apology and take her back."

Casey had been slouched down in his chair, only half-listening, but now he sat up straighter and started to pay attention. Frankie's words were getting through to him, and it was starting to make sense.

He continued, "Now here comes the hard part, sport. You're making a huge mistake with your parents. Your mom and dad are two of the best damn people I know. I know you don't see it that way, but it's the truth. Without everything they've given you, there's no scholarship, no NFL, no Esprit. Damn, Casey, there's no way you and I would be even having this conversation without them. I don't give a rat's ass about your father's drinking. I know your dad and that's his business, not yours. You should just butt out. It's not like he is an alcoholic for Christ's sake."

Frankie had set the hook and Casey was taking the bait. "All right, I hear what you're saying, but what do I do about this morning?"

"Well, kid, that's both the toughest and the easiest part. The easy part is you get your ass back to school and do just what Coach told you to do, and you better be fucking humble and sincere when you do it! The hard part is convincing Shawn Murphy that you're sorry and then him seeing fit to let you stay on the team. From what you told me, you embarrassed him on Friday, and then you went and fucked him up good this morning. He's bound to be a little pissed, don't cha' think?"

Casey's body language began to speak volumes. He was

coming back to life. His eyes brightened as his sense of purpose was restored. “Frankie, I’ve thought about everything you’ve said and a lot of it makes sense. I still want to play for Penn State, but if not, I guess it’s not really the end of the world, and now at least I know what I have to do. I’m going back over to the school right now and take care of this mess I got myself into. I don’t know what I’m going to say Shawn, but I’ll think of something. Thanks for being here for me. I don’t know what I would’ve done without you!”

“That’s what I’m here for buddy. Now get the hell out of here.”

Frankie came around the desk and put his arm around Casey’s shoulder. He wished him luck and told him to call him later, then he wrapped up the talk by telling Casey he expected to see his sorry ass back in the gym the next day at seven to make up for his missed workout today.

Casey smiled for the first time that day and was out the door like a shot on his way back to school. Frankie watched Casey walk away through his office window and prayed to God the kid would do the right thing. He had a lot riding on him.

As Casey drove back to school, he was piecing together in his head what he was going to say to Shawn and the rest of the team when his cell phone rang. He assumed it was Esprit. He still wasn’t ready to talk to her yet so he didn’t intend on answering it, but when he looked down at the screen he noticed it was her parents’ home number, not her cell, and he was surprised. She never used her home phone, and she was probably still at school. There was no way she could be home yet, so more than a little curious, he answered it.

To his surprise, on the other end of the line was Ethan Burke. He couldn’t recall ever receiving a single phone call from Ethan or Mrs. Burke. *It must be about last night’s fiasco.* He cautiously said, “Hello?”

“Casey, is that you? This is Ethan Burke.”

"Yes, sir, it's me. If you're calling about last night, I'm truly sorry. I feel responsible for Esprit's behavior. I should have stopped her from drinking so much. You and Mrs. Burke must be furious with her over that picture in the paper."

"Actually, Casey, that's why I'm calling. To tell you the truth, I wasn't pleased when I first saw it. Casey, you have a sharp mind and are quite astute when it comes to the delicate nuances of politics. I'm sure you can understand the political fallout from something like this, but she's still my daughter and I love her very much. Casey, Esprit made a terrible mistake last night; one that hurt the people she loves very badly, and that includes you, young man. I want you to know that she and I talked it all out this morning and I've forgiven her, and quite frankly, I'm worried about her. She was deeply distressed by the thought of you breaking off your relationship with her over this unfortunate affair. I called hoping to convince you to forgive here as I have and move on from this. Jordan and I are quite fond of you, and you've always been a stabilizing influence on our daughter. We'd hate to see you out of her and out of our lives."

Casey couldn't believe what he was hearing. Ethan Burke had accepted Esprit's apology and even felt bad for her. The political consequences from the photograph alone should have sent him right over the edge. Well, if Ethan Burke was a big enough man to forgive his daughter after what she had done to damage his political career, then maybe he should too.

"Sir, I can't lie to you, I was really upset by that picture. I've already taken a lot of crap for…sorry…a lot of teasing about it from my friends, but seeing that you're willing to forgive her has made me rethink the whole thing. To be honest, I wasn't planning on speaking to her today, but since you called, I think maybe I should come by your house later this afternoon around, say, around six and see her…if that's all right with you?"

"Why, Casey, that's more than all right, that's exactly what I was hoping for. You are a young man of great character. Thank you, son, I am very grateful. I'll tell Esprit that we've spoken and to expect you at the house around six. Jordan and I will be looking forward to seeing you as well. Goodbye, Casey."

"Goodbye, sir."

Casey hung up the phone, scratched his head and thought about the last twenty-four hours. None of it made any sense. It seemed like every time he turned around something unexpected happened. At the moment he was feeling better, but he was still very confused. He was still angry and disappointed with Esprit, and he was still devastated by the call from Coach Williams. And most importantly, he was still worried about what was about to happen at school, but all things considered, he had to admit that he did feel better. His confidence was returning, and he was starting to believe that he could work it all out. Bits and pieces of his talks with Frankie and Ethan were flashing through his head, and they inspired him to see the rest of this day through, whatever it would bring.

He pulled into the school parking lot at twelve forty-five p.m., fifteen minutes before the scheduled start of the afternoon session. He got out of his car and stared up at the building. He began walking, but then he paused to take in several deep breaths. "Well, here goes nothing." Then he marched determinedly into the locker room.

The second he walked through the door every head turned in his direction. As he walked resolutely towards the coaches' office, he only made eye contact with two faces – Kevin's and Shawn Murphy's. Kevin looked up and gave him a small wave of encouragement and a timid smile, but Shawn Murphy just glared back at him with pure hatred in his eyes. Casey winced when he saw the finger-shaped bruises on the boy's neck and his confidence melted away. It was like a ten-pound brick just hit him in the gut.

Without a word, he continued on to the coaches' office and knocked on the door. He heard an abrupt, "Come in," so he stepped gingerly through the door. All of the coaches were in there finishing their lunch and preparing for the afternoon session.

Coach Callahan, with a mouthful of ham and cheese sandwich, mumbled, "Good afternoon, Mr. Collins, I suspect that you're here to apologize to Shawn Murphy and the rest of the team?"

"Yes, sir."

Coach Martin eyeballed Casey with a menacing glare. Martin had always liked Casey and was impressed by his ability, but he was furious with him about what happened this morning and leery of whatever Casey had to say. He knew Casey was using steroids, he'd seen all the signs before. Ten years ago when he was a promising running back at Rutgers University he'd experimented with them himself for one cycle, but he found the negative effects were not worth the results. After he finished the cycle he walked away from them and never looked back, but he'd known many other players that did them, and he'd witnessed firsthand the severity of their altered behavior. He was able to recognize the volatile mood swings that came with steroid abuse, and Casey was definitely juicing. He didn't want Casey off the team, but he did want his problem dealt with.

With all the coaches silently staring at him, Casey began his apology. "Sir, before I go out and speak to Shawn, I want to apologize to all of you, especially to you, Coach Martin. My behavior at practice this week has been crazy and reckless. I've been thinking only about myself and my scholarship and not about the team. What I did this morning was completely out of bounds, and I deserve to be kicked off the team. Ultimately, if that's what you all decide, I will accept your decision."

Casey choked up a little and his eyes started to water. "But," he continued, "Football's my whole life, so I hope you, Shawn and the rest of the team will see fit to give me another chance."

He wiped his eyes on his sleeve and waited for a response. Coach Callahan didn't let him wait long. He looked around at his other coaches and said, "Casey, we've talked about it and nothing's changed. As I said earlier, if you apologize to Shawn

Murphy and he accepts your apology and agrees that you can come back, then you are welcome back on the team. But let me make this one point crystal clear, if you're allowed back and you step out of line just once, just once, you are gone from this team and you can say bye bye to your college scholarship. Do you understand me?"

"Yes, sir, I do."

Coach Callahan looked around at his coaches to see if anyone else had anything else to add. Coach Martin looked as if he was going to speak but then checked himself. This wasn't the time. When no one else spoke up he said, "Okay then, Coach Martin, since you were the one involved in the incident, would you bring Casey and Shawn outside the building and let the two of them talk this out. I want you to be there to witness the conversation so we have an accurate record of the outcome."

Coach Martin, looking not at all pleased with the responsibility, frowned and stood up. "Let's go, Casey." The two walked back through the locker room where Coach Martin signaled Shawn to join them outside.

Shawn Murphy was angry and scared, but he reluctantly followed them. Coach Martin walked the two boys across the parking lot, far enough away from any potential listening ears. Once they were out of earshot he turned to Shawn and said, "Casey wants to speak to you about what happened this morning, and I'm here to make sure that nothing else happens between the two of you. Shawn, are you okay with this?"

Shawn barely nodded his head; he just stood there looking down at the ground with his arms folded across his chest, nervously scuffing his cleats back and forth across the asphalt.

A lot was riding on what happened over the next couple of minutes and Casey floundered at the start. "Shawn…I…I…don't know what to say…I'm sorry just doesn't seem to cut it. I can see the bruises I put on your neck and I feel like a total asshole."

Shawn vehemently nodded his assent.

"Listen, Shawn, I know I've been a real jerk this week,

especially to you and you have every right to throw me off the team…I deserve it for what I did…but I'm begging you…please…please give me another chance! That's all I'm asking, whatever you want, just please let me stay on the team."

Casey didn't know the boy well, but he did know that Shawn Murphy was a pretty good kid and a decent football player. He was a three-year varsity starter at offensive tackle. His grades weren't very good, so he wasn't scholarship material, and he lived in a rough blue-collar part of town so he didn't travel much in Casey's circle of friends, but he loved the game of football and he played it well.

But Murphy was also really pissed off. Casey had embarrassed him twice this week, and his neck hurt like hell. He had the power to get Casey thrown off the team, and he knew that. Coach Callahan told him it was his call, but he also realized that without Casey, the team's chances for another State Championship were slim to none. Besides, if he had Casey thrown off the team, the rest of the team probably wouldn't speak to him for the rest of the season. He was stuck between a big rock and another big rock.

Shawn looked up from the ground for the first time. He looked Casey right in the eye and screamed at him, "Why the fuck have you been picking on me? I didn't do anything to you. I was just doing my job on the field with that block, and I sure as hell didn't stick those pictures up on your locker."

It was Casey's turn to lower his head and stare at the ground. "Shawn, I'm sorry. What else can I say? I found out right before practice that I didn't get the Penn State scholarship, and then I saw those pictures and I snapped. I heard you laugh and I thought for sure you put them there. That doesn't excuse what I did, nothing does. I'm just trying to tell you what happened."

Shawn looked first at Coach Martin and then at Casey. "You know what? This whole thing sucks! My neck hurts like hell, and you're an asshole, but you're the best fucking player on the team, so if I get your ass booted off, then I'm in the shits with the rest of the guys and our season's ruined. This really, really sucks!"

Casey listened to Shawn and understood his predicament. "Shawn, I'll make you a promise right now, if you don't want me back on the team, I'll go back in there right now and I'll tell the team to lay off you because this whole thing was all my fault, and I deserve to be kicked out. I'll make sure the guys don't hold it against you, I promise."

A little surprised and shocked by Casey's offer, Shawn kicked it around in his head for a minute and then he said, "Okay, Casey, here's the deal, you can stay on the team, and I won't say another word, but there are two conditions. First, you have to promise me you won't pull any more of this shit, because if you do, I swear to God, next time I'll call the cops and get your ass busted."

Casey nodded.

"And second, I know we don't usually hang out together, you being the big man on campus, and me just a poor fat kid from Hillside, but starting today, you better make sure that me and the rest off the offensive linemen get invited to all the good parties this year…starting with the one on Friday after the game. We never get invited to shit!"

Coach Martin, standing a few paces away, laughed at the second condition.

Casey listened and smiled. The relief was overwhelming. He shook Shawn's hand then grabbed him and delivered a bear hug that caused the boy to wince in pain. "Shawn, you have a deal. Thank you so much! I promise, you will not regret this, and I'll tell you what, I will personally pick you up and drive you to the party on Friday myself!"

Shawn smiled and readily agreed to Casey's offer. The three shook hands one final time and walked directly back into the locker room, where Coach Callahan, assuming a positive outcome, had gathered the coaches and the team together to await the news. When Casey walked in and saw the team all together, he realized the coach wanted him to speak to the rest of the team right then and there. He was back on the team and more than ready reassume his role as captain, so he stepped up to the plate.

"Hey, guys, I just want to say there is no excuse for what I did this morning. Coach Callahan and Shawn had every right to throw me off the team. I've been out of control and angry all week, and I've taken it out on a lot of you guys. For that I'm sorry, especially to you, Shawn. I'm supposed to be the captain of this football team, but I sure haven't been acting like it. I'm sorry. I've spoken to the coaches and to Shawn and they've agreed to let me stay on the team as long as it is okay with you guys…."

A wild cheer broke out all over the room. Casey quieted them down and continued, "I promise all of you I won't pull any more crap for the rest of the season, and if you let me, I will lead this team to another State Championship, starting with Friday night against Red Bank Regional!"

The entire team started screaming and banging their helmets against the lockers. Coach Callahan stepped up beside Casey. He gave the team their moment and then settled them down.

"Okay, boys…I think we've had enough drama for one day. Casey, go suit up. Listen up, boys, today and tomorrow are the last of the double sessions because school starts on Thursday…" There came a loud mixture of both boos and cheers because the players didn't know which was worse, double-session practices or starting classes. "So let's get out there and make them count! Let's Go! Let's Go! Time's a wasting!"

Casey, feeling more than a little pleased with himself, suited up and headed out on the field with the rest of the team for the afternoon practice. As the coaches followed the players out, Coach Martin pulled Coach Callahan aside. "I guess this all worked out pretty well for Casey, but are you going talk to him about the steroids like we discussed?"

Coach Callahan looked at Coach Martin and said, "One

thing at time, Coach, one thing at a time." Then he ran off and began blowing his whistle, signifying the start of practice.

While Casey busted his butt and behaved himself out on the practice field during the afternoon practice session, Esprit and Jamie finished their rehearsal and Jamie drove Esprit home. The hit of X had temporarily alleviated Esprit's pain and depression, but the effects were wearing off and she felt worse than ever. Esprit had only halfheartedly gone through the motions at rehearsal. Thank God they were only stage-blocking because if she had to do any of her lines, she would have failed miserably. Jamie dropped her off and she dragged herself into the house, up the stairs, and she crawled back into bed. Her thoughts turned to Casey and the scene in front of the school. He was going to dump her for sure, and who could blame him? He was so pissed, and on top of everything else he'd somehow lost his scholarship to Penn State. At least one positive thing had happened but even that made her feel shitty. She'd heard near the end of rehearsal through the school grapevine that he wasn't kicked off the team after all. Thank God for that. Being thrown off the team would have destroyed him and destroyed any remaining hope of their future together.

Her relationship with Casey was so extraordinary. She didn't know another couple her age that had such a secure relationship. They could really talk to each other. They were so relaxed together, no jealousy, no games, and no bullshit. And the sex was phenomenal. The best part about the two of them together was that their differences seemed to balance each other out. They were great together and she knew it. Until this morning she'd assumed they would always be together and someday down the road when Casey was playing in the NFL they'd get married and have a bunch of kids. Now she had totally fucked it all up.

Esprit was so drained she could barely keep her eyes open. All she wanted to do was sleep. Just before she drifted off she heard the distant murmur of her parents' voices. They were just down the hall working out in their state-of-the-art home gymnasium. A few months ago the two of them decided to go on a health kick, and of course they had to do it in a very big way. The exercising would probably last another month or so and then the gym would sit empty, collecting dust, until their next big idea came along.

Esprit listened to the whirr of the spinning wheels of their stationary bikes just above the drone of their voices as they pedaled and chatted away, but she couldn't care less. She wasn't in any mood for them right now. She was too tired and too consumed with a combination of guilt and feeling sorry for herself. She wondered if her father had been serious about calling Casey, or had he just said that to make her feel better? Within a few minutes she drifted off to sleep, but her nap was short-lived because not more then ten minutes later, her father, wearing a shiny, silver, Adidas warm-up suit and a sweaty hand towel around his neck, walked by and noticed her sleeping. He entered her room and nudged her to consciousness.

"Hey, baby, are you awake?"

"Oh…hi, Daddy…I…am now." She tried to focus on her father's sweaty face, but she was still under the lingering effects of the ecstasy and couldn't seem to center in on anything in front of her.

He shook her gently. "Honey, you don't look so good."

"I'm all right. I'm just real tired and still a little queasy from last night."

"Well, I've got some news that's bound to make you feel better. I spoke to Casey a couple of hours ago. We had a real nice talk, and he is coming over to see you in a little while."

She looked up at him incredulously. "What did you say?"

Chapter Ten

All Quiet on the Eastern Front

Monday Evening, September 3rd

After Casey left so abruptly in the morning, Lisa wandered aimlessly around the big empty house for quite some time. She straightened the family room, did the dishes, even vacuumed the pool in an effort to clear her head, but she couldn't get Casey out of her mind. His angry outburst and fragile state of mind had left her more than a little anxious. After a couple hours of intense reflection, she'd resigned herself to the fact that there was little she could do for him at the moment.

It didn't make a difference. No matter how hard she tried to get back on track for the day, she just couldn't shake the uneasy feeling deep in her gut. At around noon she left the house for a short time to run a few errands, hoping it would get her out of her funk – it didn't. She picked up some groceries and dropped off the dry-cleaning, but she soon felt an urgent need to track Casey down and make sure he was all right, so she drove right back home.

She dropped the groceries bags on the kitchen table and then listened to a few phone messages, hoping there was one from Casey, but they were either desperate calls from Esprit or calls from colleges wanting to know if they were still in the running. By around one thirty Lisa still hadn't heard from Casey or Frankie. She was starting to climb the walls. She needed to hear her son's voice; she needed to know he was okay, so she picked up the phone and called around looking for him. She tried to reach him on his cell, she called Frankie twice, she tried Kevin's house. She even left a message at the school. Nothing. With no more calls to make she dejectedly sat down at the kitchen counter, stared at the phone, and willed it to ring.

Frankie Giordano eventually returned her call around two-thirty and gave her a blow-by-blow account of his earlier conversation with Casey. He was obviously concerned and attempted to reassure her that Casey was going to be okay. When he got to the part about what Casey had done at school Lisa gasped. She couldn't believe what she was hearing. There was no way Casey could ever have done something like that. She was devastated. Frankie then told her that Casey had gone back to school to try and repair the damage done from his morning escapade. Lisa remained silent. Her son had committed another violent act, and on a fellow teammate no less.

Try as she might, she couldn't remember a single instance where he'd been violent outside of organized sports. She had no knowledge of the episode that had occurred in his freshman year. A profound sense of loss began creeping through her as she absent-mindedly listened to the rest of Frankie's call. By the time she hung up the phone, Lisa had sadly come to the realization that today she'd lost something very dear to her, something she'd never have again – her son's innocence.

After she hung up she walked aimlessly around her empty house. She looked at all her stuff, the pool, her brand-new kitchen, at the expensive Coach handbag lying on the table, at her diamond-studded Rolex, at all the material things that surrounded her and comforted her and right then and there it all meant nothing. Everything that had happened was forcing her to question her life, and she began to wonder if Casey had been right.

Had she really become someone spoiled and sedated by money? Had her failures as a mother and as a loving and giving human being actually led her to this? Was she the one most responsible for Casey's problems and pain?

These questions left her confused and floundering in self-doubt and guilt. Lisa had always pictured herself as the quintessential 'super-mom'. She'd always believed that she went well beyond what was expected when it came to her son. Over the years she'd been the recipient of tremendous amounts personal satisfaction and gratification that came directly from Casey's accomplishments, and God knows there were many.

More thoughts and questions came flooding out.

Maybe that was the problem! Maybe being the super-mom had been the very thing that pushed him over the edge. Was her constant presence and support for him in reality the very thing that led him to this heartbreaking point? Had her constant prodding and pushing him to be the best at everything gone way to far? Casey was a driven young man, that was for sure. He could never be satisfied with not being the best at everything he set out to do. Casey was not capable of accepting or even understanding the nature of mediocrity. Was he so driven to succeed that he would actually commit and act of violence rather than accept failure? Apparently so, because Casey never failed – Casey didn't know how to fail.

Lisa again thought back to his behavior this morning. He had scared the hell out of her when he banged his fists on the table in a fit of anger. Could it be that this whole thing was her fault?

Alone, with a head full of conflicting and tortured thoughts, Lisa picked up the portable phone and went outside to the patio, hoping that some fresh air would calm her frayed nerves. It was almost five and she expected Steve to get home from work very soon, and with any luck Casey would follow soon there after. She was desperate for contact with the two men she loved. She had never felt so alone and helpless.

As she sat down on the patio a strong breeze began to blow in from the ocean. She listened to the gentle wind rustling through the leaves of the ancient Elm trees that surrounded her yard. She turned her head to listen to the swooshing sound of the long slender branches of the willow tree softly slapping against the side of the house. She looked up at the tree and was comforted only a little by the familiar sight of the two doves cooing in their nest. She knew how much Casey loved those birds and thinking again of Casey made her want to cry.

When Esprit learned that Casey was on his way over, the change in her was instantaneous. Her eyes lit up at once and the fatigue she'd been feeling all day mysteriously drifted away like the early morning fog on the river dissipating under the searing rays of a hot summer sun. Everything that had been so bleak and dark just moments before was now bright and sunny, her endless day of darkness soon forgotten.

Esprit considered her father's behavior. She could not begin to fathom the change in him. In just one day he had gone from world-class shit-heel to father of the year. Esprit didn't quite know what to make of the change. It was hard to believe, but she was actually feeling love and a deep sense of gratitude towards him, and it was a shock to her system.

Maybe he was actually becoming the father she had always dreamed he could be; one that really loved her and one that would always be there for her. Maybe it took this kind of crisis for him to see the light. After he told her he had spoken to Casey he actually invited her to go to lunch with him the next day. Esprit readily accepted the invitation. She hadn't been out to lunch with just him in years.

Casey was supposed to arrive around six. Esprit needed to put her thoughts about her dad aside and get ready. It was time to get a move on. She moved into her bathroom to make herself presentable. First, she brushed out her long golden tresses and then she brushed her teeth. It was time to work on her face. Because of the dark circles and puffiness under her eyes, her face was barely recognizable. She applied more make-up than usual to hide the telltale signs of her many hours of crying.

When she was satisfied, she spritzed on a small amount of Casey's favorite perfume near some of his favorite places. Just as she was applying the final touches to her hair she heard the doorbell chime.

Casey rang the bell and was greeted at the door by both Ethan and Jordan. Ethan welcomed him into the living room, and he went out of his way, perhaps because he was feeling a little guilty, to express his empathy over Casey's difficult day. Casey was unaccustomed to receiving sympathy of any kind; he awkwardly accepted Ethan's words of encouragement.

When Esprit walked down the stairs and entered the living room, Jordan and Ethan tactfully staged their exit, telling the kids they were going out to dinner and would be home later. Alone for the first time since last night's disaster, neither Esprit nor Casey could find the right words. Casey, still sitting on the couch, looked up at Esprit. She was so beautiful standing there, silent, face lowered, eyes burning a hole through the deep pile of the Persian rug, her hands slightly trembling at her sides.

Casey savored the moment, wanting it to last forever, but then he finally broke the ice. "Spree, it's a little stuffy in here. Can we go for a walk down by the river so we can talk?"

She silently nodded.

He rose and took her hand. The two, hand in hand, left the house through the solarium and walked slowly across the garden terrace. They paused for a moment to savior the view when they reached the far edge of the lawn where it became a steep bluff overlooking the river. About ten feet in front of them there was a sharp vertical drop down through the rocky terrain of the bluff. The face of the cliff was nothing but boulders and scrub bushes all the way down some eighty feet until it reached the banks of the river. Winding its way down through the bluff was a steep set of wooden stairs that switched back on itself about halfway down the embankment, and then descended again the rest of the way down to the boathouse and floating dock below. Casey and

Esprit gradually and carefully made there way down the precipitous wooden steps to the river while holding on to both the railing and each other's hand for support.

The stairs ended at the base of the bluff and opened up onto a large wooden platform deck. To their left was a beautiful white gazebo that looked like it should have sat atop a wedding cake, and straight ahead was the boathouse. Inside the boathouse Casey spied Ethan's rarely used, thirty-six-foot Hunter Sailboat and a couple of jet-skis. The sun was just starting to descend in the western sky, but it was still a good hour away from a full sunset. Casey thought about the many times he and Esprit had come down here just like this to watch the sunset. The gazebo was such a private place, the view was dazzling, and it always seemed so peaceful and romantic.

He led her by the hand into the gazebo and sat her down next to him. They both sat facing west so they could follow the sun slowly falling in the sky. The sky was a pale cerulean blue with just a few scattered clouds slowly drifting away to the west. Out at the far end of the horizon as far as the eye could see the white sails of the boats melded together with the light puffy clouds in the sky. It was so calm and so still that neither wanted to break the silence, instead they took in the brief moment of serenity and gathered their thoughts.

Casey eventually broke the silence. "Esprit, this has been a really bad day, maybe the worst day of my life. I'm pretty sure I lost my scholarship to Penn State, I was almost thrown off the football team, and you made me look like a fool with that damn photograph."

Esprit dropped her eyes. She couldn't look at him.

"But you know what? I'm okay." He smiled and gently raised her chin with his hand. "This morning I thought my whole world was coming to an end. It seemed like everything I've worked so hard for was being taken from me – football, you, my future! I really wanted to strangle you this morning. But then I learned something important, something I never realized before.

I learned there are people out there who care about me and just maybe I can't do everything alone."

He paused for a moment. "Talking to Frankie and your father today really helped me to understand that maybe I'm not Superman. I guess what I'm trying to say is…nobody's perfect and everybody makes mistakes…even me."

"Oh…Casey!" She reached and hugged him with tears streaming down her face.

As they clung to each other he continued, "Frankie helped me to realize that losing the Penn State scholarship's not the end of the world, and your father showed me that we all make mistakes. He admitted that he used me to make you go to the party. Then he told me he was willing to forgive you for last night, even though it would probably hurt his campaign. That took guts. Maybe there's more to courage than just tackling people on a football field. Anyway, the way I see it, if your father can forgive you so easily, then so can I."

She buried her head in his neck.

"Esprit, I love you and I'm sorry about the way I spoke to you at school. Please forgive me." Casey took her face in his hands and looked down at the tears on her cheeks. Right then he thought she had never looked more beautiful. His eyes welled with tears, but he quickly rubbed them away. Esprit couldn't seem to get close enough to him as she nudged closer and closer into his waiting arms.

"Casey, I never meant to hurt you. I was drunk and angry, and I wanted to get back at my father. I didn't know what I was doing. If I had known the photographers were there, I never would have done something so foolish. I feel like such a jerk. I really hurt you, the one person I truly love. And then my father goes and forgives me right away and then he even calls you! What kind of person am I? I don't deserve you or my father. Casey, I am so sorry! Can you ever forgive me?" Once again she burst into tears.

Casey held her and wiped away her tears, "Esprit…it's okay.

It's over. Let's just forget about what happened, I mean it. I know it was a mistake, and I love you."

He kissed her, softly at first, but then with a swelling urgency that soon became unquenchable. She responded to his kiss with a heat and passion she had never known before. In no time they were tearing off each other's clothes and tumbling together onto the cushioned bench of the gazebo. Neither Casey nor Esprit had as yet experienced the delirious and deliciously gratifying netherworld of make-up sex and couldn't possibly know what was in store. But they soon found out.

Steve got home from work around six fifteen and found an empty house. Lisa's Volvo was in the driveway, but when he called her name she didn't answer his repeated calls. The last time they'd spoken was a couple of hours ago. At that point she had still sounded upset. Steve searched the house from room to room until he finally looked outside and saw her lying on a lounge chair on the far side of the patio by the pool. She looked like she was sleeping. Before he made his way outside he stopped in the kitchen when he noticed the message light flashing on the phone. He stopped and listened to the messages. The last one was from Casey saying that he was okay and that he was going over to talk to Esprit. He would be home some time after that. Steve thought his son sounded okay considering all he'd been through.

He walked out to the patio and gently kissed Lisa on the forehead as she lay sleeping. At first she murmured in her sleep, but when he kissed her again she bolted upright, startled and frightened.

"Steve, thank God you're home! Where's Casey? I haven't heard from him all day, and I haven't been able to find him." She held her husband close as she looked around trying to focus and gain her bearings. "Oh my God…I must have fallen asleep…Oh my God! Steve, where is Casey?"

Steve held her a little tighter and said, "Calm down, honey.

There's a message on the machine. He's at Esprit's and will be home in a little while." He held her for a moment and caressed her arms, hoping to calm her down.

"He called? Here? That can't be. I have the portable right here. I would have heard the phone." Lisa looked down on the ground at the phone. When she had drifted off to sleep the portable phone had fallen from her hand, and when it hit the fieldstone patio the back had popped off and the re-chargeable battery had become detached. "Shit…I hate these damn portable phones!"

Steve chuckled softly. "Honey, Casey sounded just fine on the message, and he said he'd be home in a little while. Are you okay?"

"I don't know. I must have fallen asleep for a few minutes. What time is it anyway?"

"A little after six."

"I can't believe I fell asleep. The last thing I remember I was watching those stupid doves in the willow tree and I started balling. I guess all this stress just wore me out. What did Casey's message say?"

"Just that he was going over to Esprit's after practice and he'd be home later. Lisa, you're taking this a little too hard. Casey losing the scholarship is not the end of the world. Hell…USC is a better team anyway, and it appears from his message that things with Esprit are being worked out even as we speak."

Lisa sat up straight. "Wait a minute, you haven't heard the whole story. By the time I found out what happened to Casey at school today, you'd already left the office and I couldn't reach you on your cell."

"What are you talking about?"

"When Casey went to practice this morning someone taped the pictures from the paper on his locker, and he went berserk. He chocked Shawn Murphy so hard the boy almost passed out! And, Steve, you should have seen his rage when he first saw the picture. He slammed his fists down so hard I thought he was going to break the table. I was frightened." She began to choke up. "Steve…I was afraid of him…my own son!"

"Lisa, calm down and tell me the whole thing. I'm not following you. What happened when he fought with the Murphy boy?"

After taking a minute to calm herself Lisa shared with Steve her entire conversation with Frankie. When she was done he didn't know what to think. His first thought was that teenage boys fought all the time, but then again Casey was not the average boy. He had always demonstrated an unusually high level of self-control and he was wise beyond his years. Casey never pulled any of the shenanigans that most kids his age tried. Hell, he was more responsible than just about anyone. But then again, his behavior over the last several months had been puzzling. Casey was growing more intolerant and more prone to angry outbursts as each week went by. Lately, he was quick to go off on every little thing that bothered him, things like a meal that he didn't like, or a certain shirt that that he wanted to wear that hadn't been washed. Until recently he had always let this type of small stuff just roll of his back, but lately?

"Lisa, I'm not sure what's going on here, but lately Casey's anger and mood swings have been way out of proportion to the problem. He's always dealt with stress incredibly well. Do you think this is just about that damn scholarship, or is something else going on here?"

"Steve, I don't know, but something is definitely not right. He really frightened me this morning, and I think we need to talk to him about it."

"So do I, and I think we need to do it as soon as he comes home."

Casey left Esprit's around seven thirty. As he made the short trip home, he thought about their lovemaking. It had been without a doubt the best sex they'd ever had. Esprit had been insatiable. And all the while, in between her gasps and moans, there had been a constant stream of 'I'm sorrys' and 'forgive mes'. Casey didn't know quite what to make of the whole experience. He was thrilled by the erotic combination of her submissiveness and passion, but there was something akin to guilt or shame lingering around the periphery of his consciousness. He couldn't quite put his finger on it.

As soon he drove up the driveway he stopped thinking about the sex. Because of everything that had happened today he had reached a place in his mind where he could accept life on life's terms. He still wanted very much to play for Penn State and would show Coach Paterno just how much on Friday, but if that didn't happen, he was prepared to move on to USC and succeed there. As for Esprit, her indiscretion was behind them, and her guilt had tipped the balance of power between them. He would try and use her new attitude to get her to come around to his way of thinking in terms of her partying and her friends.

But he still had one more test. His parents would be waiting to talk to him as soon as he walked through the door. His mom had talked to Frankie, so she knew the whole damn story, and so would his father by now. He wished Frankie hadn't gone and run his big mouth to her, but he was just trying to help. Casey felt terrible that his mother had tried to call him at least a dozen times and he hadn't returned her calls. He just wasn't ready to face her yet. *Well,* Casey thought, *at least I called and left her a message.*

Casey entered the house through the front door, and as expected he found his parents sitting at the kitchen counter drinking coffee and eating strawberry cheesecake for dessert. Everything seemed okay until he looked closely at his mother and noticed that she looked like she'd been crying all day. A twinge of guilt stabbed his chest when he kissed her hello.

"Hey, Mom, hey, Dad," he said, hoping to keep the mood light.

At the sound of his voice, Lisa stood up and hugged him as

tears again welled up in her eyes. "Oh, Casey, I'm so glad you're home. Your father and I have been worried sick about you. Honey, are you okay?" She brushed her fingers through his hair while she held him tightly.

Steve, not one for big displays of affection, didn't get up, but he did get right to the point. "Casey, your mother and I have been trying to reach you all day. Why didn't you call and let us know what was going on? We had to learn about what happened at school secondhand from Frankie."

"I'm sorry I didn't call, but everything happened so fast. I just didn't have time this morning, and besides, I did call this afternoon, but Mom didn't pick up, so I just left a message. Anyway, everything that happened today was my problem, not yours. I'm not a kid anymore, and I screwed up royally this morning, but I worked it all out. I'm back on the team, and Esprit and I had a long talk. She apologized for last night and I have forgiven her so it's all good."

"Casey, your mother and I are happy that everything worked out and 'its all good', but you scared the hell out of your mother this morning, and then you attacked Shawn Murphy, and from what we heard, almost seriously hurt the poor kid."

"I didn't really hurt him."

"Casey, the violent outbursts, it's not just today, you've been on a very short fuse for months now. Your mother and I have noticed it more and more. Casey, off the playing field you've never been violent in your life. What's going on? Please talk to us. We want to understand, and we want to help you deal with whatever it is that you're dealing with."

Lisa, still crying, chimed in, "Honey, I was terrified today. Please talk to your father and me and tell us how we can help you. Please don't keep telling us it was just the stress of the scholarship, it's more than that and we know it."

Casey looked at the two of them and saw their concern and determination to find out what was really bothering him. Part of him was angry that he had to deal with this, but part of him also knew that they were sincerely worried and only wanted to help.

"Mom, Dad, listen, today was a pretty rough day, don't you think? It was the worst day of my life. How would you feel if you woke up to find your girlfriend kissing a movie star in the newspaper? Then on top of that, the call from Penn State. Dad, it would be like you walking into work and getting fired from your job. And as if that wasn't enough, I walk into the locker room and the whole damn team is laughing at me because of that stupid picture taped to my locker. I just snapped…Jesus, what the hell would you two have done if you were in my place? I know what I did was wrong. I already apologized to Shawn and the rest of the team, and now I am apologizing to you. This will never happen again. I won't let it."

"Honey, we believe you, and we know it was a rotten day for you, but until lately you have always demonstrated such complete self-control, and you still haven't explained the reason for the change in your behavior over the couple of months. We're only trying to figure out what's wrong so we can help you." Lisa reached over to him and again ran her fingers through his curly mop of hair. "Honey, please tell us if there's anything else. We really want to know."

"Honestly, Mom, there's nothing else. This is about football. Maybe it's just that I'm getting closer and closer to reaching the next step and I'm a little afraid. I'm afraid that maybe I won't be as good a player in college, I'm afraid that if I get hurt the way Frankie did, my career could be over in a minute. Sometimes I'm afraid that I might not make it to the pros. I can't begin to imagine what life would be like if I don't make it to the NFL. I'm just worried that's all. Can't you guys understand that?"

Lisa smiled, but only for second. "Casey, I must say I'm surprised by your honesty. Thank you for finally talking to us. Now I think we understand a little better what you've been going though. But, honey, I am worried that maybe your father and I have pushed you too hard over these past few years. There is more to life than football."

It was Steve's turn. He was seeing his son in a very different light. "Casey, thank you for finally sharing your fears, that goes a long way in helping us to understand what's been eating at you lately. I know that must have been hard for you, but I'm glad you did. And, son, you are going to be the best college linebacker in the country, and you're going to play in the NFL. I know it in my heart because you deserve it. As for injuries, all you can do is keep yourself in the best shape possible and play smart football, and God willing you'll be fine. Just remember that we are always here for you; so from now on don't hold things back. If you talk to us, I promise we'll listen." He got up and gave Casey a hug.

Casey sighed with relief. "Thanks, Dad. I promise I'll talk to you guys if I need help from now on. I think I'm gonna go up to bed and get some shuteye. This has been a really long day."

He went to give his mother a hug, but Lisa, still a little emotional, felt the need to make one final point. "Casey, I just want you to know that if for any reason, any reason at all, you don't make it to the NFL, you are still a gifted and unique young man that has much to offer this world. Please never forget that, okay?"

Casey looked at her and smiled. "You're absolutely right, Mom. I do know that." He kissed her again to reassure her and went up the stairs to his bedroom thinking that what he had just said to his mother was absolute bullshit. If he didn't make it to the NFL, his life would have no meaning whatsoever.

Chapter Eleven

Memos & Mayhem

Tuesday Morning, September 4th

Esprit woke earlier than usual, feeling light in spirit and ready to meet the day. Gone were yesterday's guilt and shame, replaced this morning by a sense of well-being and serenity. Today was a brand-new day and everything was right with the world except for one thing; she still hadn't shaken the queasiness in her stomach that had been lingering there for several days now. She walked out through the French doors of her bedroom onto the balcony and embraced the soft breeze. The warm sun bathed her bare skin, and it felt delicious. The morning was still cool enough, but it promised to be a scorcher later on as there wasn't a cloud in the sky.

Esprit daydreamed, staring lazily off in the distance until her trance was disturbed by a deep rumbling sound. It was a mechanical sound drifting over from the other side of the river. She followed the unpleasant noise until she spied several large construction tractors moving huge piles of earth at a new construction site on the former Thompson Estate. The ugly sight brought a frown to her face when she thought about the beautiful old mansion bulldozed last week to make way for a few more McMansions.

What was once a magnificent, riverfront farm was about to become ten brick monstrosities, each with dozens of ugly little casement windows, and all crammed up together on single acre lots. Esprit cherished the esthetic beauty of the old place and thought it a shame that these grotesque three-million-dollar homes had become the rage with the 'Nuevo riche' Wall Street crowd.

Last week she had laughed when driving by another such development, Jamie had referred to them as 'tract houses on steroids'. Esprit laughed because Jamie lived in a small tract house and knew exactly what she was talking about. She lamented that the river was losing its elegance and tranquility, but she was not about to dwell on the subject and let it ruin her day.

Her father had to leave for Washington tomorrow morning so the two of them were having lunch together later on. Esprit couldn't believe she was actually looking forward to it. She'd never thought it possible until yesterday, but Ethan had gone and done the unthinkable and put her ahead of his political career. She smiled when she thought about how he'd come to her bedroom to comfort her and to apologize when she'd expected him to do just the opposite.

It was such a wonderful morning that she would have much preferred to stay home and sunbathe on her balcony, but she had to pick up Jamie for play rehearsal in less than an hour. They were running through the first four scenes of Act One and Esprit was still a little unsure of some of her lines.

Before she left the balcony she took one last look down to the river and it made her think back to the sex with Casey the day before. She and Casey had both been virgins when they began dating, so even though they were very comfortable with each other sexually, they both probably still had a lot to learn. Make-up sex was definitely something new. Then thinking about the sex made her remember she'd forgotten to take her birth control pill again last night. *Oh well, it's only been a few hours*, she thought. *I'll just take it now*. And with that thought she left the balcony for the bathroom to take her pill and prepare for a very busy day.

Casey, a creature of habit, woke at seven on the dot. His first thought was that he hoped today would be far less eventful than yesterday. He looked out the window and saw a bright blue sky. It looked like it was going to be another hot one. He needed to really hydrate at practice because it was going to be brutal out there, especially the afternoon session.

As he rolled out of bed he felt a little dizzy, and then when he stood up the headache that had plagued him yesterday came back with a vengeance. Maybe the headache was coming from the new cycle. He pushed the thought out of his head and started his exercises. The routine always cleared away the cobwebs and today was no exception. By the time he started the last set of crunches the headache had receded, and he'd moved on to other things.

When he finished the set he went to his desk and administered his next injection. He concluded the morning ritual by checking himself out in the mirror. His muscles were long and taught and perfectly sculpted. They weren't the bulging hunks of translucent tissue that popped through the stretched-out skin of bodybuilders or pro wrestlers, no, sir. They were clearly defined, perfectly symmetrical, and lay just beneath his healthy unblemished skin, except of course for the two small patches of acne on his shoulders. He believed the acne on his shoulders had to be caused by the constant rubbing of his shoulder pads, not the steroids. After all, he did take every precaution: his regulated diet, his exercise regimen, even his sleep patterns, they were all designed for maximum results and minimum risks.

Casey left his room for the bathroom to take a shower. He stepped on the bathroom scale to check his weight. This was just another part of his training routine, and of course he would chart the weight in his training log. He was up two pounds in just over a week. That was very good.

He stepped off the scale and over to the toilet to urinate when he felt a sharp, knife-like twinge of pain in his side, and he was having difficulty peeing. He thought maybe it was because of the sex last night, but then when his urine stream finally began to flow the water in the bowl began turning a pinkish red color. He looked closer at his stream and it was definitely not its normal color. It looked like a small amount of blood had mixed in.

"Oh shit, this isn't good." His mind raced through the possibilities. "Let's see, I started the new cycle two days ago, and since then I've had a headache and now this morning I have pain in my side and blood in my urine. It's got to be the high dosage. Or...maybe it's the dosage combined with a little bit of dehydration. Maybe I'm just overworking my kidneys. Either way I can't fool around with this."

Casey decided to monitor his urine for the next twenty-four hours. If necessary he would skip the next injection. He'd also make sure to hydrate much more than usual to flush out his system. Then he would play it from there. This was just a small problem and he would fix it. That's what he always did. He would talk to Kevin about it later.

Lisa had already been up for about an hour. She had started out in a much better frame of mind than the day before, that was until she read the paper. On the front page of the sports section there was yet another story of a Major League baseball player caught using steroids. The story made her wonder if Casey had ever tried them. She didn't know much about steroids, but some of the things she read made her curious.

When she heard Casey get into the shower she got up and began to prepare his shake. As she was scooping the powder out of the bags she considered the ongoing Balco steroid scandal. She remembered reading something about steroids causing a lot of health problems, including severe mood swings and irritability and then she of course thought about Casey and his recent behavior.

But then she laughed. There was no conceivable way that her son would ever do something like that. Not Casey, no way!

He was so anti-drug and anti-alcohol that there was no way he would even consider it. Besides, he lived in the gym. No one worked as hard as Casey did in the gym, and that was the honest to goodness truth. She laughed again for even thinking it in the first place and finished making his breakfast shake.

Casey came down a few minutes later. He gave his mom a hug, drank down the shake in a couple of gulps and was preparing to leave for the gym when Lisa called out, "Casey, hold on a minute."

He turned around with an annoyed look that quickly evaporated and said, "Yah, Mom, what's up?"

"I know yesterday is over and done with and today's a new day, but I just want you to know that I love you, and you will always be the most important person in my life, football or no football. Casey, you are a gifted young man, and you're going to accomplish great things in the future and not just on the football field. Please remember that?"

Instead of his usual "Sure, Mom," followed by a smirk and a quick exit, Casey put down his bag and gave her a long, hard squeeze. "Thanks, Mom, I mean that. But you don't have to worry about me. I'm okay and yesterday's long forgotten. I probably won't be home till around dinner. Please stop worrying about me and go out and have a nice day. I love you!"

She smiled as he walked out the door, but as she watched him leave she thought briefly about the steroid story again then discarded it as just paranoid nonsense.

Casey left and went directly to the gym. After a grueling workout he went on to pick up Kevin for practice. He'd urinated again before leaving the gym, and there were still some traces of blood, but not nearly as much as this morning. That was a good sign, but even so, he still planed on talking to Kevin about it. He'd thought about talking to Frankie but decided against it because he didn't want to raise his suspicions. Besides, he could talk to Kevin about this sort of thing.

Casey was a little apprehensive before he picked up Kevin. He and Kevin didn't get a chance to talk at the afternoon practice the day before. Casey wanted to make sure that they were cool after everything that had happened. He pulled into Kevin's driveway and hit the horn. Like always, Kevin came bounding out the front door a moment later. His bruises from the surfing accident were already starting to yellow and fade, and he was walking with a much less noticeable limp. However, as he walked up to the car, Casey couldn't help but gawk at his friend because there was something very different about him – something shocking and amazing.

Kevin had always been known as the surfer-dude with the attitude and the long locks of beached blonde hair, but for some reason, between yesterday afternoon and this morning he'd gotten his hair cut, and not just any old haircut, an honest to goodness, prep-school, military type haircut. For the first time in his life, at least since Casey had known him, Kevin had short hair, and it was even parted on the side. As he climbed in the car Casey looked at him in dumbfounded amazement and then burst out laughing.

"Kevin, what the fuck happened to you? Do you have to go to court or something? Shit, I didn't even recognize you! Dude, your father must have fallen off his surfboard laughing when he saw you."

Kevin's mother and father were former professional surfers who now owned a small chain of surf shops along the Jersey shore. They were both hip and casual, and everyone thought they were the coolest parents around, but the real truth was that they were attentive and loving parents who made sure their son kept on the straight and narrow. No drugs, no bad habits, and none of the wacky friends that usually ran with the surfing crowd.

"I got it cut this morning, my dad hasn't even seen it yet, but my mom laughed her ass off. She said I wasn't allowed to surf again until it grew back."

Casey buckled over with laughter as he ran his hand through

Kevin's bristling hair. "So what's the deal? Why'd you do it?"

"Think about it. You know why. I really want that scholarship to Monmouth. I figure that if I have a great game on Friday, and I look like the all-American boy, it will help my chances with the scouts."

"Kevin, are you nuts? Nobody's even going to recognize you!" He burst out laughing again.

Kevin got a little miffed so Casey eased up a little.

"I'm just busting you. It actually looks pretty good. And you know damn well I like your reason for doing it. I really want to see you play college ball, and Monmouth's got a good program."

"Yeah, it's a decent school and the campus is only a couple blocks from the beach in Long Branch. Besides, I don't know if I told you, but my father's stores aren't doing so hot this year and money's tight. He might not have the cash to send me to school, so I don't have a whole lot of choices here."

Casey decided to switch the topic. "Listen, Kev, I want to clear the air about yesterday. I'm sorry about what I did. When I saw those pictures I just went nuts. I couldn't control myself. I know you were upset, and I'm really sorry, okay?"

"That's okay by me, but yesterday that wasn't you, it was the roids talking. I'm telling you, Casey, you've got to get off that shit! You don't need them anymore. All they are doing is fucking with your head. Maybe you don't see it, but, dog, I'm your best friend and I see it, you're heading for trouble."

Casey thought about what Kevin had said. "Dude, you might be surprised to hear this, but I think you might be right. This morning when I took a piss, there was blood in the bowl, and I had a real bad pain in my side. I think I need to take at least a day or two off the stuff and give my kidneys a break."

Kevin was nonplussed. "Are you a fucking idiot? Take a couple of days off? You need to stop for good, Casey. You don't know what the hell that crap is doing to your insides. Listen, I'm not your mother or your father, I'm just your best friend, but I can't sit back and watch you do this anymore. Now you're pissing blood and acting all crazy and shit. You've got to promise me you're going to stop this shit today, or I'm going to talk to Frankie, and I mean it. I don't care if you don't speak to me again or even if you decide to kick my ass. If you don't promise to quit right now, I'm going to call him. I swear it."

Casey was a little freaked by Kevin's threatening tone. Kevin never spoke to him this way and it scared him. Maybe he didn't really see what the steroids were doing to him. Maybe this was more serious than he thought. He knew Kevin loved him like a brother and was only doing what he thought was right, but even so it was a little rough to hear.

As they pulled into the parking lot Casey said, "Kevin, I hear you loud and clear so back off with the threats. You're right, and seeing as I'm pissing blood, it's probably a good time to stop anyway. So stop with the Frankie shit, all right?"

Kevin nodded.

"When I get home tonight I'm going to throw the rest of the cycle away."

Kevin looked right at Casey and wanted to believe him. What else could he do? He couldn't really turn him in, could he? He prayed to God that Casey wasn't just bullshitting him. "Casey, it's the right thing to do, bud. I was getting worried about you!" The two boys shook hands, jumped out of the car and ran off to practice.

Esprit picked up Jamie a little after nine a.m. and then they drove to the school for a nine-thirty rehearsal. On the way they talked about everything that went down the day before. Esprit seemed almost manic with her newfound enthusiasm for life, especially when it came to talking about Casey and her father. By the end of the fifteen-minute ride Jamie was about ready to strangle her seriously hyper friend.

After the rehearsal when Esprit drove Jamie home she was a little better. They chatted about the play and evaluated each other's performance, but then Esprit changed the subject back to her father. By the time they pulled into her driveway Jamie had heard enough. She became serious and let into friend, "Spree, I know you're pretty happy about this thing with your father and that's good, but be careful and don't set your expectations too high. I know he did the right thing yesterday, but he's still the same guy he always was, so don't think he's gonna drop all the shit that always used to piss you off."

Esprit didn't want to hear it. She replied, "Jamie, why are you telling me this? You're my best friend, and you're really starting to bum me out! Can't you just be happy for me?"

Jamie softened a little. "Listen, girl, I am happy for you. I just don't want to see you get hurt. God knows the SOB has hurt you before. That's all. Forget about it. I'm sorry I brought it up. Anyway, I'm just going to be hanging out here today, so call me later and let me know how the big lunch goes. Maybe we can get together tonight since it's one of our last nights of the summer together. I can't believe school starts the day after tomorrow."

"Me neither. I'll call you later. I'm not sure what I'm doing tonight. I'll let you know after I talk to Casey."

"Later."

As Esprit drove home she wondered what the heck that was all about. She figured that it was just Jamie getting a little jealous because she didn't have a very good relationship with her own father. Her dad was kind of a macho guy who was much more comfortable around her brothers than around her. He wasn't particularly mean to her or anything; he just didn't seem to talk to her very much.

Esprit drove up her driveway and saw her father's long black Mercedes E500 in the circular drive. She was surprised that it pleased her to see him home, and even more surprised that she couldn't wait to have lunch with him. She wondered what restaurant he would take her to, hopefully one of the new places over in Red Bank and not the stuffy dining room of his silly old country club.

As soon as she entered the house she called out his name a

few times, but no one answered. Figuring he was probably up in the gym or his office, she climbed the stairs to find him. She passed by the gym, but it was empty, so she ventured further down the hall and around the corner to his office. The door was closed so she knocked a couple of times but again, no one answered. She heard the ring of his fax machine so she entered the room.

Her father wasn't there. She peeked into the adjoining bathroom to be sure, but he wasn't in there either. She'd only been in his office a handful of times in the past, and usually under negative circumstances, so she'd never taken the time to look around. She walked slowly around the room taking in all of her father's personal effects. There were photographs and books and stacks of documents lying all around his desk, they all looked very important and very official.

But he wasn't there, so she was just about to leave and look elsewhere when she spied the pile of newspapers left on his desk from yesterday, each one opened to her photo, and a flood of guilt washed over her. With a slight frown, she turned to walk out of the room, but then something caught her eye and drew her back in. Esprit looked over at the chirping fax machine on the credenza behind Ethan's desk and recognized her own name on the first line of the fax coming through the machine. Curious, she walked back around the desk and casually picked up the incoming memo. As she read it, surprise and anger began rising from the pit of her stomach.

FACSIMILE
To: Ethan Burke 8/28/07
From: Blaine Caswell
RE: 5-POINT BOUNCE, GOD BLESS ESPRIT!

Ethan,

Here are yesterday's polling results. I think you will be very pleased.

Quinnipiac	**Integrity +4**	**Leadership +4**	**Compassion +6**
Eagleton	**Integrity+5**	**Leadership +5**	**Compassion +6**
Time/News	**Integrity+5**	**Leadership +5**	**Compassion +6**
AOL-online	**Integrity+4**	**Leadership +5**	**Compassion +5**
Aggregate	**+4**	**+ 5**	**+5**

I know you didn't believe me, but the proof is in the pudding. Amazing, isn't it? We don't want to lose momentum with this. Here are a couple of ideas you may want to consider seeing that you are now Esprit's hero for keeping the boyfriend from dumping her. A possible family interview with *Time* or *People Magazine*. I have spoken to them and they would jump at the chance for an interview. Just make sure the boyfriend is there, the kid looks great on camera. Also I have spoken to Katie Courik's assistant at CBS. They are willing to do a live remote from your home on Monday or Tuesday of next week. We might even have a shot at Oprah with a cameo appearance by Dr. Phil. That could be risky, but the ratings would be huge. Think about it, Ethan Burke, the compassionate congressman. Keep Esprit in line and you could sustain these numbers well past this year's election and into your Senate campaign next year. Call me this afternoon to confirm. Again, congratulations.
Blaine

Esprit read the fax twice before taking a single breath. She felt like she'd just been hit by a brick right in her solar plexus. She didn't know whether to scream or cry. How could he do this to her? He had done it again! The son of a bitch was using her to boost his goddamn political career. Now it all made sense. This wasn't about love; it was about points on a fucking political poll. As tears formed in the corners of her eyes, she looked out the window and saw her parents walking across the back lawn from the dock. The son of a bitch must have been down there working on his sailboat. How could he do something like this?

Esprit quickly made a copy the fax. Then she put the original back on the machine and stuffed the copy into her pocket. She had to think fast, she was supposed to go to lunch with her father any minute. What the hell was she going to do? She hastily left his office and went to her bedroom to give herself some time to think.

Feeling betrayed and angrier than she'd ever been, Esprit ran to her bathroom to fix her face. She looked in the mirror and spoke out loud, "All right, Esprit, you're a damn good actress. You can make it through this fucking lunch without that scumbag ever suspecting a thing, at least until you have had some time to figure this all out. I can't believe he used me this way!"

Her anger intensified even as she regained her composure and put on her game face. As she put on the last touches of mascara and dabs of blush, she whispered, "I'll show that motherfucker," and then she headed for the door when she heard him calling her name.

Ethan came happily bounding up the stairs in search of his daughter. He peeked into his office before going on to Esprit's room. He'd been waiting all morning for a fax from his campaign manager, and there it was sitting on the fax machine, the memo from Blaine with the much anticipated polling results. He looked at the figures with great pleasure, but then his eyebrows arched and narrowed as he read the subsequent paragraph.

To no one in particular he said, "Is Blaine out of his mind? There's no way I would subject my family to this kind of public scrutiny. Who does he think we are, the Clintons, for Christ's sake? Just when I'm starting to make some headway with my daughter, he wants me to put her on television and embarrass her in front of fifty million viewers. I don't think so."

Ethan folded the fax and placed it face down inside the desk drawer so that his daughter would not inadvertently come across it. If she ever saw this fax, it would completely undo all the progress he had made with her in the past twenty-four hours.

He left his office, remembering to shut the door, walked directly to Esprit's bedroom and knocked on her door.

At football practice Casey was a model citizen. In the morning session during a live scrimmage there had been dozens of opportunities for him to exert his physical presence on the field by either making solo tackles or giving crushing blocks, but in each instance he had backed off the opposing teammate at the last moment and then patted the player on the back. Throughout the morning session he encouraged the other players and in every way he had behaved like the captain of his team. All the while he was being closely watched by the coaching staff, especially by Martin and Callahan.

When the first session ended Casey did something unusual. Instead of going off to Kevin's house for an hour of video games and lunch, he hopped in Shawn Murphy's pick-up truck and went off with him to Chris's delicatessen, a local variety store close to the school. He ended up having lunch with Shawn and a couple of the offensive lineman.

Somehow he forgot to ask Kevin to join them. After they left, Kevin was a little hurt by Casey's slight, but he was happy about the way Casey behaved on the field. He hoped his earlier threat had gotten through to Casey's thick skull. He worshiped his friend and he would do anything to save Casey from himself, even if it meant jeopardizing their long-standing friendship.

Martin and Callahan walked back into the locker room after they noticed that Casey and the linemen had left without Kevin. They spied Kevin sitting at his locker still getting dressed and came over to speak to him.

Kevin looked up as they approached and said, "Hey, Coach, oh…oh, what'd I do now?" thinking he was about to receive some more 'instructional' criticism for his efforts this morning.

Coach Callahan spoke first. "Hey, surfer boy, what happened, you and your shadow have a fight? I can't remember a single day you and Casey didn't leave together for lunch. I thought you two lovebirds were joined at the hip, by the way, nice haircut. I wasn't sure it was even you out there this morning."

"I think Casey's still feeling a little guilty about yesterday, and he just wanted to show Shawn and those guys that he's a team player."

"Listen, Kevin, there's something Coach Martin and I want to talk to you about. You got a few minutes?"

"Sure, I was just going to run home and grab a sandwich, but I'll get one in the cafeteria after we're done."

The three of them walked back to the coaches' office. When Kevin sat down he began to feel a little uncomfortable as Coach Martin closed the office door. A meeting behind closed doors with the coaches was not something any athlete looked forward to. Nervously, Kevin said, "What's up?"

"Well a couple of things, actually. First of all, both Coach Martin and I want to let you know how well you're doing. You've come a long way in the last two years. You're throwing the ball better, and you're playing real smart out there. We like the way you're using your head and reading the defenses on the play-action calls. Last year if you lost your primary receiver we were in big trouble. This year you're checking off and finding the second receiver and sometimes even the third. At the next level it's all about reads, and you are really improving in that department. That's real heady football, and we wanted to tell you that we are proud of you."

Coach Martin chimed in, "We also wanted to let you know that we got a call from the head coach at Monmouth. He's real excited about the possibility of you playing for them next year. He's coming Friday to watch you play, so we are really going to open up the offense for you and let you show off that arm of yours. Just make sure you're ready to play. How are you feeling from your surfing accident? Is your shoulder okay?"

"I'm fine, Coach. The whirlpool's taken away most of the

stiffness. I'm going to get in the tub again after practice, but it felt fine this morning, really."

Coach Callahan scratched his chin and said, "That's great, Kevin, just make sure you get plenty of rest between now and Friday, and no more surfing. Is that clear?"

"Yes, sir. I put my boards away yesterday. I'm done until next summer."

The two coaches looked at each other for a moment and then Coach Callahan continued. "There is one other thing that we want to talk to you about. We know that you and Casey are best friends, and quite frankly his behavior this past week has got us all concerned. He hasn't been himself. He seems a lot better today, thank the lord, but I got to tell you, Kevin, he's got us all worried here."

Coach Martin chimed in again. "Listen, Kevin, we know he's your best friend, and we don't expect you to rat on him or anything, but if something's wrong, we want to help him, and we know that you being his best friend and all that, well, you might know what's been bothering him. We all know he had a bad day yesterday, but that doesn't explain his aggressive attitude and reckless behavior all week. Is there anything you want to tell us?"

Kevin froze with indecision. Part of him wanted to tell the coaches everything because he was so worried about Casey, and telling them would put an end to it. But he also knew that if he divulged Casey's steroid use to the coaches, they'd have no choice but to kick him off the team. He couldn't be responsible for that. No way. Besides, Casey had just promised him that he was stopping the injections and if he was going to talk to anyone it should be Frankie, not the coaches, so he said, "Well, I know he's been having some problems with his dad. Casey told me that he thinks his father has a drinking problem and they've been fighting a lot, but please don't tell him I told you. He would kill me if he found out."

"Don't worry, Kevin, whatever is said in this room, stays in this room. Like I said, we only want to help him. But thanks for being honest with us. Why don't you go run along and get some lunch? We appreciate you taking a few minutes to talk to us. We'll see you at practice in a half-hour."

"Thanks, Coach," said Kevin. He breathed a sigh of relief and quickly left the office.

Once Kevin was gone Coach Callahan said, "I don't know, Bobby, maybe it is just a problem with his dad and not steroids after all. What do you think?"

"That's wishful thinking. I think Kevin was scared shitless, and he didn't give us anything close to the whole story. Sorry, Coach, I'm still convinced Casey's juicing and that conversation did nothing to change my mind."

"You've got to admit that he seemed back to his old self today. I think we have to watch him for at least a few more days before we decide if we're going to confront him on this. I'm not going to jeopardize this kid's future on the basis of one bad week. I won't do it."

Coach Martin rubbed his chin and said, "I agree with you that he seemed better today, but after everything that happened yesterday, what choice did he have? He's a smart kid, and he knows what's at stake. I think you're making a big mistake, but you're the boss. So we watch him for a few more days, but I promise you, we haven't seen the end of this."

Esprit opened her bedroom door and with her blood pumping, she calmly said, "Hello, Daddy, are you ready to go to lunch?"

Ethan gave her hug. "Honey, you look so much better today. I can't wait. I thought I would take you to the country club so I can show off my beautiful daughter to the other members. Would that be all right with you?"

"Sure, Daddy, that would be great," she said sweetly, but inside she was seething. Not only had he betrayed her, but now he was taking her to the one place that she absolutely hated. This was going to be a true test of her will and her ability as an actress.

Ethan was a long-standing member of the Navasink Country Club. The exclusive, private golf and tennis club was situated just a mile or so down the road from his estate, nestled in the rolling hills that bordered the Navesink River to the south. There were many expensive country clubs in the area, but Navasink was the most exclusive because it catered primarily to the old money crowd. To become a full standing member with all the rights and privileges, it could take as many as fifteen years, but first you had to be sponsored by at least two current members in good standing, and then only if you were willing to give up several hundred thousand dollars in bonds and initiation fees plus your firstborn child.

The imposing clubhouse stood high up on a hill smack dab in the center of the one-hundred-and-twenty-acre property. The clubhouse was a grand old building in the federal style with large white Doric columns and dozens of large shuttered windows dotting the four-story, white brick façade.

As Ethan drove up the long and winding driveway he commented on the beauty of the grounds. “Honey, did you know that our family has held a membership here since 1917? In fact, we are the oldest surviving family membership. Now that’s something to be proud of.”

Esprit had heard her father brag of this a dozen times before but she responded, “Oh, I didn’t know that, how wonderful.”

As soon as father and daughter entered the austere dining room, Ethan was greeted by the tuxedoed maître d’ and taken immediately over to his favorite table. It was a corner table by a large bay window overlooking the first tee. The cavernous dining room was mostly empty. The room was paneled in traditional dark oak, but quite frankly, the decor had seen better days. The carpet was a little natty and the accompanying fixtures and furnishings probably dated back to the early sixties. This was surprising considering the amount of money generated by the club's fees, but the senior members liked it this way. Old money is as old money does, and the older members like Ethan were big on tradition and fervently opposed to anything that reeked of new.

Ethan held Esprit's chair as she sat and then as he sat himself he softly whispered in her ear, as if it was some dark and mysterious deep secret, "This is my table, only senior members are afforded a table by the window." He was desperately trying to impress her, but in fact, he was doing just the opposite.

Esprit smiled.

The waiter arrived and they ordered lunch, he the house specialty, Dover sole, and she a chicken Caesar salad. When the waiter left Ethan said, "Honey, I can't remember the last time you and I had lunch here. With you being so busy at school and your acting, and me always down in Washington. So tell me, how did everything work out with you and Casey? He was already gone when your mother and I returned from dinner."

Esprit was having difficulty holding back her feelings. The truth was that she had not gone to lunch at the club with her father in eight years. She remembered the last time.

It had been a disaster. He'd taken her to this very place for her tenth birthday. It had been just the two of them because her mother had been away traipsing across Europe with her snotty women friends and she hadn't thought Esprit's birthday important enough to come home for. Esprit vividly remembered her last lunch here. She remembered her father being distinctly uncomfortable and moody, barely speaking to her for the entire meal, and then rather than ordering her a birthday cake, he'd suggested an ice cream sundae for dessert.

That was when the shit hit the proverbial fan. She had been thoroughly enjoying her sundae when she accidentally spilled the crystal parfait glass down the front of her frilly pink dress and covered herself in ice cream, chocolate sauce, and whipped cream.

Being just a kid, she laughed at first, but then when she saw the look on her father's face, she could tell he was mortified so she started to cry. Ethan, angry and embarrassed, roughly picked her up out of the chair and rushed her out of the dining room without even cleaning her up. He hurried her to the car, hoping that none of the other members would see his filthy, ice-cream-covered daughter.

He never said a word as she cried hysterically on the short drive home. As soon as they pulled up to the house he passed her off to the housekeeper with orders to bathe her. She never saw him again that day and just before bedtime she joylessly opened her presents in front of her nanny without a parent anywhere in sight.

Esprit returned to the moment and attempted to answer her father's question. "Casey and I made up last night and everything is fine now. Thank you for calling him. It meant a lot to him, and it helped get us back together."

When their lunch arrived she thought about the memo in her pocket and decided she would probe a little to see just how full of shit he was and what he was planning next.

"Daddy, I know that you've forgiven me already, but I want you to know how sorry I am. I hope I haven't done serious damage to your campaign. I would feel terrible if my stupidity and bad behavior hurt you in the election."

Ethan appeared lost in thought. "Actually, honey, it is probably way too early to know just how what you did will effect my campaign, but don't worry about that. That stuff doesn't matter now. What matters is that you and I are here talking for the first time in years, and that you and Casey are back together. If my political career takes a few lumps, so be it. It's worth the cost to see you feeling better and us being a family again. I am leaving for Washington tomorrow, and I'll deal with whatever happens then. For now it's just me and you, okay?"

There it was.

He lied. He knew damn well that she hadn't hurt his campaign, but he lied anyway. Esprit wanted to ring his ridiculously tanned neck. He knew the polls were up, but he was one sneaky son of bitch and he wanted to take this thing and run with it.

"I really am sorry, so if there is anything I can do to repair the damage you just have to ask." She opened the door for him. *What's it going to be, Oprah, or CBS and Katie Couric? Knowing you, probably both. Come on, Daddy, what's it gonna be? Are you going ask me to embarrass myself again in front of the whole world?*

His answer surprised her. "Honestly, honey, I don't want you to worry about it. If something comes up where I think you could help, I'll let you know, but please, get it out of your mind. The incident is over and done with, and as far as I'm concerned, long forgotten."

Esprit was confused. She opened the door to try and get him to show his cards. She knew he couldn't possibly forgo an opportunity to get his face in the press, yet he had said nothing. The only thing she could come up with was that maybe he hadn't seen the fax yet, but she had heard him going into his office before he knocked on her door. What the hell was he up to? She couldn't figure it out, but she was damn sure that whatever he tried to pull, whatever show he tried to put her on, he would rue the day he asked her to do it.

By the end of the lunch Ethan was quite pleased with himself. He'd done the right thing by his daughter and taken the moral high ground. He thought there might come a time in the future when he would call in her debt, but certainly not for one of those silly TV shows. She was happy with him for the first time in years, and for now that was all that mattered.

The two ended their lunch with some small talk about Casey, football and Esprit's upcoming play, which Ethan promised not to miss. They returned home with Esprit convinced that her father was a selfish manipulating shit heel with something up his sleeve, and Ethan totally clueless to his daughter's anger and venom.

Chapter Twelve

Strategic Planning

Tuesday Evening, September 4th

Until this afternoon the stifling, month-long, heat wave that had gripped the Northeast in early August had shown no signs of letting up, even though September 1st had come and gone. Between the two rivers, the fourth week of oppressive heat had created a seemingly endless funk of sweat and ill tempers. The temperature, which hadn't fallen below the mid-eighties for almost a month, even at night, finally broke late in the afternoon. A cold front had mercifully swooped down from Canada, pushing the super-heated Jet Stream a little off to the south, leaving behind it refreshingly cool breezes and nerve-calming temperatures in the low to mid-seventies. For many weeks people had been avoiding the outdoors, but on this particular night it appeared as if the entire county was making up for their month-long air-conditioned confinement.

Broad Street, the main thoroughfare through the city of Red Bank, was jam-packed with high-spirited people from all walks of life. The sidewalk cafés on the east side were bristling with the over-thirty crowd, while the many coffeehouses that dotted Broad Street's west side were overflowing with milling groups of the younger set. It was easy to define the many local subcultures that peacefully co-existed here by simply looking at who was sitting at what café. Starbucks had the twenty-something, urban professional wannabes. 'No ordinary Joes' was the home for the artists and musicians, and the Internet café had its cyber-geeks and the Goth kids.

Ethan and Jordan strolled down the sidewalk in the direction of their dining destination, Reds, a trendy and popular restaurant. They passed several of the coffeehouses. Ethan glanced around at the different crowds with a look akin to disgust.

As they approached the entrance to the restaurant a gaggle of teenage boys came skimming around the corner on their roaring skateboards, almost knocking Ethan over. Once they had passed he warily looked around and said, "Those skater kids are a damn nuisance; I should call the mayor about this." He continued muttering to himself as he brushed off his crisp silk golf shirt and pressed linen trousers to remove all the imagined soiling he'd received from his brief but too-close contact with the grimy street urchins.

Once they entered the busy restaurant, they were immediately greeted by an attractive hostess and taken directly to their table in the rear of the restaurant. When Ethan called for the reservation, he'd requested a quiet table in the back. In the past he'd become irritated with Reds' noisy crowd because he couldn't hear the conversation at the table, and he was too vain to where his hearing aid in public.

"You know, Jordan, I'm glad the city of Red Bank is doing so well, but there are times when I miss the days when you could take a quiet stroll down Broad Street without being accosted by a bunch of scruffy punks. I don't understand why some of the better stores and restaurants don't band together and go before the town council to demand something be done about it."

Jordan looked at him with feigned sympathy.

He continued his diatribe. "Well, there is a silver lining hiding behind this black cloud. If this kind of nonsense continues, the problem will eventually solve itself because people like us will stop coming here. Then business will eventually drop off, and then, my dear, the stores will start to disappear, just like they did back in the seventies when Red

Bank was a veritable ghost town. It's all cyclical, but the damn town council still doesn't see it coming."

"Aren't you the eternal optimist tonight? It was just some kids having fun for Pete's sake. What happened to your wonderful mood this evening? Why don't you just let that stuff go so you can have a nice quiet dinner with your wife?"

The waitress came by the table and they ordered cocktails – Jordan, a Cosmopolitan, and Ethan, a dry Bombay Martini with extra olives.

As they looked at the menu, Jordan continued, "Why don't you tell me about your day? Did you hear back from Blaine? And…Oh, how did your lunch go with Esprit?"

After getting his drink Ethan seemed to settle down. "I actually had a great day. Blaine sent me the numbers and they looked terrific. He was right on the money. That damn photo gave me a solid five-point bounce in all the areas where I was doing poorly. With the election only nine weeks away, if I sustain these numbers, I should win by at least a thirty-point margin. That would mean even more money from the national party coffers. Arthur called this afternoon to congratulate me – can you believe he'd already seen the polls?"

"Ethan, Arthur didn't get where he is today by being stupid and ill-informed. That man is as smart as they come. I'm not surprised at all. In fact, I would have been more surprised if he hadn't seen them. Arthur's the one man that can get you to the Senate. Don't ever forget that even for a minute."

The waitress came back and took their dinner order. Ethan ordered a NY Strip steak, extra rare, topped with a Portobello mushroom demi-glace, and polenta on the side. Jordan decided to have the locally caught, grilled yellow-fin tuna with roasted pineapple salsa.

After the girl left Ethan stayed on topic. "There is one small problem with this whole Esprit episode. Blaine has strongly recommended that I try to exploit the situation further by doing some TV, or possibly even a magazine interview. Can you believe it? He wants me of all people to go on CBS Nightly News or Oprah and expose you and Esprit in that way. It's absurd, I couldn't do that."

Jordan perked up. "Now hold on a minute, Ethan. I'm not so sure I agree with you here. You're right about Oprah, her audience is not your demographic, so there's really no point, but the Nightly News with Katie Couric is a different animal altogether. That could be a wonderful vehicle for you. What did they propose?"

"When I spoke with Blaine, he said that Katie Couric's personal assistant conveyed an offer to do a live remote from our home next Monday or Tuesday. But honestly, Jordan, I'm uncomfortable with that kind of publicity. It reeks of Clintonesque opportunism at its worst. And besides, I wouldn't want to put Esprit through that, though she feels so bad about what happened she'd probably be willing to do it."

"Don't be so hasty with your decision here. I kind of like the idea of a Katie Couric interview, but absolutely not a remote from the house. That would be all wrong. The last thing your campaign needs is the whole world getting an inside peek at our home. No, that wouldn't do at all."

Jordan thought about the dilemma. "Here's an idea! How about a taped interview from Casey's football game on Friday? We're planning to go anyway. You could invite Arthur to join us! What a backdrop that would be, the most powerful Republican in the country, side by side with the hometown congressman. Now that's pure magic!"

Their dinners arrived and they heartily began to eat. Ethan thought about what she'd said. "Your plan does have merit. It would be so easy to pull the whole thing off. Esprit's so ridden with guilt that she's eating out of my hand, and getting Arthur to attend won't be a problem. The other night Arthur was drooling over the prospect of spending time with Casey. This is definitely something to think about."

Jordan just smiled and continued eating. Ethan laughed and

said, "You know, honey, the quality and tenacity of your mind never ceases to amaze me. You are by far the most politically astute person I know. It's a shame you decided to leave the world of politics when we married. You would have been something to behold in Washington."

"Ethan, I get more than enough of Washington through you. Why would I ever want to be a member of that old boys club? No, sir, I like where I am just fine. I'm much happier being the loving wife behind the future senator from New Jersey, thank you very much!"

Ethan smiled because he liked it when Jordan played the subservient wife of a politician. However, Jordan knew damn well that the few women presently holding office were such a small minority that they suffered greatly, and because of this they were, for the most part, totally ineffective. She wielded much greater power behind the scenes, pulling on her husband's strings.

"Jordan, I think you may be right about the interview on Friday. It might just work. We could keep the interview brief and have them splice in scenes from the game. This could actually work if it's done circumspectly. But remember, I don't want to come across as if I'm seeking America's pity. What Esprit did was not that big a deal for Christ sake, its not like she was caught doing drugs or anything, God forbid."

"That's the Ethan I know and love. When you get into Washington tomorrow, meet with Blaine first thing and get this plan rolling. This could be a home run for you, honey. I can feel it."

"Do you think I ought to discuss it with Esprit first? I could speak to her tonight. I'm telling you Jordan, our lunch today was wonderful. We talked like we haven't in years. I think she finally sees that I'm not the bad guy. I should at least prepare her for what to expect, don't you?"

Jordan couldn't believe her husband's naiveté. "Ethan, I don't want to rain on your parade, but don't put too much stock in your new and improved relationship lasting too long with your daughter. Right now she feels guilty as hell about what she did, and she's grateful for your help with Casey, but she's not stupid. She's bound to find out that what she did actually helped your campaign, and then she'll probably begin to question your motives, no matter how noble they might have been. My advice to you is not to even bring it up until this whole thing is set up by Blaine, and then only after you've had a chance to review the questions they're preparing to ask her. You'll be in Washington until Friday. Once everything is settled, call her on Thursday night and run it by her. Hopefully, she'll still be of the mind to do whatever you ask, but don't count on it. You need be prepared to pull the plug at the last minute if she doesn't respond to your request the way you hope."

"As always, dear, your advice is sound. I guess I have a lot to do over these next few days."

Ethan and Jordan continued on with their dinner. Their conversation turned to the more mundane topics of campaign schedules and upcoming events.

While the Burkes were enjoying their dinner at Reds, unbeknownst to them, just two blocks away Esprit and Casey were sitting in No Ordinary Joes Coffeehouse sharing a cappuccino and a pastry. Because of the pleasant weather they decided to drive over to Red Bank and walk around town to enjoy the refreshingly cool night air. Casey was feeling better. He had a good day of practice with no problems and no flare-ups, and best of all, no more blood in his urine.

He'd consumed at least a couple of gallons of water and Gatorade throughout the day, and by doing so he had completely flushed out his system. One thing was bothering him though. Kevin's had been unusually distant at the afternoon practice. Casey attributed his odd behavior to the fact that he'd gone to lunch with Shawn instead of going back to Kevin's house like he usually did. He apologized to him before the afternoon session, but Kevin barely acknowledged his apology with a small shrug of a shoulders and a "That's cool." After practice they hardly spoke in the locker room, and when Kevin left all that Casey got was a "Later."

He'd work it out with Kevin, and everything else was good. His parents were off his back, and Frankie had been right about Esprit. She was being so nice to him he almost felt guilty. When he called her after practice this afternoon, she begged him to take her out. She even offered to pay for their date, which was good because Casey was a little strapped for cash and didn't want borrow any more from his parents just yet.

Before meeting up with Casey, Esprit had been in anything but a good frame of mind. She'd returned from lunch with her father still reeling from the memo. She tried to call Jamie, but she'd already left for the city to go clubbing with some friends and wouldn't be home until late. There was no one else around she could trust, so she'd just sat at home alone in her room all afternoon, deliberating on what to do about her father.

She had to tell Casey about the memo, but she had be careful how she presented it to him because even though she had all the evidence she needed, Casey still worshiped the ground he walked on, especially since his phone call yesterday. However, Esprit trusted that ultimately Casey would see the truth. This whole thing would be hanging over both of their heads until it was brought out in the open, and she couldn't deal with that.

At the coffeehouse Esprit was leery about bringing up her father too early in the conversation. She wanted to establish a comfortable dialogue between them first, so she asked Casey how everything had gone with his parents when he got home the night before.

Casey was open and honest with her. He filled her in on the conversation and finished by saying, "I think the worst part was that I could see I really frightened my mom yesterday. I feel pretty lousy about that. I want to make her feel better, so maybe I'll have another talk with her tomorrow night. I assume you're still going to that drama club party with Jamie tomorrow, right?"

"I was planning on it…unless…unless you don't want me to."

"No, of course I want you to go. That's your big night. Tomorrow night I'm just gonna chill. I'll hang out at home, talk to my mom, and maybe watch the Yankees game or something. I think I need a break. I feel like I've been going non-stop all summer. I'm a little run down and a quiet night at home might be just the thing I need."

"Good for you. How was practice?"

Again Casey was honest with her. He told her about practice and about his lunch with Shawn and the other lineman. She laughed when he told he was bringing them to the party on Friday. He laughed too, and he joked that he would have to responsible for their behavior. He told her everything except the cold shoulder he got from Kevin in the afternoon. He was still working that whole thing out in his head.

When he finished he asked Esprit about her day, specifically about lunch with her father. This was the opening that she had been hoping for. She reached across the table and covered Casey's hand in her own before looking him in the eye. Tears began to form at the corners of her eyes. She used her free hand to wipe them away, but not quick enough to keep Casey from noticing.

"Spree, why are you crying? What's wrong?"

She let go of Casey's hand and reached into her purse. Clutching the folded fax in her hand she began to tell him about lunch with her father.

"Casey, please don't get mad because I don't think that I can handle that again. I…I have to show you something. Something I found this morning in my father's office. I know you think he's wonderful. After everything he did to help us get back together I was starting to think so too but…."

"Esprit, what's going on?"

"I…I…found this!" She couldn't stop herself from crying as

she handed Casey the folded piece of paper. Casey unfolded the paper and read the fax. Halfway through his eyes narrowed and without even realizing it he reached across the table and took her hand. When he finished reading it, he set it face down on the table, and he was speechless as he looked into her teary eyes.

"I don't know what to say. Maybe there's a mistake. I can't believe that he'd lie to you, to both of us. Yesterday he told me that he was very concerned about the possible damage to his campaign, but that he'd deal with it later because you had to come first. Holy shit! Esprit, where did you get this?"

Esprit stopped crying and told him the whole story. When she finished she said, "Casey, I wouldn't normally read my father's private papers, I couldn't give a crap about what he does in there, but I saw my name in bold letters across the top of the page, and I was surprised. After I read it I was sick to my stomach."

Desperately grasping for straws, Casey replied, "Spree, I'm sorry. Is there any chance that he hadn't seen the fax yet, that maybe his concern was genuine and this all took place after the fact?"

"Casey, he talks to his damn campaign manager three or four times a day. I thought that might be the case at first because I desperately wanted to believe that he really loved me after all, but there's no way he didn't know about this before the fax came in. Besides, the first line of the fax says it all. They'd already discussed it over the phone. The fax was just confirmation of an earlier discussion!"

"Spree, I don't know what to say. This is awful!"

She had never looked so sad and angry. "Yesterday, I thought for the first time in my life that the SOB might actually really love me. I've never felt that before. It was so good. He held me and told me how much he loved me, and that his campaign didn't matter; only I mattered, and I believed him. He promised he would call you and fix it between us and he did! I loved him so much right then. I forgave him for everything he'd ever done to me. Casey, this hurts so badly!" She cringed and began to sob again.

Casey came around the table and sat next to her. He wrapped his arms around her and gently placed her head on his shoulder, her body was wracking with spasms of grief over her father's betrayal. "Oh my God, Esprit, lunch, how the hell did you go through with it?"

"It all happened so fast. I didn't know what to do. Right after I saw the memo he came up the stairs calling for me, so I ran to my bathroom to get my shit together. What could I do? If I confronted him, he would have accused me of snooping around in his office, and then all hell would have broken loose. I just pretended I didn't know anything and then went to lunch with him. And then it gets better; I let the asshole take me to his bullshit country club. It was awful, sitting there listening to him brag about his family history like we were descendents of Thomas Jefferson or something, and then he rambled on and on about how much he loved me. Ohhh…I just want to strangle that son of a bitch!"

Casey was torn between his concern for Esprit and his own despair over the deceitful and cruel actions by a man he fervently admired. How could he have been so wrong about Ethan? Was he really the calculating and manipulating asshole Esprit believed him to be? Or was this just the continuation of the horrible nightmare he'd found himself in over the past forty-eight hours. Casey's head was swimming. He didn't know what to think, he didn't know what to believe, and he didn't know who trust. The only thing he was really sure of was that he loved Esprit, and right now he had to help her.

"Casey, all during our lunch he kept telling me not to worry about what happened, that whatever political problems developed didn't matter, that he would deal with them later, that I came first, the whole time knowing full well that what I did had actually helped him. Why couldn't he have just been honest with me? I still would have appreciated what he was doing just as much. God! He's a devious bastard!"

"So what do you think he's going to do now? Is he really going to try and get you to go on TV and beg forgiveness in front of Oprah, Dr. Phil, and the rest of America?"

"I don't know. I tried to trick him into telling me by offering to help him fix whatever damage I'd done, but said he couldn't think of anything and not to worry about it. But then damn if he didn't leave the door wide open by saying that if anything came up in the future, he'd let me know. You just watch, he's leaving for Washington tonight, so tomorrow or the next day he'll call me up all sweet on the phone and say something like, 'Oh, by the way, honey, how would you like to do an interview with me on Oprah?' And then he'll try to convince me it will be short and painless. You just watch, it will happen just like that, I guarantee it!"

"So what are you going to do?"

In a Jekyll and Hyde kind of moment, Esprit's face morphed from sad to angry. "I'm going to blast the motherfucker and his campaign right out of the water! That's what I'm going to do! I've been thinking about revenge all afternoon. And, Casey, don't you try to stop me! I'm going to agree to do whatever he asks. I'll begin the interview acting every bit the chastised and contrite daughter that he wants me to be. Then when he least expects it, I'll break from the script and let him have it right in front of Katie Couric, or Oprah, or whoever the hell it is. I'm going to tell the whole world what kind of father I have and what kind of man he really is. Those shows are live, so they won't attempt to stop me unless I use profanity. You just watch, the ratings will go through the roof and they will love it. Then let's see how Daddy's fucking campaign does!"

Casey wanted to support Esprit, but what she was planning could be disastrous for not only Ethan but for her as well. She was acting on anger and impulse. Her fragile emotional state was not allowing her to think about the consequences of what she had in mind. He wanted to support her, but also to temper her rage with some rational thought.

"Esprit, I know you're angry, and I'll support whatever you want to do, but have you thought this whole thing through?" He continued, "At this point I don't care what happens to your father. He deserves whatever happens to him, but doing this…this thing…on national TV, it's gonna haunt you forever. For the rest of your life you'll be treated like all those white trash freaks on the Gerry Springer Show. Is this what you really want? What about your acting career, what about our future?"

"Casey, I hear you, I do, but somehow, some way I am not going to let him get away with this! I will make him pay!"

Back at the Collins' home, Lisa had just finished making dinner when Steve came home from work. He set down his briefcase in the hallway like he always did and walked towards the kitchen to say hello, but then he stopped and did a double take when he saw that Lisa had set up a fancy dinner in the dining room.

"Hi, honey, I'm home. What's with the dining room?"

Lisa was busy in the kitchen and didn't hear him. She'd spent the better part of the day reevaluating herself and her family. The first few hours had been spent trying to assuage her guilt, but after several hours of painful soul-searching, she'd come to some hard conclusions as to what needed to be done to set things right, and now she was determined to do them. There was a lot to discuss with Steve, some of it a bit dicey, so she had setup dinner in the dining room to create an appropriate atmosphere for what was to be a serious talk.

Steve called out a second time. This time Lisa answered back. "I'm just finishing up dinner. Go wash up and meet me in the dining room."

She had set an elegant dinner for two, using her finest English china and Waterford crystal. The chandelier was dimmed low and the flames from two slender tapers flickered in the center of the table. The Collins' dining room was the most elegant and austere room in the house; a house that but for this one room was designed for casual comfort and for fun.

After washing his hands, Steve walked back to the dining room, scratched his head and sat down alone at the uncomfortable Chippendale dinning room set. He warily looked around and called out, "Honey, what's up, why'd you go to all this trouble for a Tuesday dinner?" If Lisa replied, he didn't hear her.

Lisa entered the dining room carrying a large platter of deftly prepared food and set it down in front of him. Delicately laid out on the dish were two large portions of grilled salmon, topped with a cilantro, citrus compound butter, and surrounded by an assortment of lightly grilled garden vegetables. Also at the center of the table were a chilled bottle of Simi Chardonnay and a crystal pitcher of ice water with slices of fresh lemon bobbing on the top.

She silently served the food, carefully placing a generous portion of food on each plate. Then she poured each of them a healthy glass of wine. Finally, after her surprisingly formal service, she sat down across the table from Steve and told her husband what was on her mind.

With a pained yet determined expression on her face Lisa began, "Steve, I've spent the whole day thinking about this family and the course of events of the last few days, and I need to tell you that I am more than a little worried."

Steve sipped his wine and smiled. "Honey, don't you think you're overdoing this just a little bit? Casey's going to be fine. In fact, I kind of think that the last few days were probably good for him. Up till now he's lived in a fairytale world. Maybe he needed to face some adversity to help him grow up a little bit."

"Steve, it's not just Casey that I'm worried about, it's all of us…you, me, and Casey. What has happened to us?"

"I don't understand; what are you trying to say?"

This time Lisa averted her eyes when she spoke. "I'm not sure, but things seem to have gotten way out of control in this family, and some of the things Casey said the other day are hitting a little too close to home. Maybe he was right about a few things, maybe we do need to take a closer look at ourselves."

Steve's face drained of color. "Lisa, what the hell are you talking about?"

"Steve, don't get angry," replied Lisa with a bit more force. "Here's what I am talking about. What the heck have I done for the past five years of my life other than cart Casey around to his sporting events, redecorate the damn house and party with you on the weekends?"

Steve unbuttoned his collar and loosened his tie. "Lisa, now you're just being ridiculous. You're rationalizing and simplifying down everything you do around here because of some misguided sense of guilt. You're a great wife and an even better mother. You're not responsible for our son's recent problems. He's eighteen years old, a grown man. You have to let all this stuff go. It's going to drive you crazy."

Lisa responded with more confidence. "You're right about that, Steve. I do have to let Casey go and allow him to make decisions for himself. But more importantly, I have to come to terms with the roll that I've played in shaping Casey into who he is today. I've thought a lot about this, and I've come to the conclusion that while I may have pushed Casey too hard to be the best, I did the best job with him that I could, and he's a damn terrific kid. But you just said something important. You said I'm not responsible for his problems, well, if that's the case, then I'm not responsible for his successes either, and you know what, Steve? I've spent the last five years basking in the spotlight of my very talented son. I can't do that anymore. I've got to let him experience life on his own terms, and I've also got to restart mine."

"Okay, that sounds like the right attitude, but what are we talking about? Let's not overreact here. What do mean when you say 'restart your life'?"

Lisa was now on a roll. "A couple of things: first, I need to stop being a spoiled housewife. I need to do something meaningful with my life now that Casey's almost out of the house. As Casey so sarcastically, yet correctly, pointed out the other day, I've never used my teaching degree. He's right. Maybe I should go back to school and get my teaching certificate re-certified so I can start teaching at one of the public schools. God knows there's a shortage of quality teachers in this town."

Steve furiously rubbed his temples, and then he looked his wife straight in the eye.

"Lisa, are you nuts? You've spent the last eighteen years raising our son and taking care of this family. Now just when you're finally in the position to kick back and enjoy the fruits of your hard labor, you want to go and take care of other people's kids. Are you crazy? This is totally insane! The next few years were supposed to be our time together, a time when you and I can really begin to enjoy our lives. Lisa, we are still young. This is the time that we've worked for over the last twenty years. What about traveling and what about buying a summer house and parties and all of the other things that we've always talked about?"

Lisa went on the attack. "Thank you! That leads me to my second point. Hear me out on this before you jump down my throat. Honey, our lifestyle needs to change. Think about it, what do we do with our free time? I'll tell you what we do. We drink, we eat, and we party. Every weekend and every social event we go to involves partying and drinking. I tried to think of the last time you and I spent a weekend or a vacation without drinking, and I couldn't. At the beach club, at the football games…even out at the pool for Christ's sake. It's all we ever do, and it's beginning to take its toll."

Steve pounded his fist on the table. "What the hell do you mean by that?"

Lisa was frightened but determined to see this through. "Okay, Steve, answer me this. When was the last time you went without a drink for more than forty-eight hours? When was the last weekend we didn't get drunk at least once? How many forty-four-year-old men do you know that still smoke pot three or four times a week? Come on, Steve, look in the mirror! You're a beautiful man but look at what this lifestyle is doing to you! You're a good twenty pounds overweight and your face is always bloated from the alcohol. Honey, you take medication for your high blood pressure, you're not in good shape, and I'm worried that you're heading for a heart attack."

"Lisa, this is nonsense. You make it sound like I'm an alcoholic for Christ's sake. Jesus, my father was an alcoholic. He drank his booze straight out of the bottle in a brown paper bag. Sure, drinking is a big part of our social lives, but so what? Everybody we know likes to drink. What are you proposing we do, find a whole new set of friends and abandon the ones that we have because they like to have a martini or two on the weekend? This whole thing is absurd!"

Lisa attempted to soften her tone. "Steve, it's not absurd, it is the truth, and we have to face it. Honey, I'm not saying you're an alcoholic. I am saying that alcoholism runs rampant in both our families, and drinking and partying have become way too important in both of our lives. We need to do something about it before it's too late!"

"Great! Just great! Our son has a bad couple of days so now I'm an alcoholic and you want to change the entire lifestyle of this family, a lifestyle that I've worked damn hard to create, mind you, and one that I'm not so willing to give up because Casey lost his temper for the first time in his life. Lisa, you are way out of line, and this whole thing is bullshit!"

He slammed his crystal wine glass down on the table and the stem shattered in his hand. Lisa watched in silence.

When he looked down at the broken glass he only got angrier. "I'm going out for a while. Don't wait up for me!" He stood up and stormed out of the room.

A few moments later Lisa sadly watched from the dining room window as Steve peeled down the driveway in his car.

Chapter Thirteen

Paying the Piper

Wednesday Morning, September 5th

Beep…Beep…Beep… Casey forced himself awake and slapped off the alarm. He rolled over to step out of bed but something wasn't right, something was amiss, he just couldn't seem to put his finger on it. His head felt a little foggy. As he stood up he felt a mounting sense of unease and confusion. Gone was the absolute confidence that the world would yield to his every whim. This morning it had been replaced by uncertainty, by a feeling that he was losing control over everything around him.

As he knelt down on the floor to start his exercises, his thoughts continued their downward spiral. He really felt like shit this morning. The pain in his side was throbbing, and he had another kick-ass headache. He had a pretty good idea his physical problems were the result of overdoing the steroids. He thought about his pain and the promise to Kevin, but there was another invisible voice deep inside his head telling him to keep up the injections until after Friday's game. This ever-present voice attempted to seduce him into believing that there was still a chance to change Coach Paterno's mind. It said to him that he needed every edge to make that change happen. Casey whispered to himself, "I'm sorry, Kevin; I can't stop right now. I need to do this."

His morning exercise routine usually helped to relieve any

pain, but not this morning. With each and every crunch, the pain became more intense. It was now a hot searing pain just below his rib cage, and it stung like a bee with each repetition of the exercise. By the time he finished, he'd told himself that if there were even just a little blood in his urine, he wouldn't take the injection today.

When he finally stood up again he was a bit lightheaded, and he wavered slightly as he made his way to the bathroom. However, as soon as he began to pee relief washed over him because there was not a trace of blood in his urine. So, instead of jumping right in the shower, he quietly tiptoed back to his room and administered his next shot, the pain from just moments before a forgotten memory.

While Casey was upstairs taking his shower, Lisa was downstairs in the kitchen sipping her coffee. She had a full day of school shopping planned, but she was struggling to get on track. Last night Steve left the house angry and didn't return until well after midnight. When he finally crawled into bed he smelled like a brewery.

Steve woke up as usual at five-fifteen and kissed her on the forehead on his way out the door to catch the six o'clock ferry, but he didn't say a single word; not good morning, not I love you…nothing. He never left without saying something. He was obviously still angry.

While she was making Casey's shake, her eyes wandered over to her niece's wedding invitation posted on the refrigerator door. She thought about her crazy family and then a surprising thought suddenly came to her. It was about her uncle Phil. Once a raging alcoholic, he was now a member of Alcoholics Anonymous. He'd been involved with the group for a number of years, and he was a totally different man because of it.

AA had transformed him from an angry, raving, vodka-chugging lunatic into a soft spoken, loving and compassionate man. He'd turned into one of the most kind and responsible men that she knew. As Lisa delved deeper into her past she remembered a discussion that she and her uncle had a year or two after he got sober. At the time he'd been so emphatic about how the twelve-step AA program had changed his life. Maybe there was something to it. All these years later and he was still doing great, and as far as she knew, he was still active in the AA program.

Lisa weighed the pros and cons of calling her uncle for advice. If Steve ever found out she called someone about his drinking, especially someone in her family, he would surely kill her. And besides, she wasn't sure if Steve was an alcoholic. He drank too much, but wasn't it just a case of his social drinking going a little too far? An alcoholic was someone that drank straight from a bottle or some homeless person lying semi-conscious on a sidewalk, like those poor people on the streets of New York City. She'd think about it.

She snapped back to the present when she heard Casey bounding down the stairs and finished preparing his breakfast shake. As Casey walked into the kitchen she turned to him and said, "Good morning, Casey. I'm just finishing your shake. I was reading the paper and didn't realize how late it was. Sorry, hon."

"Actually, Mom, don't worry about the shake. My stomach's a little upset this morning. I'll just grab something a little later after my workout. I just came in to say good morning. I'm on my way over to the gym and then to football practice. I'll be home for dinner around six." He came over and gave her a crushing bear hug and then surprisingly he blurted out, "I love you, Mom." He kissed her on the cheek and walked out the door before she even had a chance to respond.

Lisa loved hearing those words but thought it very odd that he would pass on his morning shake. He never left without it…ever. He also looked a little pale. She hoped he wasn't coming down with something. It was probably just the lingering effects of the stress of the last few days. She shook her head and began putting the milk and fruit back in the refrigerator, but out of nowhere, she was hit by a stabbing wave of anxiety deep within her chest. She didn't know where it came from, so she took several deep breaths to calm herself and then said a silent prayer.

Esprit had tossed and turned throughout the night. This morning she woke up early, around six, but didn't leave her bedroom. Her father was scheduled to leave early this morning for Washington, and she didn't want to run into him. However, once she heard his car roll down the gravel drive she dragged herself out of bed. As she shuffled over to the bathroom for a shower her thoughts turned to Casey. Finally, after all this time he was seeing the truth about her father – seeing him for the jerk he really was.

She smiled, but then she thought about Casey's warning. He made a good point when he cautioned her about her future and warned her not to make a fool of herself on national TV. He was right. This had to be the key to any plan for revenge. She had to do it right so she didn't come off as a total bitch. The big question was; how could she humiliate her father without coming across as the stereotypical, vindictive and wild politician's daughter? She had at least a couple of days to mull it over. He wasn't due back from Washington until Friday. The control freak and egomaniac that he was, there was no way that he'd plan an interview for TV without being present, so Esprit still had a couple of days to plan.

When it came to this kind of thing Jamie was the best. She had a devious mind and she really got off on fucking with other people's heads. Esprit had called her the night before and invited her to join her today for a day of beauty at their favorite salon. Esprit's revenge dilemma would give them something fun to do while they were there. Jamie had been more than happy to oblige her friend. In about an hour the girls were scheduled to get a facial, a manicure and have their hair done in preparation for tonight's big end-of-summer cast party. Tonight's party was something the two of them had looked forward to all summer. The cast party was a long-standing tradition and the girls wouldn't miss it for the world.

As Esprit stepped into the shower she thought that spending the day at the salon was just what the doctor ordered. There couldn't be a better setting for her and Jamie to brainstorm strategies on what to do about dear old Dad. They would be at the salon for hours being totally pampered by her friend Carla, the owner of the salon, with little to do but connive and scheme Ethan's very public fall from grace.

Casey arrived at the gym at eight thirty sharp. He rubbed his aching side and wiped a light film of sweat from his brow. His forehead was hot; he might have a slight fever. He'd actually considered blowing off the workout, but his training schedule had already been screwed up enough this week, he couldn't afford to miss another session. Once school started he'd be forced to go down to lifting only twice a week, so today would be his last full-time session, and he wanted to make the most of it. Frankie's car was parked right there next to the front door as Casey walked in, and sure enough, his trainer and mentor was standing just inside the front door waiting for him.

"Hey, sport, you're two minutes late," Frankie said jokingly, but then he looked at Casey's pale face and the dark circles beneath his eyes. "Casey, you feeling okay? You really look like crap!"

"I'm all right; I just didn't sleep too good last night. No problem." Casey averted his eyes when he spoke, and Frankie frowned.

"You sure you're okay? You really don't look so hot." Casey nodded so Frankie added, "Okay, then let's get started."

The two walked over to the mats to stretch. Frankie watched intently as Casey warmed up for any telltale signs of a problem, but Casey seemed to be okay so after they finished he grabbed Casey by the shirt and they walked over to the squat rack.

"Since it's your last full-time session, I'm gonna go easy on you today. Instead of a full workout, I'm going to measure your maxes on half a dozen lifts. I haven't measured you since July, and I want to see what progress we've made. I'm thinking we'll start with squats, then dead-lifts, then bench presses, and just go on from there."

Casey's dour expression evidenced the fact that he wasn't happy with Frankie's plan. He was in no shape for a max test. His head wasn't into it, and his body felt shitty and sluggish, but at the moment it seemed he didn't have much of a choice.

"Whatever you say, but I'm warning you, I'm feeling a little tired, so don't start riding my ass if there isn't much improvement."

Frankie began putting plates on the squat rack. Casey winced at the sound of the plates clanging. His head was really starting to pound. After Frankie finished loading the bar he said, "Why don't you warm up with a few light lifts while I go get your chart from the office?"

Casey reluctantly got under the bar and began doing a set of squats with about three hundred and fifty pounds while Frankie ran across the room to his office to get the chart. When Frankie returned moments later there were more than a few beads of perspiration forming on Casey's brow as he finished the set and struggled to rest the bar back on the rack.

"Dude, how come you're breaking a sweat? Three-fifty should be a piece of cake." His concern was growing. "You sure you're up for this? We can do it another time if you really aren't feeling well."

Casey was getting irritated with all of Frankie's comments and the pain in his side was getting worse, but he said, "No damn it. Let's do it, Frankie. Maybe it'll help me feel a little better."

"Whatever you say, pal?" He looked down at the chart. "In July you maxed out your squat at five hundred and twenty-five pounds, so why don't we start you at four-fifty and work up from there?"

Together they added the additional plates. Casey tightened his belt, and positioned himself beneath the massive weight of the bar. Frankie put down the chart and stood behind Casey to spot him in case he had any trouble with the lift. Casey took a few deep breaths and focused all of his attention on the bar resting behind his shoulders. Then, with a deep gasp, he pushed up on the bar using only the strength of his legs and shoulders and lifted the four hundred and fifty pounds off the rack. The immense weight on the bar now rested squarely across his neck and shoulders behind his head.

He wobbled a bit to get his balance as he attempted to settle comfortably in before completing the squat. A successful squat requires the weightlifter to first establish control of the weight across his shoulders while standing straight up, and then to squat down to a point where the knees are completely bent, and finally, to rise back up to the original position. The leg, thigh, back, and shoulder muscle groups are all used in this type of lift. Casey took another deep breath and went down into the squat position with the weight. He descended fine, but when he tried to rise back up, the strain was too much and he couldn't manage the heavy weight.

Frankie, being the professional that he was, quickly saw Casey's distress and stepped in to help him with the bar. Together they placed the bar back on the rack while Casey sucked in large gulps of air. Even though Casey had just started, he was sweating like a pig, and he wiped his face and neck with a hand towel.

"Sorry about that, I just don't feel like I have it today. I don't know what the hell is the matter with me. I'm just not feeling it." Standing there panting like an overheated dog, Casey looked both fatigued and dejected by his failed effort.

"I agree, I've seen you have bad days before, but you've never given up, and, buddy, you really don't look so hot. Maybe today's not the day to do this. Do you want to shit can the max test and just do a light workout instead?"

Casey frowned. "No, let's keep going; maybe I'll do better on the bench."

"You're the boss."

They walked over to the bench and began to set up the bar. Frankie stood close by as Casey warmed up with a set of two hundred and twenty-five pounds. He knocked off twelve reps with no problem.

As Frankie stood by, one of his trainers came over carrying a small brown package and said, "Hey, Frankie, FedEx just dropped this off. What do you want me to do with it?"

Frankie looked at the package and noticed that it was shipped from Ener-Tech, his steroid supplier, so he lied and said that it was a new shipment of promotional supplements and to put it on his desk in the office, but then as an afterthought he added, "Make sure my office door is closed and locked on your way out. I don't want anybody messing with them till after I have a chance to see what they are."

The trainer replied, "Sure, boss, no problem," and left with the package.

Frankie turned his attention back to Casey. "Casey, you looked all right on that set. Do you want to give it try?"

Casey was bouncing up and down, finally feeling the adrenaline rush kick in. His headache now masked by the adrenaline, and the pain in his side temporarily forgotten.

"You're starting look a little better. Your eyes are brighter, and you've got some color back. So what do you think? Are you ready to do this?"

Casey said, "Hell yes. How much did I bench in July?"

Frankie checked the chart and noted that three hundred and ninety pounds was his maximum bench-press. Bench-pressing was Casey's strongest lift, and this was an incredible amount of weight. He said, "Casey, you benched three-ninety in July, but I don't want you to start anywhere near that. Let's put on three-forty and go from there." Casey loaded the bar with three hundred and forty pounds of plates. He then got back under the bar and positioned himself on the bench for the lift. Again Frankie positioned himself behind the rack to support Casey's lift if necessary.

Casey took a deep breath and struggled as he lifted the bar of the rack. The bar wobbled back and forth a couple of times until he positioned it directly above his head with his arms totally extended. Then with one motion he lowered the bar to his heaving chest and with a ferocious grunt he began his attempt to raise the bar back up.

Slowly, inch-by-inch, the bar moved upward from his chest as he labored to raise and lock his arms to a fully extended position. His entire body shook and wobbled as he lifted the great weight, and after what seemed like an eternity, with Frankie's ready hands just beneath the shifting bar, Casey finally managed to fully raise the bar and lock his arms. Frankie then grabbed hold of the bar and helped Casey to gently rest it back on the cradles of the rack.

Casey sat up on the bench looking dejected. "There's no way I'm doing three-ninety today. I barely got up three-forty. Jesus, what the hell is wrong with me?"

Frankie shook his head. "Dude, I'm growing a little more concerned here. I've seen you lift that weight a dozen times before. I don't know, Casey, maybe you're just having an off day. We'll do this again next Saturday after the game. It's no sweat. Maybe you should knock it off for the day. Maybe you're coming down with a bug or something."

"Yeah, maybe you're right. I got my last double session practice today and I haven't even had anything to eat yet. Maybe I'll just knock off for now, grab a shower, and then go get a bite to eat before practice, I'm starving."

Frankie looked at him, incredulous. "Don't even tell me you didn't eat this morning! Not even a shake? No wonder you couldn't lift shit today! Casey, you know better than that! How are you supposed to lift that much weight with no fuel? Now it's all starting to make some sense. Jesus, kid, I thought something was really wrong with you. You scared the shit out of me just now. Why didn't you fuel up this morning?"

"I told you, I didn't sleep too good last night and my stomach was a little queasy this morning."

"You asshole! Go get something to eat and take care of yourself. Maybe you are coming down with something. You got a big game in two days and you need to be ready, so go get your ass something to eat and don't overdo it at practice today. I'll see you at the game on Friday, and if you don't play the best game off your life, I'm going to work you like a dog on Saturday. You got that!"

"I hear you, Frankie, I'm out of here."

"Later."

After Casey left the gym, Frankie wondered what was going on inside the head of his prized protégé. Casey had always been so strict with his workout schedule and dietary regimen, yet in the span of a week he'd blown off two workouts and had seemingly abandoned his diet. Frankie was beginning to think that all the crap that had happened on Sunday and Monday had done more damage to the kid's psyche than he'd previously thought. Maybe it was time for the two of them to have another heart to heart.

When he returned to his office to drop off Casey's chart, he spied the FedEx package sitting on his desk. Frankie picked up the box and opened the cabinet behind his desk to stow them away. When he unlocked and opened the case at the bottom where he stored his steroids, he scratched his head and then looked in a second time. There were only two boxes of steroids left in the case when there should have been three, and a package of hypodermic syringes was missing. He was always careful to keep an exact inventory of his supplements, especially the steroids, since they were illegal, and he knew without a doubt a cycle was missing. He was furious. Only he and two of his trainers knew where he stored the steroids, and both of them had been with him a long time. They were loyal beyond question. He wondered what the hell could have happened! Fear and panic began to set in. He locked his office and went out to the gym to find and question his two employees.

Esprit picked Jamie up from her house at nine forty-five. They made a quick pit stop at Starbucks before going on to their final destination, TrimZ Salon.

Esprit was a frequent guest at TrimZ and had been so since she was six.

From the very first visit, Esprit had fallen in love with the place, or more to the point, the owner of the salon – a vivacious and wacky women named of Carla O'Donnell. Carla was two parts fashion maven and one part Lucille Ball. She was also an extraordinarily successful entrepreneur and skilled stylist. She was well known throughout the community for her off-kilter sense of humor, her ever-changing hair color, her irrepressible laughter, and most importantly, her amazing talent with scissors and a comb.

And when it came top Carla's hair, from one visit to the next Carla's regulars never quite knew what to expect when they entered the salon and saw her prancing around the shop – this visit, burnt Sienna – the next, platinum blonde.

Over the years Carla and Esprit had developed a special bond. They shared a closeness that Esprit didn't share with anyone else. Carla had become her confidant and mentor of sorts, and Esprit often looked to Carla for advice when it came to her love life or dealing with her wretched family. There had been more than a few occasions when Esprit had gone to her desperate for help, and Carla had offered her discreet and worthwhile direction.

On the ride over, Esprit tried to imagine what Carla would say about her current mess. She wasn't really sure, but for no apparent reason her mind wandered back to her first fateful visit to Carla when she was just a little girl. She remembered the day as if it was only yesterday.

Esprit's mother had incessantly lectured her on the drive over about behaving like a proper young lady in the salon, emphasizing that she was not to embarrass her in front of her friends. The last thing that six-year-old Esprit wanted to do on that beautiful summer day was sit around a beauty parlor with a bunch of old ladies she didn't know getting her hair cut. She was miserable, kicking and screaming, as her mother literally dragged her by the arm across the parking lot and into the salon.

But to her surprise, everything changed as soon as she walked through the door. Entering TrimZ was like entering another world; she likened it to *The Wizard Of Oz* when Dorothy walked out of the broken-down house and first met Belinda, the Good Witch of the North. Her initial anger and apprehension were swiftly replaced by curiosity and inquisitiveness because just like in the movie, from out of nowhere, this crazy woman with yellow and orange pigtails and matching eye make-up and nails came running up to her. Then without even stopping, the crazy lady picked Esprit up and gave her a big hug. In that moment Esprit didn't know whether to laugh or scream.

"Sooo…this is my new friend Esprit! Hello, young lady. I have been dying to meet you. Your mother told me a lot about you…but I don't believe a word she tells me."

Carla gave Esprit a conspiratorial wink and continued, "So why don't you and I just go over to the sink so I can wash your hair, and then you can tell me the real truth about you without your nosey mother hanging around."

Esprit fell in love with her right then and there. She couldn't help but laugh as this crazy woman led her away by the hand. For the next hour Carla talked to Esprit about everything – cool toys, cartoons, school, she even made fun of Esprit's grumpy mother and mean father. From that day forward, Esprit thought of Carla as a big sister and a co-conspirator in the war against her mean old parents.

Esprit's thoughts drifted away from that long ago visit and fast-forwarded to the last time Carla had helped her with a major problem. It was about a year and a half ago. Once again she was in crisis with her mother, and once again Carla had been there for her. At the time Esprit had been dating Casey for only a short while, but they were getting serious. Esprit was thinking about having sex with Casey so she had asked her mother the day before to take her to the gynecologist because she wanted to begin taking the pill. Jordan had not only refused, she'd grounded Esprit for two weeks for even considering such a preposterous idea.

The following day Esprit had a scheduled appointment to see Carla. Jordan dropped her off at the salon and then went shopping. As soon as Esprit walked through the doors and saw her wacky friend, she broke down in tears. Carla ran to her. "Okay, honey. What did that mean old bitch of mother do now?"

Carla didn't have a clue as to what was wrong, but she knew Esprit well enough to know that if the girl was upset, it most definitely had something to do with her mother or her father. She walked the sobbing Esprit over to the chair, sat her down and made her spill the beans. "So what's up, girlfriend? What's with all those tears?"

Esprit sobbed, "Carla, I'm sixteen years old, and I've been dating Casey for a couple of months now. I really love him and he loves me and…."

Carla interrupted her and smiled. "Hold it right there, honey! I think I know where this is going! Let me guess. You want to start having sex with your boyfriend so you asked your mother about going on the pill, and she went nuts…am I right?"

Esprit's eyes lit up! "Carla, how could you possibly know that? I haven't told anyone. Not even Casey. You are amazing!"

"What…you don't think I was sixteen once and all hot to trot over some guy? Come on, Esprit, what do you take me for, some old broad who doesn't know what it's like to be a horny kid? Hell, girl, I'm only thirty-eight. Sixteen wasn't all that long ago."

Esprit smiled through the tears. "Carla, I really want to be with him. I thought I was doing the responsible thing talking to my mother about it, but she went crazy and grounded me for two weeks. How old were you when you lost your virginity?"

Carla laughed when she thought about it. "Well, Esprit, to tell you the truth, I was only fifteen. It was with this seventeen-year-old guy who I thought was the next best thing to Stephen Tyler...."

"Who's Stephen Tyler?" interrupted Esprit.

Carla laughed again and said, "Maybe I am getting old. He's the lead singer of Aerosmith. Come on...you know who he is...that skinny old guy with the long hair and funky clothes. He's on MTV all the time. Anyway, I was crazy about this guy, and he and I went to the drive-in in his old beat-up Camaro...."

Esprit interrupted again, "Carla, what the hell are you talking about? What's a drive-in?"

Carla frowned, pretending to be annoyed. "Damn, girl, it's an outdoor movie theatre – you are really making me feel old – never mind the questions, just listen. Anyway, so there I was with this hunk of a guy at the drive-in, and we climbed into the back seat of his car, which has about enough room for a small suitcase. He started kissing me, and I was feeling like the damn seat was on fire, my panties were getting soaked and all I wanted to do was rip off his and my clothes."

Esprit was totally mesmerized.

"So he and I were scrambling around in the back seat, getting naked and trying to figure out a way to do the deed, but there just wasn't enough space in the damn car. The top of my head was all smashed up against the window; one leg over the seat, and the other propped up against the back window. He's trying to climb on top of me and his ass and legs were bumping against the roof and front seat."

Both girls were laughing hysterically at this point. Carla continued her story. "So after a few minutes of shear panic and frustration, we finally figured out that there was just no way that we could do it like this. But then this guy, he had an inspiration. We parked in the last row of the far corner of the drive-in, as far from everyone else as possible, and he remembered that he had an old raggedy blanket in the trunk, so both of us, as naked as jaybirds, slipped out of the car. He gets the blanket out and lays it behind the car right up next to a fence so that the car would block the view of anyone passing by.

"Now by this point I'm so horny I couldn't give a shit if anyone saw us or not. All I wanted was to have him on top of me and to feel what it was like with him inside me. At that moment I could have had sex with him on the fifty-yard line of the Super Bowl at half-time and it wouldn't have mattered. Anyway, so we finally got comfortable and started doing it, and you'll never guess what happened?"

Esprit, engrossed in the story, said, "What? Tell me…tell me please!"

"Well, just as he was about to…you know…he was about to come, a security guy with a flashlight came walking right up to us and shined the light right down on the two of us, me with my legs sprawled apart and this guy pumping up and down like an oil well on top of me. The security guy coughed a couple of times and then suggested that maybe we should go get a hotel room."

Esprit looked absolutely stunned.

"Well, let me tell you, in that moment, the urge was gone and I was mortified. As soon as he rolled off of me I jumped up and got back in the car. I tried to put my clothes back on, but that darn back seat was so tight that I hit my face against the front seat and got a bloody lip for my trouble. Then, when my wonderful date finally came back to the car, he took one look at me with blood dripping down my chin and started laughing. Boy, was I pissed. Needless to say, he took me straight home and he and I never went out again. But even with all that, I got to tell you. It still felt wonderful the first time!"

Esprit laughed and laughed, but then she finally said, “Carla, do you think I’m old enough?”

Carla stopped laughing and became serious. She replied, “Listen, Esprit, you are old enough, biologically speaking, but that’s not the point. The question is; are you emotionally ready to do this, and do you really care about Casey so much that you want to share this with him? If the answer to those questions is yes, then I will tell you that I think you’re ready.”

Excited, Esprit replied, “Carla, the answer is yes. I’m definitely ready. But what should I do about my mother? I don’t want to have sex without being on the pill.”

“You’re damn right you don’t! And let me give you another little piece of advice, young lady, even if you’re on the pill, don’t you dare have unprotected sex, even if it’s just with Casey. You never know what you can catch out there.”

“I promise, but what should I do, Carla? I really need your help.”

“Listen, kiddo, when your mother comes back, I’ll pull her into my office and speak to her about this, but I can’t promise you that I’ll be able to change her mind. But I’ll give it my all, so why don’t we finish up with your hair while I think about what I’m going to say to your mother.”

Carla spent the next half-hour giving Esprit another beautiful hair cut, and when Jordan finally returned, Carla met her at the door and as promised walked her into her office, closing the door. Esprit sat in the waiting area biting her nails for the next ten minutes. It was the longest ten minutes of her life, waiting for them to finish their conversation.

Inside the office, Carla convinced Jordan that Esprit was likely to have sex very soon whether she was on the pill or not, so getting her to see the gynecologist was the only responsible thing for a mother to do. When the two women came out, a solemn Jordan came out first, and behind her a grinning Carla, discreetly waving a thumbs-up sign. Esprit started to smile, but then Carla held up one finger over her mouth and Esprit caught herself.

Jordan said, "Okay, Esprit, let's go home. We have some things to talk about."

Esprit was released from her grounding that afternoon and her mother took her to the gynecologist the next day.

Esprit's mind returned to the here and now as she and Jamie pulled into the parking lot of the salon. She was confident that between Carla and Jamie, they'd be able to help her come up with a good plan for revenge.

As they walked in Carla came bounding out from behind the counter dressed in a pair of skin-tight black satin Capri pants and a semi see-through red lace halter-top. She was adorned from head to toe with bangles, bracelets, necklaces, rings, and a wild assortment of other bobbles and trinkets. Her flaming red and gold hair was spiked high above her head. At first glance it appeared as if there was a raging conflagration rising from her forehead, but somehow on Carla the bizarre fashion statement worked.

She came over and offered Esprit a warm and friendly hug. Teasingly, she said, "So how is my favorite celebrity tramp? I want the truth; did Rob Cronin slip you the tongue or what?" This was followed by hardy laugh that started somewhere down near her belly and rumbled all the way up through her insides until it burst forth from her ruby-red lips. Carla had a deep and husky voice so when she spoke you couldn't help but pay attention.

Esprit returned the hug and held her tightly. She blushed at the comment, but then she too began to laugh. In a mock-serious tone she replied, "Carla that's not at all funny, but if you must know…yes, he did slip me the tongue." All three girls burst out laughing.

When the laughter subsided, Carla escorted them over to the manicure tables, while informing them she wanted to do their manicures first so she could get all the dirty details without any interruptions.

As Carla and one of her girls began the tedious process of removing the old nail polish from the girl's outstretched fingertips, Esprit shared with them the whole story, starting with the sorted details of the fundraiser, followed by her finding the memo on the fax machine, and then finally, the dreadful lunch with her father that followed.

When Esprit finished, Carla sat there quiet for a moment with a peculiar look on her face. Then the effervescent hairstylist scratched her chin. "Well, honey, it sounds to me like you got no choice but to teach your dear old Daddy a lesson! Who the hell does that big old jerk think he is anyway? Don't you worry, Spree. Your old friend Carla ain't gonna let that son of a bitch get away with this!"

Jamie chimed in, "Damn right! It's high time that asshole gets what's coming to him!"

"Carla, I desperately want to get even with him, but I don't want to make a fool of myself on national TV in the process. I'm not sure what I should do, what do you think?"

Carla thought about the situation for a moment and then asked a question. "So which show do you think he's going to do, Oprah or Katie?"

Esprit had thought a lot about this question and she figured it this way. "If I had to guess I would say the live remote from the CBS show. My father just adores Katie Couric, and I know he thinks Oprah and her audience – to use his word – are 'tawdry', whatever the hell that's supposed to mean. But, Carla, I don't know when or where it will go down. I suppose he'll want to do it soon, and so will CBS, while the damn photo is still fresh on everyone's mind. My father's supposed to be in Washington until Friday, but I'm betting he's going to sneak home tomorrow night and spring it on me at the last minute. That's why I need to come up with a plan fast."

Jamie added her two cents. "Carla, I think Esprit should agree to do the interview and go right for his jugular as soon as

Katie hits her with the first question. Just blast him right then and there and tell the whole world exactly what she thinks of him! What do you say?"

Carla shook her head fervidly. "No, no, no! That would just make you look like some spoiled bratty rich kid. Honey, you've got to be way more subtle than that. You don't want to come out of this thing looking like Paris Hilton…God forbid! You're an actress for Christ's sake, start thinking like one!" This was both funny and ironic coming from Carla because there was nothing remotely subtle about her.

Carla continued, "You listen to me, you tell your daddy that you'll do whatever he wants you to do. You go with him on that show, and you play the role of the loving and remorseful daughter to the hilt, straight through the interview, then you wait for the subject of his campaign to come up, and you bet your ass it will…then BAM! When you get the opportunity, you read that memo on live TV. That'll do it! Girl, I can't wait to see the old fart's eyes pop out of his head when you read that shit on TV. It'll floor him, I swear it will!"

Esprit grinned from ear to ear, just as she'd done some twelve years before when she'd first met Carla. "Carla, as always you're right on the money! That's it! I just play the role and time it just right, and then wham, I read the memo! Then I look him in the eye and say something like, 'Dad, how could you do this to me? You said you loved me!' And I walk off the set in tears. Carla, I love you! I knew that you'd help me." There were tears in her eyes.

Carla stood back and looked Esprit right in the eye. "No problem, sweetie, and don't let me rain on your parade here, but have you thought about what's going to happen afterwards? I mean, what are you going to do? He's bound to be pretty ticked off."

Esprit wiped away the tears and folded her arms across her chest. "I don't care! I'm eighteen years old, and I only have a short while before I leave for college anyway. What's he going to do, stop speaking to me? Big fucking deal! Hell, we haven't spoken for years until this past week anyway. He won't throw me out of the house. That would hurt his political career even more. Besides, I have access to my trust fund as soon as I start college, so I really don't give a flying fuck what he does."

"If worst comes to worst, you can come live with me for the rest of the school year. My parents love you," added Jamie.

"Well, girls, it sounds like you have a plan, and a damn good one at that! Why don't we just finish up those nails and then get your hair done up so you two can look really hot for your big party tonight?"

After Casey left the gym he stopped at Chris's, a local delicatessen, for a pork roll, egg and cheese sandwich on a hard roll and a carton of orange juice before picking up Kevin for practice. He loved pork roll, though he rarely ever ate it because of his strict dietary regimen. However, this morning he couldn't possibly feel any worse so what the hell, he ordered one anyway.

He wolfed down the greasy sandwich and the quart of juice in the short time that it took to drive to Kevin's. He hit the horn and Kevin and came right out. Within five seconds of getting in the car Kevin began to grill him about the day before and how he felt this morning.

"Dude, I want the truth. Did you trash the rest of the stuff like you said or were you just bullshitting me?"

Casey hated lying to his friend, but he couldn't help it. He couldn't tell him the truth, not yet anyway, at least not until after the game. Then, he promised himself, only then would he tell Kevin everything. So in response to the question he lied. "I sure did." Before Kevin had a chance to grill him any further they pulled into the school parking lot.

Today was the last day of double sessions. Coach Callahan had planned an intense and grueling schedule for the team that included a morning of rigorous hitting drills and an afternoon of full-contact scrimmaging. Tomorrow's practice, because it was the day before a game, would be limited to a game-plan walkthrough without pads and some light stretching, so today the coach was going to exact his pound of flesh from each and every one of his players.

By the start of the morning practice the heat wave had returned. The temperature was already hovering around ninety degrees, and there was not a breeze to be found anywhere. The practice-field turf, if you could even call it that because it was really nothing more than caked mud with a few tufts of grass scattered here and there, was as hard as rock because there'd been so little rain.

Casey and Kevin dressed for practice without any further discussion and joined the rest of the team out on the field. When Callahan blew the whistle, practice began in earnest. As the morning session progressed, every time Casey hit the bone jarring, rock-hard turf, his body ached and his muscles reverberated with pain. With each punishing hit, he worried a little bit more about his degenerating condition. His body failing him was a new experience, and it frightened the hell out of him. It had never happened before, and he began to contemplate the notion that something might be very wrong.

However, to his credit, he sucked up the pain and executed each drill with his usual intensity and ferocity, and not one of the coaches was the wiser, or so he thought. The truth was that Coach Martin had been keeping a watchful eye on him all morning, and he was very much aware of Casey's pain.

Mercifully, the two excruciating hours of the morning session came to an end. When the boys returned to the locker room between practices, Casey stayed in the shower for at least fifteen minutes longer than any of his teammates in an effort to steam away the pain. When he finally came out Kevin was the only one left, waiting at his locker.

"What's up with the long shower, dog? You got a hot date for lunch you didn't tell me about?"

Casey grimaced more than laughed, "Yah, with you, sweet

cheeks!" He reached over and tried to grab Kevin and give him a kiss, but Kevin was too fast and jumped out of the way.

As he backed off he saw Casey wince. "Casey, what's the deal? Are you hurt? You just looked like you were in a lot of pain."

"No, I'm okay. I think I pulled a muscle in my lower back during the bullring drill. That's why I was in the shower so long."

"Maybe you should tell Coach and take it easy this afternoon. You need to be ready to play on Friday."

Casey turned unexpectedly defensive. "Relax, dude! There's no way I'm telling Coach I'm not scrimmaging this afternoon. I'm the captain, remember? How would it look if I skipped the last double-session practice because of a little pulled muscle? No way! I'll suck it up and I'll be fine."

Kevin looked at his friend and said, "Okay, I give up! There's no talking to you, you stubborn son of a bitch." He sat quietly while Casey finished dressing.

When they left the locker room to head over to Kevin's, Shawn Murphy was waiting outside in the parking lot. He walked over for a word with the two of them. "Hey, guys, I know this is kind of last minute, but I want to invite you over to my house tonight for some poker. Me and some of the guys started playing a weekly game of Texas hold 'em. We've been playing every Wednesday all summer, and it's been pretty cool. My dad and I set up our basement into a makeshift card room, complete with a half-dozen tables and a bar stocked with brews and cigars. What do you think?"

Casey looked at Kevin. "What do you think, dude? I was just planning on kicking back and resting tonight, but this could be fun."

Kevin was indifferent, but he looked at Casey and said, "Sure, why not? I don't have any plans, sounds cool. Shawn, how much money we need to bring?"

"Twenty bucks ought to cover it unless you really suck at

poker. In that case maybe you ought to bring a little more."

Casey glanced at Kevin's way. "Count us in for the game, but we'll take a pass on the brews…and the cigars…you guys should too if you know what's good for you."

Shawn laughed. "Give me a break!"

During the break Kevin tried again to talk to Casey about the steroids. He wanted Casey to know that the coaches suspected something was up, and they were sniffing around for information, but Casey was in no mood for a serious conversation, especially about steroids.

By the end of the break Casey's mood had lifted, and he seemed much more his old self. As they were getting dressed for the afternoon session, Casey turned to Kevin with his usual swagger and said, "Okay, pal, it's time to separate the men from the boys. I'm going to be in your face the whole scrimmage. In fact, I'll bet you a ten-spot that you don't complete a single pass, and oh, don't get too comfortable back there in the pocket because you're wearing that silly red shirt. I may not be allowed to tackle you, but I can sure as hell knock into you a few times and maybe even accidentally knock you on your ass."

Kevin laughed. "Okay L.T., you're on for ten bucks! Let's see what you got!"

They dressed in a hurry and ran out to join the rest of the team on the practice field. Casey was true to his word during the afternoon scrimmage. Coach Callahan, already confident in the skill and execution of his defense, had structured the afternoon scrimmage as a test to see how the offense would react under pressure. He informed Casey that he had free reign on the defensive side of the ball, but warned him not to get too rough. Casey would not only call the defenses from the field, but as middle linebacker, he was also free to roam the line and attack the offense from any angle.

Callahan cautioned Casey that he wanted him and the rest of the defense to put pressure on the offense, not obliterate them. Casey took the coach at his word, and for the first hour the defensive unit flew after the ball like a flock of seagulls to a fish carcass – they completely shut down the offense. In the first hour Kevin attempted six passes, three had been batted down, two had been intercepted, and only one even came close to the wide receiver, but it was dropped after the boy took a ferocious hit from Casey.

By the end of the hour, both Coach Martin and Kevin were fed up with being bullied by the defense, so they took a time-out to talk it over. Coach Martin called for a weak-side play-action pass where Kevin would fake a handoff to the strong side of the line and then simultaneously both guards would pull to the strong side so they could take out Casey, who they assumed would see the offset line and charge up from that side of the ball.

This was a play that they rarely used, but this time when they ran it, Kevin and the offense executed it to perfection, and it worked exactly as planned. Kevin brilliantly faked the handoff to the halfback, who then lowered his shoulder and charged directly into the strong side of the line. Casey bit hard on the handoff and charged around the end looking to stop the halfback before he crossed the line of scrimmage. He came on so fast that he didn't see the two pulling guards steamrolling directly at him. The two massive linemen caught him off guard and hit him simultaneously, square in the chest. They leveled him to the turf. At the same time Kevin rolled out to the opposite side and threw a perfect forty-yard spiral to his wide receiver, who had already beaten both the safety and the cornerback because they too had bitten on the well-executed fake. The wide receiver caught the ball and scampered across the goal line untouched. He slammed the ball to the ground with a loud yell.

Seeing the touchdown, Kevin raised his fists in the air and ran over to Casey, who was still lying on the ground, and howled, "That's ten bucks motherfucker! How'd you like that play?"

Kevin looked down in triumph at his friend, but Casey didn't say a word. Kevin immediately lowered his raised fists when he realized something was wrong. He bent down, rolled Casey over to his back and saw that he was unconscious. Casey's eyes were open, but they were unfocused and drifting to the left. There was long spittle of drool dangling from the corner of his open mouth.

The two offensive linemen that delivered the ferocious hit on Casey were both standing over him too, almost in shock. Kevin screamed for the coaches as he tried to take off Casey's helmet. Within seconds all of the coaches and the trainer ran over as the rest of the team, in utter disbelief and shock, surrounded their fallen captain. Coach Martin blew his whistle and yelled for the team to get back and give the coaches room. The players, one by one, took off their helmets and slowly stepped backwards as they watched the unthinkable – their best player lying unconscious on the turf.

Coach Callahan, gently but firmly, pushed Kevin out of the way and finished taking off Casey's helmet. Then the trainer knelt down and shined a light into Casey's eyes. They were still unfocused and drifting. Casey wasn't responding at all, so without further delay, he opened his kit and handed the coach an ampoule of smelling salts. Callahan cracked open the seal and placed the strong salts directly under Casey's nose.

Casey's olfactory sensors picked up on the strong ammonia odor right away, and he began to stir. First his eyes fluttered as they tried to refocus, and then he coughed several times to remove the phlegm from his throat.

"Casey…Casey…you okay?" asked the coach, but Casey didn't respond.

Coach Callahan waited a few seconds and tried again. "Casey…it's Coach Callahan, what day is it?"

Casey finally began to come around. He coughed a couple more times then responded weakly, "Wednesday, Coach…it's Wednesday. What happened?"

Callahan let out a big sigh of relief. "Whew! All right, Casey, you just lie back down and take it easy for a couple of minutes. Does anything hurt?"

Casey took a moment to respond as he felt around his body for signs of pain. Then he said groggily, "I think I'm okay. I just got the wind knocked out of me is all."

"Good! Good!" Callahan turned to the other coaches standing behind him. "Coach Martin, I think we've had enough for today. Tell the rest of the team Casey's fine and to go hit the showers. I'll bring him along in a few minutes."

Coach Martin frowned, but he did as he'd been directed and left with the rest of the team for the locker room, leaving only Casey, Callahan and the trainer out on the field. Kevin lingered behind the rest of the team, wanting to make sure his friend was okay until Coach Martin grabbed him by the shoulder pads and made him leave as well.

"Casey, are you sure you're okay? You want to try and sit up?"

Casey nodded his head, so the coach helped Casey up to a sitting position while the trainer came around behind him and supported his back.

"I'm just a little dizzy, that's all. I'll be okay in a couple of minutes. What happened?"

Coach Callahan breathed a sigh of relief and then laughed. "You got your ass kicked is what happened! The offense ran a play-action pass with two pulling guards, and you bit hard from the strong side. The guards cleaned your clock."

"Shit! Did they complete the pass?"

"They sure did, for a fifty-yard touchdown."

"Damn, now I owe Kevin ten bucks!"

Coach Callahan smiled when he saw Casey was more worried about making a bad play and losing ten bucks than about his own physical condition. He was now guessing that it wasn't anything serious. "Casey, does your head hurt? Do you think it might be a concussion? Because if you want, we'll take you over to the hospital and get you checked out." He was silently praying Casey would say no because if the kid had to go the hospital, he probably wouldn't be allowed to play on Friday.

"No way, Coach. It's not a concussion. I'm okay, really! I just got the wind knocked out of me. I'm feeling better already. Here, let me try and stand up."

Casey gradually rose to his feet with the aid of both the coach and the trainer. He bent over and coughed a few more times, and then he tried to unhook his shoulder pads. He wanted to get them off because his chest hurt when he tried to breath. Finally, he began to walk around a bit in an attempt to clear his head.

As he walked it off, the trainer whispered to the coach, "It doesn't appear to be a concussion. I think he's telling the truth. He just got hit hard and got the wind knocked out of him." The trainer laughed. "If I didn't see it with my own eyes, I wouldn't believe it. Casey Collins knocked on his ass by a couple of offensive linemen."

"Well…it was a hell of a block by those two boys," said the coach.

They stopped talking when Casey walked back over. He picked up his helmet and pads and said, "Coach, I think I'm okay now, really. I just need to take a shower and a whirlpool, and then I'll be as good as new."

Coach Callahan nodded, put his arm around Casey's shoulder and the three of them unhurriedly walked off the practice field.

When Casey entered the locker room a large whoop of relief could be heard coming from the entire team. They all crowded around him as he made his way to his locker until Callahan blew his whistle and yelled at them to give Casey a little space.

When he finally reached his locker Kevin was sitting there with red-rimmed eyes staring up at him. Casey looked down at his anxious friend. "Kevin, I'm okay. I just got the wind knocked out of me, that's it."

Kevin barely whispered, "Casey, I thought you were in trouble out there, man! This kind of shit never happens to you.

Are you sure you're okay?"

Casey reached down and gave his friend a hug. "Dude, I'm fine, really. Lighten up, it was just a good hit, and I didn't see it coming."

Kevin came in close and whispered in Casey's ear, "Casey, I'm worried about you, dog! You didn't look good all day and now this happens. You promise you threw the roids away like you said? Promise me, dude, because you're scaring the shit out of me, and I don't want to see nothing happen to you!"

Casey angrily whispered back. "Shut the fuck up, you idiot, before you get me into deep shit. I told you I threw them away and I did, give it a rest!"

Coach Martin walked up and said, "Casey, sure you're okay? That was some hit. Sure you don't won't to go to the hospital and get checked our just in case?"

"No thanks, Coach. I'm good. Nothing a half-hour in the whirlpool won't cure."

Coach Martin looked at them suspiciously, but only said, "All right then, if you're sure?"

"I'm sure, Coach, thanks."

Coach Martin walked away back towards the office.

Casey angrily turned back to Kevin. "Listen to me, you stupid fuck, you almost got my ass busted with your big mouth. I told you before; I'm done with the steroids. I don't want to hear another word about it, especially in here!"

Casey reached into his locker and pulled out his wallet. "Now here, take your ten bucks, you earned it, and let me go get into the whirlpool."

Kevin took the money and shoved it in his pocket. He looked at his friend with a sad expression, "Casey…you want me to wait around till you're done?"

"No, I'm going to be in there for a while. I'll catch up with you later. If I still feel up to it, I'll see you later at the poker game and try to win my money back."

"You sure?"

"Kev, I'm sure. Now get out of here." Casey picked up his towel and gingerly walked towards the trainer's room.

When Coach Martin left Kevin and Casey, he went directly to Callahan's office. He walked in and closed the door. "Coach, you still thinking Casey don't have a problem?"

Callahan sat up straight. "What the hell are you talking about? He just took a hit and got the wind knocked out of him for Christ sakes!"

"Bullshit!" Coach Martin sounded off. "Casey was hurting all day today, and you know it! Didn't you watch him at all today? He looked like crap, and he was totally off his game all day. This morning he was slow getting up off the turf during the drills, and you know damn well a kid with his ability never gets completely blindsided by a double-team. Coach, I've been right where he is, the sweats, the clammy skin, the slowed motor responses. I'm telling you, he's showing all the signs of a kid going over the edge on roids!"

"All right...All right! Stop yelling at me and tell me what the hell you want me to do about it! We're two days away from our first game of the year, and if I blow the whistle on Casey, his football career's over! There ain't no way I'm willing to do that. So, just what the hell do you think I should do, Coach?"

"I've told you already. Call Frank Giordano. If Casey is using, and I'll bet you my next paycheck he is, he's getting the stuff from Giordano. Call that son of bitch and confront him! Make him stop Casey for Christ's sake! I know you don't want to kill the kid's football career, and neither do I, but this has to be done! He's already beyond the danger point and something bad's gonna happen, real bad. I can feel it!"

Coach Callahan rubbed his temples. He knew Coach Martin was right. He had to deal with this and deal with it now. He just hoped he could fix the problem quickly and quietly so that he didn't jeopardize Casey's, or more importantly, his own career.

"Okay, Coach, I am going to call Giordano right now," he

reached for the phone, "and I promise to keep you in the loop, but you'd better keep your mouth shut and not breath a word of this to anyone because my ass is on the line here…and if my ass is on the line…so is yours. You got that?"

"I hear you loud and clear. You're doing the right thing, thank you." Coach Martin left the office.

Callahan knew he had no choice so he looked up Giordano's number at the gym in his Rolodex and dialed.

After the third ring an answering machine picked up. "You have reached Frank Giordano at PowerHouse. I'm not available right now, but if you leave a message, I'll get back to as soon as possible."

Callahan waited for the beep and said, "Frankie, Coach Callahan here. We've got a big problem over here with Casey Collins, and I think you might be involved – if you know what I mean. I need to talk to you right away. Please call me as soon as possible. You've got my numbers." He hung up the phone wondering what he had just gotten himself into.

Casey sat low in the stainless steel tub of the whirlpool bath, his nose barely peaking above the swirling froth. He had been soaking his agonizing body for a good forty minutes. The hot pulsating jets of blue green water and white, frothy foam swirling around his pink and tender skin provided him with a cocoon-like feeling of safety and transitory comfort, a feeling that he was in no hurry to abandon. When he decided to pull his flushed and wrinkled body out of the tub, he was the last player left in locker-room.

On his first attempt to get out he got seriously dizzy and almost fell. Fortunately for him, none of the coaches or the trainer saw him. He quickly pulled himself together, stepped out of the tub and cautiously walked back to his locker to get dressed. Every part of him ached as he put on his clothes. When he finished dressing he walked into the bathroom and looked in the mirror. He was about to brush his hair, but then he just stopped and stared at his reflection. “Is all this really worth it? I could be really fucked up inside…” He flexed his chest. “You’re damn right it’s worth it!” He finished brushing his hair, went back to his locker and grabbed his gym bag before leaving for home.

Chapter Fourteen

Fear, Loathing, & Texas Hold 'em

Wednesday Evening, September 5th

When Casey got back home around six o'clock, he found the house to be unusually quiet. This was normally the time when his mother was buzzing around preparing dinner and setting the kitchen table. The news or some other talk show should have been blaring from the TV in the kitchen, but not today, today there was only silence.

Casey walked down the hall to the kitchen and found his mother sitting quietly at the already-set kitchen table with her reading glasses on reading a little blue book. As soon as she noticed him, she closed the book and slipped it into her purse.

Casey noticed her slip the book away. "Hey, Mom, what's going on? The house is so quiet."

Lisa stood up. "Hi, Casey, I finished making dinner a little early so I was reading, that's all. How are you feeling? You had me worried this morning and…" she looked at him closely, "…and quite frankly, honey, you still don't look too hot. In fact, you still look flushed. Are you feeling okay?"

"I'm fine. I'm flushed because I took a pretty good shot in the back at practice, so I spent about a half-hour in the whirlpool trying to loosen up the muscles. He changed the subject. "What were you reading just now? I can't remember the last time I saw you reading anything other than a paper or a magazine."

Lisa blushed. She flustered a little before answering him.

"Oh, honey, it's nothing, just some trashy romance novel that Mrs. Kimball gave me to read." Then she nervously changed the subject. "Casey, are you hungry? I made your favorite meal – spaghetti and meatballs with some garlic bread, and a nice salad."

Casey sensed something was amiss. His mother was acting kind of weird. She never read that kind of crap, but he decided not to press the issue. He looked at her again a little closer, and he could tell that she was sad. "That sounds great, I'm going upstairs to make a couple of phone calls and wash up for dinner, by then Dad should be home and we can eat."

He turned to go up the stairs, but Lisa called after him, "Casey, your dad's not going to be home for dinner. He called a little while ago and said he had to stay late at the office. He won't be home till around eight thirty or nine, so as soon as you're done, come back down and just the two of us can have a nice dinner."

Casey thought this very odd. His father never had meetings after work, and he usually only stayed late in the city on Thursday or Friday nights. He felt a distinctly weird vibe in his mother's voice but he just said, "That's cool. I'll be down in about ten minutes." Then he went up to his room.

Only part of what Lisa told Casey was the truth. Steve had called about an hour before to say that he wasn't coming home for dinner. He said he was still really ticked off about their conversation last night. He said he needed a little more time to think about everything she'd said. He was going to grab a quick bite on the way home and then go for a walk on the beach by himself. After Lisa didn't respond, he sarcastically assured her that he wasn't going to a bar and hung up the phone.

Casey went up to his room, threw his gym bag in the corner and went to his desk to make a couple of calls. He called Esprit to see how she was doing. She told him all about her day with Jamie at the salon and about her plan for revenge.

Casey offered her his two cents. "Spree, I told you last night that I'll support whatever you decide to do, but I'm worried this whole thing is going backfire on you, and you could be the one to end up looking like a fool instead of your father. Think whatever you like about your dad, Esprit, but don't underestimate him. He's a very smart man."

"I know that, I will, I promise. I love you so much for backing me on this. I really do."

"I love you too," he said quietly.

Esprit turned the subject around and asked Casey about his day. He told her about the remarkable double-team hit that he'd taken at practice, and he told he was sore as hell, but he intentionally neglected to tell her about his passing out after the hit, or the fact that he'd been sick as a dog all day. Esprit asked about his plans for tonight.

Casey mentioned that Kevin and he were going over to Shawn's for a poker game for a little while, but that he intended to be home early and in bed by eleven since tomorrow was the first day of school.

Esprit giggled a little bit. "Casey, you might be the only kid in the whole school who's worried about being prepared the first day of class. Hell, it's only a half-day, and most of that is taken up by your silly pep rally. Sometimes I don't get you. I mean, it's a tradition for kids to party on the last night of summer, and here you are worried about getting home to bed on time. I guess that's why I love you so much. You are just soooo responsible!"

Casey's anger starting to rise, but then he caught himself. She was just teasing him. "Hey, you're not the one who has to give a speech in front of the entire student body tomorrow at the pep rally, and besides, I haven't even thought about what I'm going to say yet."

"You haven't written your speech yet? Oh my God! Stop the presses! Casey, whatever is the matter with you? I would've guessed that you'd written and thrown away at least twenty drafts of that stupid speech by now. You're slipping, big boy." She giggled.

Casey laughed along with her. "Very funny!" But then he got serious and said, "Listen, please don't get wasted tonight. I know it's a big night for you and your friends, but you've got a lot going on right now, and I don't want to see you get into any more trouble."

"Don't worry, Casey, I promise to be a very, very good girl tonight," she assured him in her best little-girl voice. "I'll see you at school in the morning, okay? You go out and have a little fun tonight too, and don't worry about me or that stupid speech. Love you."

"I Love you too. Later."

Casey hung up the phone and dialed Kevin's number. He picked up after the second ring. "What's up, dog?"

Kevin let out a sigh of relief when he heard Casey sounding like his old self. "Hey, Casey, I was so worried about you. How're you feeling?"

"I'm fine, bud, just a little sore is all. Stop worrying about me so much for Christ's sake. You sound like my mother sometimes," he said, laughing.

"Dude, don't make fun of me. Somebody has to keep you in line. Listen, I know you don't want to talk about this anymore, but I need to hear it from you one last time. Promise me you've stopped this cycle and swear to it. If you promise, I won't bring in up again for the rest of the season."

This irritated Casey, but he knew it was only because Kevin cared about him so much. "Kevin…goddamn it! Look, I told you yesterday and then again this morning. How many times do I have to tell you? I stopped the injections, and I threw the rest of the cycle away. I don't plan on doing any more for the rest of the season, and maybe never again. Are you happy now?"

Relieved, Kevin said, "Thanks, dude, I won't bring it up again, promise."

"Good, now that we got that out of the way, do you still want to come with me to the poker game? I'm not going to stay there real late, but it sounds like it might be fun. What do you say?"

Kevin replied, "What the hell, I've got nothing better to do. Sure, what time?"

"I still have to eat dinner so figure around seven thirtyish. Cool?"

"Great! See you then."

Casey went to the bathroom to wash up for dinner, but first he took a leak. To his dismay, there was once again a pink tint to his urine, and this time the pain in his side flared up when he started to pee. That was it; he was done with the cycle. Something was very wrong. Right then and there he decided that after the game on Friday he'd fess up to Frankie about stealing the new cycle and apologize for what he'd done. Then he'd ask him for help. He was in trouble. Frankie would get crazy pissed about him stealing the cycle, but after the tantrum he would help him.

Casey zipped up his fly and washed his hands. Then he closed his eyes, clasped his hands tightly together and with complete and utter sincerity, and more than a little bit of fear, he prayed to God that he was going to be okay. When he was done he looked in the mirror once again, dried his face and hands and went downstairs to join his mother for dinner.

Lisa was standing over at the stove stirring the spaghetti sauce. A center island of cabinets divided the cooking area from the dining area of the kitchen, so as Casey walked over and sat down at the table Lisa bent down under the cabinets, looked over and said, "Hey, good timing. I was just getting ready to make you a plate," and then she continued on with her task.

Casey, sitting by himself at the table, looked down at the chair next to him and spied his mother's purse with the little blue book peaking out of the top. Since Lisa's view was obstructed by the cabinets he took the opportunity to peek at the title of the book to find out what she was reading. When he turned it over and read the two words printed on the cover, he was taken back. He put the book back and sat back in his chair, wondering just what to think about his mother reading a book entitled *Alcoholics Anonymous*.

Casey had a vague understanding of the iconic twelve-step program. He knew from health class that AA supposedly helped millions of alcoholics, but why was she reading it? Was it for her or for his father? It must be for his father, but maybe…maybe it was for the both of them. Casey wondered if his talk the other day had got the two of them thinking. Or was there something else going on that he wasn't aware off? At least the book explained his mother's odd behavior, and his father's absence from dinner.

Lisa came over with a couple of plates of spaghetti and meatballs along with a basket of piping hot garlic bread, dripping with butter and melted mozzarella cheese. The plate that she handed to Casey was piled high with a mountain of spaghetti and three mammoth meatballs. Casey dug in to his plate with relish, happily devouring the food at an astonishing rate. Lisa, on the other hand, only picked at her food, and after a few minutes Casey noticed her lethargy. He asked, "Mom, what's the matter? You're not eating."

"Oh, I don't know, Casey. I guess I'm not real hungry," Lisa sighed.

"You seem a little down, is something wrong?"

She was a little short with her response. "No, Casey, nothing's wrong. It has just been a rough couple of days with everything that has happened, okay?"

"Okay, don't get angry, you just seem a little upset is all."

"Casey, I'm sorry. I know you're just concerned. If you want to know the truth, your father and I had an argument last night, and he's still pretty angry with me. That's why he isn't home for dinner. But we'll work it out when he gets home later."

Casey thought about the book in her purse, and his dad's heavy drinking lately. He said testily, "Not if he comes home drunk you won't."

Lisa got angry. "Listen, mister, with your behavior over the last few days, you've no room to talk, but if you must know the truth, the argument had very little to do with your father's drinking. He was upset because I told him I was thinking about taking a course over at the university to renew my teaching certificate, and then maybe getting a job teaching at one of the local public schools. He was upset because he felt that after you graduate it would be better for the two of us to start doing more things for ourselves; you know, enjoying our empty nest years together instead of me going back to work."

Casey was caught off guard by his mother's words. He was about to confront her about the book, but he couldn't believe she was actually thinking about going back to teaching, and he was real happy to hear it. He decided to apologize. "Mom, I'm sorry about the drinking comment. It was out of line, but I'm happy for you about the teaching thing. I think you'd be a wonderful teacher."

"Thanks, Casey, that means a lot to me. Don't worry about me and your father. We'll work it out. So how are you feeling and what are your plans for your last night off before school starts?"

Casey and Lisa spent the rest of dinner with small talk about school and football. Casey had two large helpings of spaghetti, and by the end of dinner he was feeling much better. A full belly and the notion that his mother was planning to teach again were good medicine. His anxiety over the blood in his urine and the intense headache were, for the time being, forgotten.

Esprit dropped Jamie off at home after the salon and some last-minute shopping around five p.m. with the promise to pick her back up at eight for the party. When she got home she was greeted with nothing but silence. She spied a note card from her mother on the foyer table. It said she'd be out till around ten at dinner with some friends and that the cook had prepared Esprit a little something for dinner and left it in the fridge.

Esprit was thankful for the solitude. She rightfully thought that her mother was just as culpable as her father in this whole sordid affair because she was the one in the background pulling her father's strings from behind that phony Southern belle façade of hers. Not having to deal with her mother before her big night out was an unexpected bonus to what was turning out to be a pretty good day after all.

Esprit spent the next two hours luxuriating in the tranquility of her large, empty house. First she went to the kitchen and scarped down the plate of fried chicken left for her by the cook. She didn't even bother to heat it up because she was so famished. It was her first decent meal in a while because of the bouts of nausea that had plagued her for most of the week. She washed down the chicken with a couple of glasses of a 1994 Cakebread Chardonnay, courtesy of her parents' wine cellar. Then, after speaking to Casey on the phone, she went upstairs for a quiet bubble bath in her parents' oversized, marble whirlpool tub. This left her with a full hour for dressing and make-up.

At seven forty-five, she looked up from her dressing table and saw it was getting late. She took one last sip from her third glass of wine and then finished what was left of a joint she and Jamie had fired up earlier in the day. She was a little lightheaded when she stood up, but it was a good kind of buzz. She turned and smiled in the mirror, pleased with the results of her two hours of primping.

By eight o'clock she was working a glowing buzz as she pulled up into Jamie's driveway in her shiny black BMW convertible. The buzz had put her in a good place, and she didn't want to spoil it by having to talk with Jamie's parents, so she just beeped the horn a couple of times from the driveway and waited for her friend to come out.

A minute later Jamie came strutting out the front door looking the total diva. She sashayed over to the car showing off her new hairdo and outfit and hopped in laughing.

Esprit smiled. "Girlfriend, damn you look hot!"

"Damn right!" Jamie blew her a kiss. "You too, now let's blow this pop stand!" Esprit peeled out of the driveway with a screech of the tires.

The end of the summer cast party was a big deal for the kids in the drama club, and each year everyone tried their best to top the previous year's glam and style. This year's party was being held at the palatial, ultra-modern home of fellow cast member Evan Cook. Evan's parents just happened to be vacationing in Europe for a month, so he had accepted the honor and responsibility of throwing the bash.

The Cook home was an enormous, angular wonder. At first glance the house appeared to be a series of white stucco cubes precariously stacked one on top of the other. The geometrically challenged home also had dozens of odd-shaped windows, and what seemed like miles and miles of burnished nickel railings that wrapped around the many balconies that protruded from the dwelling.

The exterior lines of the house reminded Esprit of a sleek cruise ship or large yacht. Evan's house probably would have been more at home in a place like Malibu, overlooking the Pacific Ocean, than in the old money section of Middletown, New Jersey, but there it was, just a few miles down the road from her house. The girls found a parking spot on the long and winding drive and exited the car.

After checking their make-up one final time, Esprit and Jamie coquettishly made their grand entrance, Esprit, with her dazzling fair-haired locks and complimenting shimmering gold lame halter dress, and Jamie, with her luxurious dark tresses, looking absolutely stunning in a black lace camisole with matching black and red pleated mini skirt.

For the girls, the party wasn't about getting done up nice and hooking up with a guy – they could do that any time – it was all about style. They strutted into the crowded house like they were walking down the red carpet at the Oscars, and all eyes, male and female, turned to stare at them. They said their hellos as they waltzed their way through the house in search of Evan, and the bar. Gradually, they wound their way through the crowd, careening around dozens of glass tables and soft leather couches, until they eventually wound up outside on the patio, where the bar was set up.

The party was going strong. There were probably at least fifty kids inside the house and double that outside on the bluestone veranda that surrounded the pool. Floodlights were blazing, multicolored strobe lights were pulsating, and hip-hop music was pounding out a steady beat from a wireless speaker system that ran throughout the house. The girls danced out onto the patio and made their way up to the bar.

The bar was set up on a banquet table with the obligatory keg strategically placed right next to it, but surprisingly there was also a large assortment of wines and liquor to choose from sitting right there on the table alongside hundreds of assorted sizes of plastic cups.

Esprit commented, "Nice set-up!"

She poured herself a glass of chardonnay while Jamie opted for a beer and a shot of tequila. Without hesitation, Jamie tilted her head back and drained the shot, then she bit into a thick slice of lime. She grimaced for a second, wiped her mouth with a cocktail napkin, and said, "Spree, you already got a pretty good buzz going, want to do a hit of X? It'll help keep you going all night."

Esprit thought about the offer. "No thanks, I think I'm gonna take a pass. I promised Casey I'd take it easy tonight, and I don't want to break a promise."

"Suit yourself, sweetie, but you better take it easy on the booze then. You're already pretty lit."

She reached into her purse, took out a hit of ecstasy, swallowed it and washed it down with her beer. Then the girls began to work their way around the party, stopping here and there to talk with friends until they ran into Tom Carton, a boy on the football team who was there because he dated a girl from the drama club.

"Esprit, Jamie, nice party. You girls look dope!" He turned to Esprit. "I guess Casey didn't feel up to coming tonight after what happened at practice. Man, he doesn't have a clue what he's missing here tonight."

Esprit's eyebrows narrowed. "Tom, what are you talking about? Casey didn't mention anything bad about practice today; he just said it was a tough one. What happened?"

"That's what he said? That's just like Casey," laughed Tom.

"Esprit, he was blindsided by two offensive linemen. They hit him so hard they knocked him unconscious! Coach Callahan had to stop practice because Casey was out cold. He was still lying on the ground five minutes later when the coach sent the rest of us to the showers. About ten minutes later Casey walked back in, helped by the coaches, and he didn't look so hot."

Esprit was relieved to hear that Casey didn't get in any more trouble, but she was worried and more than a little miffed that he hadn't told her about what happened.

Jamie tried to make light of the situation, "Chill out, Spree, you talked to him an hour ago and he was fine, right?"

"Yah, but…."

"No butts, girl. He told you he was going to a stupid poker game tonight. How hurt could he be? Besides, he is one tough SOB, so stop worrying about him and try to have a little fun here. We're at a party, remember?"

Still worried, Esprit replied, "I don't know…maybe I should call him and see if he's okay."

Jamie glared at Tom and grabbed Esprit by the arm. As they walked away she turned back and said, "Thanks a lot, Tom, you jerk! Come on, Esprit. Let's go get another beer, and then you can call your baby if you must."

Tom just stood there dumfounded with his girlfriend at his side, wondering what exactly he'd done wrong.

Over the last few years poker, or more specifically a game

called Texas hold 'em, had taken the country by a storm, and the teenage boys of Middletown, New Jersey were no exception. The Texas hold 'em craze started a couple years ago when a relatively obscure cable channel started airing a celebrity poker show featuring young and beautiful Hollywood stars playing cards with house money at a popular Las Vegas casino. Surprisingly, from the very first episode, the show garnered remarkably high ratings, especially with the seventeen to twenty-five male audience.

Media giant ESPN, who had been televising the World Series of Poker Tournament for years to appallingly low ratings, saw the opportunity to capitalize on the other show's success. The key to generating high viewer interest was to mount tiny cameras around the lip of the gaming table. The cameras discreetly picked up the individual player's hidden cards. This allowed the audience to see in advance what was in each player's hand and whether or not they were bluffing. This simple trick of modern video technology made for decidedly fascinating television because it gave the television viewer an inside look into the strategy of the game and into the psyche of the players.

Armed with this new camera technology ESPN dumped millions of dollars into show production and ten times that amount into marketing and promotion. And presto, a few months later it was impossible to turn on the TV without seeing another new poker show. America bit the hook and bit hard, especially teenage boys. Poker had become so hot it was impossible to walk into any local store without bumping right into a Texas hold 'em merchandise display complete with T-shirts, hats, kits, cards, instructional videos, the works. Kids across America began playing Texas hold 'em, and playing a lot, some winning a few dollars now and then, but most losing their shirts.

When Casey and Kevin walked into Shawn's house they were flabbergasted by the spectacle. First of all, there were cars lined up and down both sides of the street. As if that wasn't enough, when they walked down into the basement from a well lit outside entrance, they were amazed. This wasn't just a poker night with a few high school buddies in Shawn's unfinished basement. No way. This was an event.

The boys walked into a raucous and brightly lit paneled room. The large basement was swirling with cigar smoke and perfumed by the odor of stale beer and sweat. Spread around the room were six poker tables with four to five guys at a table. Casey couldn't believe that Shawn and his father had actually set up their basement as a full-blown poker parlor. Scattered throughout the room were busy tables and only a few empty chairs. Over in the far corner next to a couple of neon beer signs there was a huge refrigerator fully stocked with beer and soda. Next to the fridge there was a man standing behind a portable bar-like counter who appeared to be the bartender. He was the guy you went to see to buy into a game, get a beer or a cigar, and of course, to cash in your chips at the end of the night…that is if you were lucky enough to still have any.

Casey looked around and saw a group of men he recognized at one table. They were some of his teammates' fathers. Shawn's dad was sitting with them. At the other tables there were a lot of kids from school and many of them from the football team. Casey scanned the room and found Shawn sitting at the center table; in front of him there was a big stack of poker chips and a frosty mug of beer. Shawn looked up with a shit-eating grin and a fat, unlit stogie dangling from his mouth when he noticed Casey and Kevin.

He stopped his game right in the middle of the deal, stood up and ran over to greet them. "Hey, guys, glad you made it. Casey, we were worried about you, man! How you feeling?"

"I'm okay," said Casey, still looking around with amazement. "This is unbelievable. Dude, this is crazy! Isn't your dad worried about getting busted?"

Shawn laughed. "Hell no! See those guys playing at my dad's table?" He pointed. "Two of them are cops. Besides, the house ain't making any money. We just charge for the cost of the beer and the cigars. Dude, it's just about having a little fun, that's all."

Kevin scratched his chin. "Right."

Shawn was eager to impress. "So, are you guys ready to play or what? Come on over to the bar with me, and we'll get you some chips. Then you guys can join my table."

He took them over to the bar, where they each purchased twenty dollars worth of chips. Neither wanted a beer, so Shawn gave them each a bottle of water on the house. Then they came back to Shawn's table, but before they could all sit down Shawn had to throw a couple of other players off the table. He pointed to a couple of guys that Casey didn't know and flipped his thumb. The two rejected players pissed and moaned, but they eventually stood up and shuffled off to another table. Once everyone had a seat, Shawn asked Kevin and Casey if they'd ever played Texas hold 'em before. Both said no.

"It's a pretty simple game. I'll explain it." Shawn took them through the fundamentals of the game in just a couple of minutes, and then they did a practice hand. Casey ended up with three queens. Not bad. Shawn looked at the two boys. "No gimmicks, no wild cards, just good old-fashioned poker, pretty simple, right?"

Casey and Kevin looked at each other and nodded.

"Okay boys! Let's play poker!"

He dealt the first hand. As the game progressed Kevin got on a hot streak and started to win hand after hand. After about an hour or so he was up almost forty dollars. Casey, on the other hand, won a couple of hands early but had hit a rough streak and was now watching his chips steadily move across the table, most of them in Kevin's direction.

Casey was down to only eight dollars in chips when he felt his cell phone vibrate in his pocket. He pulled it out and looked at the number. It was Esprit. Thinking that it was probably a good time for a break, he decided to take the call. He excused himself and walked outside the smoky room. The fresh night air felt cool against his warm skin. He walked down the driveway and answered the phone.

"Hey, Spree, what's up?"

"Hi, Casey, it's me. I…I just ran into Tom…from the football team…he told me you were knocked unconscious at practice. I…when I heard I got worried, I wanted to make sure you were…you know…okay."

Casey could tell by the pauses in her speech that she'd already had a lot to drink. He could also tell she was pretty upset by the news and very worried about him.

"Esprit, I'm fine. Really! It wasn't a big deal. I was only out for a minute or two. I just got the wind knocked out of me. It was a tough hit, that's all."

"Why didn't you tell me? God…Casey, I freaked when Tom told me what happened. I love you…please don't keep secrets from me. Are you sssure you're okkkay?

Now she was slurring her words. Damn it, she was wasted again. Casey was pissed. "Goddamn it, Esprit, I didn't keep any secrets from you. I told you that I took a hard hit and was still a little sore, so let it go for Christ's sake. By the way, you sound pretty fucked up again. What happened to, 'I'm going to take it easy tonight, Casey'?"

Esprit panicked. "I…I've only had a couple glasses of wine. I'm…fine. I was worried about you." Trying to change the subject she said, "So how's the poker game. Are you having fun?"

Casey, in no mood to argue, said, "It's pretty cool. Shawn and his dad have quite a set-up here. It's just like a real casino. There's probably fifty guys over here playing cards. I'm losing a little, but Kevin's up about forty bucks." Casey thought about her drinking again, and he just couldn't let it go. "But what's with the partying tonight? You promised me you'd take it easy tonight. Esprit, this is bullshit!"

"Casey…I just told you. I've only had a couple glasses of wine…I promise. I was just worried about you…that's all. Don't get mad at me…please!"

"Esprit, you sound pretty hammered, so no more wine. I mean it. Don't forget what happened the last time, all right?"

"I promise, Casey. I'm glad you're okay. I'll see you at school in the morning. I love you!"

"Me too."

He hung up the phone. Here she was, just a couple of days later and she was already partying her ass off again. Tonight was a big deal for her and her friends, but what the fuck? Casey walked around for a bit trying to dump the anger, but he couldn't, and now he wasn't much in the mood to play cards any longer, but he walked back into the basement anyway.

He rejoined the game and took his seat. Kevin had won another hand while he was on the phone and was grinning from ear to ear. When the next hand came up Casey was sitting to Shawn's left, and it was Shawn's turn to deal so Casey would be the first to bet. He was dealt a pair of queens for his two down cards. These were the best down cards he'd had all night so he bet two dollars. The next two guys folded and then it was Kevin's turn. Kevin, feeling more than a little cocky, matched Casey's bet before he even looked at his cards. When he did look he was holding a pair of kings. As the hand went around the table everyone else folded and watched the aggressive betting between the two friends. The hand came down to just the two of them. Shawn dealt the flop.

The three up cards were a queen, a king, and a three. Casey now had three queens with two cards still to be dealt. He thought he couldn't lose. There was no way Kevin could possibly hold kings, no way. He had a lot less money than Kevin so he had only one play to make. He called, "All in," and moved his small pile of chips into the center.

When a player believes he has a good hand but is low on chips the best move is to go 'All In', forcing the other players to match what he has put in or fold. Casey had gambled all his remaining chips. There would be no more raises. Kevin, without the slightest hesitation, matched Casey's pot and the die was cast.

Both of them flipped their down cards over and watched with great anticipation as Shawn prepared to turn over the final the two cards. When Casey saw Kevin's kings he winced. He knew that unless another queen came up in the last two cards he'd lose, and the odds of that happening were pretty slim. Shawn flipped the next card; it was the six of diamonds, no help to either player. Shawn was relishing his moment as the dealer on the big hand. He deliberately flipped over the last card. To add injury to insult, he turned over Kevin's fourth king. Kevin laughed out loud as he raked in the large pot. "Damn, I'm good!"

Casey, still angry from the phone call, was none too happy about losing the hand. In fact, the surge of anger he felt when he saw the final card was surprising even to him. He hated to lose at anything. He cursed under his breath and smacked his hand on the table, but he quickly regained his composure and looked at Kevin. "Looks like I'm all tapped out, Shit head. Nice job. I'm pretty sure most of that money in your stack is mine. Now I'm into you for thirty bucks today.

Kevin smiled. "Sorry, dude!"

Casey stood up from the table. "It's cool. I'm going to hit the road. You want to come with or do you want to hang for a while and catch a ride with someone else?"

Kevin was having a great time and didn't want to leave. He said, "If it's okay by you, Casey, I'd like to keep playing a little longer."

"Sure, bud, no problem. I'll see you in the morning."

Casey got up from the table and thanked Shawn and his father. Then he left the smoky room and made his way out to the car. On the drive home he couldn't stop all the negative stuff swirling around in his head; the stolen steroids, the headaches, the blood in his urine, Esprit, his parents, her parents, Penn State, and getting knocked out at practice. All this bad shit was leading up to something very unpleasant. He could sense it.

After Esprit got off the phone with Casey she felt better, but she was worried that he was pissed at her because she was partying again. So, even though she knew he was okay, her mood soured. Jamie picked up on the change right away. When Esprit put her phone back in her purse Jamie rushed over with a couple of shots of tequila and said, "He's fine, right? Now it's time to party!"

She handed Esprit the shot and a piece of lime, then picked up her own.

"Bottoms up!"

Jamie downed the shot, but Esprit hesitated.

"Come on, bitch! What're you waiting for?" She lifted Esprit's hand with the shot glass up towards her face until it reached a point where either Esprit drank it or it was going to spill down the front of her dress. Having little choice, Esprit downed the shot and gagged a couple of times before biting into the sour lime.

"That's my girl, now don't you feel better?"

The shot did make Esprit feel a whole lot better. The tequila immediately spread a warm fuzzy feeling throughout her body, and that sensation temporarily washed away the guilt she'd been feeling just a moment before. Esprit smiled.

For the next two hours she and Jamie did a bunch more shots. They partied and laughed with their friends till around midnight, when Esprit found that her buzz had evolved into a tremendous headache. She grabbed Jamie and said it was time to head for home.

Jamie reluctantly agreed, and after saying their goodbyes, the two of them set off to find the car, which was parked way down the drive from Evan's house. They finally found it and giggled and gossiped on the short drive home. Mercifully, it wasn't far; Esprit almost drove off the winding road twice. Jamie had planned ahead for the night. She'd planned on getting wasted so she'd already told her parents she was crashing at Esprit's and that she would go to school with her in the morning.

It was a little past one when the girls finally made it back to Esprit's house. Thinking her mother long fast asleep, Esprit and Jamie stumbled into the house and made quite a racket as they climbed the stairs to her bedroom. At one point Jamie tripped and dropped her bag. It clunked down several steps before she was able to retrieve it.

Jordan woke because of the loud noise. She sat up in bed and listened intently to the whispered conversation of the two obviously drunk girls as they stumbled down the hall into Esprit's bedroom.

She could just barely make out a few little snippets of conversation, and what she heard disturbed her. "...Can't wait...screw that...asshole father... On fucking national TV...Holy shit!...ha ha ha..." The whispers were followed by drunken laughter. Jordan heard enough to ascertain two things: one, her daughter was smashed again, and two, Ethan's new relationship with his lovely daughter was most definitely not as secure as he thought it was. She decided not to do anything just now. She would let her daughter sleep it off and then confront her in the morning.

Chapter Fifteen

A False Calm before the Storm

Thursday Morning, September 6th

It was six fifteen when Jordan woke to the horrible sound of the phone jangling on the night table. She reached across the king-sized bed and picked up the phone. As she expected, it was Ethan.

"Good morning, honey, did I wake you?"

Jordan wiped the sleep from her eyes and testily replied, "Why no, dear, I've been up since five doing the laundry…of course you woke me, you idiot! Why are you calling so early?"

"I'm sorry, but I'm meeting with Blaine in about a half-hour, and I wanted to let you know what I've decided to do with the TV interview before I told him."

A red light went off in Jordan's head. Her thoughts jumped back to the snippets of Esprit's conversation she'd overheard last night. Her mind leaped to attention.

"Okay, Ethan, so what've you decided to do?"

"Well…you're probably not going to agree me, but at least hear me out before you jump down my throat."

She rolled her eyes. "Okay."

"Well…I told you the other night that I was uncomfortable with this idea from the start. You know how much I don't approve of the political exploitation of one's family problems just for the sake of getting votes. I never have. I didn't like it when Clinton did it, and I'd feel like a hypocrite if I went through with the interview. Besides, I thought about this whole thing a great deal last night. Now that I have Arthur to support my campaign and with my current polling numbers improving…well…I am so far ahead of my opponent…and in all likelihood it will stay that way with only eight weeks to go…."

Jordan became frustrated with his blathering. "Honey, just get to the point?"

"Okay. I know that you're going to say that the interview is not about this campaign, it's about the Senate run next year, but I still don't like the idea of it. It just feels sleazy to me, and more importantly, I don't want to do anything to upset Esprit. I haven't felt this good about our relationship in years, and I don't want to do anything that might jeopardize it. Surely you can understand that."

Jordan chuckled at the irony of the situation. "Ethan, regrettably, at this point what I think is irrelevant. It seems you've already made up your mind on this issue."

"That's not true…."

"Ethan, please be quiet and let me finish. What I was trying to say before you rudely interrupted was that unfortunately, I have no choice but to agree with your decision, but not for the reasons you're thinking. I believe your darling daughter may not be as deeply entrenched in your political camp as you would like to believe."

"Jordan, what the hell are you talking about?"

"Last night when Esprit and that miserable little tramp Jamie came home, they were drunk, again! I overheard part of their conversation as they came up the stairs. Now understand, I only heard a few bits and pieces, but what I heard wasn't good. They must have assumed that I was sleeping because they were whispering, but they were so drunk they couldn't help but make quite a racket. Anyway, I heard Esprit say something like, 'I can't wait' and then something I couldn't make out, and then 'on national TV'. Then her horrible little friend used some profanity with your name in the middle that I would rather not repeat, at which point they both started laughing. So it would seem, my dear Ethan, that Esprit somehow has got wind of your planned interview, and she's got something nasty up her sleeve."

"Oh…my…God…Jordan! Thank God I decided not to do it. She could have ruined me! But how the hell could she possibly know about the interview? The only people that knew about it were you, me and Blaine. Are you sure you heard it right?"

"Honey, I couldn't help but overhear them. They made enough noise coming up those stairs to wake the dead. I intend on getting to the bottom of this as soon as she gets up for school. I'm going to speak to her this morning, and I promise you I'll get the truth out of her."

"Oh this is just awful. I can't tell you how disappointed I am. Everything was falling so perfectly into place: Arthur's support, the upcoming election, the Senate campaign, and most importantly, my relationship with Esprit…and now in the span of a single phone call my relationship with her is once again a fucking disaster!"

Ethan rarely used profanity. This fact signaled to Jordan that he was really upset.

"Now hold on a minute, Ethan. Let's not get carried away here. The only thing that's changed is that you're not doing the interview. And let me remind you that it was one you didn't really want to do in the first place. As for Esprit, I warned you not to get too excited by her enthusiasm and warmth towards you. She's a rebellious teenager and one good deed by dear old Daddy doesn't wash away years of you coming in last place as father of the year, at least not in your daughter's eyes."

"Well, that's a bit harsh don't you think?"

"Maybe so, Ethan, but someone has to be the voice of reason, and that someone is me. I'll speak to her later this morning, and then we'll know the truth. For now you need to focus on what's really important, your career, and I'll deal with our ill-tempered daughter."

"Okay, dear, I guess you're right. I'll call you later this

afternoon."

"Bye."

Jordan hung up the phone wondering how her husband could be so intelligent and savvy when it came to running his political career and so woefully ignorant and naïve when it came to his relationship with his daughter.

Steve got out of bed at five-thirty, as he usually did, and went to the bathroom to shower and dress for work. Lisa hadn't slept very well and was wide-awake when he came out of the bathroom. He was surprised to see her sitting up in bed. He paused before coming over to her.

She broke the ice. "Listen, Steve, I can see that our conversation is still bothering you, but I can't go through another day not talking. I'm sorry if what I said upset you. Please accept my apology and let's move on from this. I let you have the whole night to yourself last night. And what happened? You came home late and went right to bed without even saying a word. I love you, and I can't stand us not communicating. If it will make you feel better, I will let the whole thing go and not bring it up again."

Steve sat down on the edge of the bed next to his wife. He bent down, took her in his arms and kissed her. "Lisa, I love you, and I'm sorry I got so angry. Some of the things you said really pissed me off, and I needed time to think them over. I don't think we can just forget about the conversation. I think you and I need to talk this out and come to an understanding about our future. I have to go to work now, and you know I'm going to the Yankee game tonight after work, but I promise I'll only work a half-day tomorrow. We can continue this conversation tomorrow afternoon. I'll take you out to lunch before Casey's game."

"Can't we talk later today?"

"Lisa, you know we can't talk about this while I'm at work. My partners are sitting right there next to me. They can hear every word of my calls."

Lisa, a pained expression on her face, answered, "I know that…but…."

"Honey, I know this is important to you, and it's important to me too. I love you more than anything, but if I don't hurry I'm going to miss my boat. I promise I'll call you later from the office, and we'll work this all out tomorrow afternoon. But now I've got to run." He gave her one final kiss and was out the bedroom door.

Lisa stared after the empty doorway, wondering if Steve meant what he said. Maybe they would be able to work things out. Maybe he was starting to see that his drinking was becoming a problem. She was feeling a little better when she heard Casey walk down the hall and enter the bathroom. Why was he up so early? She heard the sound of running water when he turned on the shower. She decided it was futile to try and go back to sleep since the rest of her household was up, so she threw on her robe and went downstairs to the kitchen to make a pot of coffee and start her day.

Casey couldn't sleep. He woke up at about five with a lot on his mind. Everything was tumbling around in his head like wet clothes in a dryer – steroids, Esprit, his parents. And on top of everything else, in just a few hours he had to deliver the captain's speech at the pep rally, and he had no fucking idea what he was going to say. Thirteen hundred kids sitting there waiting for him to give them something to cheer about, and he hadn't been able come up with shit! He was mad at the world and couldn't shake it. Everything was pissing him off. Even Kevin had managed to get under his skin at the stupid poker game last night. Well, one thing was for sure, he was going to take Kevin's advice – no more steroids.

For the second time in as many days, Casey closed his eyes and prayed that he hadn't done any really serious damage to his body. He slipped out of bed and set about doing his morning exercises. His body felt a hell of a lot better this morning than it had yesterday. That was something. He breezed through his sets and then got up and went to the open window. He took in several big gulps of fresh air as he looked out at the willow tree. His gaze wandered to the doves' nest. It was empty. His two beautiful birds must have departed to wherever it was they went at the end of each summer. Normally their leaving would have stirred little emotion in Casey, but for some reason their absence this morning made him very sad. He sighed and left the window to take a shower. Afterwards he'd get cracking on writing something that would resemble a speech for the pep rally.

Before entering the shower, Casey guardedly relieved his bladder. To his enormous relief there was no sign of blood and no pain when he peed. Feeling almost happy for the first time in a couple days, he climbed into the hot steamy shower, and it felt wonderful. The hot spray not only woke him up, it cleared his head of all the crap that had been festering up there.

When he left the bathroom he heard the radio playing downstairs in the kitchen and assumed that his mother was already up. He threw on a pair of sweats and went down to get his breakfast shake. He was surprised by the strong hunger pangs he was feeling and took it as a good sign that he was better. Maybe the negative effects of the new cycle of steroids were finally wearing off.

Casey entered the kitchen and smiled, seeing his mother there preparing his shake.

"Good morning, honey, I heard you were up, so I figured I'd surprise you and fix your breakfast early. I was going to bring it up to you. You look a lot better today than yesterday. How are you feeling?"

"A lot better, and I'm starving." He took the shake from her and kissed her on the cheek. "Thanks. I've got to get back upstairs and finish writing my speech before school starts."

"Oh…that's right. I forgot, today's your big speech. I'm surprised you haven't finished it yet. It's not like you to wait till the last minute, but I guess with everything that's happened this week, it's understandable. Do you want anything else with your shake? Some toast or maybe a bagel?"

"Actually, a bagel with cream cheese would be great."

Casey took a seat at the counter while Lisa went about making it for him. "So how did things go with Dad when he got home last night? Are you two still fighting?"

Without looking up from what she was doing she said, "Casey, your father and I are not fighting. I told you…we just aren't in agreement on a few things about the future. We talked a little bit this morning and everything's fine."

Casey looked over on the counter and spied the blue book sticking out of the top of her purse, but this time the title was clearly visible. "Mom, what's going on? Your acting a little weird, and I can see the trashy novel you were reading yesterday sticking out of your purse. *Alcoholics Anonymous*, now that's a catchy title for a novel."

Lisa was caught off guard.

"Casey, what I'm reading is none of your business. But since you're so nosey, I'll tell you. I am a little concerned that both your father and I have been drinking too much lately. You know as well as I do that there's drinking problems on both sides of our family, so I decided to read up on it. That's it! No big deal!"

"If it's not a big deal, why'd you lie yesterday?" He questioned her further. "I'm not a little kid anymore, Mom. You know Dad's drinking has bothered me for a long time."

"Casey, don't start up on that this morning, I'm in no mood to listen to you attack your father…."

He interrupted. "Mom, I'm not trying to piss you off, okay? I just want you to know that what you're doing is a good thing and that if you need my help, I'm here." He got up and went around the counter and offered her a hug.

Lisa looked up into her son's eyes and saw sincerity. "Thanks, Casey, but I'm serious, everything's going to be fine. Your father's not an alcoholic; he just needs to cut back a little, that's all. And it wouldn't hurt for you to try being nice to him for a change."

She handed him his bagel and said, "Now you've got a lot to do this morning so why don't you take your breakfast up to your room and get that speech ready? And for Pete's sake, stop worrying about your father and me. We're okay!"

"Okay, I'll be upstairs." Casey picked up his breakfast and went back to his room.

Lisa watched him leave with mixed emotions. She was pleased that Casey was feeling better and that he seemed back to his old self, but she was still worried about the fragile state of her household, especially as it pertained to her husband.

Last night Jamie and Esprit had fallen into bed still wearing their party clothes. Anticipating a late night, Esprit had been smart enough to set the alarm clock before going out for the evening, so at six thirty sharp it went off. It began blaring right in Jamie's ear because she happened to pass out on that side of the bed. Jamie tried to open her painfully swollen eyes. She looked over at her passed out friend. All she could discern was a snoring nose and a pair of dry cracked lips desperately in need of some Chap Stick peeking out from under a cluster of tangled golden hair.

"Oh my God, Esprit, wake up! Your breath stinks like tequila." Then she moaned once more as she reached over to shut off the alarm.

Esprit grumbled but gradually came awake and said, "Ohhh…my head's killing me! I need some Tylenol."

Esprit struggled to climb out of bed. She dragged herself to the bathroom and looked in the mirror. Staring back at her was that stranger again – that someone she barely recognized. It wasn't the glamorous Esprit from last night; it was an ugly girl with matted hair, bloodshot eyes, and a red and puffy face. Her once perfectly applied make-up was now just a mishmash of smears and blotches haphazardly lacquered across her face.

Jamie came up behind her to stare in the mirror, and faring

not much better, she said, "Girl, you look like shit!" and she began to laugh as she squatted on the toilet to pee. Jamie looked up at her friend and saw that she was crying. "Spree, what's the problem? It's just a little hangover. Why are you crying?"

"Look at me! Look at me, Jamie! I can't do this anymore. I feel like crap. I look like shit, and Casey's mad at me again! Why do I do this to myself?" she shrieked and started to sob again.

Jamie, after finishing her ablutions, stood up and put her arm around Esprit. She looked in the mirror, trying to make eye contact with Esprit. "What's the dealio? You're a little hung over. Nothing a hot shower and a cup of coffee won't cure. You had fun last night, didn't you?"

Esprit was not to be consoled. "No, Jamie, I didn't have fun. I just got wasted, and I don't even remember the rest of the night once we started doing the shots. I can't do this anymore!" she sobbed and rested her head on her friend's shoulder.

"Okay…okay, Esprit, no more drinking and drugging, all right? Why don't we both take a break for a week or two? I know we've been partying our asses off, but hell, girl, it's the end of the summer. That's what we're supposed to do! Why don't you get in the shower first, and then we'll get dressed and run to Starbucks before school? Come on, what do you say?" Jamie forcibly pushed Esprit towards the shower and turned up the water so that the shower was piping hot.

It took about forty-five minutes, but both girls managed to shower, dress, and apply a new veneer of make-up that went a long way towards covering up the telltale signs of the damage done the night before. While Jamie was perfectly normal and ready to start the new day, Esprit struggled with the demons in her head and was sluggish and non-communicative.

"Esprit, what do you say, kid, let's go get us a couple of double-espressos and start the new school year off with a bang?" chirped the irrepressible Jamie.

"Why not?" replied Esprit as they picked up their purses and headed for the bedroom door.

Jordan was out of bed as soon as she got off the phone with Ethan. She no longer had the desire to sleep, so she went to her dressing room, fixed her hair and slipped on a white silk robe. She intended on being downstairs waiting when her darling daughter and her miserable tramp of a friend made their grand appearance before leaving for school. There was no way Esprit was going step one foot out the house before Jordan got to the bottom of last night's antics. First, she went to the kitchen and informed the cook that she wanted a poached egg with an English muffin for breakfast. Then she made herself a cup of English breakfast tea and marched directly into the living room. She planned on waiting there until Esprit and her friend came down. She picked up the *New York Times* and began skimming the pages as she simmered with anger over her daughter's behavior.

After waiting testily for almost an hour, Jordan finally heard the girls coming down the stairs. Both were wearing those clunky, ridiculously high platform sandals, so popular with kids these days. When they reached the bottom landing she coughed and said, "Esprit, darling, could you come in here for a minute. I want to have a word with you." Then she added in a malicious tone, "Alone!"

Esprit froze. "Christ, she's the last thing I need right now." She turned to Jamie. "Just wait here and don't say a word!"

Jamie nodded.

Esprit cautiously entered the room, and when she saw her mother's dour expression she knew the conversation wasn't going to be pleasant.

"What's up, Mom? We're kind of in hurry. We don't want to be late for the first day of school."

"Esprit, I don't give a damn about you being late for school, but I will get right to the point. I heard the two of you come in last night. You were drunk again. It was one in the morning for God's sake. What the hell's the matter with you? You'd think after the stunt you pulled Sunday, getting drunk again just three days later would be that last thing that you'd want to do. What were you thinking?"

"Mom, I don't have time for this, all right?"

"Young lady, you'd better make time because when I tell your father about this, especially after what he did for you with Casey, he's going to be furious...and what about Casey? Does he know that you got drunk again? I bet if he did, he would be none too happy about it!"

Esprit's eyes narrowed. "Mom, are you threatening me? I'm sorry if we woke you up last night, but it was the last night of the summer and you knew damn well I was planning on going to the party for weeks. So give me a fucking break! What did you think was going to happen at the party? I don't know, maybe we were going to just sit around reading Shakespeare's soliloquies or play scrabble!"

"Don't get smart with me, young lady. I'm in no mood for it! And what was that I heard the two of you talking about when you came up the stairs...something about you screwing with your father on national TV. What are you up to Esprit?"

Esprit couldn't hide her look of shock. She had no memory of her conversation coming up the stairs, but right then and there she knew that the two of them had let the proverbial cat out of the bag. Now her plan for revenge was gone like the wind. "Mother, I don't have any idea what you're talking about. Jamie and I came home and went to bed, that's it, and now I am going to school!" She turned on her heels and marched out of the room, signaling Jamie to follow.

Jordan, in her nightgown and slippers, traipsed after them, and as they got into Esprit's car she called out, "Esprit, we aren't finished with this conversation. When your father gets home tonight we will talk of this again, I promise you!"

"Great, just great! My father's coming home tonight!" said Esprit as she tore down the driveway and turned in the general direction of Starbucks.

Casey drove up to school and parked in the lot. When he stepped into school he looked all around the sprawling brick structure, just like he did every morning, but for some reason today it looked a little different. For some reason looking at the school pleased him today, but he couldn't put his finger on why.

Perhaps it was because the first day of school is different than all the others. The first day had a unique flavor and esthetic all of its own, a feeling not experienced by students or faculty for any of the remaining 181 days of the school calendar year. Maybe it was the lingering sweet, yet somehow hygienic smell of the freshly applied Johnson's wax to the mirror-like miles of linoleum hallways and hardwood gymnasium floors. Or possibly, it was the uniformly decorated bulletin boards that ran along the hallways, neatly trimmed with brightly colored construction paper. Bulletin boards that in the not-to-distant future would show a lot of signs of wear and tear, replete with the student-sponsored graffiti and the curling brown edges of scotch tape that would hold up the hundreds of unread pages of useless information.

It could have been the glass, all that shiny glass, the glistening mirrors, the classroom windows, the doors; all recently squeegeed by the school janitors to a sparkling shine, yet destined to be smeared by the marks of a thousand fingerprints in less than a week. Then again, maybe it was seeing for the first time the gaggle of cautiously optimistic teachers, each one sitting in their classroom, waiting to greet this year's students. Each one hoping against all odds that they would get that one student; one that would challenge their intellect with intelligence and promise and wash away the weariness of battling the other ninety kids day after day just to complete their homework assignments.

But for Casey, more than likely, it was seeing all of the students for the first time in several months: the jocks, sporting their varsity jackets even though it was eighty-five degrees outside, the high-society kids self-consciously sporting their trendy new outfits, praying no one thought their clothes were brand-new and hoping that everyone thought they were cool. Or, last but not least, the remaining seventy percent of the student body, milling about aimlessly, hoping to find a place to fit in.

As Casey joined the throng of frenetic activity that was the first day of school, he could feel the static electricity coming off the other students and wafting into the thick air of the hallways. The scene worked its magic on him. He smiled as he said hello to a group of kids that he hadn't seen all summer, and then he spied Jamie and Esprit standing in front of Esprit's locker just down the hall.

The two of them were whispering in each other's ears, all the while carefully holding their insulated Starbucks cups. He walked over. When Esprit looked up and saw him she handed her cup to Jamie and ran to greet him with a hug and a more than casual kiss.

Casey quickly broke the passionate embrace and said, "Hey, how you feeling this morning?" in a tone that evidenced less concern and more anger.

"Casey, don't start. I told you last night on the phone that I only had a couple of glasses of wine, and that's the truth. After I got off the phone with you I had one more and that's it," she lied. "Jamie and I were home in bed by a little after midnight. So please don't be angry with me…not on the first day of school. By the way, how do I look?" She twirled around in front of him.

Casey had to admit that she did look pretty damn good in her skimpy, pleated, green and red, plaid miniskirt and fuzzy matching brushed cotton top. The outfit exposed her taught stomach as well as the one-carrot diamond stud that graced her belly button. "You look great, Esprit, you really do."

"Now that's better, you ready for your big speech?"

"Yeah, I suppose so. I wrote something up this morning. I mean…it's not like I haven't done this before," he said with a bogus look of ambivalence. "I've got to get to class, but before I forget, my dad's going to the Yankees game tonight, and my mom's going out for a few hours to her yoga class and then coffee with her friends afterwards. It looks like it's going to be a sweet night, so why don't you come over and we can go for a swim. Kevin's probably going to be hanging with me, so bring Jamie along if you want."

She looked over at Jamie, who enthusiastically nodded. "That sounds perfect, Casey. We'll come by around seven. By the way, how're you feeling? Are you still sore?"

Casey frowned. "I'm fine. It wasn't a big deal! Now I've got to get to class. I'll see you at the pep rally."

"Okay, good luck with your speech!"

As Casey walked away, Esprit turned to Jamie. "That went better than I expected. I thought he was really going to bitch me out for drinking last night. God, Jamie, I could kill you! I really feel like crap!"

"Hey, I didn't force you to drink those last three shots of tequila!"

"Yeah, but you did make me drink the first one! Well, at least we didn't have another fight, and I'm sure when he finds out I'm not going to screw my father, he's going to be very happy. Now all I have to do is figure out what to do about my pain-in-the-ass mother and everything will be back to normal, right?"

"That's my girl. Don't worry about your mom. We'll deal with her later, but for now we've got to get to class." They picked up their books and arm in arm, strolled down the corridor to their first class.

Across town, Frankie Giordano had just arrived at the gym, and he was in his office listening to his phone messages. He was already in a foul mood because he'd not been able to figure out what happened to the steroids he discovered missing yesterday, but when he heard Coach Callahan's message, his ill mood darkened considerably. Frankie shut off the machine and put two and two together. Even though Callahan's message was somewhat vague as to the specific problem, it became all too clear to him.

This was about the steroids; it had to be! Damn it! It had been Casey! It must have been. That would explain why he'd been all fucked up this week! He stole the cycle, and he'd been loading up all week. Christ, he was going to really fuck himself up! *I fucking don't believe this, Casey, of all people!* he thought.

The last person Frankie wanted to talk to was his former coach. He loved Callahan like a father, but he was frantic that this whole thing was about to blow up in his face. He thought about it for a couple of minutes and concluded that he didn't have a choice. If he didn't deal with this quickly and quietly, he could lose everything – his clients, his gym, and his livelihood. Not to mention the possible legal problems that could come his way. He picked up the phone and reluctantly dialed the coach's number.

Coach Callahan picked up the phone in his office on the second ring. "Coach Callahan."

"Hey, Coach, Frank Giordano returning your call."

"Hold on a minute," said the coach. He turned to the two students sitting across from him in his office and said, "Could you boys excuse me for about ten minutes? I need to take this call." After the boys left Coach Callahan closed and locked his office door and before coming back to the phone.

"Frankie, thanks for getting back to me. Let me get right to the point. You and I have got a major fucking problem on our hands, and if we don't deal straight up with each other right now, the shit is going to hit the fan. Do you hear what I'm saying?"

"Yes, Coach," was all that Frankie could muster.

Callahan didn't beat around the bush. "Casey has been doing steroids for quite a while, and you and I both know it, so don't even try to deny it. I know damn well that he is getting them from you! I've suspected it for a long time, but I've turned a blind eye to it because, like you, I think Casey's a once in a lifetime athlete, and I want to see him go all the way. I also kind of figured that if he was getting them from you, that you'd be responsible enough to regulate him. But, Frankie, the kid is spiraling out of control. First it was the violent outbursts at practice from a kid who never loses it! I tried to deal with them quietly, but now he's showing all the signs of overdosing on the stuff. Hell, yesterday he got knocked unconscious at practice!"

"What?"

"Yup, it's true. This is Casey Collins we're talking about here! And Frankie, I'm telling you, he looks bad, real bad! He's pale and sweating all the time, and his motor skills are way off. I got to tell you. I think he's in big trouble. You and I have to take care of this, and fast, or else all three of us are heading for a fall."

Frankie, knowing that a denial was useless at this point and trusting that the coach would do the right thing, decided to deal with him straight up.

"Coach, it's true. Casey's been doing steroids, and yes, he's been getting them from me, but I swear to God, and you've got to believe me, I didn't know he was doing them now! He finished what I thought was his last cycle a week ago, and as you well know; the steroid dosage is minimal near the end of the cycle. As far as I knew, he was fine. He didn't have much left in his system, at least that's what I thought."

"Well, Frankie, you were wrong."

"Coach, no bullshit, I swear it. Our plan was always that he wouldn't do steroids during the season. However, yesterday afternoon I noticed a cycle missing from a locked cabinet in my office, and now it's all starting to make sense. Casey's got free reign around the here. Everyone here knows he's like my little brother for Christ's sake. He must have snuck into my office and stole a cycle on a day that I wasn't around. He knew where I kept my keys, and he knew the exact times when I was going to be gone for a while. It all fits! Jesus, what the fuck has gotten into him?"

"I don't know, Frankie, but I do know this, we are all in

deep shit unless we figure out away to stop this mess from getting any worse. Casey could be in serious danger here."

"No…no way, Coach. He hasn't been doing them that long, and he's a tough kid. As long as he stops the new cycle right away, he should be okay. I promise. He's in great shape. You've got to trust me on this. If we get him to stop, he'll be fine."

"I don't know about that, from the looks of him, he might already have screwed up something inside, but I'll take your word for it. But listen, Frankie, you've got to be the one to confront him and get him to stop. If I even suspect the problem, I'm supposed to report it, so I can't have anything to do with this. This phone call never took place, you got that?"

"Loud and clear, we never had this call."

"Good. So when are you going to talk to him. You need to do it ASAP. Tomorrow's the Red Bank game, and I don't want his head all screwed up from talking to you right before the game. Christ, this is the most important game of his life. Penn State's going to be there. USC is going to be there. Everything is hanging on how he plays tomorrow. You've got to handle him just right so that he doesn't go over the edge."

Frankie thought about his dilemma. "Knowing Casey, he wouldn't risk a shot on the day of a game. He knows the doses early in the cycle are really strong and can come with some nasty side effects. That probably explains all the problems he's been having this week. There is no way he'll do one tomorrow, and if he did one today, it's already in his system, so talking to him now won't change a thing. I think it's best if I wait till Saturday morning when he comes in for his workout. By then the game will be history and the pressure will be off. To me that seems like the best time to talk to him. What do you think?"

Callahan didn't like it. "Damn it! I don't know, Frankie! I don't have a clue what that garbage is really doing to him. I've got to trust that you know what the fuck you're talking about. But hear me and hear me good, if anything happens to Casey, I'm coming looking for you. And one more thing, if I ever hear of you supplying that shit to another one of my players, I will call the fucking police myself!"

"I hear you," said a contrite Frankie. "I'll call you on Saturday to let you know how this all turns out. Good luck with the game tomorrow and don't worry, Casey will be fine."

"Yeah…right!" The coach hung up the phone. Just as he did the phone rang again. He picked it up and gruffly said hello.

"Hi, Coach Callahan. This is Donna from Pete Carroll's office. I hope I didn't catch you at a bad time. I was wondering if you could arrange a brief phone call before your practice today between Pete and your boy, Casey Collins…."

School spirit at Middletown South High School was something of a throwback to an earlier day and age. At a time when most high school student bodies, especially those in affluent communities like Middletown, couldn't give a rat's ass about tradition and school spirit, Middletown South, because of its exceptional history of championship football, was the rare exception. The majority of students not only bought into the hype, they actively participated in school-sponsored events like pep rallies, homecoming weeks, and the like. The school had held an opening day pep rally for the past ten years, and it was always met with unbridled enthusiasm. This year was no exception. At twelve o'clock on the dot, thirteen hundred students and seventy-five faculty members slowly filed out of their classrooms, all heading directly for the bleachers of the adjacent football stadium. By twelve fifteen almost every seat was filled on the home side of the field.

Sitting smack-dab on the fifty-yard line next to a microphone and podium atop a small wagon was the good luck totem for the South football team, a three-foot-tall plaster of Paris replica of an American bald eagle sporting South's blue and white colors. The old eagle had seen better days. The paint was peeling in spots and the entire statue was covered with the built-up residue of the thousands of dirt-covered hands of past football players that had faithfully rubbed on it for luck before every game going back over fifteen years. The eagle icon was never far from the action, sitting on the southeast end of the sidelines at every home game. There had been some talk a few years ago about replacing the old eagle with a newer version, but the team would have none of it. This particular eagle had brought ten State Championships to the Eagle football team over the last sixteen years, so it wasn't going anywhere.

As the crowd stirred in the bleachers, a drum roll began softly in the distance, and it continued to get louder and louder as the marching band mysteriously began to appear in the center of the field, mysterious because they were entering the field from a partially hidden tunnel beneath the stands. As the band continued its rhythmic march into formation at mid-field, they were followed first by the flag and baton twirlers, and then by a screaming gaggle of frenzied cheerleaders who bounced, tumbled, and rolled, all while screaming cheers at the rest of the student body to join them in the fun. The area surrounding the fifty-yard line was slowly turning from grass green to royal blue and white as it filled with rally participants.

The crowd soon caught the fever and began screaming and chanting, "Beat Red Bank," right along with those already on the field. Esprit and Jamie had taken their seats on the fifty-yard line right up in the first row. The spot was saved for Esprit because she was dating the team's captain. While Esprit was getting into the fun, screaming and chanting with the crowd, Jamie was oblivious to it all. She had her head buried in the script of the play they were rehearsing.

The members of the band's percussion section relentlessly pounded their chosen instruments as if their very life depended on it. They elevated the rhythmic beating and thumping to a fever pitch, when suddenly Coach Callahan sprinted onto the field from beneath the stands, his open windbreaker flapping out behind him in the breeze.

He reached the podium and raised his hands. As one, the

band, the twirlers, the cheerleaders, and the rest of the teaming crowd came to an abrupt silence. The jam-packed stadium was so quiet you could hear a mouse fart.

Coach Callahan stepped up to the microphone and cleared his throat. "Ladies, gentleman, Principal Lesko, Vice-Principal Monroe, and faculty, I would like to personally welcome you back to the greatest high school in the State of New Jersey."

The crowd, only seconds before totally silent, erupted again with a deafening roar of approval. After maybe twenty seconds of euphoric applause, the coach once again raised his arms, and once again there was instantaneous silence.

"Ladies and gentleman, it is once again my honor and my privilege to introduce you to one of the finest groups of young men that I have ever coached."

As the coach began his team's introduction, the student body responded like a rising storm. First came a low rumbling, and then with each new word spoken, the rumbling grew louder and louder. "Ranked number six in the nation by *USA TODAY*, ranked number one in the State of New Jersey by both the *Gannet* and the *Newark Star Ledger* Pre-Season polls. Last year's Division 3 defending State Champions, and this year's soon to be Division 3 Repeat Champions, the Middletown South Screaming Eagles, led by this year's offensive and defensive captains, Kevin Hahn and Casey Collins!"

The students began stamping their feet in rhythm to the pounding drums, all the while clapping and screaming with every ounce of energy they could muster. The cacophony of sound reached a crescendo when the whole team, wearing their blue game jersey's and led by Kevin and Casey, came barreling around the east end of the stands and charged out onto the center of the field like a herd of frenzied water buffalo being chased by a pride of hungry lions.

Starting with the two captains, as each boy reached the fifty-yard line, they stroked the head of the legendary eagle, and then in military fashion, they snapped to attention in crisp rows directly behind the podium. Casey and Kevin stood in the center of the team out in front of the first row, yet respectfully a few paces behind their coach. Every member of the team was smiling and beaming with pride as they looked up in the stands at the screaming crowd.

Casey experienced a pang in his stomach when he thought that in just a moment he'd be addressing this wildly enthusiastic crowd. He needed to give an unforgettable speech and wondered if he was up to the task. Coach Callahan allowed the crowd what seemed like forever before once again raising his hands to restore order.

"Students and faculty, as you know, I have been coaching football here for seventeen years. In that time we have won ten State Championships! I've had dozens of player's receive full scholarships to division one colleges; I have even had the good fortune to see three of my players make it to the NFL! But never, in all those years, I repeat, never, have I coached an athlete…" The crowd, anticipating Casey's introduction, exploded into an even higher state of euphoria. "…with more talent, more physical ability, more intelligence, more heart, and more commitment to leadership than the young man that I am about to introduce. I can say without hesitation that this young man is not only the finest athlete I have ever coached, but that he is perhaps the best high school football player in this country today! Ladies and gentlemen, please allow me to introduce our team co-captain and two-time *Parade All-American*, Casey Collins!"

Casey looked up in the stands at Esprit. As the crowd around her stood on their feet and cheered wildly, Esprit openly wept with pride. Casey nervously stepped up to the podium beside Coach Callahan, the noise around him deafening. The coach put his arm around Casey and whispered in his ear, "I'm proud of you, son! When the rally's over, I need you to come directly to my office before practice. There's someone that wants to have a word with you." Then Callahan turned back to the crowd. Listening to Callahan, Casey experienced a brief feeling of apprehension, but then the crowd noise pulled him back in the moment.

He stepped up to the microphone, cleared his throat, and waited patiently for the clapping to die down. As he waited, he thought, *This must be what it's like to run for political office.* The unbridled enthusiasm and adoration of thousands was most definitely an aphrodisiac, and he most certainly liked the feeling. Finally, after several minutes, the crowd noise began to subside and Casey started his speech.

"Thank you, Coach Callahan. And thank you to all our fans and supporters! Kevin Hahn, my co-captain, has asked me to speak on behalf of the team today. I think that I might be the luckiest kid on earth. I am so fortunate that my parents passed on to me their good genes and all the love and support a kid could ever want. I have worked very hard to be a good football player, but I haven't done it alone. I am so blessed to go to school in Middletown, where we have the best coaches and the best high school players in the whole darn state, hell, maybe the country!"

The rest of the team started going crazy listening to Casey's flattering words. "I am not the only good football player on this team, and I am not the only one who is going off to college next year with a scholarship. I am surrounded by the best bunch of players in the world, especially my best friend and our quarterback, Kevin Hahn!"

He turned and winked at Kevin, who was blushing with the unexpected attention. Again the crowd amplified its roar. Casey paused for a minute to savor the moment and then he continued. He raised his arms to calm the crowd. "But the season is just starting, and we have a lot to accomplish! It's great that everyone recognizes the talent on this team, and that we are ranked number one. We earned that right because of what we did last year, but it doesn't mean anything! We have yet to play a single down. We have twelve games to play before we have truly earned anything, and we have a lot of competition this year, starting with Red Bank!"

The crowd roared.

"Red Bank has three of the best players in the shore conference, and nothing would make them happier than to knock the Eagles off our lofty perch. But we are not going to let that happen, are we, boys?"

He turned and raised his fists to his teammates, who were all screaming and high-fiveing one another. Casey turned back to the crowd. "This could be the Eagles' greatest year ever in a long and proud history! The coaches have us ready, but we still need a couple of things before we can win. We need to not buy into the hype about our national ranking, we need to focus on one game at a time and not worry about games down the road. We need to play smart and tough! And most importantly…" Casey paused for effect. "We need all of you to come out and support us at each and every game!" The crowd was instantly on their feet clapping and screaming in response to Casey's challenge.

Suddenly from around the east end zone came the cheerleading squad pulling a wagon with a seven-foot, stuffed effigy of a Buccaneer, the mascot for the Red Bank regional team. They pulled the wagon right up between the crowd and the podium and began chanting, "Here we go Eagles…Here we go!"

The crowd joined in. Casey reached down beside the podium and picked up the unlit torch and lighter that had been left there for him. The captains traditionally lit the bonfire together, but Casey decided he was going to let his best friend Kevin do it alone, so before he lit the torch he called Kevin over. Then he ignited the torch and handed it to Kevin, who walked over and lit the effigy on fire. To the delight of the hysterical crowd it burst into flames and the crowd continued to scream for the time that it took to burn away.

After several minutes of fiery pandemonium, Principal Lesko finally walked back up to the podium and began to calm the crowd. "Let's hear it for Coach Callahan and his Screaming Eagles! I would like to welcome you all back to school, and I look forward to seeing everyone tomorrow morning at eight o'clock sharp, ready to hit the books. Class dismissed!"

As the principal walked away from the podium signaling the event was officially over, not a single student stopped clapping. Only after a while did the crowds stop clapping and begin to slowly exit the stadium.

The football team, in groups of threes and fours, worked their way off the field, heading back to the front entrance of the school so they could retrieve their belongings before heading off to practice. Casey peeled off from his group and turned in the direction of the rear entrance to the locker room. The coach had told him to come to his office right after the rally, and that's what he intended to do.

Casey took a seat outside the office and waited a few of minutes until Coach Callahan returned. When he came up Callahan eyed Casey closely, looking for signs of any lingering effects from yesterday's debacle, but he saw none. Casey looked as strong and as healthy as ever. He wasn't pale or clammy, and his eyes were bright and clear, a very different picture than yesterday. Callahan had agreed with Frankie not to bring up the steroids until after the game on Friday, but he couldn't help worrying about the kid.

"Casey, that was a great speech, I would expect nothing less from you!"

"Thanks, Coach, and thank you for all those nice things you said."

"Casey, I meant every word out there. You are by far the best player I've ever coached, but I'm still a little concerned about yesterday. How are you feeling? And I want the absolute truth! Don't even think about bullshitting me!"

"Coach, I feel great, really! I went to bed early last night, and I don't have any pain at all from yesterday. I'm ready to play, I swear."

"Good! The reason I wanted you to come to my office is because I got a pretty special phone call this morning. Pete

Carroll called personally and asked me to arrange a phone call with you for this afternoon. Now I know you have your heart set on Penn State, and there's still a slight chance that it might happen, but when the head coach of the NCAA National Champion calls to speak with you, you damn well better take the call." He smiled at Casey.

Casey was feeling much better about the idea of playing at USC and he enthusiastically said, "Wow, you're kidding?"

"No, Casey, I'm not. He is expecting my call right now. Are you ready?"

Casey nodded his head as the coach dialed the number. Casey got on the phone and spoke to Coach Carroll for the next ten minutes. They talked about everything from football to possible majors, even about places where Casey could live off campus if he decided to come out to USC. By the time he finished the call, Casey thought Coach Carroll sounded like a hell of a nice guy, and he was feeling even better about playing at USC. He was beaming when he got off the phone.

Coach Callahan smiled just for a moment and then gruffly said, "Okay, superstar, don't let it go to your head! Now get out there and get ready for practice. We've got a game to play tomorrow."

Chapter Sixteen

There's Friends and Then There's Family

Thursday Evening, September 6th

The pep rally and the phone call from Coach Carroll had been just what Casey needed. By the start of practice he was feeling a hundred times better in both body and spirit than he had in several days. Knowing that someone as important to college football as Pete Carroll thought he was a good football player had gone a long way towards making Casey forget his recent problems. He glided through the afternoon practice on a cloud. There wasn't any dwelling on his ailments. Esprit and her problems with her father never crossed his mind. There wasn't even any anger or resentment towards his own father, and most importantly, there was no more angst or anxiety over the apparent loss of his Penn State scholarship. Not today, for a couple of hours on a warm early September afternoon, Casey, running around on the sun-baked turf, was oblivious to all the harsh realities of the outside world.

As the team ran through the final preparations for its big game against Red Bank, Casey blocked everything else out and simply followed his coach's instructions. He led his teammates through all the minute details of their game plan without distraction or interruption. When practice was over, Casey was surprised it had gone by so quickly because he had been having fun.

He and Kevin trotted for the showers without a care in the

world. As they made their way to the locker room Casey said, “Dude, that was a great practice. You were awesome out there. Why don’t you come over and hang with me tonight? My parents are both out of the house. I thought we would order a pizza, take a swim in the pool, and then maybe watch a movie or something.”

“That’s sounds cool. I wouldn’t mind a quiet evening with just the two of us. Count me in.”

“Great, but it’s not gonna to be just the two of us, Esprit’s coming over with Jamie.”

Kevin frowned. “So much for that idea, damn, Casey, every time Jamie gets around me she starts rubbing up against me like she’s a fucking cat or something. She makes me crazy!”

“So what’s the problem with that, dog? She’s a hottie for Christ’s sake. You know, if I didn’t know better, bud, I’d swear you’re gay.” Casey laughed and punched Kevin lightly in the shoulder.

Kevin’s face reddened and he reacted a little harshly. “Hey, asshole, that’s my throwing arm. Knock it off!”

Casey laughed. “Whoa…dude, take it easy. So you coming or what?”

Kevin didn’t answer for a second. “Yah…I’ll be there.”

Esprit’s afternoon was nowhere near as carefree as Casey’s. She’d spent the entire afternoon dreading the inevitable face to face with her parents that was coming later on. Try as she might she couldn’t remember a single word of her conversation with Jamie the night before. She found it disconcerting that she couldn’t remember anything of what her mother said she overheard. As she and Jamie plodded along through their play rehearsal she couldn’t find a way to shake her troubles. She’d already resigned herself to the fact that she’d lost the opportunity to get even with her father, but now how was she going to handle what was bound to be a rather uncomfortable confrontation with her parents tonight?

She was totally distracted by this question as she and her fellow cast members practiced their lines from the opening scene of the second act of William Shakespeare's *The Taming of the Shrew.* There was a flurry of activity going on all around her on the stage, but her thoughts kept drifting, and she was barely going through the motions. About a half-hour into the rehearsal, from somewhere deep in the back of her mind she heard voices; one was definitely Jamie's and the other sounded like it might be her drama coach, but she wasn't quite sure... '*which I could fancy more than any other.*' "Hello! Esprit. Earth to Esprit, it's your line!"

"Esprit, dear, I believe your next line is, '*Minion, thou liest: Is't not Hortensio*'...Esprit, honey, are you still with us?"

The voices shocked Esprit out of her reverie and back to reality, and she looked around the stage until she spied the two people speaking to her, and with complete bewilderment, she said, "Oh...I'm sorry, guys. Is it my line?"

"Esprit, what's the problem? You've been missing your lines all afternoon. Are you all right? Do you need a break?" asked her drama coach.

"No, Miss Healy, I'm fine. I was just daydreaming, that's all. I'm sorry, it won't happen again."

"Okay, if you're sure, but let's all take a ten-minute break anyway. Everyone please be back on stage and in position by two forty-five."

Jamie and Esprit walked away and took a seat in the rear of the auditorium. Jamie looked at her friend with concern. "Esprit, what the hell is the matter with you? You've been missing your cues all afternoon."

"I don't know. I guess I'm still feeling shitty from last night, and I'm totally bummed about having to deal with my parents later. Listening to them yelling and screaming at me is really going to suck."

"Oh brother."

"Jamie, I don't think I can't take this anymore. I really have to get my shit together. I keep screwing up, and I keep feeling like something really bad is about to happen. Have you ever felt like that?"

Jamie cuffed her on the shoulder and said, "Listen to me, you idiot! Stop being so paranoid! Casey's not mad at you, and to hell with your parents. Don't go home until late tonight. Maybe, with a little luck, they'll be in bed when you get home. Stop acting like such a baby for Christ's sake!"

"No, you're wrong. I know my parents. I could tell that my mother was really pissed. You just watch, the two of them will be sitting there in the living room, all holier than thou, waiting for me the minute I get in the door, I know it!"

"So what? What happened to that tough girl yesterday at the salon? The one who said she didn't give a shit about what her parents would do? The one who was going to finally make her father pay for all the crap she's put up with? Where did she go?"

"I…I don't know."

Jamie put her arm around Esprit's shoulder. "Listen, girl, when all else fails, deny, deny…Deny! It's that simple! You said so yourself yesterday, what are they going to do, throw you out of the house? I don't think so!"

Esprit picked her head up. "You know what? You're right, Fuck 'em! Let's just go to Casey's later for pizza and a swim, and if the shit hits the fan when I get home, I'll deal with it."

"That's my girl! Besides, I want to get another shot at that hot body of Kevin's. Damn, he's so cute, even if he is a little shy and a jock." They both laughed as Miss Healy called the cast members back to the stage.

When the rehearsal was over Esprit called home, hoping and praying that her mother was still out of the house so she could just leave a message that she planned on going to Casey's after rehearsal and would be home later. To her enormous relief, the machine picked up after three rings. She hurriedly left the message and then she and Jamie drove back to Jamie's to change into bathing suits before going on to Casey's house.

Back at the Collins' home, Lisa had just showered and was getting dressed in her workout clothes in preparation for going to her favorite yoga class when she heard Casey pull up the driveway. She was feeling a little better. Steve had called around five o'clock and the two of them at least had a nice, if short, conversation.

Steve called to let her know that he'd decided to take the whole day off tomorrow so that they could spend the morning together. That was a good start. Then he went on to tell her that he loved her and that after a whole lot of thinking, he had taken to heart some of the things she'd said. His words had encouraged her, but when next she asked him to explain, he hastily replied that he didn't have time to go into it. He and his partners were getting ready to leave the office for the Red Sox–Yankees game. He apologized and said they would have to wait and talk about it in the morning.

At least he sounded sincere, and he did tell her that he loved her…something he rarely ever did from his phone at work. She took that as a very good sign. Before Steve got off the phone he promised not to overdo it at the game, and that he expected to be home some time around midnight. Lisa took that as another good sign. He usually didn't get home until two or three in the morning when he went to a Yankees game.

She always worried when he went to games. He and his buddies from work always seemed to get a little crazy at those damn baseball games, and the South Bronx could be a very dangerous place. Lisa clearly understood the passions of a sports fan, she was one herself, especially a Yankees fan, but she also knew that passion and beer were sometimes a really bad mix for a sports fanatic like Steve. However, he had promised to take it easy. All in all, he had said the right things, so as she finished dressing she was in a relatively good and peaceful frame of mind. As she came downstairs she heard Casey on the phone in the kitchen, so she went down the hall to say hello and to ask about his day.

"Hey, Casey, I thought I heard you come in. Are you hungry? There's plenty of spaghetti and meatballs left over from last night. I can heat some up for you before I go if you want."

"Oh hey, Mom, no that's okay. I just ordered a couple of pizzas. Kevin and Esprit are coming over for a swim, but thanks anyway." He noticed that she was dressed in her workout clothes. "Mom, you look great! You are really taking good care of yourself. All those yoga and Pilates classes are paying off."

Surprised because Casey was not one to toss out compliments lightly, let alone even notice such things, she replied, "Well thank you, Casey. It's nice of you to notice. I have to get going to my class and then afterwards I'm going out with a couple of the girls for coffee and a bite to eat at the diner. I'll probably be home around eleven."

Casey watched his mother smile, and he looked surprised. "Mom, you really do look great and you seem so happy. Did you and Dad have your talk today?"

"Yes, Casey, we did. And like I told you this morning, everything's fine with your father and me. So like I said before, there's nothing for you to be concerned about. In fact, your father called me a little while ago to tell me that he's taking tomorrow off so that we can spend the whole day together and then go to your game. You know your father is so proud of you; he can't wait to watch you play tomorrow night. By the way, the Kimballs are coming with us to the game.

"That's great! You go ahead and have fun tonight with your girlfriends. I love you." He reached over and gave Lisa a kiss on the cheek.

For the second time in just a few minutes, Lisa was taken aback by Casey's newfound sensitivity. This kind of caring and affectionate behavior was certainly very unlike him, but she was enjoying it. She smiled at him and with a wink said, "I don't want any hanky-panky going on here while I'm out, mister, and that's an order!"

Casey laughed. "On the night before a game, are you kidding? No way!"

"All right then, I guess I'll see you later. I'll have my cell phone on if you need me."

"Bye, Mom, have a nice time."

As Casey watched her leave he had a feeling that maybe, just maybe, things were beginning to rearrange themselves back into the well-ordered state of his universe. His usual sense of expectation and that comfortable feeling that he was in total control; feelings that until recently he had taken for granted, but as of late had gone haywire, seemed to be returning, and it felt wonderful. The chaos and uncertainty of the previous five days were finally beginning to wash away. His mother was happy again and he was feeling healthier than he had all week.

He stood in the hallway savoring the moment because just as important, the two people closest to him in the whole world were on their way over to spend the evening with him, and everything seemed just perfect. He snapped out of his reverie at the sound of the doorbell.

Standing at the front door was Kevin, wearing a grimy *Phish* T-shirt and a pair of sun-bleached, QuickSilver board-shorts. And coming up the walk right behind him were the two girls, both sporting skimpy cropped T-shirts barely covering even skimpier string bikinis.

"Hey, guys, come on in. I just ordered the pizzas."

Casey, after kissing Esprit hello, took the three of them through the house and out to the pool. Jamie had only been to Casey's house once before during the winter, so she'd never seen his backyard or the pool. She looked around in wonder at the sparkling azure pool, the stylishly appointed cabana, replete with its thick Berber carpeting, ridiculously expensive Sony entertainment center, and of course the fully stocked bar. She was stunned by the beauty and decadence of it all. Her eyes wandered around the secluded yard. She saw a veritable oasis; the pristine pool and the meticulous yard surrounded by a dense twelve-foot privet hedge and professionally manicured flowerbeds that were bursting with late-blooming lilies, roses, and African impatiens.

"Oh…my…God! Casey, it is so beautiful back here! It's like having your own Caribbean resort right in the fucking back yard! It's unbelievable and totally private! Club Collins…that's what you should call it!" she said enthusiastically as she dropped her bag on a lounge chair, tore off her shirt, and leaped into the pool, making a huge splash.

Casey laughed at her enthusiasm. He sometimes took his surroundings for granted and was a little surprised by her behavior. When Jamie swam up from the bottom and burst through the water in the deep end of the pool, she yelled, "Man, Casey, this sure ain't nothing like my neighborhood."

He laughed and called back to her, "I'm glad you like my house, Jamie, but please…please don't be shy. You just go and make yourself right at home!" The three of them not in the pool broke into laughter as they watched Jamie, who at the moment looked more like a slippery seal at an aquarium than a pretty teenage girl swimming in a pool. Totally carefree and unselfconscious, Jamie dove back and forth around the pool in utter delight.

Kevin turned to Casey. "Hey, Casey, I ended up winning ninety bucks last night and a good amount of it was yours, so at least let me pay for the pizza."

Casey smiled. "That, my friend, is not a problem. I would be more than happy to let you buy since you kicked my ass, not once but twice yesterday, first on the football field and then at the poker game.

While the boys were talking, Esprit followed Jamie into the pool. The boys began to watch with lustful pleasure as the girls wrestled and frolicked with each other like little schoolgirls on a playground. Casey glanced at Kevin and said, "What are we, idiots? What are we doing standing here ogling when we could be right in there with them?"

He tore off his shirt, revealing his finely sculpted chest, and dove into the pool. Kevin, though not on Casey's genetic level, was a physical specimen in his own right. Where Casey looked like a professional bodybuilder, Kevin had more of a swimmer's physique, but his build was impressive just the same. He followed Casey in, his Phish T-shirt and sandals carelessly cast away on a chair. He trotted around the pool to the diving board and then perfectly executed a forward one and a half summersault into the deep end of the pool. He landed with a big splash almost on top of the girls and scared the crap out of them. When he finally broke the surface both girls began splashing him mercilessly until he swam away to the shallow end of the pool, where Casey was just floating around, watching the fun.

Casey paddled over to Kevin and conspiratorially whispered in his ear, "What do you say to a round of chicken fights? You take Jamie and I'll take Esprit. Jamie looks like she's a lot stronger than Esprit, so that should balance it out. I'll bet you double or nothing on the money I lost last night that they will both be out of their tops in less than five minutes."

Kevin, who up till this point seemed to be having a pretty good time, frowned. "Dude, I don't know. I don't want to give Jamie any ideas. In five minutes she'll be crawling all over me just like she did on the ski trip last winter."

"Kevin, you're scaring me, dude! You don't have a girlfriend and there's a hottie at the other end of the pool who in five minutes will have her top off, and you're worried because she's hot for your ass. What the hell is wrong with you?"

Kevin pouted a little. "Nothing, she's just not my type." Then he smiled a little. "Oh, fuck it, let's do this!" and the two boys raced to the deep end, where the girls were still playing. Kevin, because of his years of surfing, was the much more skilled swimmer, and he arrived there first with Casey furiously beating the water right behind him.

As they treaded water, Casey said, "Since you girls are so frisky tonight, what do you say to a round of chicken fights, best out of three falls? It will be me and Esprit against you and Kevin. Come on, what do you say?"

The girls looked at each other and started giggling. Esprit said, "Casey, she's a lot stronger than me, but hey, why not?"

"Great!"

They all swam to the shallow end of the pool. The sun was just setting over the top of the hedges and the shallow end was beginning to fall into shadow. Casey went under the water first and swam up between Esprit's legs. He grabbed her high on her thighs and hoisted her out of the water with little effort. As he stood waiting, and while Esprit adjusted the straps to her top, Kevin swam beneath the water and positioned himself behind Jamie. She flirtatiously wiggled her ass at him as his head passed through her legs, and then he too hoisted her up onto his shoulders. Like Casey, he grabbed the front of her thighs and effortlessly lifted her out of the water.

The two couples then squared off and began to circle around one another in the shallow end of the pool. Esprit was taking this whole thing very seriously, aggressively positioning her arms in an outstretched attack position while she listened intently to Casey's battle instructions. Jamie on the other hand, was having way too much fun teasing Kevin. She squirmed around on his shoulders, tickling him under his arms and shielding his eyes so that he couldn't see the direction of the enemy. Kevin soon became frustrated with her antics. He had money riding on this, and he wanted her to stop fooling around.

"Come on, Jamie, knock it off, I got money riding on you!"

She laughed and said, "Okay, big boy, take it easy. I'm going to kick her butt, and then afterwards we will see who's riding who!" Jamie laughed, then she attacked.

The girls flailed around and grabbed for each others arms as the boys kicked and bumped into each other, hoping to assist in the opposing girl's fall. Jamie, with her longer arms, reached around the back of Esprit's neck and yanked with all her might. Esprit began to wobble and Casey had to use all of his strength just to keep her upright. But in the end she was just too wet and slippery, and she fell from his shoulders with a dramatic splash into the pool for the first fall of the event.

Casey frowned as he helped her up and put her back onto his shoulders. At that same moment on the other side of the pool, the excited and victorious Jamie grabbed the top of Kevin's head and pulled it back to kiss him, but she could only reach the top of his face with her lips, so she kissed him on the forehead. Then she whispered, "If we win the next one, there are more of those to come!" Kevin brushed off her comment. He was only focused on one thing, winning.

Once again the couples began to circle around one another. Casey, not one to suffer losing at anything, shouted words of encouragement to his partner as they cautiously circled for the second round. This time Casey was determined to win at any cost, so he went directly at the other couple and released one of Esprit's legs so that he could grab hold of one of Jamie's. He hastily latched onto her thigh with his vice-like grip while she battled above with Esprit, and with all his might he shoved her backwards from Kevin's struggling but overmatched shoulders.

As Jamie tumbled into the water she screamed, "Hey, no-fair, Casey! That was cheating!"

"Bullshit," laughed Casey. "All's fair in love and chicken fights!"

He patted Esprit on the thighs. Jamie swam around for a minute then made her way back over to Kevin and whispered again in his ear as she climbed back up on his shoulders. "Watch this, Kev. That bitch is about to lose her top!" Kevin got her up and settled, and then the two couples squared off for the third time.

This time Kevin winked at Casey. Casey wasn't sure what he meant, but they converged on each other anyway. The grabbing and pulling became vicious between the two girls. As Jamie began to get the upper hand both boys just stood there, as still as possible, smiling at each other. They were allowing the girls to battle it out on their own, hoping for the much desired and much anticipated end result.

Jamie managed to turn Esprit with a little devious assistance from Casey, and as she did so she grabbed for the tie at the back of Esprit's bikini top. She leaned in and pulled furiously, but when she did, Esprit reached over with her own free hand and worked the same strategy. After what seemed like an eternity, but in reality was only about twenty seconds, both girls had succeeded in loosening the other's top, but by then they had both tilted so far forward that the boys could no longer support them. At virtually the exact same moment, the boys had no choice but to release their partner's legs, and the girls toppled forward, falling into the pool and clutching the other's ripped-off bikini top.

Jamie broke the water first. She jumped high in the air, her small, bare breasts glistening with moisture, her taught nipples saluting the chill in the air. She smiled, triumphantly holding Esprit's top. Within a second Esprit followed, her fist also raised high, clutching Jamie's top and claiming victory. Her more voluptuous breasts were quivering as rivulets of water cascaded down between them. The boys just stood there, frozen in amazement as the girls shouted words of victory and unselfconsciously pranced around the shallow end of the pool like carnival ponies.

After a short period of celebration, Esprit made her way over to Casey with a smirk on her face and a provocative look in her eye. She kissed him hungrily. He responded to her uninhibited display of affection by wrapping his arms around her.

Jamie watched the erotic entanglement for a moment and then made her way back over to Kevin. This was the moment she'd been waiting for. It was time to make her move. Slowly and seductively she walked up to him. Shamelessly she stood before him, her breasts rising and falling only inches from his, her nipples leaping forth with desire. She looked directly into his eyes, waiting for him to touch her, but Kevin just stood there mesmerized, not knowing what to do next.

The pause became awkward so Jamie seized the moment. She assertively reached up for his face and began to kiss him softly on the mouth, first gently, but soon with a greater force and urgency. As she opened her mouth to his and probed his lips with her tongue, he reluctantly responded and she, without her lips ever leaving his, began to grin.

Slowly she dropped one hand from around his neck and feverishly began exploring the water below his waist as if searching for buried treasure. Kevin's eyes were still closed, and he didn't realize what she was up to until her hand had found its mark. She reached inside his suit and gently caressed him. He was startled by her touch. Just as he was about to pull away from her the doorbell chimed at the front door. All four of them jumped at the sound, and as quickly as it had started, the erotic moment was lost.

"Holy shit, I totally forgot about the pizza!" exclaimed Casey as he jumped out of the pool.

Kevin broke from Jamie's embrace and said, "Hold on a minute, Casey, I'm paying, remember." Then he too jumped out of the pool to fetch his wallet.

Jamie, frowning, unable to hide her disappointment, looked dejectedly over at Esprit. For Jamie, Kevin was a huge mystery. On the one hand he was the star quarterback of the football team, a position that symbolized everything she found distasteful about high school, but on the other hand, he was a kind and gentle, free-spirited boy who was obviously sensitive and shy. And on top of everything else he was good-looking as hell with his messy sun-bleached locks, golden tan, and crystal blue eyes.

Esprit patted her friend on the shoulder. "Don't be disappointed. It's a start."

"Yeah…whatever," Jamie replied as they both put back on their bathing suit tops and watched the boys go off through the house to fetch the pizza.

The girls climbed out of the pool and grabbed a couple of

the fluffy cotton beach towels out of the cabana. As they were drying themselves the boys came back outside with the pizzas.

Casey set them out on the table along with some paper plates and napkins. "I got one pepperoni and one ham and pineapple. If you guys want something to drink, there's all kinds of stuff in the fridge in the cabana. Take whatever you like. Esprit, could you grab me a bottle of Evian?"

Esprit and Jamie walked into the cabana and over to the fridge. Jamie opened the door and was amazed to see it stocked with several different types of beer and a half-dozen bottles of wine. She called out to Kevin, "Hey, Kev, you want a beer?"

"No thanks, I'll have an Evian too please."

"Suit yourself, Boy Scout," she chided and grabbed a bottle of Evian for him and a Corona for herself.

As Jamie opened the bottle of beer on the opener on the side of the fridge, Esprit stared at her friend in disbelief, then crossed her arms, frowned and said, "Hey, girl, what happened to the two of us going on the wagon for a couple of weeks? It's only been a few hours, and you're already breaking your promise."

"Oh Christ, Esprit, you're not going to hold me to that, are you? I just said that to make you feel better. You really didn't believe I was going to go through with it, did you?"

Esprit laughed. "Jamie, not only did I not expect you to go through with it, I would have bet a thousand dollars that you wouldn't last two days trying, especially with all the parties tomorrow night after the game." She laughed once more. "You're still planning on coming with me to Kim's party, aren't you?"

Jamie, sulking, replied, "I don't know…maybe. It depends on whether the choirboy over there decides to kiss me again tonight or not."

Esprit looked at her friend. "Why don't you try not being so pushy for a change? He's very shy!"

"Great, now I have Marge Simpson giving me advice on how to hook up with a guy! Get the hell out of here!" She jokingly punched Esprit in the arm. "Don't worry about me. Let's go get some pizza before those two pigs finish it all. And by the way, is your boyfriend nuts or what? Who the hell eats pineapple and ham on pizza?" They laughed and left the cabana, joining the boys at the table.

Casey, sounding barely intelligible because he was trying to speak while simultaneously shoving a whole slice of pizza into his mouth, said thanks when Esprit handed him the bottle of water and then followed up with, "Kevin, that was a blast. That was the most fun I've had in a long time."

Esprit arched her eyebrows and glared in the direction of her boyfriend. Casey caught the look and immediately attempted to rectify his transgression. "I…I meant the most fun just hanging out, Esprit. I'm not talking about when I'm alone with you!"

His halfhearted words didn't seem to rectify his faux pas, so a grinning Jamie took the opportunity to stick it to him a little further. "Casey, would you maybe like to trade that slice of pizza for my shoe to stick in your big fat mouth?"

Casey looked at the girls with pleading eyes. "Aw come on, you both know what I meant!" Then he sheepishly lowered his head as both girls laughed at his obvious discomfort.

After a minute or so he couldn't take their laughing anymore, so he looked at Jamie and said, "Oh, by the way, Jamie, you've got a pretty decent rack for a dyke with a drug habit." Kevin joined in on the laughter.

Casey's crude remark caused Esprit to turn and swat him with her towel. "Don't you start acting like a pig. We're having a nice night, don't spoil it!"

"Okay…okay. Hey, I didn't get a chance to ask you this morning. What's the deal with your father? What've you decided to do about the TV interview?"

Esprit was slow to reply. "I've decided not to do anything, Casey. I'm just not going to do any interview, that's it. If he doesn't like it, well, that's too damn bad!"

Casey was astonished by her decision. "Wow, Esprit. Why

did you change your mind? You seemed so determined for revenge yesterday. I have to tell you that even though I think you're doing the right thing, I'm shocked that you're backing down on this. What's the deal?"

Esprit looked over at Jamie, wondering what she should tell him. She didn't want him to know how drunk she got last night, or that she was in big trouble with her parents so she just said, "I just decided that it wasn't worth it. It's no big deal, really. Can we change the subject please?"

Kevin, ever the peacemaker, picked up on her discomfort and attempted to redirect the conversation. "So, Jamie, are you going to Kim and Joey's party tomorrow night after the game? You know they throw the best parties."

There was usually at least one big party every weekend during the school year, especially during the football season. This week the party was being thrown by Kim DeFazio, one of the cheerleaders. Kim's parents were avid golfers, and they owned a condo down in Myrtle Beach. They flew down there for a round of golf almost every weekend in the fall and in the spring, leaving Kim and her older brother Joey at home by themselves. Kim and Joey's parties were legendary. There was always plenty of beer, good music, and usually a pretty well behaved crowd.

"I don't know, Kevin, are you asking me out on a date?" said Jamie in a mischievous and playful tone.

Kevin swallowed a couple of times. "Uh…sure…why not?"

Jamie snuggled up closer to him at the table, making him feel even more uncomfortable.

Meanwhile, Casey wasn't finished with Esprit. "Come on, Spree, tell me, why did you change your mind?"

Not wanting to discuss this any further, Esprit testily replied, "I took your advice okay? Now could you please give it a rest?"

"Okay…Okay…I'm just curious, that's all. One moment you want to kill your father, and the next you're letting everything go. I'm just surprised. Don't get mad." Then he reached over, picked up another slice and began to inhale his fourth piece.

Over the next hour the four of them finished most of the pizza and the talk turned to school: classes, teachers, gossip, and of course to the big game the following day.

When they began to clean up the table Jamie impishly looked across the table at Casey. She poked him in the side and said, "Casey, that was some speech today at the pep rally. When you're done with football maybe you should become a motivational speaker…you know…like that guy on the TV infomercials with the big teeth… what's his name…Robbins…yeah, Tony Robbins!"

Kevin and Esprit fell to the ground laughing. Casey ran around the other side of the table, picked Jamie up over his head like a rag doll and walked her over to the deep end of the pool. He effortlessly tossed her in even though she fought him with all her might. Casey stood there triumphantly at the edge of the pool watching for her to come up to the surface with his hands on his hips, when suddenly Kevin snuck up behind him and pushed him into the pool as well. Both Kevin and Esprit quickly followed and they all began to swim around, splashing and dunking each other. However, the sexual tension from before was long gone so after about a half-hour or so they called it quits and they left the pool to dry off.

After she finished toweling off, Esprit tiptoed up to Casey and said quietly, "It's still pretty early, why don't I send Jamie home with Kevin so you and I can snuggle for a while? I really don't feel like going home yet."

Kevin was standing near enough to overhear her and silently pleaded with his eyes for Casey to say no. But his plea wasn't necessary. Casey was a firm believer in the old adage that athletes should never have sex the night before a big game. So even though he was horny as hell he said, "Not tonight, Spree, let's save it for tomorrow okay?"

Esprit was a little dejected but not surprised, so she decided not to press the issue. "Okay, then I guess we're going to hit the road. God…I dread going home tonight."

She turned to her friend. "Jamie, why don't we stop at Starbucks on the way for a couple of cappuccinos?"

The always-agreeable Jamie replied, "Sounds like a plan." The two of them gathered up their things.

The boys walked them out to Esprit's car. Casey gave Esprit a long and passionate kiss. Again there was another awkward moment between Kevin and Jamie, and once again Jamie took the lead. She reached over to Kevin and put her arms on his waist. "I had a lot of fun tonight. I really did, but Kevin, you don't have to be so shy. I like you okay? And I'm really looking forward to being with you tomorrow night." Then she winked.

Kevin fumbled for something to say, but Jamie didn't give him a chance. She just kissed him quickly on the mouth and stepped into the car, leaving Kevin standing there speechless and bewildered.

The girls drove away and the boys walked back in the house. Casey flipped on the TV to catch the score of the Yankees game. The Yankees were losing to the Red Sox by the score of nine to zero, and the game was already in the eighth inning.

"Holy Shit! The Yankees are getting crushed! Dude, my dad's at the game. He wanted me to go with him, but I took a pass because of our game tomorrow. I guess I didn't miss much. Oh well." And he turned off the television.

Casey turned to Kevin with a serious look on his face. "Kev, I've got to ask you a question. What is the deal with you and Jamie? Do you like her or what, buddy? Christ, the girl is falling all over you and you're acting like she's got syphilis or something. What's wrong with you, dog?"

"I don't know. She's just not my type. She's way too aggressive, and she makes me feel weird."

"Too aggressive? Jesus, dude, I know a hundred guys that would kill to be with her! I know she's a bit weird, and she parties too much, but Kev, she's a hottie! You don't have to marry her for Christ's sake."

Kevin, unwilling to look Casey in the eye, mumbled, "I don't know…she's just not my type…."

"Whatever, dude. Listen, I think I'm going to crash on the couch and catch a movie. I'm not tired yet. You're welcome to hang with me if you want."

Kevin, looking relieved that the subject had changed, said, "No, not tonight, I'm a little tired. I think I'm going to head home and get a good night's sleep."

"That's cool." He walked Kevin back towards the front door.

Just as they were about to open it; in walked Lisa with a smile. "Hey, guys, did you have a nice night?"

"Hi, Mrs. C, sure did. Are you coming to the game tomorrow?" said Kevin.

Lisa laughed. "Kevin, when have I ever missed one of your games? Casey's father and I will be there rooting the two you on. Casey tells me there's going to be some scouts there watching you too. I hope you play your best game ever!" She rubbed her hand through his messy hair.

"Thanks, Mrs. C. Casey, I'm gonna run. I'll catch up with you in the a.m."

"Later, dude!" and Casey closed the door.

Lisa said to her son. "Well, I guess you guys had an early night. What time did the girls leave?"

"Just a few minutes ago, how was your night?"

"It was great, but I'm tired after that yoga class. The instructor worked us like dogs tonight. I think I'm going to take a shower and go to bed. Your father is going to be home pretty late because of the Yankees game."

"Don't count on it; the game's already in the eighth inning, and the Yankees are getting shelled. Knowing Dad, he's probably already in the limo and on his way home."

"Oh, you're probably right. That's too bad about the Yankees, but at least now your dad will be able to get up early tomorrow. Are you coming up?"

"No, I'm still wide awake. I think I'm going to watch *Remember the Titans* again. I love that movie."

"Okay, honey, but don't stay up to late. Remember you've got a big game tomorrow."

"Yes, Mom."

He kissed her before she headed up the stairs, and then he walked back to the big comfortable couch in the family room. He took out his favorite DVD, put it in the player and then settled down to watch his all-time favorite sports movie. He'd probably watched it a hundred times. He thought for sure Denzel Washington should have earned the academy award for his gritty portrayal of the racially challenged 1960s high school football coach.

Esprit attempted to drag out the night as long as she could. After leaving Casey's she and Jamie went to Starbucks, and they sipped a couple of cappuccinos for well over an hour, gossiping about the evening and making plans for tomorrow. They also spent a good part of the hour talking about Kevin.

"You know what I think? I think Kevin is just a really shy kid, and you're scaring him off with your aggressive personality. I honestly think he's afraid of you!"

"Come on, give me a break. You're making it sound like I tore off my clothes and jumped on him the minute we got to Casey's. I don't think I was that aggressive, I mean, he knows I like him. What was I supposed to do? Stand there next to him in the pool twiddling my thumbs while you and Casey were going at it all hot and heavy?"

"No, of course not, but maybe you could have at least allowed him to make the first move. I saw what you did. I saw you going right after his junk as soon as he started to kiss you…."

"What? Are you out of your mind? First of all you didn't see shit because you were too busy trying not to choke because

Casey's tongue was jammed so far down your throat it tickled your tummy." She laughed and continued, "Besides, I couldn't help myself. That boy is delicious. Once I got started I got a little crazy, is all."

Esprit again tried to make her point. "I'm just saying that maybe you need to cool it a little bit. I've known Kevin pretty well for a couple of years, and I can't even remember him ever having a steady girlfriend. Hell, Jamie, he might still be a virgin for all we know."

Jamie slapped her hand on the table. "See, now that's what I'm thinking. Here's this great-looking surfer dude, right? And there are probably at least a hundred girls in our school alone that would kill to have him jump their bones, but neither you nor I have ever heard one single story about him. This whole thing just doesn't add up. When I first kissed him tonight in the pool, he was like all nervous and shaking and shit, but then after a couple of seconds he seemed like he was starting to get into it. So I figured what the hell, and I reached down into his bathing suit to find out what he was really about. Well, I got to tell you, Spree, he was most definitely happy to see me, if you know what I mean!" Both girls started laughing.

"But then that damn doorbell started ringing and it was over, just like that. He pulled away from me so fast you would have thought I had VD or something. I just don't get it. Maybe he's gay! You know I have heard that rumor before."

Esprit looked shocked. "Don't even think that Jamie! Are you crazy? There is no way that Kevin is gay…."

"Oh yah, you ever see the way he looks at your big hunky boyfriend when he thinks no one's watching?" Jamie started laughing again.

Esprit started to get angry. "Jamie, that's bullshit and you know it. God, sometimes I can't believe the stuff that comes out of your mouth. Why don't you try just being nice to him tomorrow and see what happens? Get him alone off in a corner somewhere and just be nice to him. Let him make the first move, and then see how it goes from there."

"Spree, that's just not my style, but I will tell you this. One way or another, tomorrow night I am going to hook up with him, and then we will know the truth. Anyhow I'm starting to feel a little ragged. I think I'm ready to go home. But listen, if you don't want to deal with your folks tonight, just crash at my house. You can wear some of my clothes to school tomorrow."

"Thanks, but if I don't face them tonight, the whole thing will still be hanging over my head tomorrow. I might as well just get it over with."

"Suit yourself."

They left the coffee shop and Esprit reluctantly drove Jamie home. A few minutes later as she drove through the gates and turned up her long gravel driveway she looked at her watch, which read eleven fifteen. She prayed that her parents had already gone to bed.

Esprit turned off the car and tiptoed into the house through the giant front doors, trying desperately not to make a sound. She jumped a little as she opened the doors because the old hinges creaked from lack of oil. She crept into the foyer and looked around. There was only one small table lamp lit in the living room, and she didn't hear a sound so she began to quietly make her way up the stairs, but as soon she reached the second step, she heard a soft voice coming from the general direction of the living room.

"Esprit, darling, could you come in here and talk with me for a minute? It's Daddy."

She slowly turned around and spied her father sitting on a club chair at the far side of the room. Her eyes adjusted to the dark, and she could see that he was just sitting there, still wearing his pinstripe suit and regent tie. His legs were elegantly crossed, exposing his black silk stockings and highly polished cordovan brogues. She trembled a bit when she looked at him because the low light coming from the small table lamp was casting an ominous shadow across his face. At that moment he looked less like her father and more like some kind of eerie undertaker.

She gathered up her courage. "Oh, Daddy, you startled me! I'm tired and I have to get up for school in the morning. Do you think we could wait and have this little talk tomorrow?"

Ethan spoke in a soft, yet somehow very forceful tone. "No, Spree, I don't believe this conversation can wait till tomorrow. In fact, I flew home from Washington this evening just so you and I could talk. Your mother has already gone to bed, so she will not be disturbing us. Please, Esprit, come in here and take a seat." He patted the chair next to his. "I think it's time that you and I cleared the air once and for all, don't you?"

Esprit, sensing the seriousness of his tone, obediently entered the room and sat opposite him in the other club chair. When she looked at him, she had difficulty reading his face. She expected anger, but what she saw was more distressing. Instead of the predictable fury she saw in his drawn face, there was abject sadness. The normally stoic and outwardly collected Ethan Burke looked utterly depressed and defeated. Esprit was confused. *What the hell is going on here?*

Ethan waited almost ten seconds, adding even more tension, before he began to speak, and when he did, it was in a voice that wasn't much more than a soft whisper. "Esprit, I really need you to listen to me for a few minutes without any interruption or argument. You are my only child, and this conversation is of vital importance to me, so please promise that you will do as I request."

Esprit's head was spinning. This whole scene was so surreal and so out of character for her father that she simply replied, "Yes, father."

"Your mother told me about the conversation she overheard last night between you and your friend when you came home drunk again. She was really quite upset by it. She seems to think that you are planning to take some kind of revenge against me on a TV interview. Now when she told me this morning I had no idea what could have possibly been said between you and your friend that would have prompted your mother to think such a thing. But then I began to really think about it. I know that I didn't speak to you yesterday, nor did I ask you to do any television for my campaign at our lunch the other day. I also know your mother didn't speak to you about any of this either, so at first, I couldn't figure out what you were up to."

"Daddy, I can explain...."

"No, Esprit, not yet, please let me continue. When I left on Tuesday, everything seemed to be so good between us. So for me this whole thing just didn't make sense. At first I was very confused, and I must say more than a little hurt. But the more I thought about it, the more I was able to put some of the pieces together. I started thinking about our day together on Tuesday, and I recalled that when I took you to lunch you seemed very distracted through most of it...that is, until we began to talk about my campaign. Then suddenly you were focused and so inquisitive. I remember you insisted on knowing what, if anything, I wanted you to do to help fix the problems within my campaign because of what happened at the fundraiser. Then I remembered thinking that you seemed incredibly surprised when I told you that I couldn't think of anything." Ethan paused as he remembered exactly what happened. "But then...then when I said if something came up, I'd let you know, right then something changed in you. At that point your facial expression changed as if you were thinking; '*okay, there it is. I know he's planning something. He just isn't sure what it is yet',* but at the time I let it go. I was too busy trying to impress you with my stupid club. Obviously that didn't work, did it?"

"No, it didn't."

"Anyway, this morning, about an hour after I got off the phone with your mother, I began to organize my papers for a meeting with Blaine, and suddenly it all became clear. I came across a certain fax that I received on Tuesday at home, the morning of our lunch. It is the only thing that makes any sense of all this. Esprit, did you read that fax?"

Stunned by his question, Esprit managed only a soft, "Yes."

"I thought so. Esprit, honey, now you really need to listen to me. I beg you. On Monday morning after the party, when I found you in your room so upset, it was true that I already knew your stunt at the party hadn't really hurt my campaign. In fact, Blaine had already called to assure me that the photos not only weren't going to hurt my election, but in fact they were probably going to give it a small boost. And yes, Esprit, I was pleased about that, but when I came to your room and found you so devastated by what you'd done..." Ethan choked up a little. "Well...seeing you laying there like that nearly broke my heart."

Esprit's skin was getting warm because she sensed an emotional outburst was probably going to follow. Here was her father, expressing what seemed to be truly honest feelings for possibly the first time in her life.

"Esprit, I know that I have been a horrible father to you. I have never been involved in your life, and I have never taken the time to get to know who you really are. I have always tried to mold you into the person that I wanted you to be, and only God knows how much I regret that now. I know how much you resent that your mother and I have paraded you around like some kind of trophy since you were six years old. I can't tell you how much it hurts when I see you look at me with such hatred in your eyes. You are my only child, and when you hugged me the other day and said that you loved me something inside me woke up. Esprit, I loved that feeling, and I don't ever want to not feel it again. Everything in my life now, my campaign, our wealth, it all seems pale by comparison...Esprit...it's all meaningless if I believe that you still hate me."

Esprit did not want to believe a word, but her emotional walls were beginning to crumble. In a jumble of confused anger and hope, she burst out, "But, Dad, what about that goddamn memo? How the hell do you explain that? You were going to put me in front of millions of people and force me to humiliate myself just so you could get more votes."

"Esprit, that's just not true. Please let me explain. It is Blaine's job to get me re-elected. It is why I pay him a great deal of money. That fax was just a list of his possible ideas to exploit the opportunity that presented itself with the publishing of those photographs. Honey, Blaine was just doing his job. The truth is that your mother and I did discuss the possibility of doing a TV interview. We weighed the pros and cons of going on TV with you, and I decided against it right at the outset."

Esprit wanted desperately to believe him, but she struggled. "I don't believe you! You only changed your mind about the interview because Mom figured out what I was going to do! You're lying to me again…I know it!" She started to sob.

Ethan tried to reach out and hug her, but he realized she wasn't ready. "Esprit, I swear to you I decided well before I knew anything about your intended plans, you must believe me!"

"It's true, Esprit," came a soft feminine voice from the stairs as Jordan entered the living room in her pajamas and dressing gown.

"I'm sorry to say it, but it was me who pushed your father to do the interview. He didn't want anything to do with it from the very beginning. I thought doing a family interview would not only help his election, but that it might also help you to recognize that lately you have been treading down a dangerous path with all of your drinking and partying. Honey, I'm so sorry. It was a bad idea, and I should have never supported it."

She came to Esprit and put her arms around her. Esprit cried uncontrollably.

"Honey, your father and I had a long talk this evening…a talk about you. And we both agreed that we have done an awful job raising you, but despite our selfish behavior and our best efforts to screw you up, you have become an amazing young woman."

Ethan moved closer, and he too put his arms around his daughter. "Esprit, please find it in your heart to forgive us. We know that we have been selfish and neglectful with you, but we have always loved you, and we honestly never meant to hurt you."

"Esprit, your father and I promise that from this day forward, nothing will get in the way of the two of us being there for you. Not your father's career, not our social lives, not anything. Whenever you need us, we will be right there. If only you are willing to forgive us for the past and let us prove to you that we are sincere."

Esprit's thoughts were spinning around like a carnival merry-go-round. She wanted desperately to believe what they were saying, but the past kept rearing its ugly head, making her even more confused and disoriented.

She burst out, "I love you both! Please…please…don't be lying to me now. It would kill me! There have been so many lies. And, Daddy, I want you to know that I wasn't snooping around in your office when I found the memo, I swear it! I was just looking for you because I was so happy that you were really taking me to lunch. I went into your office to find you, and I would have left, but then I heard you and Mom through the open window coming up from the boat so I went over to look. And that's when I saw the fax coming through with my name on it – please believe me!"

Ethan looked sadly at his wife. "Of course we believe you. It all makes sense. No wonder you were so distant at lunch, you probably wanted to kill me right then and there!"

"Honey, can you ever forgive us? Is it possible for the three of us to start over and really become a family again? Please say yes, Esprit, your father and I need to hear it."

Esprit wiped the tears from her eyes and looked up at the hopeful faces of her parents and simply said, "Yes."

The joy and relief was instantaneous. Ethan smiled, first at his wife and then at his daughter. He stood up and said, "Thank the lord! You have made us so happy, Esprit!" He hugged his daughter again, and as he looked at her he saw she was exhausted. "Well, this has been a most trying and emotional day, but all to a wonderful end. Why don't the three of us go up and get a good night's sleep? I think we could all use it."

Esprit nodded. The three of them got up and walked up the grand staircase and down the second story hall until they reached Esprit's bedroom door. There Esprit turned and faced her parents, and with as big smile she said, "I love you both very much, good night."

It was almost eleven thirty and *Remember the Titans* was just about over. Casey had been struggling to keep his eyes open when suddenly he heard the screech of tires and a small crash, followed by a string of muttered expletives coming from outside in the driveway. He leaped up from the couch and looked out the window, where he spied his father staggering up the walkway towards the front door. With a frown, Casey walked to the door to open it.

When Casey opened the door his father stumbled through, reeking of beer and looking like death warmed over. Steve's shirt was covered with yellowish stains, and his suit jacket was wrinkled and covered in crumbs of food. His eyes were bloodshot and glazed over. Casey had never seen his father look worse. He disgustedly stood aside and watched his father stumble through the door into the family room.

Steve began to ramble and his words slurred together from the alcohol. "CCasey…those GGod-damn Yankees…can't hit for shit…. That…wass…the…wwworst…fucking…game…I ever…and…oh ssshit! I think I hit your…mmother's car."

Steve vomited a little left over beer and then he began to giggle uncontrollably. Casey went from being disgusted to angry in the span of about five seconds. "Dad shut the hell up! You're going to wake up Mom, you stupid drunk!"

Steve stopped the moronic chuckling and slowly cocked his head to the side. He opened his red-rimmed eyes wide in an attempt to focus them on his son, and then he staggered right up to within an inch of Casey's face. So close that the stench of his vomit and beer breath coated his son like an oily film. "What…did…you…say…to…me? Why…you little shshshit!" He then stepped forward and tried to take a swing at Casey, but he missed completely and staggered backward.

Casey took a step back to get away from his father's stench and tried to control his anger. With gritted teeth he said, "Dad, you're drunk. Knock it off and let me get you up to bed."

Steve bellowed. "Fuck you!" He moved forward to strike his son again, but Casey's anger took over, and he reacted without thought. With both arms extended, Casey grabbed his father's shoulders and hurled him backwards with a mighty shove.

The force of the push caused Steve's feet to leave the ground. With arms flailing out to his sides, he flew backwards across the room. Everything seemed to be happening in slow motion as Casey watched his father in horror. As Steve landed he crashed right through a glass coffee table and dropped to the floor in a heap.

The sound of glass and metal breaking under his weight was deafening. Within seconds Lisa came running down the stairs in only her nightgown screaming, "What happened? What happened?"

She reached the bottom and peered into the family room only to find her husband passed out on the floor, lying atop a mound of broken glass and metal, a trickle of blood slowly dripping down the left side of his face, and Casey standing menacingly over him, his fists clenched and teeth bared in anger.

Lisa screamed. "Oh my God, Casey, what have you done?" She ran to her husband's side.

Casey snapped out of his anger and looked at his mother with a combination of shame and confusion, "Me?…Mom…I didn't do anything! He came home drunk and started screaming at me and swinging at me. What was I supposed to do…let him hit me?"

Lisa looked up at her angry son with both fear and fury in

her eyes. "Casey, shut up!" She tried to pick up her husband's head in an effort to help him regain consciousness.

"Casey, your father's bleeding! Go get me the medicine kit!"

Casey just stood there dumfounded.

"Now, damn it!" she yelled.

He snapped out of it and ran to the kitchen to get the kit for his mother.

As Lisa held up Steve's head, he began to come around and he mumbled, "What…happened?"

Then Lisa began to cry.

Casey came running back into the room with the medicine kit, but he stopped in his tracks when he saw the scene; his mother crying in her nightgown, down on her knees, cradling his father's lolling and bleeding head, spit dribbling down the side of his mouth. He hesitantly handed her the kit and stepped back out of the way. While Steve mumbled a bunch of gibberish, Lisa looked up in anguish at no one in particular and screamed, "What is happening to this family!" Then she turned to her son. "Casey, how could you do this to your father?"

"But, Mom, he came home drunk and…."

She abruptly cut him off. "I don't want to hear it! Your temper is so far out of control! How could you do this to your father? Help me get him up to the bedroom so I can clean him up, and don't you say another word to me!"

There was no sense trying to defend himself; his mother was in no condition to hear it. He helped her pick up his delirious father and together they carried him up the stairs and laid him on the bed.

Lisa was still furious. She turned back to Casey and said, "Casey, I want you to go to bed right now! I will take care of your father, and then I'll clean up downstairs in the morning. Do you hear me?"

He couldn't help it. He tried once more. "But, Mom, he attacked me…I was just…."

"Casey, we will discuss it in the morning!" she shrieked at

him. "This family is coming apart at the seams, and I can't take it anymore! Now go to bed and let me take care of your father!"

Casey left the room and walked slowly to his bedroom. He closed the door and slipped into bed. He was frightened and angry and confused. His mother had never spoken to him like that before. He desperately wanted to tell her what really happened downstairs, but she wouldn't listen to him. He tried to go to sleep, but his adrenaline was still pumping fiercely so he laid in bed for the next two hours just staring up at the ceiling and listening while his mother quietly moved about the house, attempting to fix first her broken husband, and then her broken home.

Chapter Seventeen

Pains, Plans, & Missed Opportunities

Friday, the Day of the Game

Well before his alarm went off, Casey woke up from his restless sleep, if you could even call it that. He'd tossed and turned in the darkness for most of the night. However, around three a.m., when he finally succumbed to fatigue, his dreams were fraught with fragmented and violent images of him and his father. As he shook off the last vestiges of sleep and woke, chilled and damp in a sweat-soaked bed, he tried to shake the violent imagery, but it stayed with him long after he was awake.

Goddamn his father! Today was supposed to be his big day. It was still probably the most important day of his life. He'd had pretty much come to terms with the reality of not playing football at Penn State, and he was actually beginning to get excited about playing for the national champions, USC Trojans, especially since the phone call from Coach Carroll. But there was still something inside him gnawing at his gut. It was that voice telling him that unless he played the best game of his life and proved Coach Paterno wrong, then things just wouldn't be right with his world.

Casey banged the side of his head with his fist a couple of times in an effort to shake off the dark thoughts about the fight with his father. He was angry – no he was more than angry, he was down right furious. But more importantly, he was worried about his mom. *How could that asshole come home drunk and pick a fight for no reason when he knew damn well that Mom's been so upset about his drinking? Because he's a drunk, that's why! Mom knows it and I know it! Well I'm not going to let the shithead stop me from playing one hell of a game tonight!*

With a rejuvenated sense of determination, fueled by his anger towards his father, Casey leaped out of bed, sped through his exercises, and then showered and dressed for school. Before going downstairs, he looked over at his desk drawer, and for a moment he actually considered taking another steroid injection, but then he discarded the notion because he couldn't take the risk that he might get sick again right before the game.

The house was quiet when Casey made his way down to the kitchen. He looked into the family room as he went by and noticed that the room was spotless. There wasn't a shard of glass to be found anywhere on the rug where his father had crashed through the coffee table. The room was completely back to normal except for the large open space in the center of the room where the coffee table once stood. The missing table created an strange void and left Casey with an unsettling pit in his stomach.

Casey shook his head and left the family room for the kitchen. Thinking his mother still asleep, he planned on making his own shake, but when he went to open the fridge there was a note from his mother tacked on the front. It read:

Dear Casey,

I was up most of the night cleaning up the family room and taking care of your father. If you are concerned, he is fine now. The cut on his face was really just a scratch, but he has a very bad hangover, and though he deserves it, he is still your father and I love him. I know that you didn't mean to hurt your father, and I'm sure you are sorry about what happened. Try not to think about any of this today. I know that tonight's game is very important to you. Please focus on that and not on what happened last night. I also know in my heart that

you are going to play great tonight, and of course, your father and I will be there to cheer you on. I promise you that things are going to get better with this family, so please just hang in there and do the best you can.
I love you always, Mom
P.s. I made your shake early this morning. It's in the fridge.

Casey choked back a small cough and rubbed his eyes as he read the note. She was one hell of a good person, and she deserved so much better than the bullshit that happened last night. Later on he would call her to tell her that he loved her and see how she was doing. He gulped down the shake and headed for the front door.

Esprit woke up to her alarm feeling fabulous – no hangover, no nausea, and no fight with Casey hanging over her head, and even possibly, the newfound love and respect of her parents. Nothing could possibly go wrong on such a glorious day. Last night's talk had lifted a great weight from her shoulders, and this morning she felt awesome. She leaped out of bed and ran across the room to open the French doors that led to her balcony. As she stepped outside in just her T-shirt, the early morning rays of sun warmed her face. She felt invigorated as she deeply breathed in the fresh summer air coming up off the river.

Last night had gone a long way in helping Esprit to finally understand what her parents were all about. They didn't really hate her after all. This morning she was no longer her parents' accidental birth child, their afterthought, the one burden in their wonderful lives. Everything she had always believed in the past simply wasn't true. Last night she had learned two very important truths: first, her parents really did love her, and second, that they were only human and made mistakes. She understood for the first time that her parents had flaws of character just like everyone else, and that they admittedly were often selfish and egocentric in their dealings with her, but never evil.

From now on they would be different. Now she could begin to develop an honest dialogue with her parents. She cherished the thought of getting closer to them.

However, Esprit was first and foremost a pragmatist, and she tempered her enthusiasm with the understanding that some of those character flaws would still be there today, and so would hers. She cautioned herself not to expect miracles overnight, but at least now she understood where her parents were coming from.

Downstairs her parents were just sitting down to breakfast out on the veranda. Ethan was nattily dressed in a summer-weight, powder blue cardigan and gray, gabardine slacks, and Jordan in her fashionable yet conservative white tennis togs. This was Friday morning after all. Every Friday Jordan played in her round-robin house tournament at the country club.

"Jordan, I can't tell you how wonderful I feel this morning! It's as if the last two miserable years with Esprit have simply been washed away."

Jordan smiled.

"There is so much I need to do today, but first I need to call Arthur to make sure that he's still planning to join us for Casey's football game tonight. Do you think that perhaps Esprit would like to sit with the three of us at the game?"

Jordan set down her coffee cup. "Ethan, please don't get carried away. Esprit knows how sorry we both are, and that we really love her, and that's what counts. If you push her to hard too soon, she's likely to pull away again. Don't even think about asking her to come and sit with us at the game. I'm sure she plans on sitting with her friends like she always does. If by chance she decides to come up and see us at some point, well, that will be enough."

"You're right, as always. I just want her to know that we really meant what we said last night. I want to show her. That's all."

Out of the corner of her eye Jordan spied Esprit approaching. "Oh my…look who has decided to join us for breakfast?"

They both turned towards the house and watched as Esprit walked over to their table. She was absolutely radiant in a simple pink cotton skirt and sleeveless white top. The ringlets of her flaxen hair cascaded down around her beautiful face, and she was beaming from ear to ear. Her crystal blue eyes shone bright in the morning sun, and she seemed happier than her parents had seen her in such a long time.

"Hi, guys. I thought I'd join you for a bite to eat before school. Is that okay?"

"What a pleasant surprise! It's more than okay, it's wonderful!" said Ethan as he stood to kiss her good morning. He signaled for the maid to come over and then said, "Esprit, I don't think I have ever seen you looking more beautiful than you do right now! I mean that."

Esprit blushed. "Thanks, Daddy. I just wanted you both to know how much last night meant to me. I feel wonderful this morning because for the first time in my life, I honestly believe that we can finally be a family, a real family."

By the time she finished her little speech, tears formed in her eyes, but they were tears of joy rather than of sadness.

"Today is a new day, and we want you to know that we are really looking forward to going to Casey's game tonight. By the way, I don't know if your father told you, but Arthur will be joining us."

Esprit paused for a minute before replying, "That's…that's great, Mom. I'll look for you guys and maybe I'll come up at half-time and sit with you for a while. That is, if that's okay?" She beamed.

Ethan looked to Jordan and winked. "Esprit, I can't think of anything that would make me happier. I have a feeling that today is going to be a really great day. One that I won't soon forget."

Not long after Casey left for school, Lisa lethargically dragged herself out of bed. She was up most of the night cleaning the house and taking care of Steve, and she was dog-tired. Not wanting to wake him, she tiptoed over to the bathroom and put on her bathrobe. Then she snuck quietly downstairs. She made a pot of coffee and sat down at the kitchen table. After a few minutes she reached over to her purse and pulled out the little blue book. She paged through it for a while and then picked up a blank card and a pen from the table. She began to write what was perhaps the most difficult letter of her life.

Dear Steve,
I am writing this letter to you, not out of sadness, or even out of anger. Rather, I am writing it to you with love, determination, and hope. Hope because I know that you are a loving and sensitive man, and a man that places his family above all else. A man who is willing to recognize his faults and frailties, and one who is willing to do something about them for the sake of his family.
What happened last night must never happen again. It is that simple. Steve, your drinking has spun way out of control, and I think deep down that you know it. If it continues, it is going to tear this family apart, and that is something I will never allow to happen. I am a very tough woman, and I will do anything to fight for the two men that I love. You and Casey mean more to me than life itself. I will not stand idly by and watch the two of you tear each other apart. It is time for you to admit that alcoholism is in your genes, and it is time for you to finally admit that you have a problem. If you can find it in your heart to accept this, then I will be there right beside you, and together we will get help. Here is a book to help you begin to understand the nature of your problem. Steve, if you truly love me, then you will at

least take a look at this book, and then afterwards we can talk. Please do this for me, for Casey, and most importantly, for yourself.
Your loving wife, forever, Lisa

She read over the letter over a couple of times with tears in her eyes, and then she placed it in an envelope. She set down her coffee, picked up both the book and the letter, and resolutely she walked back upstairs to her bedroom. When she entered the room the odor of stale beer and the stink of her husband's foul breath, along with smell of his soiled clothes, engulfed her senses. She stood there for a moment looking at him while he slept. This only reinforced for her that she was doing the right thing.

As she gently placed the book and the letter on the pillow next to his battered and snoring head, she knew she was embarking down a life-altering path, and she also knew that he would probably fight her tooth and nail at the beginning. But to save her family she had no other choice. She wept for a minute, and then she grabbed her clothes and left to take her shower in Casey's bathroom so as not to wake her ailing husband.

About an hour later, Steve stirred for the first time. As soon he opened his eyes, throbbing stabs of pain erupted in both his temples. The left side of his head was swollen and sore. He lightly touched the left side of his forehead and felt a large bandage there instead of his skin. He winced at the touch, and suddenly he was filled with a sense of dread, bordering on shear panic. He had no recollection of what happened.

Did I have a car accident?

He tried to shake the fog from his brain. The last thing he remembered was getting into the car-service limo at Yankee Stadium and spilling a beer all over himself, and all over the back seat of the car.

What the fuck happened last night?

He struggled to think coherently and to gather his thoughts. He tried to sit up, but his whole body unexpectedly racked with pain. He collapsed back down on the pillow, and when he looked to his right he spied what appeared to be an envelope sitting atop a book not six inches from his face.

What the hell is this?

He slowly reached across the bed and picked up the envelope and panic began to set in. As he struggled to open the letter, a fleeting image of Casey menacingly standing above him as he lay in a heap of broken glass, flashed through his mind.

Oh my God! What have I done now?

He began to read the letter and his question was partially answered. He read each line deliberately, and then he read it a second, and then a third time. He dropped the letter on the bed and closed his eyes. He stayed that way for a good five minutes before he warily picked up the book. Incredulously, he read the title.

Alcoholics Anonymous, is she fucking serious?

His mind began to race faster and faster as he tried to piece together what had happened last night and then to form some kind of response to address his predicament. He was still foggy on the details of what had actually occurred, but it obviously involved a fight with Casey, and Lisa was really pissed.

Come on, this is ridiculous! She actually thinks I'm a fucking alcoholic! Hell, she drinks almost as much as I do! What the fuck does she want me to do with this Goddamn book? What does she want me to do, start going to those meetings over at the Methodist church on Tuesday nights with the rest of the town drunks? This is Bullshit! So I got drunk at a damn Yankees game; me and half of New York for Christ sakes!

He breathed deeply for a minute or so, trying to calm himself, and then he picked up the letter again and read it for the fourth time. Lisa's words had struck a nerve. He did love his family more than anything. That was true. He began to think that maybe his drinking was the reason his family seemed to be coming apart at the seams.

Steve laid his head back down on the pillow. He rubbed his swollen eyes and began to think. He thought about the people in his life that he knew had alcohol problems, and of course his father came to mind, but then he thought about Dick Morris, a man that he worked with. Dick was the senior partner over on the equity desk.

Five years ago Dick was considered one of the best damn equity traders on the street. He was a real up and comer and just about everyone at Merrill thought he was well on his way to senior management. Morris was rare, an Ivy League hotshot with a ton of brains and a set of balls to match.

This guy was absolutely fearless. He would find markets and make trades that everyone else thought were pure suicide, but somehow he would come out on top every time. Morris's timing was uncanny, and he was the ultimate risk taker. By the time the guy was thirty he was pulling down well over three million a year just in bonuses.

But then two years ago the guy just imploded. He was partying every night, and then it went from booze to cocaine, and who knew what else. After a couple of months Morris was showing up late for work looking like shit, but more importantly, he was starting to really fuck up his financial position. Then as the months went on, in an attempt to try and cover his mounting losses, he began taking greater and greater risks, with only greater losses to show for it. Then when the inevitable corporate heat really started coming down on him, his partying only intensified, until finally, one day, he just cashed in his chips and went out in a blaze of glory.

Steve thought about that day. He remembered it like it was yesterday. Morris stumbled onto the trading floor at eight thirty, well after everyone else was already there and working. He had apparently come directly from an all-nighter, looking like crap and reeking like a brewery. He bobbed and weaved over to his desk, picked up his headset and a cup of coffee and proceeded to throw them across the trading floor. They smashed up against a window and shattered everywhere. After he had the entire trading floor's undivided attention, he simply crawled under his desk, curled up in a ball and wept like a baby until an ambulance called by management came and took him up the east side highway to Bellview.

No one on the trading floor knew the whole story about what happened afterward, but bits and pieces of gossip had made their way around the room. From what Steve had heard, Dick spent the next few days in the Detox ward at Bellview, and then he entered a rehab clinic in New Jersey.

He spent a month there and then he took another month off after that, but then one day he just showed back up at work. He came in on a Monday morning, took his old seat on the Equity desk, and he started trading again like nothing had happened. From what Steve had heard, the company had decided to give him a second chance on the condition that he completed his stay in rehab. This wasn't done out of the kindness of their proverbial corporate hearts, but because Morris had made the firm millions in the past, and they hoped that he could do once it again.

When Dick came back to work after his sabbatical, he was a different guy. First of all he had shed at least twenty pounds and looked a whole lot healthier than ever before. But he had also shed his cocky, master-of-the-universe attitude. In its place was this quiet and reflective guy that never made a peep. He would come to work, make his trades and then at five o'clock he would just disappear. He never went out with the other traders after work, and he never attended work-related social functions. However, he did, from time to time, joke around with the other guys on his desk, and now that Steve thought about it, the guy genuinely seemed to be okay.

Three years had passed since Dick's breakdown on the trading floor, and he had already worked his way back to being the senior partner on the desk and was once again making millions. Because of what happened, Morris would never be considered a candidate for top-level management again, but it appeared that he couldn't care less about that. Steve thought about it. The guy today was a hard-working productive trader, and according to the other guys on his desk, he owed it all to AA. They say he still went to meetings every day right after work.

Steve compared himself to Dick. He wasn't screwing up at work, and the only thing he did besides drink was smoke a little pot. But things were getting a little squirrelly in his personal life. He was overweight, and he was starting to have some pretty major problems at home, and yes, he had to admit that he was drinking pretty much damn near every day. Lisa was adamant in her letter that she thought he had a problem, and Casey had been riding him about his drinking for months.

Okay, I screwed up big time last night. So maybe if I take a look at this book, promise to cut back on my drinking, and apologize to Lisa and Casey, I can pull this whole mess back together, but I'll be dammed if I am going to those meetings!

Determined to start setting things right, Steve slowly got out of bed. Wobbling with pain, dizziness, and nausea, and with book in hand, he made his way to the bathroom to take a shower before going downstairs for the dreaded confrontation with his wife.

The atmosphere at the high school was festive and upbeat in anticipation of tonight's game. Between classes, the students milled about in the hallways, talking with friends and making plans where to meet before the game. Esprit had been grinning from ear to ear all morning. Between each class she searched for Casey because she wanted to share the big news of her amazing reconciliation with her parents. She'd tried to call him on his cell but only reached his voicemail. He would be so happy for her. She couldn't wait to tell him. As she glanced up and down the hall she finally spotted him, his head towering over most of the other students. He was making his way directly toward her locker. She watched him as he chatted with a couple of boys while walking up the hall. At that moment, just seeing his handsome smiling face, she knew that nothing could possibly spoil this simply perfect morning.

When Casey finally saw her standing there, he broke away from his friends and trotted over.

"Hey, I've been looking for you all morning. I really need to talk to you. I have some wonderful news!" she said with a burst of energy.

"Hey, Spree." Casey gave her a peck on the lips. "Okay, okay, calm down. So what's the big news?"

"Casey, you're not going to believe this…I swear, but when I got home last night, my father was sitting there waiting for me and I thought, oh shit, here we go again, another argument, but, Casey, he and I had the best talk. We talked about everything…and he was so sweet. He apologized for the first time ever, and he explained everything about that damn fax, and…."

"Whoa, slow down, Spree. You're not making a whole lot of sense."

Esprit couldn't get the words out fast enough. "Casey, he was never going to put me on TV! That was just something dreamed up by his campaign manager. And then, Casey, he almost started to cry…I swear it! He was so sad that I was angry with him again. There's no way he was faking – no way! Anyway, it was amazing! Then my mother came down and joined us and we talked about everything! God, I feel wonderful this morning – and oohh, I love you so much!"

She leaped up into his arms and hugged him again. She was so happy she was practically hyperventilating. Casey attempted to smile at her good fortune, but he did so with a heavy heart and real sadness in his eyes because of his own troubles.

Esprit picked up on it right away. "Casey, what's wrong? I thought you'd be so happy for me?"

He took a step back and looked at her. "Esprit, I am. I really am happy for you. I swear it. You know how much I like your parents. I'm glad everything worked out for you. I really am. It's just that…."

"Just what? Casey? What's wrong?"

"Listen, Spree, you're in such a great mood, I don't want to spoil it…it's nothing." He looked down at his feet.

Sensing his distress, she grabbed the front of his shirt with both hands. "Casey Collins, you had better tell me what's wrong right now, or I am going to beat the shit out of you!"

"Okay, okay. The end of my night wasn't quite as happy as yours. My father came home wasted from the Yankee game and…."

He told her the whole sordid story; she couldn't believe any of it. She didn't know what to say. Finally she managed to blurt out, "Oh my God, Casey! Is your father all right?"

"He's fine. The blood was from a small cut on his forehead. It wasn't big deal. He was so drunk he just lost his balance and fell over. I didn't mean to push him – he was just being such a fucking asshole! But my mother…she was so upset…" Casey stopped. He was struggling to get the rest of the words out.

"Oh, Casey, I'm so sorry! Are you okay?"

The warning bell rang for class. Casey wiped his eyes and said in a somber tone, "I'm okay, Spree, really. My mom left me a note this morning saying she understood what happened last night and for me not to worry about it. Can you believe it? She told me to just focus on the game. So that's what I'm going to do – fuck my asshole father!" he said angrily.

Esprit felt terrible for him. "Is there anything I can do?"

"No, Spree, I'm fine…really. And I really am happy for you. We have to get to class. Please don't worry. Nothing's changed. I'm going to play the best game of my life tonight, and then you and I are going to have a blast at Kim's party, okay?"

"All right, Casey, I love you!"

"I love you too!"

He kissed her lightly on the lips and walked away towards

his class. She watched him leave, and she felt terribly sad for him. He deserved so much better. Then she closed her locker door and left to make her way to her own class before she was late.

An hour had passed between the time Steve crawled out of bed and when he at last made it downstairs. Earlier, when he finally mustered up enough courage to drag himself into the bathroom, he'd been overcome by a nasty bout of nausea. The sickening feeling overwhelmed him, forcing him to sit on the toilet with his head between his legs and both his hands white-knuckling the towel rack for dear life, the book he'd holding dropped and forgotten.

When the waves of nausea finally subsided he picked up the book, sat down on the toilet and read the first two pages, but then he abruptly slammed it shut and set it on the sink. The first few pages of the book describe the typical behaviors of an alcoholic and the words hit him a little too close to home. He wasn't ready to deal with his drinking yet. He stood up slowly and shuffled his stiff and aching body over to the tub to take a long hot shower.

Some forty minutes later, when he finely emerged from the bathroom, he was feeling only marginally better than when he'd first gone in. He labored to put on a pair of khakis and a T-shirt, and then feebly combed his hair. Finally, he brushed his teeth for an awfully long time in an effort to remove the foul stench and cottony feeling in his mouth. Then with a heavy sigh, he left the bedroom to go and find Lisa.

When he walked into the kitchen he looked out through the French doors and spied her out on the patio, reading the paper and sipping her coffee. Before he went out to face the music he fixed himself a cup of coffee, black with just a little sugar. Then for the second time that morning, he tried to muster up some courage by taking some deep breaths. *Here goes nothing.*

He walked out into the back yard and quietly walked over to

her. When she heard his footsteps she set the paper down and looked up at him with a mix of worry and anger in her eyes.

"Can I sit down?" He pointed to the end of her chair. She reluctantly pulled up her legs and wrapped her arms tightly around them as soon he sat down in front of her on the lounge. She rested her chin on the top of her knees and silently waited for him to speak.

Steve's eyes were still severely bloodshot and swollen. He blinked rapidly, trying to adjust his eyes to the sun. The bright rays of light were causing him insufferable pain, but he knew this was no time to put on his sunglasses. He needed to look Lisa in the eye – that was important. He stared at her frozen features for a moment but couldn't read what she was thinking. This was bad. He could always gage her mood just by looking at her, but not this morning.

Lisa had no intention of saying anything. She patiently waited for him to speak, and it seemed like an eternity before he gathered up the courage to do so.

"Honey, I really don't know what to say. I'm not even sure what happened last night. The last thing I remember was getting into the limo at Yankee Stadium. Everything else is kind of a blur…." He trailed off, not knowing what to say next.

His pause really pissed her off. "All right, Steve, let me fill you in on the rest of your evening. After soaking yourself with beer in the back seat of the limo, you passed out somewhere along the NJ turnpike on the way home. The car-service driver gave me the whole story when he called this morning to make sure that you got home okay."

Steve winced.

"Anyway, the driver drove you home and woke you up in the ferry parking lot, and then he helped you to your car because you insisted on driving your car home. He said you threatened to fire him if he didn't let you."

Steve, hearing her cutting tone, lowered his head in shame.

Lisa continued, "So then, even though you were barely able

to stand, you got in your car and drove home from the ferry – thank God it's only a mile away. And then when somehow you managed to drive yourself home, you pulled up the driveway and plowed right into the back of my car. As you staggered out of your car the noise woke up Casey, who was sleeping on the couch. He heard you crash into my car so he ran to the door to see what was wrong, and then he helped you inside."

"Oh my God…."

"Oh just wait, Steve, it gets much better. Casey said that when you came into the house, you were all fucked up – my words not his – and you started raving about the Yankees losing to the Red Sox. Jesus, Steve, it was a stupid baseball game!"

She then proceeded to fill him in on the rest of the sordid details. When she finished, with more than a little sarcasm in her voice, she said, "Does any of that ring a bell?"

Steve lightly touched the cut on his forehead. It hurt like hell. "Honey, I am so sorry. Please forgive me. I had no idea that's what happened. I read your note, and now I understand why you are so upset. I know I've been drinking too much, but don't you think…?"

Lisa jumped up from the chair and stood over him with her arms tightly crossed against her chest. "No, Steve, no buts, not this time! You haven't just been drinking too much; you've been drinking every day! You have a drinking problem! Steve, do you hear me? I think you're an alcoholic, and I think you need to get some help, now! That's why I bought you the book. Did you even look at it?" She pointed at the book in his hand. "Because I sure did, and right there in the first chapter it describes an alcoholic, and, honey, you most definitely fit the bill!"

Steve was beginning to feel angry and defensive, but this was not the time to escalate this little scene into a full-blown argument. Instead he calmed himself and tried to appease her. "Honey, I looked at the book, and I am taking what you wrote in your letter to heart. Maybe I do have a problem. Maybe I do need to get some help. I know that my drinking is out of control, and I know that I am hurting you and Casey…and…I'm sorry!"

Steve's eyes were focused on the ground and beginning to water as he spoke the words.

When Lisa saw the hurt on his face she sat back down and reached over to hug him. "Steve, just promise me that you will get some help – promise me that you will try to stop drinking. I don't want to watch our family fall apart!" She sobbed and buried her head in his shoulder.

He put his arms around her and held her tightly. After a moment he looked at her and said, "Lisa, I promise you that my drinking will not cause this family pain ever again – ever. I will read the book and I swear to you, I will try and get some help!"

This wasn't the way it was supposed to go. His intention coming out here was to pacify her and tell her what she needed to hear, but something had clicked inside his brain, or maybe inside his heart, because real emotions suddenly came pouring out. He welled up with tears and sobbed, "I'm so sorry that I hurt you and Casey! Can the two of you ever forgive me?"

Lisa pulled away from him, wiped the tears from her eyes and looked at him with resolute determination in her face. "Steve, I will forgive you right now as long as you promise to get some help, and then you actually do it! If you don't, then all bets are off! As for Casey forgiving you, well, that's up to him. You owe your son one hell of an apology, so you better plan on being at that game tonight, no matter how shitty you feel, and when it's over you, better go to him and tell him what you just told me. Because Steve, I'm telling you, I saw him last night. If you don't get through to him soon and admit you have a problem, then you're going to lose him forever."

Chapter Eighteen

Friday Night Football

Friday Night, the Big Game

Although there was more than an hour to go before the kickoff, the stadium at Middletown South High School, affectionately called the 'Swamp' because of its poor drainage and persistent wet condition in the fall and winter months, was bursting at the seams. It was still early, but every seat was filled on the home side of the field, except of course those places of honor reserved for the local dignitaries, who because of their status were able amble in just minutes before the start of the game.

The opposing team's bleachers on the far side of the field, which almost never filled for a home game, were crammed to capacity. This was probably for two reasons: one, Red Bank was the next town over, just a short, five-minute drive for the Buccaneer faithful, and two, the Bucs were expected to be a really good team this year. They were one of only a handful of the state's public schools that could boast three division-one prospects on their team. They had a six-foot-three, two-hundred-and-ten-pound, rocket-armed, quarterback, who'd just yesterday signed a letter of intent to play at Pittsburg. They also had a six-foot-four-inch, lightning-fast wide receiver, who'd orally committed to Syracuse. And finally, they had their own version of Casey, Tyrone Banks, an All-American, blue-chip monster. He was a behemoth, two-way tackle, standing just over six feet five and weighing in at over three hundred and thirty pounds.

Banks, like Casey, was being recruited by virtually every major school in the country. There were rumors circulating that the big lineman had orally committed to Miami, but no one really knew for sure.

The beautiful sunny day had evolved into a warm and breezy night with the temperatures hovering in the mid-seventies. A steady ten to twelve-knot breeze was blowing from right to left across the field. By six fifteen, still forty-five minutes before the game, every parking space and every inch of available asphalt was filled to capacity with cars. Dozens of these were covered with paint and paper streamers that matched the school colors of the team that the owners were rooting for.

Those few cars still arriving without parking passes were being forced to turn around and park almost a quarter of a mile away at the municipal parking lot down the road.

Behind the home bleachers hundreds of kids were milling around searching for their friends. The lines at both the home and the away concession stands were already winding down around the back end of the field. The long lines were filled with hungry, boisterous fans waiting to buy a hot dog and a soda, or a cup of coffee.

Both teams had already finished their pre-game warm-ups and were at the moment huddled up with their coaches back in the school locker rooms going over last-minute game strategies.

Out on the field, the marching band was playing a bizarre, yet somehow intriguing arrangement of Bruce Springsteen's greatest hits for the buzzing crowd. Because of Springsteen's local roots, this was a popular medley, but there was something just a little odd hearing marching band renditions of *Born to Run*, *Rosalita* and *Tenth Avenue Freeze Out.* The growing crowd seemed to be paying the band's musical efforts little heed. On the other hand, the cheerleaders were running along the sidelines, screaming and tossing each other two stories high into the air to the rapt attention and screaming applause of many of the fans.

As the clock approached the magical hour of seven and the sun began to set in the western sky, the bright phosphorous lights surrounding the field popped and buzzed to life, and the crowd energy began to elevate in anticipation of the start of the game.

The marching band mercifully vacated the field and ever so slowly wound its way back to their seats at the far end of the grandstand. Directly behind the band, and above the last row of seats, was the scouting deck. This large wooden-planked platform was usually reserved for other local high school coaches and the few college scouts that tended to show up, but for tonight the scouting deck was standing room only.

At least two dozen scouts and coaches wearing a colorful assortment of sweaters and golf shirts emblazoned with their school affiliations were standing around talking amongst each other while waiting to watch the talent that was about to come on the field. Some were holding cameras and clipboards while others held stopwatches. Stationed right up front were two scouts from Penn State. One of them was still setting up a large video camera. Right next to them were a couple of scouts from USC. A little father down at the other end the platform there was also a small contingent of coaches, including the head coach, from nearby Monmouth University. They were there to take a good long look at Kevin.

Ethan had called the school principal earlier in the day and reserved a VIP spot for himself, Jordan, and Arthur. Their seats were up on the top row of the stands, on the fifty-yard line, just below the press box. The Eagle games were always broadcast on a small local radio station, but because of the significance of tonight's game both CN8 and News 12, the two largest New Jersey Cable Stations, had sent film crews. The reporters and their crews were vying for space in the cramped press box, which was little more than a covered shelter that resembled a ten-year-old boy's tree house more than it did a professional media press box.

As Arthur, Jordan, and Ethan climbed up to their seats through the teeming crowd, they passed by Lisa and Steve Collins, who were sitting about ten rows below. The Collinses were surrounded by a mass of blue-clad, screaming parents. When Ethan and Jordan called over to say hello, Ethan couldn't help but notice Steve's pale, sickly appearance and downcast eyes. When they finally sat down Ethan turned to Jordan and said, "Honey, did you notice how poor Steven Collins looked? Has he been sick? He looks just awful."

"Actually, I didn't because I was looking for Esprit. Oh, there she is!" She pointed to an area directly below them, way down at the bottom of the stands. Esprit was standing and cheering with a group of her friends in the first row right behind the players' bench. Right at that moment, Esprit turned and looked up at them and smiled. She waved to them enthusiastically then turned back around and continued yelling and clapping with her friends.

Jordan turned to Ethan and finished her thought. "Ethan, if you're concerned about him, at half-time, why don't we go over there and say hello? I'm sure Esprit would appreciate the gesture, and then you can inquire about his health."

Before Ethan had a chance to reply, the bright lights began to flash on and off above the field, and the percussion section began wildly beating their drums. Then to Ethan's surprise, the whole grandstand began to shake as thousands of fans simultaneously began to stamp their feet in time with the deafening drumbeat.

Ethan, frightened by the movement of the stands, turned to Arthur and nervously inquired, "I don't know, Arthur, do you think this bloody contraption is safe? The whole damn stadium feels like it's swaying and buckling right under our feet!"

Arthur laughed. "Relax, Ethan. Haven't you been to a football game before? The bleachers are fine, I promise."

Embarrassed and trying desperately to hide both his fear and his ignorance, Ethan stood up with Arthur and began clapping as the opposing team started their frantic charge onto the field. As soon as the Red Bank team had reached the sidelines, the drumming ceased and within seconds the fans in the stands had followed suit. There was dead silence.

A few tension-packed seconds ticked by. Then there came a crackling and popping from the public address system followed by an earsplitting voice.

"Ladies and gentlemen, please welcome your defending Group Three State Champion, the Screaming Eagles of Middletown South!"

A moment later a sea of blue and white emerged from around the east end of the stadium and rampaged onto the field, screaming and cavorting like a horde of Vikings attacking an eighth-century Saxon village. As each player crossed the goal line he abruptly stopped, just for a second, to touch the beak of the weathered eagle icon before charging forth towards the fifty-yard line. At midfield the athletes merged together into one fluid and quivering entity. To the casual observer in the stands the team looked just like a writhing and wriggling mass of blue fish caught in a fishermen's net.

The players and fans were screaming and yelling in unison to the resounding blast of heavy base and drum-laden rock music that was pouring forth from the PA speakers.

"Well, this is quite the spectacle!" said Ethan as he absorbed the adrenaline-pumping atmosphere. He looked at Arthur, who appeared to be enjoying himself immensely.

Arthur replied, "That, my dear Ethan, is why football, and not baseball, has become America's favorite sport."

After several more minutes of pandemonium, a lovely young girl, a student from the school, walked out to the middle of the field. She was holding a microphone. The crowd, seeing her for the first time, settled down when she began to sing a heart-wrenching rendition of the *Star Spangled Banner*. At the end there was vigorous applause from the six thousand enthusiastic fans in attendance.

Once the pre-game festivities and the coin toss were over, the game was set to begin. The Eagles won the toss, but instead of receiving the ball, they selected to kick off with the wind. Kicking off to start the game was another tradition that had started way back with their first State Championship and no coach or player had ever dared to challenge it. So as the two teams lined up on their respective forty-yard lines for the start of the game, every fan in attendance rose to their feet in anticipation of what could be the biggest game of the year in the Shore Conference.

Casey made his presence known on the very first play. As soon as his teammate kicked off the ball from the forty-yard line Casey tore down the field with reckless abandon, knocking several would-be blockers out of his way as if they were flimsy paper cutout figures rather than live football players. He reached the Red Bank kick returner just as the boy caught the ball on the ten-yard line, and he leveled him right there on the spot. Somehow the delirious ball carrier managed to hold on to the ball, but it took him a minute just to get back up on his feet.

On the subsequent play, Red Bank's first offensive play from scrimmage, their star quarterback faked a hand-off to the tailback and rolled out to his right just short of the ten-yard line for a play action pass. This was the same type of play that Casey had been knocked unconscious on just two days before, but this time he wasn't fooled by the fake. He swept wide around the left end, avoiding the oncoming blockers, and raced after the quarterback. Just as the Red Bank quarterback was about to launch the pass, Casey leaped through the air and swiped his arm before he had a chance to cock the ball, so instead of the ball flying forward it dropped backwards and rolled toward the end zone. As Casey tumbled to the ground he spied the loose football out of the corner of his eye. He leaped from the turf in a coordinated roll, and in a flash he covered the eight or nine yards to the ball and pounced on it in the end zone well before any other player from either team even saw the fumbled ball. Casey looked up and saw the referee signaling a touchdown. He stood up, handed the ball to the official and walked off to the sidelines.

Casey hated football players that showboated after scoring a touchdown. Coach Callahan always preached that when you score a big touchdown, look like you have done it before, and Casey lived by those words. When he reached the sidelines, he looked up in the stands, first at all the college scouts buzzing over his play, and then over to where his parents were sitting. He frowned when he found his father waving and cheering for him in the crowd.

While his team was out on the field kicking the extra point, Casey sat down on the bench and grabbed a squeeze bottle of Gatorade. Kevin walked over and said jokingly, "Nice play, sport, but do you think you could ease up just a little bit out there so that maybe me and the offense can get on the field sometime in the first half, and maybe even try to score some points?"

Casey laughed.

Kevin said, "Remember, buddy, those scouts up there aren't just here to see you!" They laughed together for a moment before Casey headed back out on the field for the next kick-off. On the ensuing kick-off Casey once again was in on the tackle, but the Buccaneer's were able to run the ball up to their own thirty-yard line.

On their second offensive series the Bucs stayed in a very conservative offensive formation and did their best to marginalize Casey's superstar ability. For three straight plays they ran weak-side, off-tackle slants, gaining only about six yards for their trouble. On fourth-down they were forced to punt from their own thirty-five-yard line. As soon as the ball was snapped Casey came roaring through the line and missed blocking the ball by maybe an inch.

South's punt return man called for a fair catch and caught the ball at the Eagle forty-yard line. The offense was finally getting their chance to enter the game. As Kevin was about to trot out to the field, Coach Callahan called him over.

"Okay, son, here's a perfect time to show those scouts up there that arm of yours. Let's run Trips-Strong Side, Z-Post, Y-Corner. And, Kevin…let her rip!"

Kevin smiled. "Yes, sir!"

Kevin entered the huddle for the first time and called the play. He looked at his two eager wide receivers. "Whoever breaks first is getting the ball. I want a touchdown on this play, so don't fuck around, on three…ready…break!"

The offense approached the line of scrimmage. As Kevin came up to the line he saw Tyrone Banks, the huge defensive lineman staring right at him. The monstrous player called over from across the line of scrimmage, "Yo, surfer boy, you goin' down! No passes for you today…uh…uh...don't you even think about putting one up!" Kevin ignored the taunts as he stepped up under center and began to call the signals.

As soon as the ball was snapped he immediately dropped back and began searching for his wide receivers, but neither had separated from a defender yet and Banks, the big defensive lineman was on the verge of breaking through his double-team block. From the corner of his eye, Kevin spied him coming, so he rolled to his right and searched for an open man down field.

Suddenly, Kevin was aware of two things happening at exactly the same moment; first, he caught sight of one of his receivers breaking loose down the left side at about the fifteen-yard line, and then he saw Banks charging right at him, also from the left. At the last possible moment Kevin planted his left foot and let the ball loose. Less than a fraction of a second later, Tyrone Banks leveled him. The big man charged and hit him in the chest, brutally forcing him to the ground.

Kevin had no idea what happened after that because he was lying on the ground smothered beneath the huge lineman. However, the ball sailed through the air in a tight spiral for almost forty yards until it zeroed in on its intended receiver, who caught the ball on the fly without even breaking step and then scampered the last ten yards into the end zone untouched by a single defender.

Kevin didn't realize that he'd thrown a touchdown until he heard the rest of his teammates screaming and saw them jumping up and down with delight. He slowly got up to his feet, turned to the big lineman and said, "Nice try." Then he raised his fist high in the air and ran off the field.

Casey greeted him on the sidelines with a hug. "Not bad girly-man," and then he banged Kevin's shoulder pads with a pair of clenched fists.

With just five minutes gone in the first quarter, the Eagles were already up on the Buccaneers by a score of 14 to zero, and it looked to be the beginning of a rout, but the Eagle team suspected that Red Bank wasn't just going to roll over and play dead.

On the next series Casey and his vaunted defense once again held the Bucs to very little yardage, and once again Red Bank was forced to punt. The Red Bank punter let loose a high end-over-end kick that seemed to take forever to make its way back down to earth. It wasn't a long kick, but it was incredibly high, and it allowed for the speedy Buccaneer players to get down the field before the ball was even caught.

The Eagle punt-return man, mesmerized by the extraordinary height of the punt, forgot to signal for a fair catch. As soon as he caught the ball he was mauled by three attacking Red Bank defenders, including the giant Tyrone Banks. The ball was jarred lose by the assault and one of the Red Bank players in on the hit quickly picked it up and sprinted for the end zone. Casey, who had been at the other end of the field trying to block the punt, saw the fumble and raced after the Red Bank player with the ball. The kid had a forty-yard head start, but all heads turned as Casey charged after him with amazing speed for such a large man. He nearly caught the kid too, but he just missed as the boy crossed the goal line for the Bucs' first touchdown. With a successful extra point attempt, the score was now 14-7.

For the rest of the first quarter and through much of the second, the two offenses were stalemated in their attempts to move the ball. Casey and the Middletown defense continued to shut down the high-powered Red Bank offense. Kevin and the Eagle offense moved the ball reasonably well up and down the field, but because of a fumble by the running back and a couple of offside penalties, they'd earned no more points to show for their efforts.

With just under two minutes left in the first half and Red Bank with the ball on their own forty-two-yard line, the Bucs' star quarterback launched only his third pass of the day. Casey, reading the quarterback, dropped off into the flat for a coverage situation and began trailing the tall wide receiver, crossing the center of the field. As soon the quarterback let loose the ball, Casey kicked his speed into overdrive and at the very last possible moment, he stretched out in front of the wide-out and intercepted the pass.

He took off down the sideline in the direction of the end zone, still a good fifty-five yards away. As Casey steamrolled down the field, two Red Bank offensive linemen, one of them Banks, angled in towards Casey to make the tackle. The first player, the faster of the two, reached Casey and shoved him forcefully out of bounds, thereby ending the play. But the second one, Banks, all three hundred and thirty pounds of him, continued on and a split second later, even though the play was well over, at full speed he blindsided Casey from behind.

Casey, thinking he was safe because he was out of bounds, had already dropped both his guard and the ball, so when the hit from behind came he was completely defenseless. He went flying through the air, crashing through several players before finally coming to an abrupt halt when he crashed over the top of the trainer's table in a busted heap.

When the south players witnessed their captain on the receiving end of the brutal and illegal hit, they went berserk. Several jumped on Banks and fights between players broke out all over the Eagle sideline. As the coaches rushed over to check on their fallen star, the referees began breaking up the scuffles. It took several minutes for the melee to end, but eventually the field was quieted and Casey was slowly lifted from the ground by the trainer and coaches.

Lisa and Steve helplessly looked on from the stands. They were relieved when Casey finally stood up, took off his helmet, and waved to the crowd. Coach Callahan cautiously checked out his star player to see that he was really okay. Casey winced, but said he was okay, even though there was sharp stinging pain in his lower back, down in the area of his kidneys.

He walked around to shake off the hit, followed by jogging up and down the sidelines and stretching out his back. The referees had finally settled down the rest of the agitated players and assessed a fifteen-yard penalty on Banks for unsportsmanlike conduct. This gave the Eagles the ball on the Red Bank thirty-five-yard line with just over a minute left in the half.

Kevin ran a couple of running plays right up the gut to tighten up the linebackers and to run some time off the clock. Then on third down from the Red bank twenty-nine-yard line, with only nineteen seconds left, Kevin called his favorite play, the weak-side play action pass.

As soon as the ball was snapped Kevin brilliantly faked the hand-off to the fullback. The entire front seven on defense bit on the fake, and they bit hard. Kevin rolled out to his left he saw his rather large tight end all alone in the end zone. He fired a perfect thirty-yard spiral into the waiting hands of the tight end for his second touchdown pass of the night. By the time the whistle was blown and the extra point kicked, there was no time left on the clock.

At the sound of the horn signifying half-time, the Eagles ran to their locker room with a 21 to 7 lead. Kevin and Casey lagged behind as the team left the field. "Nice throw, Kevin. One more like that and you can bank on your full ride to Monmouth!"

"Dude, how are you feeling? That was some nasty hit. That

motherfucker Banks should have been thrown out of the game."

Casey smiled. "I'm okay. My back's a little sore, but I'll be fine, and don't worry about Banks; I'm going to teach that dumb fuck a lesson in the second half! You can bank on that too!" He laughed and then the boys picked it up and ran to catch up with the rest of the team.

The second half couldn't come fast enough for Casey and the rest of the team. To a man, they were all still really pissed off over the illegal hit delivered by Banks on their captain. Callahan used the anger to fire up his team during half-time. When they returned to the field for the second half, the team was boiling with rage and looking for revenge. During the warm-ups, taunts and jeers flew back and forth across the field.

Just before the teams lined up on their respective forty-yard lines in preparation for the second half kick-off, Casey, who didn't usually play on the receiving team, ran up to Coach Callahan and asked to go into the game as a front line blocker on the play.

The coach, realizing what Casey was up to said. "Casey, I know what you're planning to do, but I don't want to see nothing illegal out there. You want to teach Banks a lesson, fine, but you do it straight up with a hard nose block. I don't want to see any late hits or punches thrown. You got that?" Then the coach smiled and patted him on the back.

"Now go kick his ass!"

A huge cheer from the home team crowd broke out as Casey ran out to the forty-yard line. Lined up on the field some twenty yards away and directly across from him was Banks. Many of the savvier fans in the stands, especially the scouts, immediately picked up on what Casey was planning, and they held their collective breaths in anticipation of the forthcoming clash of the titans.

As soon as the ball was kicked the two hyped-up athletes charged at each other like a couple of horn-butting mountain goats vying for alpha dominance. Collins and Banks, each one a veritable mountain of muscle shielded in plastic-plated armor and cloaked in form fitting Rayon, sped directly at one another with complete and utter abandon. Neither one even remotely concerned with the play developing around them.

For both Casey and Banks this clash had nothing to do with the kick-off, this was the one play for all the marbles. This one collision would finally determine which one was the ultimate warrior. And while Banks was superior in overall size, Casey was by far the faster and stronger of the two, so when they finally crashed head-on, the earth-shattering crack of their contact could not only be heard, but felt throughout the stadium.

The crowd rose to their feet in anticipation of what ended up being a fairly routine kick-off and return, with one exception. There was a collective gasp seconds after the two giants collided. When the dust settled on the field the Eagle player who received the kick-off was tackled on the twenty-five-yard line. While a good twenty-five yards away from the play, right at the center of midfield, Casey was standing triumphantly over his opponent, who lay crumpled at his feet, his helmet still rolling, after having been jarringly parted from his head by the ferocity of Casey's assault.

Casey reached down and extended his hand to his fallen adversary. As he helped the struggling Banks to his feet he said quietly, "You're a hell of a player, Tyrone, no more cheap shots today, you got that?"

The Red Bank player just nodded, picked up his helmet and hobbled back to the sideline.

The third quarter turned into the 'Kevin Hahn Show'. Kevin took the ball on that first possession and marched his team seventy-five yards straight down the field with well-timed play-action passes and short runs up the gut of the defense. He finally scored from the twenty-five on a masterfully executed bootleg play where he faked the long pass and scampered the remaining twenty-five yards untouched into the end zone.

Casey and the defensive unit followed and once again shut down the high-powered Red Bank offense in just three plays. With time dwindling down in the third quarter, Kevin and the Eagle offense took the field and again Kevin opened it up, hitting on three of four passes, two for more than twenty yards.

When the whistle blew ending the third quarter, the Eagle's offense was sitting pretty on the Red Bank six-yard line. On the first play of the fourth quarter Kevin handed off the ball to his sure-handed running back. The swift back cut to the outside. As he began his turn up field for the end zone, he was hit hard, and of course it was Tyrone Banks doing the hitting, and the ball was jarred loose.

The monstrous lineman spied the loose ball. He picked it up and rumbled his way down the sidelines. He was a good twenty yards ahead of the nearest Eagle player. Kevin, who had rolled out to the opposite side of the field after the hand-off, was a good forty yards away, but when he saw the fumble he turned around and flew like the wind, chasing after the big lineman. He raced furiously across the field desperate to stop Banks from scoring. He finally caught up with the big tackle at the Eagle five-yard line and did the only thing he knew to do. He submarined in right under Bank's massive, churning legs. Banks never saw him coming, and he stumbled and toppled over right on top of Kevin, with the ball finally coming to rest on the Eagle one-yard line. The crowd went berserk.

As Casey and the rest of the defensive unit ran onto the field, he grabbed Kevin coming off the field and said, "Hey, dog, I'm the one who's supposed to make the great tackles. You're the quarterback, remember?" and he jokingly swatted him on the side of his helmet. Casey then ran over to his own goal line to fire up his defense.

The Eagles needed to stop the Bucs from scoring right here. If Red Bank scored, it would be 28 to 14 with almost a full quarter still to play. With the Bucs' talent on offense, one more lucky break could put them right back in the game, but Casey knew that if the Eagle defense shut them down here, it would break their spirit.

As he stalked back and forth behind the line of scrimmage before the play, Casey shouted across the line at the opposing quarterback, "You might just as well give me the rock now because you ain't moving it an inch – not in my house!" This wasn't just bragging to intimidate the other team, it was meant to fire up his defense as well.

Red Bank broke from the huddle and lined up on the ball. Casey sensed that they were gong to try and run away from him so he roved back and fourth behind the defensive line trying confuse the offense. He guessed right. The ball was snapped and the quarterback attempted to run a keeper away from Casey, but he read the play, broke through the two blockers and caught the speedy quarterback two yards behind the line of scrimmage.

On second down from the three, Red Bank tried to bull their way across the line by using Banks as a blocking fullback. As soon as the play began Casey filled the gap in the middle of the line and barely contained the charge. The Bucs picked up a yard on the play.

It was now third down from just beyond the two-yard line, and Red Bank unexpectedly lined up in a three wide receiver set. Casey was surprised that they were going to attempt to throw the ball so he dropped back a couple of yards off the line of scrimmage. When the ball was snapped the quarterback dropped back a good five steps and looked for one of his swift receivers. Casey followed the eyes of the quarterback and at the last moment he charged through the line just as the quarterback released the ball.

At that exact same moment, Casey leaped into the air, attempting to bat down the ball before it had a chance to find the wide receiver in the end zone. He didn't make contact with the ball, but he disrupted the play just enough so that the ball went well wide of the intended target and bounced harmlessly to the sidelines for an incomplete pass.

It was now forth down from the two with only eight minutes left in the game, and Red Bank sent in their field goal unit. The entire stadium was stunned. They were down by three scores and desperately needed a touchdown to get back in the game, yet here they were lining up for a lousy field goal. Casey didn't buy the field goal attempt for a minute. He knew that their quarterback was also the holder on kicks, and he was probably going to try a fake kick. Casey went up to the line and whispered into Shawn Murphy's ear that it was going to be a fake, and then he told Shawn what he wanted him to do.

Casey watched on which side of the ball that the quarterback lined up for the hold and positioned himself accordingly, not to attack the line for a block, but rather to run around the strong side of the field in an attempt to thwart the possible fake. As soon as the ball was snapped Casey knew he'd guessed right. The quarterback picked up the ball, and behind two blockers he raced around the strong side, but Casey was right there to greet them, and he threw his body into the blockers to clear the way for Shawn Murphy, who was trailing behind him. Shawn leaped over Casey and the two falling blockers and threw the Bucs' quarterback to the ground for a three-yard loss.

With a hand from Shawn, Casey stood up gingerly and slapped the euphoric Murphy on the back. With just under eight minutes to go the Eagles defense had thwarted the Bucs' last real chance of getting back in the game. Kevin and the offense took over the ball at their own five.

The crowd went crazy as Casey as the defensive unit triumphantly walked off the field. Coach Callahan greeted Casey with a big hug. "Casey, I don't know where the hell you're going to end up playing your college ball, but if that series and this game don't change Paterno's mind, well than he's a damn fool!"

"Thanks, Coach!" said an out-of-breath Casey, and then he and Shawn Murphy ran over to the bench to grab some Gatorade.

When Casey looked up into the stands and scanned the

crowd, he spied Esprit frantically waving at him trying to get his attention, and a few rows back, his mother and father beaming with pride. He waved to Esprit and then looked over to the scouting deck. He noticed the scouts from Penn State packing up their camera equipment. He said to no one in particular, "Well, I did the best I could. I guess we'll see what happens tomorrow." He took the fact that they were leaving early as a good sign. Then he took a seat on the bench to rest his very sore back and watched as Kevin and the offense again worked their magic.

Kevin had already played one hell of a game, and now he knew what needed to be done to close out the game. He took control of the offensive unit and conservatively began to chew up the remaining time on the clock. Again, using a series of runs and short play-action passes, he marched the offense straight down the field. At the two-minute warning, the Eagles were on the Red Bank twenty.

When play resumed the offense continued their grinding assault against the tired Red Bank defense and with just three seconds left to go in the game the Eagles were threatening on the Red Bank one-yard line. The receiver brought in the play from the sidelines. Kevin listened, but didn't like the play so he called a time-out. The coach wanted another touchdown, and Kevin could have easily scored on the final play to run up the score, but instead he went to the coach and asked if he could take a knee on the next play. Callahan grumbled at first but then relented. Kevin was taking the high road, he ran back out to the huddle and used the rest of the time-out to congratulate his teammates and let them know what he was going to do. On the final play of the game Kevin took the ball and knelt to the ground, and as time expired the fans in the stands went wild with applause. The Middletown South Eagles had opened their title defense season with a hard fought 28-7 victory over a very tough Red Bank opponent.

As the Eagle players lined up and marched to the center of the field to shake hands with their defeated opponents and to celebrate their victory, the stadium quickly began to empty. Hundreds of family members and friends slowly filed out and began to line themselves up along the path that led from the field to the school. They formed a gauntlet for the victorious players to walk through when they made their way back to the locker room.

Right in the middle of the swarming crowd, Esprit and Jamie were pushed and shoved until they'd situated themselves up near front where the players came off the field. Steve and Lisa took their time and lined up about halfway down the long line. Jordan, Ethan, and Arthur waited a while and decided to wait near the end of the line up by the parking lot where the crowd was sparse.

Casey and Kevin, as team captains, took their place at the tail end of the line when the players finely began to walk off the field. When the two boys finally made it to Esprit and Jamie, they were both greeted with enthusiastic hugs and kisses. Esprit screamed, "Casey, that was your best game ever! I'm so proud of you. And you too Kevin!" Then she gave Casey another kiss.

Jamie chimed in, "Okay…Okay…you two heroes, why don't you too just move along and go take a shower, you're filthy. We'll meet up with you in an hour at Kim's party."

Casey nodded as Esprit clung tightly to his soiled uniform. Finally Jamie pulled the clinging Esprit away so the boys could continue to move their way up the line.

When the boys reached Lisa and Steve, Casey stopped and gave his mother a hug. Lisa kissed both boys and praised them for their play. "I just don't know what to say. I have been watching the two of you play for six years now, and I've got to tell you, that game was something special, something to be proud of!"

They both smiled and then Steve stepped forward and tried to shake his son's hand, but Casey backed off. Steve, seeing that Casey wanted no part of him, reached for his son's arm and quietly said, "Casey, that was one hell of a game! Listen, I want to apologize for what happened last night…."

Casey angrily pulled away from his father's grasp. "Screw you, Dad!" Then he grabbed Kevin by the shirt and sped forward up the line.

After Casey's abrupt departure, Lisa put her arm on Steve's shoulder and said, "Honey, it's okay! This just wasn't the time! You can talk to him tomorrow."

Steve dejectedly lowered his gaze as they turned to leave for their car.

Once the two boys were far enough away, Kevin stopped and said, "Dude, what the hell was that all about?"

"Nothing, Kev, let's keep moving…I'll tell you about it later!"

Near the end the line the throng of enthusiastic fans had begun to thin, but there right in front of the two boys stood Jordan, Ethan and Arthur. They were standing just off to the side of the locker room door.

Arthur approached the boys first and shook both of their hands. Then he turned to Casey and said, "Casey, it's nice to see you again, and, son, that was one hell of a game! I can only hope to see you in a Giants' jersey someday."

"Thank you, sir!" said Casey, and then he turned to shake Jordan and Ethan's hands.

Ethan smiled and said, "Well, Casey, I can honestly say that I don't know much about the game of football, but from what I saw, you were pretty damn spectacular, and that goes for you too, son." He briefly looked Kevin's way but then turned back to Casey and continued, "Casey, by the way, if you are not doing anything tomorrow, Jordan and I would like to take you and Esprit out to dinner. I think we have a lot to celebrate."

Casey let go of Ethan's hand, smiled and said, "Thank you, sir. As far as I know, Esprit and I haven't made any plans. I just want you to know that she told me about last night, and I am really happy for all of you. I will be looking forward to it!" and then he waved goodbye and he and Kevin ran the last few yards to the locker room door.

Chapter Nineteen

The Party

The Eagle locker room was in chaos immediately following the game. Jerseys, pads, and helmets were flying all around the room as the boys celebrated their first victory of the season. Casey and Kevin, the last members of the team to enter the room, bobbed and weaved their way across the crowded room, high-fiving and slapping their teammates. Casey made a point of stopping by each of the lineman that he'd promised to bring to the party, assuring each one the plan was still on. When he finally reached his locker he said to Kevin, "Buddy, that was one hell of a fun game, and you were awesome! I've never seen you so fired up! If this game doesn't get you your full ride to Monmouth, nothing will!"

Kevin smiled. "Thanks, Casey. My parents will be pretty stoked if that's true. You didn't play so bad yourself. I saw the Penn State guys pack up right after your goal line stand. Probably a good sign that they thought they had enough videotape to convince Paterno."

Casey looked away and said, "Yah, that's what I thought too. I guess we'll find out soon enough."

Kevin was surprised by the blasé attitude. "So, what's the deal with you and your dad? Man, you were pretty jacked up when you saw him. I thought for a second that you were going to take a swing at him."

"It's nothing, Kevin. He just did something really fucked up last night that upset my mom. I'm just pissed off at him, that's all."

"That's cool, but your dad's a pretty solid dude as far as fathers go. I hope you guys can work it out."

"Jesus Christ, first Esprit, then Frankie, and now you? Is my father paying all you guys to be in his fan club or what? None of you know what the hell you're talking about. My father can be a real asshole sometimes, so give it a rest. Anyway, I don't want to talk about my parents right now. I just want to kick back and celebrate if that's all right with you!"

"That's cool."

"Anyway, I'm so stoked right now, I might even break my rule of no alcohol during season and have a beer or two at the party. What do you say, dog? Let's hit the showers and go have some fun!"

As the two boys peeled of their filthy, sweat-soaked uniforms, Kevin gaped at the large purple contusion around the left kidney on Casey's lower back. "Hey, you got one hell of a nasty bruise where Banks took his shot at you; you should go get it looked at by the trainer."

"No fucking way! I'll get it looked at tomorrow by Frankie's guy when I get to the gym. I want to get over to the party, besides, it doesn't really hurt that much." The truth was that it really hurt like hell, but Casey was fired up and didn't want to spoil the night nursing a bruise.

The two boys spent the next thirty minutes showering and primping for the party. Kevin finished long before Casey because Casey was much fussier with his appearance than Kevin, who, after his shower, simply threw on a pair of old jeans and a sweatshirt and then brushed his fingers through his wet hair.

Long finished, Kevin waited patiently by his locker while Casey spent another ten minutes in front of the mirror, shaving, brushing his teeth, and then gelling his hair into perfectly symmetrical ringlets.

Casey finally did emerge from the shower area looking like he was about to strut down a runway. He casually walked back to his locker and was met with a standing ovation from Kevin and the four overweight, shabbily dressed linemen, who by this time were board out of their skulls waiting for him.

Shawn Murphy laughed. "Jesus Christ, Casey, you're worse than my fucking sister. If I knew that you were going to take this long, I would have never have asked for a ride! You already got the hottest girl in school, so who the fuck are you primping for?" The rest of the boys started to laugh.

Casey smirked, "Whoa boys, take it easy. You gotta look good for the babes no matter what. And from the looks of you, Shawn, the only thing you're going home with tonight is that Vienna sausage between your legs you call a dick! Tuck in your shirt, you fat slob, and come over here and try a little of my cologne." He took out a bottle of Polo Sport from his gym bag and sprayed it in the general direction of Shawn, who leaped back out of the way to avoid the mist.

After a couple of minutes, Casey finished dressing and led the other boys out to his car.

As they were leaving Coach Callahan popped his head out of the office and said in a mock-serious tone, "Nice game, boys, don't overdo it with the beer tonight. I mean it!" To which the six of them responded in unison with a "Yes, sir!" but not one of them meant it.

In the parking lot Casey reached into the car with his keys and started his Mustang so he could put the top down while he tried to figure out just how he was going to squeeze fourteen hundred pounds of fat football players into his little car. After a minute or so of shuffling and shoving, the six boys all managed to squeeze in. Casey was of course driving and Shawn sat beside him in the passenger seat because he was the largest of the others. The other three linemen were jammed in together in to the back seat, and Kevin, who was by far the smallest of the group, was lying across their laps.

Mercifully, the party was in a neighborhood only about five minutes from the school, so the boys didn't have to suffer long. On the short ride over they did, however, pass a Middletown police officer, but because the officer recognized Casey he just waved to them as they went by rather than pull them over for driving a dangerously overcrowded vehicle.

As Casey drove up the road leading to Kim and Joey's house, he noted that the street was lined with cars still decorated with streamers and paint from the game. "Looks pretty crowded," he said. After searching for a while he found a parking spot several houses down from the party. There were more than a few groans of relief as the boys, one at a time, extracted themselves from the little Mustang.

As the group walked up the street towards the party, Shawn pulled Casey aside and whispered, "All kidding aside, dude, I want to thank you for setting up that play for me at the end of the game, and for bringing us tonight. Me and the guys never get invited to these things, it means a lot to us, I just wanted to say thanks." And he shook Casey's hand.

"No problem, Shawn. I'm glad you guys are here, but remember no rough stuff and no fighting or this will be the last one you come to!"

When they entered the house the party was already in high gear. There were hundreds of kids from school in groups of fives and tens, walking around, drinking beer and trying to talk to one another over the thumping stereo that was blasting a Drop Kick Murphy's CD. Once inside, the four big linemen ran ahead of Casey and Kevin, and like a cattle call, as a group they B-lined it straight for the keg out in the back yard. Those boys had a nose for beer and knew where to find it without asking a soul.

As Casey and Kevin made their way through the crowded living room, they were greeted with splashes of applause and a lot of pats on the back. Kim and Joey, the hosts of the party, soon took notice of their arrival and came over to pay their respects. Joey, who was already pretty lit up, said, "Well…look who's here…the two guests of honor! You guys played a hell of a game tonight. Mi casa es su casa!"

"Thanks, man! Great party! Have either of you seen Esprit and Jamie?" said Casey.

Kim chimed in, "Hi, Casey…hi, Kevin. I think I saw them a few minutes ago out back on the patio."

"Thanks, Kim, we'll catch up with you guys later, nice house!" and the two boys began to slowly make their way through the house in search of their dates.

Outside, Esprit and Jamie had each just poured a beer, and the two of them were off by themselves talking. "So what do you say, girl, do you want to do some X with me or what? Tonight's going to be a perfect night for it! Come on, what do you say?" said Jamie.

"No way, Jamie, I'm taking a pass. I haven't been feeling so great the last couple of days, and besides, I don't want anything to spoil my night with Casey."

Jamie popped one into her mouth and said, "Suit yourself – all the more for me. But listen, I got an idea. Tell me what you think. You know how Kevin's been so uptight around me, but he seems like he really wants to hook up."

"Yeah…" said Esprit, not knowing where Jamie was going.

"Well, when he gets here, I'm going to offer to go get him a beer, and then I'm going to drop a hit of X in it. I crumbled one up into powder a little while ago. I got it in a little baggy right here in my purse. I'm just going to sprinkle it in his beer. I bet that'll loosen him up, and then he and I can party all night!" Jamie grinned and danced around a little.

Esprit looked at her friend incredulously, "Jamie, are you fucking crazy? Kevin doesn't do any drugs. What if he freaks out?"

"Chill out. It's just one hit of X for Christ sakes. He probably won't even know he's on it! He'll just start feelin' really good vibes and probably think it's the beer. Christ, you've done X a hundred times, have you ever flipped out?"

"No, but…."

"Listen, Esprit, I'm doing this. I really want to get together with him, and this way maybe he'll finally relax around me. I'll take full responsibility if anything happens –which it won't – so why don't you just mind your own business and promise to keep your mouth shut? Not a word…promise!"

"I don't know, Jamie, I don't think it's such a…."

Jamie pleaded with her friend. "Come on, Spree, don't do this!"

Esprit was about to tell her not to do it when over Jamie's shoulder she spied Casey and Kevin walking out through the back door. Flustered by their sudden presence, she said, "Oh shit! I don't care, Jamie. You'll do whatever the hell you want anyway. But don't you come crying to me if this blows up in your face." Then she waved at the boys through the crowd to come over and join them.

Casey and Kevin fought their way through the crowd, it was slow going because they were stopped every few seconds by someone wanting to congratulate them on the game, finally, they made their way over to the girls. "Hello, ladies," said a jovial Casey as he hugged and kissed Esprit. "This is some party, and you two look hot! Have you been waiting long?"

"Not too long, but we're glad you're here," said a smiling Esprit.

Jamie nudged up to Kevin, put her arm around his waist and gave him a peck on the cheek. In return, he barely acknowledged her presence, but he did manage to squeak out a soft, "Hi, Jamie."

Esprit, happy to finally be with her conquering football hero, had already forgotten her conversation with Jamie from just a moment ago. She said to no one in particular, "That game was totally awesome! I am so proud of you two! And I'm stoked that you're finally here!" Then she hugged everyone a second time.

Jamie turned to Kevin. "What do you say hero, can I get you

a beer?"

Kevin finally cracked a smile. "Now that would be awesome!"

As Jamie turned and started walking away towards the keg, Casey called out after her, "Hey, Jamie, would you mind getting one for me too? I'm feeling it tonight, what the hell!"

She looked at him incredulously. "Sure, big boy, no problem."

As soon as Jamie left for the keg the other three continued to talk about the game. Esprit, a little surprised by Casey's request, looked up at him and said, "My…my…hold the presses! Hey, everyone, Casey Collins is actually going to have a beer during football season." After everyone in earshot had their laugh, she looked at him closer with a smile and whispered in his ear, "Whatever has gotten into you?"

Conspiratorially, he winked at her and said very softly so that no one else could hear, "I just want to be with you and have a good time tonight, okay?"

She hugged him tight. "Sounds good to me, stud!"

While Esprit was teasing Casey, Jamie had walked over to the keg and poured two beers for the boys. She set them down on the table, surreptitiously reached into her purse and furtively dropped the ground-up hit of ecstasy into the cup that she intended for Kevin. She was just about to pick up the cups and make her way back to them when she was interrupted by a tap on the shoulder from a friend in the drama club. Surprised, she stepped away from the table and turned to greet her friend.

"Hey, girl, what are you doing here?" said Jamie, and then the two girls spoke for a couple of minutes until the other girl left to rejoin her date. When Jamie finally turned around to the table to pick up the two cups of beer, she froze with confusion. *Oh fuck, what the hell did I just do? Which one is which?*

Jamie couldn't remember which cup she'd put the hit in. She peered into each of the cups looking for any residue from the dissolving powder, but it was too dark to see anything. She racked her brain for a minute trying to remember which cup was which while being bumped and jostled by other kids trying to get at the keg. Finally she came to the conclusion that it was definitely the one on the left – she was sure of it.

As she picked them up and turned around, Casey, Kevin, and Esprit were heading right to her. They were tired of waiting, so they had come over to join her.

"What's up, Jamie? Did you get forget about us or what?" said Casey as she handed him the cup in her right hand.

Oh shit, I hope I got them right. If not, Esprit's in for one hell of an evening, and I'm shit out of luck, she thought as she handed Kevin the other cup, still not completely sure which one was which. Each of the boys, still parched from the game, took a healthy slug. Casey drank most of his in a single gulp as Esprit watched in amazement.

"You'd better slow down, big guy, or I might actually get to see you drunk for the first time in like…oh I don't know, ever."

After they finished the beers they got another round, and then the two couples left the keg and began to meander around the party, stopping here and there, talking with friends and bullshitting about the game. Not long after they left the keg, Casey and Esprit intentionally separated from Kevin and Jamie and made their way over to the four linemen that came to the party with Casey. They were huddled together off to the side of the patio, savoring their beers.

Casey introduced Esprit to the boys, "Now, boys, I thought we talked about this on the way over. How the hell are you going to hook up with some of those fine ladies over there if you're standing all the way over here away from the rest of the party?"

Each one, looking completely embarrassed, just stood there in painful silence. Casey laughed. "Esprit, don't you think we should take these guys around and introduce them to some of your friends? I promise you they will be on their best behavior!"

Esprit looked up at Casey, a bit of surprised, but she decided to play along. She replied, "Sure, Casey, I think we can do that!"

She walked up to the four and wrapped her tiny arm around Shawn Murphy's rather large waist. He turned about three shades of red and the whole group started to laugh, but very soon the group began to make its way around the party, with Esprit and Casey acting as hosts and making introductions on behalf of the four very shy boys.

While Casey and Esprit were having their fun with Shawn and the linemen, Jamie and Kevin had wondered by themselves around the party. Jamie kept reaching for Kevin's hand, but he seemed to keep finding opportunities to pull it away, either to shake someone's hand or to pick something up from the ground. She took this as a bad sign, but she continued to watch him closely for signs that the X was starting to kick in. However, he continued to be distant and quiet. Finally, at Jamie's urging, they took a seat on some patio furniture out in the rear of the yard away from the rest of the party.

Jamie sat on his lap and looked him straight in the eye. She was determined to attract him one way or the other. She said, "Kevin, you really played a great game today…I mean it! You know I don't like football, and I really don't even understand the game…but even so, you looked really hot out there running around in those tight pants. Great ass!" She giggled.

"Thanks Jamie…I guess," said Kevin awkwardly.

Jamie continued talking, even as he looked away. "So Kevin…listen, I know you're really shy, but I want you to know that I really do like you! I don't usually go for jocks, but there's something very different about you. You're not like the rest of those macho jerks…I mean it!" As she said this she leaned into him and kissed him on the lips. He hesitated at first, but then he reciprocated for a short while before gently pulling away.

Obviously nervous, he said to her, "Why don't we get up and walk around for a while…maybe go find Casey and Spree?" Without waiting for a response he stood up and backed away.

Jamie was becoming frustrated and confused. "What's the

matter with you, Kevin? Are you all right? Here I am practically throwing myself at you, and you're blowing me off again." She wondered just when the damn X would finally work its magic.

More flustered than ever, he said, "I'm fine. I just don't feel like sitting right now. Come on let's go." And he reached for her hand.

Exasperated, she took it and got up, then they rejoined the party.

After about twenty minutes of wondering around the party playing matchmaker with Esprit and the boys, Casey started to feel a little hot and lightheaded. He turned to the group and said, "Okay, guys, Esprit and I have done all we can. You are now officially on your own, so get out there and find yourselves some girls." He then teasingly shooed them away. Each one thanked him with a smile and then the four of them left to begin their quest of finding the perfect girl at the party.

As soon as they left Casey turned to Esprit, his eyes appeared unfocused and cloudy. "Is it hot in here or is it just me?"

She noticed beads of sweat forming on his brow. "Casey, you don't look so hot. Why don't we go outside and get some fresh air?"

She wrapped her arms around him and felt the warm moisture of sweat on his back. As they made their way back out of the house and into the back yard, Esprit realized that the stereo was playing their favorite song, *When I'm with You*, a romantic ballad from Usher's last CD.

"Casey, it's our song! Are you feeling okay to dance? You know how much I love this song!" She looked up at her pale and clammy boyfriend. Casey's head was now swimming, and he was starting to feel nauseous, but he didn't want to disappoint her so he just nodded his head and wrapped his big arms around her. As they began to sway back and forth in time to the beautiful song, Esprit stood on her tiptoes so she could nuzzle her head up against his broad shoulders.

Together they danced slowly, listening to the song. She rested most of her weight against him for about a minute or so, then suddenly out of nowhere, Casey began to waver. Two seconds later he collapsed, toppling backwards to the ground like a rag doll, and Esprit, all of her weight still resting against him, toppled right over with him. Esprit, thinking at first that Casey was just fooling around, rolled over laughing, but then she looked into his eyes with horror. They were rolled back in his head, and he was unconscious.

Esprit screamed at the top of her lungs for help. Kevin was there like a shot with Jamie in tow as soon as he heard Esprit scream. He knelt down beside Casey and tried to turn him over onto his side, but when he did Casey let loose a stream of liquid vomit that looked to be mostly the beer he'd just drank. Casey moaned once and then collapsed again in Kevin's arms. Jamie tried to comfort the panic-stricken Esprit, who continued screaming for help. Kim heard the commotion from inside the house and came running out to see what was going down.

Franticly, Kevin yelled for her, "Kim, Casey's unconscious and I'm not sure if he's breathing! Call 911 right now!"

Kim turned and raced back into the house to make the call.

"Jesus Christ, he's burning up! Somebody get me something to put under his head. Esprit, how much more beer did he have after we split up?"

Esprit cried hysterically, "Just one more glass, and I don't think he even finished it! Kevin, what the hell's wrong with him? Please…get him to wake up! Please God…help him!"

Over the next few minutes Shawn and the some of the other boys began to crowd around Kevin and the unconscious Casey while Kim's brother Joey and a bunch of his friends scurried about the house and yard collecting beer cups and hiding the keg in anticipation of the immanent arrival of the police and the first-aid squad.

Everyone could hear the two-tone blast of the ambulance

siren quickly approaching. As the seconds ticked by, they seemed like hours. Kevin continued to cradle Casey's head. He kept franticly trying to ascertain if Casey was actually breathing or not and checking for his pulse. He wasn't sure about the breathing, but there was definitely a weak pulse. He could feel it in his friend's neck. Jamie continued with her futile attempts to comfort Esprit.

Kim, breathless from her run inside to the phone and back, told everyone that the rescue squad was on their way, but she needn't have wasted her energy because the booming sound of the siren was getting louder and louder by the second.

Esprit continued to scream out questions to no one in particular. "What's the matter with him? Kevin, is he going to die? Is he still breathing? Somebody please, please do something – help him!"

She was losing her grip on reality and spinning further out of control by the second.

"Jamie! Could you please take her into the house, she's only making things worse…and everybody back the fuck up and give him some room to breathe, goddamn it!" yelled Kevin, frustrated by his helplessness as he desperately tried to think of something else to help his unconscious friend.

"Fuck you, Kevin! I'm not going anywhere, you asshole! He's my boyfriend!" screamed Esprit as Jamie tried to pull her back from the crowd.

Not more than a minute later, to Kevin's great relief, two emergency medical technicians, pulling a stretcher, burst through the crowd along with two police officers. As the technicians began to urgently work on Casey, one police officer began moving the crowd back while the other pulled Kevin aside to question him.

"Okay, son, first off, who is that boy and what's your name?"

"His name is Casey Collins, and I'm Kevin Hahn," said a clearly distraught Kevin.

"Okay, Kevin, try and stay calm, your friend is going to be all right. Can you tell me what happened here?"

"I…I really don't know! One minute he was fine, just hanging out with his girlfriend, and the next he was passed out on the ground!"

"Okay, Kevin, where is his girlfriend?"

Kevin pointed to Esprit and Jamie, who were standing just a few feet away. The police officer pointed to the two girls and signaled them to come over.

As the girls walked over to the officer the first EMT called out, "His heart rate is down in the low forties and his blood pressure is dropping! Find out if he has taken anything…now!"

The officer looked at the girls and said, "Okay, girls, which one of you is this boy's girlfriend?"

Esprit meekly raised her hand and said, "I am."

"Okay, young lady, did your boyfriend take any drugs tonight and how much beer did he drink? You need to tell me the truth so we can help him."

Esprit had trouble speaking, but she managed to eek out, "Just a couple of beers, Casey doesn't do drugs?"

The other EMT, who up till this point had been on his radio talking with the hospital, overheard Esprit's denial. In disbelief he stood up and yelled to the rest of the crowd, "This kid is in big trouble; if anyone knows if he's taken anything, please speak up right now because his life is at risk!"

The crowd was stunned into complete silence. Everyone knew Casey, and anyone that knew him knew that he'd be the last person in the world to do any illegal drugs. Jamie, still holding on to Esprit, looked nervous and uncomfortable, but she didn't say a word. Finally Shawn Murphy broke the silence when he yelled from the back of the crowd that Casey was a straight arrow and there was no way he did any drugs tonight.

Kevin thought about the steroids and weighed his options. He knew Casey had stopped them several days ago, so he decided for the time being to remain quiet so that he didn't get

Casey into trouble.

Not hearing any further responses from the crowd, the second EMT began helping the first one to load Casey's lifeless body onto the stretcher. Though they were trying to appear calm so as not to excite the crowd, the technicians were in reality panicked over Casey's deteriorating condition. So much so that they rushed to get him on the stretcher and then ran him as fast as they could around to the front of the house and quickly loaded him into the ambulance.

One of the EMTs called back to the police officer, "Go get the girlfriend, she needs to come with us! We need to question her further and have her get in contact with his family!"

The officer obeyed. He found Esprit and took her by the arm, urgently walking her over to the ambulance. Esprit turned at the last moment before boarding the ambulance and shouted to Kevin, "Call his parents, Kevin…right away…please!" Then the police officer shut the door and the ambulance sped off down the hill.

Though many of the partygoers had already fled at the first sign of trouble, there was still about sixty or seventy kids milling around in the driveway. They were scared and dumbfounded, the sound of the siren growing softer and softer as the ambulance screamed towards the hospital emergency room two miles away. The two police officers remained and halfheartedly questioned those kids still present, but they knew that the time for them getting any helpful information had long past. Finally the two officers walked Kim and Joey back into their house and told the rest of the partygoers to disperse.

Kevin, as soon as the ambulance pulled away, called Casey's parents. Lisa picked up after the first ring. Kevin cried out hysterically, "Mrs. C., it's Kevin. Something has happened to Casey! An ambulance just took him to Riverview Hospital! You and Mr. C. need to get over there right away! Please!" and then he started to cry.

A shocked Lisa cried out, "Kevin! What the hell are you

talking about? Calm down and talk to me. What happened?" she pleaded with him.

"I don't know Mrs. C. One moment he was fine, he and Esprit were dancing, and then the next he was passed out cold on the ground. We called for an ambulance and when they got here Casey was barely breathing…it all happened so fast…I don't know what happened…but…but…Mrs., C., he's in trouble…you need to get over to the hospital right away."

"Kevin…this doesn't make any sense! Who is with him now?" Lisa cried, desperate for information.

Kevin sobbed, "They took Esprit with him in the ambulance. I'm on my way now!"

Lisa, now panicked, said, "Steve and I are leaving right now. We'll meet you at the hospital, but, Kevin, when we get there, you've got to tell us everything that happened. So pull yourself together! Okay?"

Before he had a chance to say another word, she hung up the phone. When he got off the phone he turned to Jamie and said, "This is sooo fucked up! We need a car to get down there!"

Jamie pulled a set of keys out of a purse. "I took Esprit's pocket book before she left with the ambulance."

"Okay, let's go!" and he started for the car,

But Jamie grabbed a hold of the sleeve of his sweatshirt and said, "Wait a minute…I have to tell you something really, really important!"

Kevin looked at her in disbelief. "Tell me in the car…we have to get to the hospital…Now!"

"NO, KEVIN, IT CAN'T WAIT!…I think…I think…I accidentally gave Casey a hit of ecstasy!"

He turned to her. "YOU DID WHAT?"

"Kevin, please listen to me for a second. I put a hit of X in one of the beers I got for the two of you at the beginning of the night. It was supposed to be for you…I thought it might help you to loosen you a bit…but I accidentally set them down on the table, and then I forgot which one was which. Casey must have drunk the one with the X. I'm so sorry, Kevin…I really am!" She started to ball hysterically.

Kevin stared at her with white-hot rage. "JAMIE, ARE YOU OUT OF YOUR FUCKING MIND? YOU STUPID BITCH! WHY DIDN'T YOU TELL THE COPS?"

"I…I…wasn't sure, and I didn't want to get in trouble!" she sobbed.

Kevin grabbed her roughly by the arm. They ran down the road and jumped into Esprit's car.

"When we get to the hospital, you are going to tell them everything…everything! And if anything happens to him, I will fucking kill you myself!" screamed Kevin as they tore down the street in the direction of the hospital.

Chapter Twenty

Emergency Room – Part Two

The violent racking spasms of the seizure came to an abrupt halt about two minutes after they began, but unfortunately, so did the few remaining beats of Casey's struggling heart. The heart monitor beside his gurney, the one that just moments before had been emitting sporadic tones and beeps, now offered only a soft monotonous hum. The LED display on the front of the machine registered only a solitary flat red line. Even though Casey's body was finally calm, his temperature was still well above the danger threshold, holding steady at one hundred and four degrees.

Dr. Foster took a deep breath as he rechecked Casey's vital signs. In doing so he soon ascertained that Casey's respiration had completely ceased as well. Only a minute ago there had been eardrum-piercing chaos surrounding the patient, now there was just an eerie stillness and quiet in the room as the two orderlies, the nurse and Esprit, waited for Dr. Foster to do something – anything!

Foster shouted, "Oh shit! We may be too late! His heart's stopped! Someone take his girlfriend out of here, and Connie, get a bag on him!" Then he took a step back from Casey's lifeless body and ran for the crash cart. It was tucked away in a corner on the other side of the room. As he ran Foster slipped on the debris scattered around the floor but quickly regained his footing. At the same time one of the two orderlies grabbed Esprit and literally dragged her kicking and screaming out of the room. While all this was going on, Nurse Jones calmly placed an oxygen bag over Casey's face. She quickly adjusted the straps and began to rhythmically squeeze it to a silent count, heard only in her head.

Dr. Foster screamed out the door to no one in particular, "GET ANOTHER DOCTOR DOWN HERE, STAT! I NEED AN ASSIST!"

Another surgical nurse, who'd just arrived on the scene, jumped into the fray and started cutting away Casey's shirt with a pair of razor-sharp surgical scissors in order to provide an open area on his chest for the shock paddles that the doctor was prepping with some kind of clear, jelly-like lubricant. The nurse, with the help of the other orderly, turned Casey over on his side so she could cut away the remaining parts of his shirt. When he was on his side she saw the enormous contusion on his lower back and then, as she glanced a little further down his torso, she also spied the needle marks on his buttocks.

"Dr. Foster, you got to come here and get a look at this! His entire lower back is one big contusion, and that ain't all! From the looks of it, this boy's been self-administering injections in his left buttocks for quite some time! There's got to be at least a dozen different marks down there, and some of them are clearly weeks, maybe even months, old!"

Foster scrambled over with the crash cart in tow and checked out Casey's backside. "Damn, this kid's no fucking diabetic, and from the looks of him, I'm pretty sure he's not main-lining heroin, so I am willing to bet the ranch that the dumb son of a bitch has been loading up on anabolic steroids. Damn it! Now it all makes sense! No wonder the epinephrine and the atropine sent him through the roof!"

Foster clapped his hands to get everyone's attention. "Okay, people, we've got to get his heart started again right now! A couple more minutes and his brain's gonna fry! Mary, keep that bag going until I tell you to stop!" the doctor screamed as he did one final check on the paddles before placing them firmly on Casey's lifeless chest.

"Okay here we go, step back everyone." Foster set the paddles down on Casey's chest and yelled, "Clear!"

Once outside the ER, the orderly hurried Esprit back to the crowded waiting room and handed her over to the waiting security officer. Then without another word, he turned right around and rushed back through the doors to the trauma room. The security officer remained silent as he kept an eye on Esprit, who was standing there in the middle of the waiting room sobbing, desperate with fear.

Not knowing what else to do or where to turn, she ran up and grabbed the officer, clutching at him and pleading for him to do something – anything. He looked down into her pleading eyes and fueled by compassion he brought her to a chair and gently sat her down. He was about to sit with her and attempt to calm her down when the emergency room doors burst open and Kevin and Jamie rushed in, breathless from their mad dash to the emergency room from the upper reaches of the adjacent multilevel parking garage.

Jamie ran up to Esprit and tried to comfort her, but Esprit turned away. She wanted nothing to do with Jamie. Instead, she turned to Kevin with her fruitless pleas for help. Kevin listened for a few seconds but couldn't make sense out of anything she was saying. It was all just hysterical gibberish, so he got up and ran over to the admissions desk to find out what was happening. When he reached the desk and inquired about Casey's condition, a less-than-accommodating hospital receptionist behind the desk only confirmed what he already knew – that Casey was in the trauma room in serious condition. No matter how much he pleaded, the stubborn and callous woman would give him nothing more. She just shook her head and told him to be patient.

Frustrated, he ran back to Esprit and tried to find out something, anything, from her, but she was beyond the ability to rationally communicate. She just kept repeating the same mantra over and over, "HE'S DEAD...I KNOW IT...CASEY'S DEAD!"

Kevin pulled Jamie away from Esprit for a moment and whispered harshly in her ear, "Jamie, I have to tell the doctors about the ecstasy! They need to know what he's taken!"

She pleaded with him not to. They'd discussed it on the ride over, and she'd begged him not to tell because she was afraid she'd be arrested, but Kevin couldn't care less then and he still couldn't.

"Fuck you, Jamie! I don't give a shit about you getting arrested." He pointed. "Casey's in there and he's in big fucking trouble!"

Jamie clutched at his shirt as he turned to leave, but he forcefully pulled away and stared back at her with pure hatred in his eyes, then he ran back over to the front desk. "Listen, miss, I really need to speak with a doctor right now! I have some information about Casey Collins that they really need. It can help them!"

The stubborn woman at the desk, unaware of the severity of Casey's condition because he'd been brought in by ambulance through a different set of doors, merely said, "Young man, I can't exactly leave my desk to waltz back into the ER and disrupt the doctors right now. As you can see, we are very busy, so why don't you just go take a seat and be patient. I'm sure the doctors will come out to speak with you in a little while."

Kevin was livid. He realized he wasn't getting anywhere with this bitch, but he had to do something, so he turned away from the desk, feigning like he was going back to his seat, but then to the woman's surprise, he took a quick left turn and darted for the door that lead to the treatment area. The security guard spied what was happening out of the corner of his eye and took after him like a shot. But Kevin, utilizing his greater speed and agility, hit the door running and was through the entrance well before the guard had a chance to catch him.

Once through the door, Kevin searched franticly up and down the large circular ward. He saw an expansive, well-lit area, flooded with hundreds of bright florescent lights. Around the entire circular perimeter of the space were a series of treatment rooms and in the center, a large circular workstation with several doctors and nurses talking and milling about. Kevin surveyed the area, trying to ascertain exactly where Casey was being treated, but he was running out of time. Suddenly he noticed on the far side of the ward a room where there seemed to be a big commotion. He took off like the wind in the general direction of the room, hastily searching each open door as he ran by. Several nurses attempted to stop him, but he was determined to get to Casey. Just as he made it around to the far side of the room where he suspected Casey was, the security guard came barrel ling through the entrance, yelling, "STOP HIM! STOP THAT KID!" But by then it was too late.

Kevin reached the room on the far side with the door marked 'Trauma'. He took a deep breath before going in. Even so, he was still unprepared for what he was about to see because when he opened the door he stepped right into hell. He looked around at the mess and confusion and was paralyzed with shock and with fear. He watched in horror as the naked, lifeless body of Casey jolted upwards in the air and arched six inches above the gurney while a half-dozen doctors and nurses franticly charged around him, holding all sorts of needles, bags, and other medical instruments. Kevin broke from his trance and looked around the rest of the room. There was blood, body fluids, and discarded instruments scattered all over the floor.

Kevin focused his attention on the machine attached to his unconscious friend. He had watched enough episodes of *ER* to know that it was a heart monitor. When he saw that the machine was not beeping, and there was only a single, unmoving flat line on the monitor, he was dumbstruck. When he finally turned and looked down directly at Casey's face he barely recognized it. Beneath the bag that a nurse was squeezing over his mouth and nose, Casey's skin was a swollen dark purple mess and Kevin could only see the whites of his eyes.

Dr. Foster, hearing the commotion at the door, looked up from his critical patient and saw Kevin. At the very same moment, the security guard ran in through the door and grabbed Kevin by the collar.

"Who the hell is this kid and how did he get all the way back here?" screamed the doctor.

Before the officer could respond, Kevin screamed out, "Casey's been on steroids for about a year, and tonight someone dropped a hit of ecstasy in his beer! Is he going to be okay?"

The doctor, with little patience and even less time, stared directly at the officer and said, "Thanks, kid. Now please get him out of here…now!" Then he went right back to work on Casey's chest, leaving Kevin frightened and bewildered.

The security guard's demeanor changed somewhat when he realized Kevin was only trying help his friend, but still, he forcefully pushed Kevin from the room and forced him to walk directly back to the waiting room.

Kevin, in tears as they walked back through the ER door into the waiting room, looked up and saw Casey's parents a few feet away, down on their knees in front of the two girls, pleading with Esprit to tell them what happened to their son.

Steve turned and saw the security guard coming towards them with Kevin in tow. He leaped up and ran to them. "Kevin, what the hell is going? Please, please, tell us something! The woman at the front desk said that Casey was brought in unconscious and in serious condition…what the hell happened?"

Kevin was too distraught to say anything at first, but when he looked into the imploring eyes of Casey's parents, he summoned the strength to tell them what he had just witnessed firsthand in the trauma room.

"When…I…ran…in…into the room, Casey was unconscious and…" He stopped for a moment to gather his strength, "and his…his heart was stopped!" That was all he could manage before bursting into tears.

Lisa fell to the carpeted floor and shrieked. Steve looked at him incredulously. He screamed, “What did you say? Oh my God! I have to get back there!” He took off for the door, but this time the security guard anticipated his reaction and was ready. He raced after Steve and blocked him well before he could pass through the door.

The officer grabbed Steve firmly by the shoulders and quietly but resolutely said to him, “Sir, I know it’s your boy in there, but I can’t let you in there right now! What the boy said is correct! There’s a team of doctors in there right now attempting to save your son’s life! They’re doing everything they can to save him, and you going in there will only distract them from doing what they need to do! Do you understand?”

Steve, crying now, shouted. “Fuck you! He’s my son!”

He tried again to break away and push through the door, but the officer wouldn’t relinquish his iron grip. “I told you…I can’t let you in there, sir!”

Steve pleaded as tears streamed down his face, but the officer wouldn’t budge. “Sir, please go back and take care of your wife and your son’s friends. I promise, I will go back there and find out what’s happening. The moment any new information comes out, I will come and tell you…I swear to you. But…please…please let the doctors do their job and try and save your son!”

As soon as the guard finished speaking, Steve’s shoulders sagged and his head dropped. He had come to the awful realization that he was utterly helpless to help Casey at the moment. He wiped the tears from his face, looked up at the officer and nodded his acceptance.

When the two of them walked back to the group Lisa saw Steve’s beaten demeanor and was bewildered. She rushed over and furiously beat on Steve’s shoulders, “NO…NO…NO…WE HAVE TO DO SOMETHING! STEVE…PLEASE… GODDAMN IT!”

After a furious minute of violent futility, she stopped and buried her head in her husband's chest and moaned in frustration. Steve began to gently stroke her hair to comfort her when in through the front doors rushed Ethan and Jordan Burke.

Ethan scanned the crowded room until he spied the hysterical group in the far corner over by the admissions desk. He looked over the crowd for his daughter; first he spied Steve with his arms wrapped around his wailing wife, tears streaming down both of their faces. Standing next to them looking helpless and crying was Casey's friend, Kevin, who was being calmed by a security guard. And finally, there sitting down right behind them on one of the hard plastic waiting room chairs was Esprit's friend Jamie with her arms wrapped around his distraught child.

Back in the trauma room, the medical staff was working feverishly, trying to restart Casey's heart. It had been over ten minutes since Casey had seized, and well over six since his heart stopped and his respiration ceased for the second time. Dr. Foster had already made two unsuccessful attempts to shock Casey's heart back into rhythm and was frantically preparing for a third. By this point he knew full well that if he didn't get Casey's heart going in the next ninety seconds, they were going to lose him.

He calmly and professionally assessed the numbers as he readied the shock paddles. *Okay, his heart had been stopped for at least six minutes, possibly more. His respiration has ceased for the same amount of time, and his fever has been well over the danger threshold for as much as half an hour. If I don't get him breathing again and his heart started right now, the odds are that he will end up, best-case scenario, with brain damage or worse, brain dead, no matter what happens!*

For the third time he firmly placed the paddles on Casey's chest and loudly shouted, "Clear!" As soon as the others stepped back Dr. Foster pressed the switch on the paddles and Casey once again arched into the air as electricity coursed through his body, but unlike the first two attempts, the LED screen on the heart monitor suddenly sprang to life. It miraculously changed from a continuous flat line to a broken line that evidenced small irregular spikes; small but spikes just the same.

Nurse Evans shouted, "Hey, I think we got something here!"

Everyone looked at the monitor and saw the faint activity on the LED display. Dr. Foster called out, "It's still way too early, and the beats are slow and irregular. Continue with chest compressions and the bag until we get more activity. And, Connie, if in the next two minutes he gets stronger, I'm going to intubate him so get the respirator ready to hook him up. He's still not breathing, and at least for now I don't think he's going to be able to on his own!"

He looked over his shoulder at the two orderlies. "You two go and find me every ice pack in the ER, as many as you can carry! We have to get him cooled down in a big hurry!"

The doctor looked up again at the monitor and indeed, Casey's heart was beginning to establish a soft but steady rhythm. "Okay, people, his heart is getting stronger, but we are a long way from being out of the woods here. We've got to get more oxygen into him right now! He's been down for almost ten minutes and with the high fever, God only knows what kind of brain damage he might have sustained."

The orderlies ran back in a minute later and began stuffing ice packs all around Casey's body to rapidly bring down his temperature. At the same time, Dr. Foster and Nurse Evans started the intubation process so that they could hook him up to the respirator. She tilted Casey's head back as far as it would go while the doctor inserted a long curved plastic tube down the back of his yielding throat.

As he ran for the ice, one of the orderlies had called out to the desk to let them know they had gotten the patient's heart restarted. A sympathetic nurse at the desk who'd witnessed

Kevin's earlier mad dash, radioed to the security guard standing with the family. He heard the call and walked away from Steve and Kevin before responding. The nurse informed him that Dr. Foster had been able to get Casey's heart restarted, but the boy was still teetering on the edge of life and death.

The guard thought for a moment about what to tell the family. They were all so distraught, but he didn't want to give them false hope. He'd seen this kind of thing many times before; it could still go either way. Quickly, he decided giving them a little something was better than nothing. It would probably be a long while before any more news came out, and these people were at their breaking point. He clicked off his radio and walked back to the group.

"Mr. and Mrs. Collins, I just received word that they were able to restart your son's heart."

Everyone leaped up at the news, but before they could ask a single question he continued, "Wait…wait a minute. I'm not a doctor…I was only informed that his heart has been restarted, and that he is still in very grave condition!" All eyes were drawn to his every word. "Now please listen to me. It could be a while before any more information comes out, so please try and stay calm! As soon as any more information comes out, I will let you know."

The security guard, sensing that the family now had at least a sliver of hope to hang on to, and knowing he had nothing else left to offer, quietly made his way off to the other side of the room.

Upon hearing the news Esprit began to pull herself together and started talking to her parents. Lisa and Steve managed to pull Kevin away from the others, and they pressed him about what happened. Lisa, between sobs asked, "Kevin, what is going on? Did Casey get hurt at the game? Please tell us what's happened. Steve and I need to know what is going on…something…anything…please!"

Kevin's head was spinning. In just mere seconds he'd

shifted from the elation of knowing Casey was still alive to the fear of having the most difficult conversation of his life. He had no idea what to say to Casey's parents. He looked over Lisa's shoulder and spied Jamie, standing alone, separated from everyone, her eyes pleading for him not to say anything.

He weighed the facts; the doctor knew about the ecstasy and the steroids, so no matter what happened, it was going to come out. But no one knew it was Jamie who had accidentally given it to him. Kevin didn't know if the X had anything to do with what was happening to Casey, but it didn't really matter. He was going to tell them everything except Jamie's part in the story.

With new tears forming, he began, "Mr. and Mrs. Collins, I'm sorry to be to the one to tell you this, but Casey's been injecting steroids for over a year now. He started his forth cycle last week, three months before he was supposed to, and he's been sick as a dog all week."

Ethan and Jordan heard Lisa gasp and turned to listen to the rest of the conversation. Steve was furious. He couldn't even begin to digest what Kevin had said. Lisa looked at Kevin and shook her head. "There's no way...Kevin, this can't be true…tell me it isn't true!"

Kevin lowered his eyes. "I'm sorry, Mrs. C…but it's true. I begged him to stop, but he wouldn't listen to me!" Kevin paused to regain some control.

Lisa went ballistic. She charged at Kevin, striking out at him as she screamed, "Why didn't you say anything? He was your best friend!"

Steve, still in shock, just stood there in frozen disbelief. Ethan jumped in to Kevin's rescue. He gently pulled Lisa away from Kevin and tried to comfort her while Jordan stayed with a stunned Esprit.

Now Kevin had no choice now but to tell them the rest. They were going to find out anyway. So as Ethan gently kept Lisa at bay, between intermittent chokes and sobs, Kevin told them everything that happened leading up to the party. Then he finished with a bang. "There's one more thing! Tonight at the party someone put ecstasy in Casey's beer…I think that he must have…." Then he was cut off.

Steve had been totally quiet to this point, not able to comprehend much of what Kevin was saying. He couldn't begin to comprehend the idea that his perfect son would ever do something like this. Not in his wildest dreams! But when Kevin mentioned the ecstasy something clicked in Steve's head. He knew what X was, and he knew that it was dangerous. He was shocked that one of Casey's supposed friends had surreptitiously drugged him, but this was something he could at least understand. This was something he could sink his teeth into. This one terrible fact gave Steve the means to reenter reality, and it allowed him to finally emote. Unfortunately, his emotion poured fourth in a gout of anger and rage.

"WHAT!" he interrupted. "Who the fuck would have done something like that to my son! I'LL KILL THE SON OF A BITCH! KEVIN! WHO DID IT? I WANT TO KNOW RIGHT NOW!"

Steve grabbed Kevin by the neck and throttled him. As the security guard came charging back over to pull Steve away from Kevin, Jamie slowly rose from her chair next to Esprit and began to slip away towards the exit doors.

Suddenly, from out of nowhere Esprit let loose an earsplitting scream that stopped everyone but Jamie in their tracks. "NOOO! JAMIEEEEEEE! NOOOO! OH MY GOD… YOU DIDN'T!"

The moment Jamie heard the scream she bolted out the emergency room doors before anyone could stop her. Esprit collapsed on the floor, her body wracking and heaving. As Ethan and Jordan rushed to their daughter's aid, Steve turned to Lisa in utter disbelief and said, "I don't fucking believe any of this! This can't be true!"

He grabbed Lisa and held her tightly, both of them desperately clinging to the hope that their son would survive, while attempting to digest what they'd just been told – information that only yesterday would have seamed so totally absurd.

A little after one in the morning, not long after Esprit's surprising outburst and Jamie's hasty exit, a police detective entered the emergency room. He identified himself as Detective Morrongiello to the women at the desk and inquired on the status of the teenage patient that had been transported in by the Middletown rescue squad just over an hour before. He informed the hospital that since the victim was found unconscious at a party, the police were investigating the cause. The now suddenly convivial women at the desk provided the detective with Casey's full name and address and then informed him of his critical condition.

"That name sounds very familiar," said the detective. "Isn't he the star football player over at Middletown South?"

She replied, "Well, sir, I couldn't possibly know that, but his family is right over there." She pointed in the direction of the distraught group.

Detective Morrongiello said, "Thank you, miss. I'll go over there to speak with them. If by chance you get an update on his condition, could you let me know right away?"

The woman smiled. "Why certainly, Detective."

Detective Morrongiello appraised the group before approaching them. They were all in pretty bad shape. *Apparently they know a hell of a lot more than the old crone at the desk*, he thought. He quietly approached a middle-aged couple who were standing apart from the rest and crying in each other's arms, thinking they had to be the parents.

"Excuse me, I'm sorry to disturb you at a time like this, but my name is Detective Morrongiello, and I'm investigating the incident involving the boy at the party over in Oak Hill. Would the two of you be the parents of…" he looked down at his notes, "…umm…Casey Collins?"

Steve looked at the detective and quietly replied, "Yes, we are his parents."

The detective again looked down at his notes and said, "I am truly sorry to disturb you, but I've been sent over to find out what's happened to your son because the two patrolmen that responded to the emergency call noted in their report that there was a large quantity of alcohol being served to underage kids, and there was also signs of marijuana and drug use. First off, what is the condition of your boy?"

Lisa pulled away from Steve and walked right up to within an inch of the Detective's face. She snarled, "Detective, my son might be dying back there! YOU WANT TO KNOW WHAT HAPPENED, GO ASK THEM!" and she pointed right at Kevin and Esprit.

"Okay, Mrs. Collins, I'm not here to upset you, so why don't you try to calm down, and I'll go and talk to the kids, all right?"

Steve tried to control his enraged wife as the detective excused himself and turned away. Detective Morrongiello walked over to where Esprit was sitting with her parents and Kevin. As he approached, Ethan stood up and protectively stepped in between the detective and his daughter.

"Detective, I'm Congressman Ethan Burke, and that young lady is my daughter Esprit," pointing at his prone and weeping daughter. "Casey Collins is her boyfriend and as you can see, she is quite distraught. I would appreciate it if you would hold off on your questioning, at least until we get some more news of Casey's condition."

Detective Morrongiello sensed that with the addition of a congressman's daughter into the mix, his investigation had just ratcheted up a notch to an entirely different level. He became very polite. "Sir, I am terribly sorry to bother you and your family at this difficult time. Maybe you could give me the facts, so that I don't have to disturb your daughter?"

Ethan appeared flustered. "Well, I really don't know all that much, but I will tell you what I do know, and then this young man can probably fill in the rest." He pointed to Kevin.

"From what we have been told so far, and it isn't much, Casey's heart stopped soon after he was brought in by ambulance, but the medical team was able to get it restarted. We were informed by the security officer about ten minutes ago that his condition was grave."

"Okay, sir, thank you. Now we are getting somewhere," said the detective. "Does anyone know what might have caused the boy's condition? Is it possibly alcohol poisoning, or maybe some kind of drug thing?"

"We were only just informed by this young man that it could possibly involve steroids and something…some drug called…oh…what was it…ecstasy. Yes, I think that was what he said, ecstasy. But, Detective, I've known Casey for a long time, and he is not the type of boy who abuses drugs. This whole thing doesn't make any sense. You really must speak with Kevin. He's Casey's best friend, he'll be able to shed some light on this whole sordid mess."

The detective thanked Ethan and turned to Kevin, who was visibly beside himself with worry.

"Okay, Kevin, my name is Detective Morrongiello. It would seem that you are the only one who can fill in the remaining blanks to this story. Why don't you and I go over to those chairs away from Casey's family, and then you can tell me what the hell happened here."

Kevin was reluctant, but the security officer prodded him on, so he walked away and sat down with the detective. Through tears and sobs he told him the whole story: Casey's history of steroid abuse, his physical problems this week, and finally, the events that occurred tonight at the party, including Jamie's accidental dosing of Casey's beer.

When he finished he slumped down in his chair with his head in his hands looking as if it was the end of the world. Casey was back in there fighting for his very life, and he had just ratted out everyone involved. Detective Morrongiello patted Kevin on the shoulder and told him he had done the right thing. He then politely excused himself from the group and went outside with the security guard. The guard informed him confidentially that Casey's chances were very slim and then left to rejoin the group inside.

Detective Morrongiello, now standing outside by himself, lit a cigarette and considered carefully how he was going to proceed with this delicate investigation. After a minute or so, he blew out a thick stream of smoke, threw the half-smoked butt on the ground and crushed it with the toe of his shoe. He then picked up his radio and called into the station telling them to issue arrest warrants and send out two squad cars to pick up one Jamie Heist and one Frank Giordano for questioning.

Back in the trauma room Casey had been successfully intubated and was now breathing, but only with the help of the respirator. The triage team led by Dr. Foster had reestablished a slow but increasingly steady heartbeat, and Casey's blood pressure was rising back out of danger. Thanks to the dozens of ice packs surrounding his body, his temperature was also down below one hundred and two, but Dr. Foster was troubled by the fact that he was still not capable of breathing on his own, only with the support of the ventilator.

Fearing that Casey had suffered severe brain damage and was now perhaps in a deep and irreversible coma, the doctor continued to check Casey for signs of cerebral and brain stem function. He began by squeezing different areas of Casey's anatomy, hoping to find a simple motor response to the pain, but there was none. Then, with a small penlight he looked closely into Casey's eyes for corneal and oculocephalic reflexes, but again there were none. He then irrigated Casey's ears with fifty CCs of ice water and looked into his eyes for the third time to check for oculovestibular reflexes, but again there was simply no response. Casey pupils remained fixed and dilated, and he was demonstrating zero motor response.

Dr. Foster, now fearing the worst, told his staff, "Okay, people, we have done everything we can, but it doesn't look good. I'm not getting any motor response whatsoever. Let's spend the next few minutes stabilizing him, and then, assuming he remains in a deep comatose state, we'll begin running him through Brain Death Criteria. Let's get ready to run an EEG."

He signaled the nurse to bring in the EEG monitor in preparation for the test. "Okay, everybody, listen up, I am starting to think that the combination of oxygen loss and high fever may have fried his brain. When we run the EEG, if there is something there, great, then we rush him right up to the OR, but if not and his brain is completely shot, well, then he becomes a candidate for an organ harvest. His kidneys and liver probably can't be used, but his heart and other organs are healthy and strong. Does anyone know where his clothes are? I need to find his wallet."

One of the nurses raised her hand.

The doctor continued, "Go through his wallet, find out how old he is, and check his driver's license to see if he checked the organ donor box."

The nurse pulled out Casey's wallet and checked the license. She confirmed that Casey was eighteen years old and that he indeed had checked off the box.

"Okay, everyone, I'm going to go call in a neurosurgeon on the off-chance that something positive happens, and we can save him, and then we'll run the EEG. Connie, get on the horn with the Share Network and let them know we might have a candidate just in case."

As the two nurses went about setting up the EEG, Dr. Foster hurried to the ER phone and called up to fourth floor to see if there was a neurologist on stand-by, or better yet, one still in the hospital. The operator took a moment to check what doctors were still in the building, but at two in the morning it was a futile exercise. She returned a minute later and informed the doctor that there was no one present but that she would call the neurologist on stand-by. Foster thanked her and hung up the phone. Then he went back to the patient.

As he began preparing for the EEG, Foster took a moment to reflect on the situation. He thought about Casey and what could possibly have caused this to happen. He had come in unconscious and in respiratory distress. When he first checked Casey's vitals, they were all dropping so fast the kid had reached a catatonic state. Administering the epinephrine and the atropine were standard operating procedures for the boy's condition, but that was before he knew about the steroids. Then there was the wildly high fever and the bruising around his kidneys. It had appeared at the time that some, if not all, of the kid's major organs were starting to shut down one at a time. Most assuredly his kidneys and liver were severely damaged. That was evidenced in the initial tox screen, but the CBC and the other blood work would confirm all of that soon enough. It was pretty clear to Foster that Casey had been abusing steroids for some time, and that in itself would have put a serious strain on the functioning of his internal organs, and then ingesting the ecstasy tonight would have only exacerbated the problem.

He assumed the drugs would explain the high fever, but what about the massive contusion? That could only have come from brute force impact. Well, the boy was a star football player. He must have taken one hell of a shot in the back. As he prepped the patient to run the EEG, he held out very little hope of seeing any brain activity. His last thought before starting the test was, *One way or another, we will get to the bottom of this when we get the tests results back.*

It took a few more minutes for the team of nurses and the doctor to properly attach each of the electrodes around Casey's head, and then they were ready to run the electroencephalogram, a test that measured brainwave activity and function. Unfortunately, a few short minutes later, just as the doctor had predicted, the test results from the EEG evidenced no brain function whatsoever. Casey was brain dead.

While the rest of the team went about unhooking Casey from the EEG, Dr. Foster looked dejectedly down at the boy's still and lifeless body. Casey's heart was beating, but his brain had been completely destroyed by the lack of oxygen and the intense fever. He would never again be able to breath on his own.

At this point Dr. Foster was quite sure they would find some pretty severe damage to the boy's liver and kidneys. However, it was his job to save lives and even though there were probably a couple of organs that couldn't be used, Casey was still a good candidate for a harvest. As a matter of course, Dr. Foster would have the neurologist run a Cerebral Blood Flow Study first, but he already knew the study would only confirm the EEG results.

However, now it was time to act. First things first, the blood flow test, and then he would have to meet the boy's next of kin and get them to agree to shut down the respirator, which in effect would be the legal cause of death. Only then would he attempt to get them to agree to the organ harvest. Foster knew this was going to be dicey. Even though the patient had signed his organ donor card, his parents could still challenge the hospital, and that would come only after they agreed to terminate his life. He walked back to the house phone and dialed the hospital's compliance office to track down the in-house attorney.

When he finished the call, he dreaded what came next. He'd just gone through the details of the patient's chart with the hospital's legal council, and council, somewhat reluctantly, gave him the go-ahead to proceed with caution with the boy's parents. The attorney begrudgingly acknowledged that, based on the facts of the case, the hospital had no liability for the boy's death, but any termination of life support was a tough call and the organ harvest request would only add an additional layer of complexity to any potential legal challenge.

Dr. Foster first went to the changing room behind the ER to change out of his soiled hospital garb, and then he washed his face and hands with cold water. He was rather fatigued, and his head was pounding. He rubbed his temples for a moment and then with a deep sigh he left the ER to go find Casey's parents.

When Dr. Foster walked through the door into the waiting room, all heads turned in his direction. By this time it was after two a.m. and they were the only ones left in the lobby.

Lisa pulled away from Steve and ran up to him. "Are you the doctor taking care of my son? Is he going to be okay?" she pleaded. Steve followed closely behind.

"Are you Mr. and Mrs. Collins?" the doctor asked.

They both nodded.

"Please come with me."

Before they had a chance to say a word, he led them just a few steps away to a private conference room off to the side of the waiting room. Steve and Lisa stepped through the door fearing the worst, but hoping and praying for something positive. They both sat on one side of the table and Foster took a seat on the other side. He folded his hands on the table and began.

"Mr. and Mrs. Collins, your son was admitted over three hours ago by ambulance. When he arrived he was unconscious, barely breathing, and he had an extraordinarily high fever – over one hundred and six degrees, and his vital signs…blood pressure and heart rate…they were dropping fast. We gave him a shot of epinephrine, hoping to stimulate his activity, and he immediately went into a bout of severe convulsions that lasted for several minutes. When they finally subsided his heart had stopped. We spent the next eight to ten minutes attempting to revive his heart. On the third attempt we finally got it beating again, but Mr. and Mrs. Collins, by then he had been deprived of oxygen for at least ten minutes, maybe more."

Lisa moaned as the tone of his voice began to change. Dr. Foster took them step-by-step through detailed process of medically determining brain death. By the time he reached his discussion of the EGG and Brain Death Criteria, both Steve and Lisa were painfully aware of where this was heading.

As they listened in shock, the doctor continued, "There is a neurologist with Casey right now running a final test called a

Cerebral Blood Flow Study. It's a test that will measure if there is any remaining blood flow to the brain, but Mr. and Mrs. Collins, I have been through this many times before, and I have to be honest with you. The EEG is rarely, if ever, wrong. I am truly sorry to inform you, but your son is brain dead."

"NOOOOOOO!" cried out Lisa. Steve sat there frozen in disbelief. "NOOOOO! NOT CASEY! PLEASE GOD…NOT MY BOY!" She banged her fist on the table over and over again until her strength failed.

Outside the conference room, the others heard Lisa's scream, and then they guessed that their worst fears had come true. Ethan tightly held his retching daughter while Jordan quickly moved to comfort Kevin.

Dr. Foster allowed Lisa and Steve a good ten minutes to vent their pain and anger before he continued. "Mr. and Mrs. Collins, I'm so sorry for your loss, but there are some things that we need to discuss, and I want you to be very clear on what is happening."

He looked at them to see if he had their attention, and even though they both were looking directly at him, he wasn't sure if either one comprehended anything he had just said.

"Legally, the Cerebral Blood Flow Study must be run twice, so it will take at least another two hours to complete. Once we have determined the results of both tests, which I believe will evidence no brain activity, I will have no choice but to declare your son brain dead. His heart will still be beating, and he will be breathing with the aid of a respirator, but his brain will have ceased to function, and, I wish it were not so, but there is no current medical science that can restore your son's brain activity, and none in the foreseeable future."

Lisa began to wail louder and louder.

Dr. Foster again allowed them time to digest his words. Then he gently continued, "Mr. and Mrs. Collins, normally, at pronouncement of death we would simply turn off the respirator and allow the patient's still-functioning systems to simply shut down on their own. But in your son's case I would like to speak with you about organ donation. He has checked on his driver's license that he is a willing donor, and he is a perfect candidate. There are thousands of critical patients around this country that could truly benefit from your tragic loss. Casey signed his organ donor card, but ultimately this decision is yours. If you were to agree, we would leave him on the respirator until we were able to ascertain which of his organs would be used. This would be for a period of no more than twenty-four hours. If the two of you would like, I can get a representative from the Share Network, the agency that handles organ donations across the country, to come in and speak with you."

"ARE YOU OUT OF YOUR MIND!" screamed Lisa. "That's my son in there, not some piece of meat, you fucking asshole!" She reached across the table in an attempt to grab the doctor.

As Steve tried to pull Lisa back, Dr. Foster calmly stood up from the table and said, "Mr. and Mrs. Collins, I am sorry if I have caused you any further pain. I'm only trying to do my job, which is to save lives…."

"FUCK YOU! YOU DIDN'T SAVE MY SON'S LIFE!" screamed the inconsolable Lisa.

The doctor lowered his head and folded his hands. "Mr. and Mrs. Collins, I am sorry. I'm going back in to the ER now to finish the Cerebral Blood Flow Study. This will give the two of you a chance to talk. I beg you to reconsider. Casey's last act could be to save someone else's life. I'll be back to speak with you as soon as the tests are completed. I am truly sorry for your loss." He then quietly left the room.

As soon as the doctor left, Esprit, her parents, and Kevin rushed in to find out what had happened. When they entered the cramped conference room, Lisa collapsed on the table with Steve standing behind her, his hand on her back, tears streaming down his face, and then they knew the truth, Casey was dead.

Esprit dropped to the floor, and as Ethan struggled to pick her up Steve signaled them to come in. He barely managed to get out what he needed to say before he burst into a series of painful sobs. "Casey is brain dead. He's on life support while they run one final test to make sure that there is absolutely no brain function, but the doctor has already told us that his brain is gone." There was little more to be said.

After a few moments, Ethan broke the dreadful silence by saying, "Lisa, Steve, I can't tell you how sorry I am. Casey was truly a unique and gifted young man. If there's anything I can do at this moment to ease your pain, please just ask."

Lisa raised her head from the table and whispered, "Thank you, Ethan, could you bring the kids home. There's nothing more for them here. Steve and I need to wait for the test results to come back, and then we have some tough decisions to make. We will call you when it's over!" Then she began to sob once more.

Ethan nodded and turned to the two teenagers. He said gently, "Come on kids, it's time to go home. There is nothing more any of us can do for Casey."

He reached for his daughter, but she pulled away fiercely and screamed, "NO…I HAVE TO SEE HIM…I HAVE TO SEE CASEY ONE MORE TIME…PLEASE!"

Ethan reached for her and wrapped her in his arms. He said softly, "I'm sorry, baby, I really am, but you can't do that right now. Please, honey, we need to get you home."

Esprit sobbed and squeezed her father tighter as he led her out the door and then out of the hospital with Jordan right behind him, half-walking, half-carrying Kevin.

Detective Morrongiello, who till this point had been quietly waiting in the shadows, saw them leave and approached the information desk, where he was informed that Casey had been pronounced brain dead. He thanked the woman behind the desk and swiftly left the hospital for the station. *Christ, wait till the media gets a hold of this.* His investigation had just been cranked up even further. Not only did the case involve a star athlete, illegal drugs, and a congressman's teenage daughter, but now there was the death to add to the already sordid mix.

For nearly an hour Steve and Lisa sat slumped together in the stuffy little conference room. The security officer came in on two separate occasions and offered to get them coffee, but on each occasion they declined with a barely nod. The two of them were completely absorbed in their own minds, futilely battling the misery of their private thoughts, and neither had the strength nor the capacity to comfort the other, or for that matter, even the ability to exchange even a few simple words.

As Lisa sat there staring off into space, her mind began to wander. Her subconscious took her back to the comfort and the safety of the past in order to escape the pressing agony of the here and now. Scenes drawn from the pleasant memories of Casey's childhood deliriously swirled around the periphery her consciousness.

They came in whirling haphazard fashion, it was like she was in the center of the tornado scene from the classic film *The Wizard of OZ*, only she was Dorothy on the spinning bed. In her mind's eye there was Casey, a newborn baby coming home from the hospital, wrapped tightly in a fluffy blue blanket to ward off the chill. He was wearing his first outfit, a thick white cotton jumper with the Yankees' interlocking NY insignia on the front. Then the image was gone with a flash and another came into focus. Casey, eleven months old, taking his first bumbling steps, followed by a fall right underneath the Christmas tree as he reached to touch a shiny ornament at grandma's house at his first Christmas. *Click*, as if by magic and with no conscious thought, the scene changed again. Lisa wanted the images to slow down. She wanted to savor each precious one, but her racing thoughts quickened to a dazzling pace, and now the images were coming so fast it was if she was watching Casey's whole life flash by before her eyes.

The images were coming on so fast they were slightly distorted, and it seemed to her as if she was now seeing them through something like the opaque, plastic lenses of a ViewMaster children's toy. *Click*, Casey's first day of T-ball…his stubby little legs churning around the bases as fast as they could go. *Click*, Casey in second grade, up on the stage at his elementary school, bowing over and over again with a big grin on his face and his two front teeth missing, while enthusiastic parents and teachers clapped for his adorable performance as Hansel in the play *Hansel and Gretel*. *Click*, Casey's first touchdown in Pop-Warner football. *Click*, his first wrestling match. *Click*, his first real date. *Click*, the Junior Prom….

One after another the scenes zoomed into Lisa's consciousness, and then after only a fleeting moment they all too quickly dissolved, only to be replaced by the next image in a long line. No matter how she tried desperately to cling to one image, they just kept changing at breakneck speed.

Steve, unlike his wife, made no attempt to find safety in the past. That was beyond him. His grief could only move him in a forward direction. Instead of focusing on the past as Lisa was, he sat there slumped over the table in the overheated tiny room fantasizing on the not-to-distant future.

In his deeply troubled mind the future was a bleak and shadowy place filled with lonely images of him and Lisa standing bewildered against a stark backdrop of empty space. There were no other images in his head, nothing, nothing but a deep and dark void. But then suddenly a picture began to materialize. The image was of him and Lisa, just the two of them, silently packing up cardboard boxes in Casey's bedroom…slowly…mechanical…like robots, methodically going through the motions of taking down the Derek Jeter and Lawrence Taylor posters – Casey's two greatest heroes. Packing up the dozens of trophies he'd accumulated over the years...filling box after cardboard box with cleats and sneakers and jerseys – schoolbooks, fitness magazines, hundreds of photographs of Casey and Kevin...of Casey and Esprit – a history in photographs of Casey's life that covered his bedroom walls. Steve couldn't even begin to come to terms with the thought that Casey's short but brilliant life had come down to this, a bunch of cardboard boxes on the floor.

As the minute hand on the wall clock directly above them slowly crept its way around the dial, not a word was spoken between them, not a tear shed – just complete and utter silence.

As the sun began to rise and shards of morning light cascaded across the calm surface of the Navesink River, Dr. Foster wearily looked up from the monitor of the completed Cerebral Blood Flow Study and thoughtfully gazed out the window of the triage room. There was a certain irony to having a large bay window with a magnificent view of the river right smack in the middle of the chaos that was the triage room. He marveled at the idea that he could still appreciate the simple beauty of a September dawn while standing amidst the chaos and ruin that was directly before him.

The blood flow studies confirmed what he'd already known. There was absolutely no sign of blood flow to the brain. He thanked the neurologist and pronounced Casey's death at 6:17 a.m., on the morning of September 8th.

Dr. Foster now had to go back out and face Casey's parents again, but this time he wasn't going solo. A representative from the Share Network had arrived at the hospital a little earlier and was waiting for him at the central desk. Speaking to the next of kin was clearly not the most favorite part of his work, especially when it involved a child, but he had been down this road many times before, and though it was never pleasant, it was still an important aspect of his job, and as always, he would try to be as compassionate as humanly possible. He walked to the desk and introduced himself to the woman waiting for him; and after a short briefing, together they went in to face Steve and Lisa.

When they walked into the small windowless conference room, Dr. Foster was not surprised to find Casey's parents in virtually the exact same positions as when he'd left them over two hours before. Both of them were just sitting there, emotionally drained, helpless, and silent. He knew from experience that there was no pain in life equal to the psychological pain and suffering of parents who have just lost a child.

Steve and Lisa barely moved when the two people entered the room, and Dr. Foster felt a jab in his gut as he sat down at the table across from them and looked into their emotionally drained faces and bloodshot eyes.

"Mr. and Mrs. Collins, we have finished the second blood flow study and as I expected, there was absolutely no blood flow to the brain. I'm sorry," he said as gently and as softly as he could.

In this situation family members sometimes would hold on to that last glimmer of hope and then be devastated a second time, but in the case of Steve and Lisa, Dr. Foster had intentionally left little room for that in his earlier conversation with them so they would not have to suffer additional pain, disappointment, and shock all over again. He wasn't surprised when they did not respond with a new outburst of emotion.

He continued, "I would like to introduce you to Anne Calahne from the Share Network. I asked her to join us in case the two of you had any questions regarding the possibility of organ donation that we discussed earlier."

Miss Calahne quickly jumped in, "Mr. and Mrs. Collins, I am so sorry for your loss, but I want you to know that the death of your son, as tragic as it is, could possibly save someone else's life this very morning. We have desperate patients all across the country, some in emergency rooms just like this one, with parents just like you, waiting, hoping, praying that someone will find a suitable organ donation for them. I know this is a most difficult time for you, but time is precious! Have the two of you decided if you will allow your son's last act to be one of charity and mercy?"

Steve lifted his head from the table and with lethal, bloodshot eyes he looked directly at the woman. "GET OUT! HOW DARE YOU LAY THAT GUILT-RIDDEN BULLSHIT SPEECH ON US! GET OUT NOW!"

Lisa barely raised her head. She showed no sign of even hearing her husband's outburst.

Not appearing the least bit flustered or upset, Miss Calahne stood up from the table, apologized for causing them any further grief and quietly left the room. Dr. Foster had tried his best, but like most next of kin, the Collinses had reacted quickly and severely to the concept of donating their son's organs. Unfortunately, this was usually the case, but as a medical professional he had to try.

"Mr. and Mrs. Collins, I respect your decision, and it will not come up again, and again I am sorry if this has caused you any further pain."

Steve and Lisa finally looked up at him.

"We would like to turn off your son's respirator in a few minutes, which will then allow his remaining bodily functions to cease. This process doesn't take long, and of course your son will not feel any pain. Would you to like to go in and spend some time with him before we do so?"

This was the moment that Steve and Lisa had been dreading, but also desperately wanting and needing for the last few hours. They both nodded their heads, so the doctor continued, "Okay then, before I bring you in to see your son, I need to discuss with you what's about to happen. By law, because illegal drugs were involved with your son's death, we are required to perform an autopsy to determine the cause of death. The autopsy report will then be forwarded to the police. I should have the initial toxicology report results later today, and I will call you with them. Because of the autopsy, we will be required to keep your son's body for at least the next forty-eight to seventy-two hours. I would guess that the earliest we could release him to you would be Tuesday morning. When the two of you decide who will be handling your son's funeral arrangements, please have them contact the hospital at their earliest convenience. Do you have any questions?"

Steve and Lisa couldn't even begin to register any of what he had said to them. They just stared off into space in total bewilderment. The whole night had evolved into nightmarish kaleidoscope of fragmented scenes and images; the game, the phone call from Kevin, the rush to the emergency room, Esprit, the doctor, the detective – none of it made any sense, and they were so emotionally drained that they couldn't begin to comprehend much of what was happening.

"Mr. and Mrs. Collins?"

Steve came out of his thick fog enough to say quietly, "No…no questions…we just want to see Casey."

Dr. Foster stood up and helped Steve raise Lisa from the table. The three of them walked slowly through the emergency room, Steve, helping the sobbing and helpless Lisa, until they reached the door to the trauma room where Casey's body lay. The medical staff had long ago cleaned up the mess and there in the room lay their son, Casey, on fresh white cotton sheets, his face partially obscured by the intubation tube, still attached to the respirator.

As soon as Lisa got her first glimpse of Casey she began to wail. She ran to his side and clutched his hands, which were lying peacefully at his sides. She buried her face into his chest and began to weep, "My baby…my baby…."

Steve went up to his son's face and repeatedly ran his fingers through Casey's curly dark hair as he watched his chest slowly rise and fall. He looked down at his son's face, and even though it was partially covered, it was calm and peaceful. Steve too began to sob.

Dr. Foster quietly walked out of the room and left them alone with their son. Some time later when Steve and Lisa finally emerged from the room, Dr. Foster was there patiently waiting for them.

"Mr. and Mrs. Collins, I am now going to shut down the respirator, and your son will stop breathing shortly thereafter. It will only take a few minutes, and as I said earlier, he will not feel any pain. Would you like to wait and see him one more time before you go?"

This time it was Lisa who responded, "Yes, doctor, I would like that," she whispered hoarsely.

"Okay, why don't you two take a seat right out here, and I will come back out for you in just a few minutes."

While doctor Foster went back into Casey's room and quickly unhooked him from the respirator, Lisa and Steve sat outside the door, crying in each other's arms, oblivious to the hectic atmosphere of the emergency room that surrounded them. Less than ten minutes later the doctor came out and informed them that it was all over and they could come back into the room.

This time when they entered, Casey was lying serenely on the gurney with no tubes or machines obscuring the view of his face. His curly dark hair was neatly brushed out of his eyes, and his face was peaceful. It seemed to Lisa that he was almost smiling. Until this very moment it had all been just a nightmare, but seeing her son lying there so still and so quiet finally brought the reality of the situation crashing down upon her. She leaned over his body and kissed his face over and over again. "No…no…" came softly from her lips as her tears moistened her son's face.

Steve stood behind his wife holding her. He watched for the rise and fall of his son's chest that he had witnessed just moments before, but now there was none. After several more minutes there was nothing left for either of them to do but cry.

Dr. Foster, sensing that they were finished, softly said, "Now it is time for the two of you to go home and let us take care of your son's body. You've had a long and terrible night. I've arranged for one of our security officers to drive you home, and another will follow in your car."

He handed Steve a small bottle containing a half-dozen pills. "The two of you are physically and emotionally drained. Here are few Valium to help you find a little bit of rest – I am sure you are going to need it. Now please go home and try to get some sleep. I will be in touch with you later today, and once again, Mr. and Mrs. Collins, I am truly sorry for your loss."

Steve and Lisa didn't have the energy to respond. They simply turned around and made their way out of the hospital with the much-needed assistance of the two officers.

Chapter Twenty-One

The Aftermath

Steve and Lisa finally made it home from the hospital around seven a.m. on Saturday morning. It was the start of another warm and sun-drenched day, but they never would have noticed. Not a word was spoken on the drive home, each of them sitting next to the door on their own side of the car, mired in their own misery and staring out the window blankly at the passing scenery as the car made the journey from the hospital to their home.

When they pulled up the driveway and got out of the car the hospital security officer helped Steve to carry Lisa into the house and upstairs to their bedroom. Steve thanked the guard as he walked him out of the house. As soon as he closed the front door he was overcome by the stillness of the house and an overpowering sense of finality brought on by the seemingly insignificant physical act of closing the door. The feeling besieged him and sent him spiraling into a deep and terrifying despair. He stood there shivering for several minutes, unsure of what to do or even where to go, but after a while he came around and dragged himself back upstairs to check on Lisa. When he looked in on her, Lisa was still fully clothed, curled up in the fetal position atop the bed, gazing listlessly out the window at the willow tree beyond.

Steve, concerned for her well-being, covered her with a comforter and then went to the bathroom and fixed her a glass of water. He took the bottle of Valium that Dr. Foster had given him out of his pocket and twisted off the cap. First he swallowed one for himself, and then he shook one out for his wife. He returned to the bedroom and went to her side. She didn't acknowledge his presence so he said, "Here, honey, take this, you need to sleep."

He had to insert the pill into her unresponsive mouth, but after a few seconds she took a sip of water, swallowed the pill, and then simply turned away from him again. He got up from the bed and watched her from the doorway for several minutes. She didn't stir so he left her there in the bedroom and went back downstairs.

Steve almost immediately became agitated by the silence of the house again. He felt a desperate need to do something, anything, or he'd go crazy, but he didn't know what to do. He walked over to the phone to call Ethan as promised, and then decided that he would start calling the rest of the family as well. But as he was about to dial Ethan's number something across the room caught his eye. He looked over at the bar and decided that he needed to dull the pain a little more, so he went straight for the liquor cabinet and pulled out his most expensive bottle of single-malt scotch and a large tumbler. He poured almost five or six ounces into the glass and drank it down in one deep gulp, then he filled the glass again. As the warmth of the alcohol washed down his gullet and spread through his veins, he trembled at the sensation, and then he released a long and heavy sigh. Only after several minutes of relishing the euphoric rush of the alcohol did he finally wobble his way back over to the phone.

When he finally placed the call to the Burke residence, Ethan picked up the phone after just two rings. "Hello, Ethan, it's Steve. I just wanted to let you know that it's all over. Casey was pronounced dead about an hour ago."

Ethan responded softly, "Steve, I am so sorry, I…I…don't know what to say."

"The hospital is not going to release his body until Tuesday at the earliest because they are required to do an autopsy. So we won't have the funeral until at least Thursday." Steve's voice began to crack a little over the phone.

"Steve, I know this is a most trying time for you and Lisa, but I need to tell you something. I just got off the phone with this Detective Morrongiello. He is coming over to interview Esprit later on this morning. I managed to get some of the story as to what happened last night out of her; although God only knows how, she's been crying and vomiting since we got home. We finally got her to take a Valium about an hour ago, and I think she's sleeping now. But I digress. It seems that at the party Esprit's friend Jamie was trying to spike Kevin's beer with some drug called ecstasy, but she inadvertently gave the drugged beer to Casey by mistake. I think the young lady is in a lot of trouble. Anyway, I thought it important to let you know what I was able to find out."

Steve remained silent on the other end of the phone. He hadn't gathered his thoughts enough to even begin to understand what had happened, let alone to start assigning responsibility for his son's death.

After a moment of uncomfortable silence Ethan continued, "Err…Steve, I want you to know that Jordan and I are here for you and Lisa. Please let us know if there's anything we can do."

Steve managed a thank you and hung up the phone. In a zombie-like trance he walked back to the bar and poured himself four more fingers of scotch. Then he returned to the phone and began to call relatives. It took well over an hour and a couple more belts of scotch before he finished making the calls, but when it was over he had sedated himself with enough booze to the point where he could barely stand, so as he fell into his big black recliner. His last conscious thought before passing out was of the missing coffee table that should have been right there at his feet.

Several hours later Lisa began to stir. Somewhere out on the very edge of her consciousness she thought she saw Casey standing before her in a black tuxedo, a curly lock of his hair dangling down just over his left eye, his blue eyes sparkling in the light, a single red rose on his lapel. Standing next two him was Esprit in a stunning white silk and lace wedding gown, holding a bouquet of dozens of perfectly formed red roses, her beautiful face framed delightfully by the multitude of golden curls that were only partially covered by a veil, her arm interlocking his, and both of them laughing merrily together as they walked down an aisle directly towards her.

Lisa thought she might be in a church. She began to look around at the hundreds of people who were standing with her. Family and friends, everyone she knew, they were all crowded around her and all staring right down the aisle at her son, who was walking towards them. Then she heard the sound of church bells ringing. At first the bells were ringing softly, but then they grew louder and louder until they were so loud the sound hurt her ears. Still half in a dream state, she squeezed her eyes tightly and covered her ears because she couldn't understand why the bells were so loud. A feeling of panic began to rise in her chest. She just wanted to make the bells stop! But they grew louder and louder…ring…ring…ring. Suddenly Lisa opened her eyes and realized that she'd been dreaming and the phone was ringing.

It took a moment for her to shake off the odd sensation of the dream, but then she rolled over with a groan and reached for the phone. She looked around for Steve, but he was nowhere to be found. She picked up the phone and in a rough, sleepy voice she whispered, "Hello."

"Good morning, Mrs. Collins, this is Joe Paterno calling. I hope I haven't woken you. I'm sorry I called so early, but I just finished watching the tape of Casey's game last night and I have some good news, I've decided to offer Casey the scholarship. After the game he played last night there was just no way I could let him get away. Could I speak with him please?"

Lisa couldn't believe what she heard and was incapable of a

response at that moment. Dead silence hung in the air for a good ten seconds.

"Mrs. Collins, are you still there?"

The image of Casey's dead body lying so still and quiet in the hospital last night ripped Lisa out of her delirium and she weakly replied, "Yes…Coach Paterno…I'm here. Um…uh…Casey won't be playing for you at Penn State next year…because…because…" she couldn't think of what to say so she just blurted it out, "…because he died last night from a drug overdose!"

Coach Paterno remained silent as Lisa began to sob, and then he realized it wasn't a joke. "Oh my God, Mrs. Collins, I am so sorr…." Before he had a chance to finish Lisa hung up the phone without saying another word.

Casey was dead. Her only son was dead. Lisa sat up in bed and tried to adjust to her surroundings. The emotional and physical fatigue combined with the lingering effects of the sedative were making her head swim. She was nauseous, disoriented, and more than a little frightened, but slowly the things around her began to come into focus and a dark reality began to take shape. Her son was dead.

She had no desire to get out of bed; she was not yet ready to face her son's death. She desperately wanted to go right back to the place in her dream, where her son was alive and smiling, but she knew that was impossible so she dragged her weary body from the warmth of the comforter and forced herself into the shower. The stinging warmth of the spray woke up her body, but her mind was still deeply entrenched in a terrible funk. Even though it was warm and sunny outside, she was chilled to the bone as she dressed in a comfortable warm-up suit and tied her hair back in a ponytail. When she brushed her teeth she couldn't even look in the mirror without tears starting to fall. Every move, every action, seemed to drain her physical strength, yet somehow she found the will to keep going and left her bedroom in search of her missing husband.

As soon she came down the stairs she heard the soft drone of the television set so she walked into the family room. Steve was lying comatose in his recliner, his head lolled to one side, an empty tumbler lying on the floor just inches from his outstretched hand. Lisa sadly looked over at the bar and figured Steve had managed to drink more than half the bottle of scotch that stood on the bar countertop. She scanned the rest of the room. She looked over at the phone and the open phone book beside it and assumed that he must have already called around to the relatives, and she began to cry again.

What the hell am I supposed to do now? God...why did this happen? The anger came rushing back in waves when she thought about the horrific nature of her son's death. The sketchy details began to consume her thoughts. *Who the hell was responsible for Casey's death? Jamie...for putting that drug in his drink? And where did he get the steroids in the first place? It must have been Frank Giordano – there's no one else! Someone is going to pay for this!*

The anger, frustration, and bitterness began to spread through her veins like a drug as she contemplated her next move. Then her thoughts turned to Steve. She looked back at the half-empty bottle and assumed the worst; that he had already retreated behind the veiled curtain of alcohol. *He's going to be useless unless I do something!* She went to the bar and poured the remaining scotch down the bar sink drain. She felt horrible. *If I'm ever going to make it through this day, I'm going to need a cup of coffee...no...a lot of coffee.*

With the empty bottle in hand, Lisa walked past her sleeping husband flashing him a look of disgust. As she headed for the kitchen the phone rang for the second time. She scurried quickly over to the portable, instinctively thinking to hurry so that the ringing wouldn't wake Steve, but then she had a second thought, *Yah right! There's a slim chance of that happening.* She picked up the phone.

"Hello."

"Hello, Mrs. Collins. It's Dr. Foster. I hope I haven't called too early. In situations like this people don't usually sleep very much, and I thought you would want to hear the results of the toxicology report as soon as I had them."

Lisa took a second to compose herself and gather her thoughts. "Yes, Doctor. Thank you. I would."

"Before I began I want to caution you that the legal cause of death has not yet been determined and will not be until the autopsy has been completed. Do you understand that that, Mrs. Collins?"

"Yes, Doctor."

He continued, "Okay then. The initial toxicology screen indicates a dangerously high concentration of anabolic steroids in Casey's bloodstream. It also indicated the presence of methylenedioxymethamphetamine, otherwise known as MDMA or ecstasy. Both of these powerful drugs are illegal, Mrs. Collins, and each by itself is quite dangerous, but when mixed together they can produce a very dangerous and life-threatening condition. Each of these drugs, if abused, can, independently of the other, produce severe dehydration, increased blood pressure, an elevated heart rate, and possible kidney and liver malfunction. Together, under the right conditions they can be lethal. Mrs. Collins, unfortunately your son was experiencing each and every one of those symptoms when he was brought in last night."

"But, Doctor…." she interrupted.

"Wait, Mrs. Collins, there is more. I promise I will answer all of your questions after I have given you the whole picture. In addition to the two illegal drugs, the toxicology screen also showed evidence of unusually high levels of caffeine, as well as a recently banned substance called ephedrine. Both of these substances can cause similar symptoms to the first two, dehydration, elevated heart rate, the works. They most definitely exacerbated his condition. Mrs. Collins, your son's system was so completely inundated with these four substances; if it wasn't for his unbelievable physical condition, you probably would have noticed the symptoms long ago."

Lisa was upset and confused so she interrupted again. "Wait a second, Doctor, I don't understand…I mean…I know how Casey got the ecstasy and I have no choice but to think that he had been on the steroids for quite some time, but I have never seen my boy drink a single cup of coffee, and I don't even know what the hell that other ephedra thing is. None of this makes any sense!"

"Mrs. Collins, both caffeine and ephedrine can be found in hundreds of over-the-counter dietary and fitness supplements. Bodybuilders have been taking this stuff for years. Do you know if your son was taking any supplements?"

Lisa's mouth opened and her chin dropped. "Oh my God! I…I made him a shake every morning with powder that he gave me. I had no idea what was in it. I thought it was just extra protein and vitamins! Oh my God…what have I done?" she cried into the phone.

"Mrs. Collins, please listen to me. I know you are distraught but those substances alone would not have put your son in the condition he was in last night, and there was no way you could have known about the others. Your son's death was not your fault."

"But…."

"Mrs. Collins, please hear me out. There is one more factor that I need to bring to your attention. When your son was brought in, we found a large contusion on his lower back. In addition to the substances that he had ingested into his system, it appears that during the football game last night he received an extremely hard hit in the region of his kidneys and liver. The impact of that trauma alone could have caused severe internal injuries all by itself. Mrs. Collins, I guess what I am trying to say to you is that no one single thing caused this tragedy to happen. Last night your son experienced a confluence of several external factors: the drugs, the supplements, and the football injury, and it was this compounding of these problems that led to your son's tragic and untimely death. Mrs. Collins, the truth is each one of these factors and their unintended consequences contributed to the death of your boy…I'm so sorry. We did everything we could to save him."

Lisa sobbed for a minute. When she regained control she said, "Thank you, Doctor. I know that you did. When do you think they will release him to us?"

"I informed your husband last night that I thought the autopsy would be concluded by Tuesday. I believe that is still the case."

"Thank you, Doctor."

"Mrs. Collins, once again I am truly sorry for your loss, and if you have any further questions, you can reach me here at the hospital."

Lisa hung up the phone and collapsed on a kitchen chair. She didn't have the strength to stand. Not yet. Her eyes wandered to her beautiful back yard, but she saw nothing – not the colorful flowerbeds surrounding the well-manicured yard or the crystal clear, aqua blue water rippling across the pool in the bright sunlight. She heard nothing – not the birds singing on the hedge or the rustling of the leaves in the trees, or even the high-pitched voices of the small children playing in the neighbor's yard, nothing. Instead, she sat there, frozen in the moment, wondering how a just and loving God would allow her whole life, a life which just days ago had seemed so perfect, to fall so far so fast. One week ago she had a beautiful, thriving son and a wonderful, adoring husband. Today her son was dead and her husband lay drunk and unconscious in the other room, and her once cozy life had been brutally ripped apart.

Esprit clung to the last vestiges of her Valium-induced sleep as she clutched tightly the soiled and scruffy Winnie-the-Pooh bear that she had cherished since she was a little girl. As she began to stir, the events of last evening came back to her in a violent rush, and when she opened her eyes the room began to spin. And for what seemed like the fifth day in a row, she got up and ran to the bathroom to throw up. After several minutes of gagging and choking, she finally felt that sense of relief when a bout of nausea finely subsides, but then she was left feeling more drained and fatigued than before.

She laid there with her head resting heavily on the edge of the toilet for several minutes, while gathering up enough strength to stand up. In between her thoughts of despair over Casey, a new thought, one having something to do with her weeklong bouts of nausea began to creep into her consciousness. Could the nausea be from the drugs and alcohol or maybe it was just her system shutting down to deal with the grief. Then another thought came to her, an unwelcome and unsettling thought, and it smacked her in the face. *Oh God, it couldn't be! I've missed taking my pill at least four times this month! Oh God...please...please...don't let me pregnant!*

After a time she feebly stood up, hands braced on the front edge of the bathroom vanity for support and looked at herself in the mirror. Unlike a few days ago when she looked in the mirror and saw someone she didn't even recognize, a girl ravaged by a night of excess, this morning she saw in her face something entirely different. This morning she saw a weariness and sadness in her swollen eyes that had never been there before. It looked to her as if she'd aged ten years overnight. Tears should have followed, but they didn't. A growing combination of fear and fatigue took the place of her sadness and depression.

Esprit had been taking the pill since the summer after her sophomore year, and over the past two years she'd forgotten to take her pill dozens of times, but recently she and Casey had been having sex quite often, and she'd begun to worry about her occasional bouts of forgetfulness. A couple of months before on a whim she'd purchased a home pregnancy test kit to keep in the closet just in case something like this happened.

With great trepidation she reached up to the back of the top shelf of her bathroom closet, behind the hundreds of bottles of make-up and nail polish, and pulled out the kit. She sat back down on the toilet and carefully read the directions on the back before quickly tearing off the plastic wrapper and opening the box.

As instructed, she urinated across the strip and then she set it down on the counter to wait the mandatory five minutes needed for a proper reading. It was perhaps the longest five minutes of her life. As she waited, thoughts of her life with Casey began to work their way into her head, beginning with their first date, when Casey had finally worked up enough courage to ask her out.

There he was shyly approaching her locker at school, he, in his varsity jacket, his head bowed so that she could only see the top of his curly black hair. "Hi, Esprit, I'm…I'm Casey, I don't know if you know me…but I was wondering...would you like to go out…maybe to a movie…or something?"

Esprit laughed and said, "Of course I know who you are. Everyone knows who you are! And yes, I would love to go out with you!"

Casey's face, just moments before flushed with anxiety, was now beaming with delight.

Then the she thought about the first time they'd made love.

Esprit's parents were gone for the weekend, and the two of them were left alone in her big house. Somehow they both knew that this was going to be the big night, and as both were virgins, it was a little tense and awkward. They were watching a movie and began to make out on the big leather sofa in Esprit's media room. Both were ready to explode with anticipation and passion, but each was unsure how to proceed and worried that the other might not reciprocate.

It wasn't long after that Casey was fumbling with her clothing, his mouth never once leaving hers, while unsuccessfully trying to unlock the secrets that were her buttons and zippers. Finally, an exasperated Esprit, desperate to feel his warm skin against hers and totally incapable of waiting a moment longer, broke their embrace. She took off her clothes and then frantically took off his before leading him by the hand up to her parents' bedroom, where they made love over and over again on her father's bed for the entire night and well into the next morning, touching, exploring, moaning, and laughing together before finally falling asleep in the morning from sheer exhaustion.

Then her thoughts turned to the night before.

The two of them, dancing at the party, holding each other so tight, it was difficult to breath, their song playing in the background. Then suddenly Casey went completely limp and fell to the ground. This morning it was all just a whirl of flashing images – the kids screaming for help, the ambulance, the police, the ride to the hospital with the paramedics desperately trying to save Casey's life, and finally, the hospital, the nurse dragging her into the room and her seeing Casey thrashing wildly around, his face contorted in agony as three men tried to hold him down.

Esprit shivered as she snapped out of her reverie and looked at her watch. The five minutes were up, and it was time to face the truth. Before looking at the test strip she closed her eyes and said a prayer. Then she slowly opened her eyes and picked up the strip. What she saw caused her to let out a gasp. She sat back down on the toilet, the test strip in one hand and the directions in the other. Her head swiveled back and forth for a moment, first rereading the instructions on the box, and then staring at the little blue strip showing on the test kit. She dropped the strip and the box carelessly on the floor and rested her head in her hands as she began to cry. The cold reality of her life had begun to sink in, Casey was dead and she was pregnant with his baby.

Lisa had decided to let Steve sleep though some of his grief. He had obviously drunk himself into a stupor, and she wasn't even remotely prepared for dealing with his drama when he finally woke up. Instead, she sat down at the kitchen table, her trembling hands rubbing at her temples, and began to consider what she should do next, but her mind was confused. It was all just a jumble of disparate, yet interconnected thoughts. She panicked because she didn't think she could handle all of this on her own. She picked up the phone and called Claire Kimball, her best friend. Claire picked up after the first ring.

"Hello."

Just hearing her friend's soothing voice made Lisa's mind take off like a rocket. The words tumbled out. "Claire, it's me, Lisa. I need you to come over right away…Casey is dead! He died last night of a drug overdose…I think I'm going crazy…Please…what the hell am I supposed to do now? Who do I call? What about the funeral arrangements? Who should I call for that? And what about his friends? Should I call them? And the school? And what about the newspaper? There's bound to be a big story about this in the paper. Should I take the phone off the hook? I don't want to talk to any damn reporters that's for sure. Oh God…God…please…please come and help me, Claire! I don't know what to do!"

Her shocked friend finally broke into the monologue, "Oh my God! Lisa, honey, I am so sorry! Oh my God! You hang on, okay, Lisa? I'll be there in twenty minutes, I promise!"

Lisa hung up the phone, crying for what seemed like the hundredth time, and rested her head on the table. Just then the doorbell rang, pulling Lisa right out of the void of her despair. *Who could that be?* She thought as she moved to go and open the front door. When she opened it there was a man standing there that she vaguely recognized from last night at the hospital. She looked at him with a bewildered expression.

Sensing that she wasn't sure who he was, he reintroduced himself.

"Hello, Mrs. Collins, I'm Detective Morrongiello. We met last night at the hospital. I waited this morning as long as I could before coming over. I hope I haven't woken you."

Lisa, still flustered, replied, "No…no…I've been up for while. I couldn't sleep."

"Mrs. Collins, I am deeply sorry for your loss, may I come in?"

"Yes."

She walked him into the living room. On his way in he trailed behind her, and he took note of Steve stirring on the couch in the family room and the bottles of liquor sitting on the bar behind him. Lisa offered him a seat on the couch and sat across from him in a club chair. Unfortunately, the seat that she offered him was directly facing a large bay window with the sun streaming right into his face, causing him to squint each time he looked in her direction.

"Mrs. Collins, I have been assigned to handle the investigation of your son's death. Since illegal drugs were involved, it has unfortunately become a criminal investigation." He saw the pain and confusion in Lisa's eyes. "Mrs. Collins, would you like to go get your husband? He should probably hear what I have to say."

"Uh…he is sleeping in the other room…let me see if I can wake him."

As she left the detective alone in the living room to go and wake Steve, Morrongiello scanned the hundreds of photos displayed around the living room. He shook his head in disgust, wondering how something as tragic as this could befall a family that on the surface seemed like it had the world by the proverbial balls. *Nice house…nice car…lots of money…a superstar kid…none of it makes any sense. How the fuck does a kid with all of this wind up on a slab down at the morgue? God must have a really fucking warped sense of humor!*

Lisa re-entered the room with Steve in tow. Detective Morrongiello's first thought was that the husband didn't look in much better shape than the son. Steve's face was a pale yellow in color, his lips were dry and crusted with a white, milky film, and his eyes were swollen almost shut. Without saying a word, Steve collapsed into the club chair opposite the one his wife was sitting in.

Lisa turned to the detective, “I’m going to get my husband a cup of coffee, would you like one?”

“Yes, thank you, Mrs. Collins, I could use a cup. I take it with a little milk and sugar if you don’t mind.”

Lisa left the room and was back shortly with three steaming cups of coffee on an unsteady tray. She carefully handed one to the detective and then one to Steve. Both Lisa and the detective couldn’t help but notice how badly Steve’s hands trembled as he took hold of the cup with two hands and raised it to his mouth.

“Mr. and Mrs. Collins, I am deeply sorry for your loss, but I’m here officially this morning for three reasons: first, to bring you up to speed on the investigation so far. Secondly, to ask you some tough questions concerning your son and his friends. And third, I would like to search your son’s room for possible evidence of a crime. I do not have a search warrant, so you can refuse to allow me into your son’s room, but I was hoping the two of you would cooperate so that together we can figure out how and why this tragedy happened.”

Both Steve and Lisa nodded their heads in weary acceptance.

Detective Morrongiello continued, “After interviewing Casey’s friend Kevin last night, who I must say seems like a fine young man and has no responsibility whatsoever for what happened to your son, we were able to ascertain two key pieces of information. The first piece, I’m sorry to say, is that your son has been taking illegal steroid injections for the better part of a year, and those steroids were being provided to him by one…” the detective paused a moment to look at his notes, “…Frank Giordano, whom I believe was your son’s personal trainer and a local gym owner. Mr. Giordano was arrested about an hour ago and charged with possession and distribution of illegally obtained pharmaceutical drugs. He is at this very moment being interviewed down at the station. Were either of you aware your son was abusing steroids? Please be honest with me. You’re not in any trouble; I’m just trying to get a clear picture of everything that happened."

Steve and Lisa looked at each other with incomprehension, and then Lisa spoke out angrily, "Detective, neither of us had a clue what Casey was doing. If we had, we would have done something about it! However, I will tell you that we both noticed a difference in his behavior recently. Over the last few months he'd become aggressive and easy to anger. This was surprising to the both of us, but we had no idea that it was because of the drugs. And as for Frank Giordano…I'm totally shocked. Frank and his wife are our friends for Christ's sake! I can't believe he would do something like this!"

"Mrs. Collins, for whatever it's worth, I don't think Mr. Giordano meant to do harm to your son. Steroid abuse, because of its popularity and high profile in professional sports, has become an epidemic with high school athletes, especially the top ones like your son. I'm sure that Mr. Giordano, even though he was breaking the law, was only trying to help Casey become the best athlete he could be. Earlier this morning we did a national medical database Internet search on steroid-related hospitalizations and teenage deaths, and I can tell you without hesitation that they are occurring each and every day and in every state across the country. California alone reported eighty-six steroid-related teenage deaths last year."

Lisa gasped, "Oh my God!"

"Mr. and Mrs. Collins, you are aware that your son also ingested a drug called ecstasy last night. Ecstasy is often referred to as a club or party drug, meaning that it is very popular and easily obtainable for teenagers and young adults. Like steroids, its use and associated problems are also rising to epidemic proportions with today's kids. Kevin informed us that Casey did not take the drug intentionally; rather, he was mistakenly given a beer that had been spiked with a hit of ecstasy, a beer that was in fact, meant for Kevin. It seems that Kevin's date for the party…one Jamie Heist…thought it would be fun to secretly dose her date. The nice young lady in question only disclosed this fact to Kevin after Casey had already been taken away in the ambulance.

"According to Kevin, as soon as he found out he rushed to the hospital and informed the doctors the minute he arrived, but by then it was too late. I just left Kevin's house a little while ago, and I can tell you that he is terribly distraught over Casey's death. He believes your son's death was his fault since he knew about the steroids, and he didn't make it to the hospital in time."

Steve looked at his wife and spoke for the first time, his voice scratchy and hoarse. "I will call Kevin later on and speak to him. This was not his fault, and he was a true friend to Casey."

"Thank you, Mr. Collins, I think that would be a good idea. As for Miss Heist, we arrested her at her home this morning and found a half-dozen more doses of ecstasy and a small amount of marijuana in her room. She, like Mr. Giordano, has been arrested for possession with intent to distribute."

Lisa asked a question, "Detective, what about Casey's girlfriend Esprit, have you spoken to her? Did she know about any of this?"

"Yes and no, Mrs. Collins. Actually, I was with her right before I came over here. She too was in terrible shape when I spoke to her, and like the two of you she was completely in the dark about the steroids. However, she admitted to doing some drugs in the past with her friend Miss Heist, but she says she didn't do any last night. We've asked her to take a blood test which will be done later today. When we pressed her on the ecstasy in the beer, she broke down and admitted that she knew what her friend was up to, but she said that she tried to talk her out of doing it, and that she had no idea that Casey had been accidentally given the laced beer instead of Kevin. Because of her father's prominent position in the community, I had no choice but to go easy on her, but I must tell you, though she's far from innocent in her own behavior, I honestly believe she told me the truth, and she had absolutely no responsibility in your son's death."

Lisa began to cry, and Steve reached over to comfort her, but she was not to be consoled.

"Mr. and Mrs. Collins, I have also spoken with Dr. Foster twice this morning, and I must tell you that depending on the cause of death as determined by the autopsy, we may be charging both Mr. Giordano and Miss Heist with the additional charge of second-degree manslaughter. However, like Dr. Foster, I'm inclined to believe that your son's death was an accident, caused more by a series of unintended, yet dire consequences than by any one single person's malfeasance."

Steve and Lisa lowered their heads, unable to respond.

The detective, sensing that the parents had indeed reached the end of their rope, concluded the interview by asking them if they had any further questions, to which they both responded with a simple, "No."

"Okay, then if it would be all right, I would like to go have a look in Casey's room."

As Lisa continued to cry, Steve pointed to the stairs and said, "Make a left at the top of the stairs. It's the first room on your right. And please be quick about it, Detective. I think my wife and I have had about as much as we can take for today."

Detective Morrongiello politely nodded and quickly bounded up the stairs. Less than five minutes later he came back down holding a plastic bag containing the remaining syringes and vials of steroids, which he'd found in Casey's desk drawer. He walked back in to the room and found Lisa and Steve exactly where he'd left them.

"Mr. and Mrs. Collins, I'll be leaving you now. I just want you to know that I did find a box in Casey's desk drawer that contained what remained of his cycle of steroids and some unused syringes. There were no other drugs to be found. I will be taking them in as evidence. And again thank you for your cooperation. I am sorry about Casey. From what I have learned it seems he was a very special young man. You know where to reach me if you have any further questions."

They didn't even look up when he left. As the detective walked out the door, a teary-eyed Claire Kimball came running up the path and entered the house. When she saw Lisa sitting there crying in the living room she burst into tears and ran to comfort her distraught best friend.

Steve stood by watching the two women cry in each other's arms for a few minutes, but watching them made him feel more alone than he had ever been in his entire life. Unacknowledged, he left the room and walked determinedly into the family room and over to the bar. He looked for his bottle of scotch. It wasn't there, so he opened a bottle of vodka and poured himself a large glass.

Epilogue

The Funeral and Beyond

The days following Casey's death and leading up to his funeral proved to be quite trying for just about everyone involved. The autopsy was completed on Tuesday as scheduled. The cause of death was ruled as acute respiratory failure; and though exhaustive tests were done, the medical examiner was not able to pin down exactly what had caused Casey's body to shut down. The steroids, the supplements, the ecstasy and the blunt trauma to his liver and kidney area all could have played a contributing or even primary role in the cause of death.

However, the autopsy report did find that Casey had a grossly enlarged heart and that there were degenerative lesions on his kidneys and necrotic tissue on his liver. It was noted in the final autopsy report that based on the deteriorating condition of Casey's internal organs, it would have been only a matter of time before he would have begun to experience life-threatening problems if not for the circumstances that combined to cause his abrupt and untimely death.

On Tuesday, when Detective Morrongiello delivered the autopsy report to the Collins' home, he informed them that the district attorney's office had made the decision not to add the additional charge of second-degree manslaughter against either Jamie Heist or Frank Giordano. They had all agreed that the autopsy did not provide enough conclusive evidence to merit the indictment of second-degree manslaughter against either party.

Lisa and Steve accepted the DA's decision. They'd done much soul-searching over the last three days, and the two of them, especially Lisa, had come to the sad conclusion that neither Frankie nor Jamie was singularly responsible for causing Casey's death. Rather, Lisa believed, that to some degree, almost everyone involved, including both of them and their dead son, had some culpability in his untimely demise.

However, Lisa had been so utterly shocked and devastated by the information from Detective Morrongiello on steroid-related deaths that she had done a few Internet searches on the subject on her own in the wee hours of the morning over the last two nights. Unable to sleep and angry as hell, she desperately needed to blame someone other than herself or her son, and the drug and supplement manufacturers soon became the target of her wrath.

As Lisa emerged from the bottom of her despair and grief and focused her attention on the myriad of details surrounding Casey's funeral, Steve moved in the opposite direction. When not completely anesthetized by alcohol, he was either sleeping or simply staring out the window from his chair in the family room. At first Lisa tried to talk to him and to get him involved with funeral arrangements so he would at least have some menial tasks to occupy his festering mind, but he wanted nothing to do with any of it. It was way too soon for him to come to terms with Casey's death. By Tuesday, Lisa had given up any hope of him snapping out of his self-induced emotional exile. She was determined to get through the funeral on Thursday in one piece, and only then would she begin to try to deal with her husband's problems.

Leading up to the funeral, the press, both local and national, because of the involvement of a prominent political figure's daughter and the death of a nationally recognized high school athlete, were an ever-present source of agitation to everyone involved. They showed a complete and utter disregard for the privacy of the grieving friends and family, showing up or calling at all times of the day and night, and then sensationalizing even the smallest detail of every aspect of the tragedy in both the electronic and the print media.

Ethan was forced to issue public statements on three separate occasions begging the press to leave his and the Collins family alone. And then finally when they wouldn't heed his repeated requests, he hired a private security firm for both his and the Collins' home. The bold disregard by the media for the family's privacy in this time of grief was beyond appalling. All for the sake of keeping the juicy story alive and running it for one more day.

Ethan also became a solid source of support for Lisa in terms of handling the hundreds of details surrounding the funeral, while Jordan focused her attention on caring for her grieving daughter. Ethan helped Lisa to find a Catholic church to conduct the funeral and even assisted her in selecting a funeral parlor.

On the night before the funeral, Esprit finally made the decision to tell her parents that she was pregnant. This would be the ultimate test to see if her parents had really meant what they said on that fateful night last week when they extolled their love and devotion for her no matter what.

For the first time that week she came out of her bedroom and joined her parents for dinner in the dining room, and rather than wait till the meal was over, she told them as soon as the cook left the dining room. She cried as she told them, and for just a moment, both Ethan and Jordan stared at each other in disbelief, but then seeing their daughter in such great distress they both stood up from their chairs and went to comfort her.

Their reaction was better than Esprit could have hoped for. They agreed to support whatever decision she made in terms of the baby, but strongly advised her that whatever she decided was best left till after the funeral was over. Esprit went to bed that night unsure of what she wanted to do, but content in the fact that her parents were really going to be there for her no matter what the decision.

Casey's death caused Kevin to suffer a deep emotional wound. He honestly believed that he alone could have prevented all of this from happening, and that he alone could have saved his friend. He hadn't slept or even eaten in the three days following the tragedy. On Monday afternoon, Lisa, remembering the conversation with Detective Morrongiello, called Kevin's house and asked his parents if they would bring him over.

She told Kevin's mother that she and Steve really needed to speak with him about what happened. Kevin's parents, fearing for their son's health, prayed that this would help to bring him back from the brink. They readily agreed.

However, Kevin was reluctant, and he had to be physically forced by his father to leave his bedroom. When the Hahns arrived at the Collins' home, Kevin's mother and father literally had to walk him through the front door. Lisa was shocked at Kevin's poor physical state. The young man was so pale and lethargic. He wouldn't even raise his head as his parents sat him down on the couch across from Steve and Lisa.

Lisa had half-expected Steve to take the lead on this discussion since he was the one that expressed so much concern about Kevin on Saturday, but Steve just sat there in his chair, listless and silent, so Lisa stepped in to handle the delicate conversation. She began by telling Kevin that they were proud of him for trying to help Casey, and that he was in no way responsible for anything that had happened.

Kevin looked up at her with tears in his eyes for the first time and tried to express his guilt and sorrow over not doing something sooner, but Lisa quickly cut him off, telling him that Casey was an intelligent young man who should have been capable of making his own rational decisions.

Lisa's comforting words were sinking in; Kevin's demeanor slowly began to change. In those few minutes it appeared as if a great weight had been lifted from his shoulders, hearing those words of absolution coming from Casey's mother were just what he needed. His eyes brightened considerably when Lisa finished the conversation by asking Kevin not only to be a pallbearer but also to speak as Casey's best friend at the funeral.

When Kevin left the Collins' home, his body language and demeanor had changed as though he had been given a new lease on life. Mr. and Mrs. Hahn couldn't begin to express their overwhelming gratitude towards Lisa for what she had just done to help Kevin, even in the midst of all of her own pain and suffering.

By Wednesday, the news of Casey's death and the subsequent funeral arrangements had spread throughout the entire community like an unchecked wildfire. The mysterious death of the local high school football legend was front-page news. The funeral arrangements, usually placed near the end of an obituary, were actually highlighted at the end of the story on page two of the paper. According to the press, there was not going to be a wake, but flowers could be sent to the John E. Day Funeral Home. The funeral mass was to be held at St. Mary's Church at three p.m. on Thursday, followed by an internment service at Mount Olivet Cemetery. Lisa and Steve decided on Mount Olivet because it was the burial home of one of Casey's biggest football heroes – the legendary coach Vince Lombardi.

On Wednesday afternoon the principal at the high school ordered the school to be closed at noon on Thursday so that all students who wished to would be allowed to attend the funeral. The school also brought in a team of outside grief-counselors to be available for any troubled students and then scheduled a memorial assembly to honor Casey for first thing Friday morning. Coach Callahan postponed the upcoming Friday night game and cancelled practice for the entire week to allow Casey's teammates an appropriate period of time to mourn their fallen teammate.

The Funeral

On Thursday morning, for the first time in weeks, the crystal clear skies thickened with menacing clouds and a light rain began to fall. By two o'clock a brisk wind had come barreling down out of Canada, and what had been up till then a light and misty downpour, turned into hard and driving rain. The wind from the north brought with it a damp chill that hadn't been felt in these parts since the early spring. In the hour before the funeral, most of those planning to attend had spent a lot of time running around searching for raincoats and umbrellas.

Steve finished putting on his only black suit and looked in the mirror. He thought he looked like shit. With a shake of his head, he stood up and silently left his wife, still dressing in the bedroom. As he walked downstairs and over to the bar to fix his fourth drink of the day, he looked out the window at the surprising weather and grimly thought that the torrential downpour was somehow fitting for what was about to take place.

He quickly downed a tumbler of scotch, not wanting Lisa to catch him with another drink and start chastising him again, and then he sprayed his breath with Binaca in a futile attempt to hide his drinking from his wife.

He peered out the window at the long dark limousine sitting in the driveway, waiting patiently to take them to their son's funeral. He laughed acerbically, thinking how very far, yet not so far at all he had come in the world. Just twenty-five years ago he and his mother barely had enough money to bury his father. The whole family had driven to his father's funeral at the county graveyard in a ten-year-old beat-up Chevy station wagon. Today he would go to his son's funeral in style, riding in a brand-new shiny black stretch limousine. But it didn't matter; nothing mattered, at least not right at this moment. The only thing that mattered to Steve was to somehow make the pain go away, and the only thing that seemed to work was a drink. He snuck back to bar and quickly poured himself one last pop for the road.

As he let out a long breathy sigh and set the glass down on the bar, Lisa walked into the room. She knew what he was up to, but rather than have another ugly confrontation, she looked disgustedly away and whispered that it was time to go. Steve wiped his mouth with his handkerchief, picked up his coat and umbrella and silently followed her out to the waiting car.

Esprit couldn't shake her deep depression. That she had told her parents about her pregnancy only had a marginal effect on lifting her spirits. Her two closest friends in the world were both gone. One was dead and the other in jail – she had no one to talk to. The daily bouts of morning sickness had done nothing to help her, and today's horrible weather had left her feeling as low as she could possibly be without crawling under a rock. She had no idea how she was going to make it through the service, but for Casey's parents and for Kevin she knew she had to try.

Ethan came to her room and knocked gently on the door, "Honey, it's time to go. We're going to pick up Arthur on the way to the church, and we don't want to be late."

"All right, Daddy, I'll be right down."

She slowly got up from her desk and slipped into her black overcoat and scarf. She walked back over to her desk and picked up a photograph. It was her favorite picture of her and Casey. It had been taken last winter in front of a roaring fire at the ski lodge up at Mount Snow. They had been hugging and smiling at each other, completely unaware of the camera. Their cheeks wore rosy from the cold, and the look of love between them was undeniable. She looked closely at the picture, into his big blue eyes. She clutched the photograph to her breast and held it there. After a moment she set it down and without even realizing it, she let out a soft moan of anguish. Then determined to get through this, she picked up her umbrella and purse and went downstairs to join her parents in the car.

The two limousines pulled into the circular driveway of the church at almost the same exact moment. The large church parking lot and the enjoining streets were overflowing with cars. There were also a couple of TV news vans indiscreetly parked a hundred yards down the street. As Lisa spied the long line of mourners attempting to get out of the rain and into the church, the limousine drivers in both vehicles gently suggested to their occupants that they wait a little while before getting out of their cars. She was a bit shocked by the spectacle of it all. She could hardly believe that hundreds of people were there, and when she saw the entire football team lining up in their khaki pants and varsity jackets to act as honorary pallbearers, it was more than she could stand. She began to cry.

Steve, peering out the opposite window looked disgustedly at the television crews across the street blatantly shooting footage of the football team for the six o'clock news. He just shook his head and reached for his wife.

After another twenty minutes the huge crowd had finally made its way into the church. The football team was now lined up on both sides of the walkway in anticipation of the arrival of the family and the hearse carrying Casey's casket. The Burke family left their limousine first and walked up the stone path. When Esprit saw Kevin she rushed up the walkway and ran to him because it was the first time that she'd seen him since that fateful night five days before. She hugged him for a very long time, and then with tears in her eyes she looked directly at his face. It seemed to her that he too had aged a lot in the last few days.

She hugged him again, and when she did she whispered in his ear, "Kevin, you were the greatest friend Casey ever had. You did everything you could to save him, and I love you for that. Please be strong for him today. That's what he would have wanted. And, Kevin…I need to tell you something important because after the funeral you may not see me for a while."

He looked at her inquisitively.

"Kevin, please, you must keep this a secret…at least for now. I'm pregnant with Casey's baby." And she started to cry.

Kevin was speechless. He looked at her incredulously as she turned away and entered the church with her parents.

As the hearse carrying Casey's casket pulled up to the front of the church, Steve and Lisa finally emerged from their limousine. Arm in arm, they slowly made their way up the walkway, making eye contact with Casey's tearful teammates, who stood at attention as they passed by. When Lisa passed Kevin, she stopped for a moment and kissed him on the cheek before she and Steve continued on.

As they entered the church they were overwhelmed. Even though it was the largest Catholic church in the area, it was overflowing with people. Every single pew was jammed with mourners, friends, family, and students from the school, Steve's co-workers, and what seemed like about half of the town. There were people lined up along both sides of the church and as they passed under the balcony where the choir usually sang, Steve noticed that it too was spilling over with humanity.

As they made their way to their seats in the first pew at the front of the church, both Steve and Lisa couldn't help but notice the hundreds of floral arrangements and sprays that had been sent by friends and family. Once they had taken their seats, the football team, fronted by Kevin and Coach Callahan solemnly led the funeral procession into the church and up to the altar. At the center of the long line of teammates was Casey's casket. It was draped with a beautiful floral blanket in the design of an Eagle.

The casket was carried by six big offensive linemen, including the weeping Shawn Murphy. As the boys slowly proceeded up the center aisle, the choir quietly encircled the altar and began to sing a strange yet beautiful up-tempo hymn called *Shout to the Lord.* The hymn was surprising because it wasn't sad or mournful. Rather, it was almost celebratory in both word and tone, and while it caught many of the older attendees a little off guard, it did wonders to lift the collective spirit of everyone in attendance.

Once the hymn was finished the pastor of Saint Mary's stood up and walked deliberately to the pulpit. All eyes were upon him as he began his sermon, and not unlike the hymn, he delivered a passionate yet upbeat sermon that focused on the joy of Casey's early ascension to heaven and on the many accomplishments of his brief but extraordinary life.

Though not churchgoers, both Lisa and Steve were spiritually moved by the pastor's sermon, and their spirits were lifted by the outpouring of love that could be felt throughout the church. When the sermon was over, it was time for the eulogy. Over the past few days Lisa had considered the idea of having several different people deliver eulogies but felt that might be overdoing it. She also didn't wish to insult Kevin, being Casey's best friend and all, so in the end she determined that Kevin would be the only speaker.

The pastor looked down at the second row and beckoned Kevin to come up to the pulpit as the choir began another spiritual hymn. Kevin, seated directly behind Steve and Lisa with his parents, took a deep breath before making his way to the altar. He looked incredibly uncomfortable in the stiff black suit that his parents had bought for him only the day before, but his eyes were dry, and he was determined to speak for his friend with dignity. Kevin reached the pulpit and rested his hands on the sides as he took a moment to compose his thoughts. He did not want to read from a prepared text. He wanted to convey his love for Casey in the most simple and natural way possible and so he began.

"Casey Collins was my best friend, and he was bigger than life. Everybody loved Casey and he loved them right back. He was the kid that all the girls loved and all the boys wanted to be like, but for some reason, no one was ever jealous of. He was friends with just about everyone, and he didn't have a mean bone in his body – except on the football field. He was smart and handsome and strong. He was all of these things, but to me he was more than all that. He was an unbelievable friend.

"When I first met Casey back in seventh grade, I was a shy little kid who had just moved here from south Jersey. I didn't know a soul. I remember him coming up to me on the first day of class out of the clear blue and he said, 'Hey, new kid, what's your name?' When I told him he said to me, 'Okay, Kevin, welcome to Middletown, I'm Casey, why don't you come over to my house after school and I'll introduce you around to some of the guys? And if you need anything – anything at all – you just come and find me!' I couldn't believe it! Here I was this shy little kid, afraid of his own shadow, in a new school and this big, happy, and obviously popular kid takes the time to make me feel welcome. I just couldn't believe it. I knew right then and there that he was going to be my best friend.

"Over the years Casey was always right there beside me. In eighth grade when I broke my leg surfing, he was at the hospital before I was even out of the emergency room with a stack of comic books and a pocketful of candy bars. When we lost the State Championship in my sophomore year because I threw that interception at the end of the game, he was right there by my side telling me it was okay, and that we would get them next year, and you know what? He was right! We did get them next year.

"I don't want to stand up here and make Casey out to be a saint. He was just a kid like the rest of us, and he had his problems too. But the difference was that he wasn't afraid to face his problems head-on. If he struggled with a class, he studied that much harder, if we lost a football game, he would outwork everybody on the practice field until we were that much better. If he had an argument with someone, he would not rest till it had been resolved and the friendship repaired. I remember one time last summer I was mad at Casey because I thought he had blown me off on a planned surfing trip to Long Beach Island to go out on date with Esprit, and I was totally pissed…er…I mean upset. He must have called me ten times the next day to apologize. I wouldn't take his phone calls, so he snuck over to my house and climbed up to my bedroom window and taped a poster on it that read, 'Dude, I'm sorry!' When I saw that stupid poster and him standing there like a jerk on my roof – and I thought about what he had done, the most popular kid in school – just to say he was sorry, I couldn't help but laugh. So I let him in and ten minutes later we were in his Mustang with our boards sticking out the back on our way down to L.B.I. That's the kind of kid he was.

"But I said before that he wasn't perfect. Nobody is. Casey's greatest strength was also perhaps his biggest weakness. He always had to be in control, and he truly believed that you could solve any problem and find the answer to anything by simply putting your mind to work. He approached everything like that, his schoolwork, his friendships, and especially football. He believed that if you did everything that you could possibly do, then things would always work out – as long as you gave it your all. And for most of Casey's life, this idea worked for him, but unfortunately it led to some problems. First of all, it led him to set unrealistic expectations for himself and also for those that were closest to him. He had no tolerance for failure, especially if he felt that the person who had failed him had not given the problem everything that they had. There were times when he was pretty tough on me and on Esprit, and he was really tough on his parents. No matter what they did, he seemed to always expect something more. I know Mr. and Mrs. Collins pretty well, and I can tell you they are two of the greatest people in the world."

Kevin paused a moment to look over at Lisa and Steve, who were sitting there weeping unashamedly.

"Perhaps Casey's biggest problem was that he just didn't know what he didn't know. He honestly believed that he could quickly find the answer to everything if he searched for it hard enough, and this was why he turned to steroids. He felt that he needed to get bigger to be the best damn football player in the country; a goal that he was determined to reach this year. I remember watching him read up on everything he could find on the subject of steroids before he started taking them, and when I begged him not to do them, he just looked at me and said, 'Kev, what's the big deal? I've looked into this, and I know what I'm doing. As long as I am careful, nothing's going to happen.' And you know what? He believed that! He wasn't just saying it. He believed every word. He just knew that he could do this the right way and that he wouldn't get sick, but he was wrong…so wrong!

"Casey had been sick for the last couple of weeks. I knew it and he knew it. Last week I begged him to stop, and I threatened to tell Coach Callahan. He didn't get mad at me, he just promised me that he would stop, so I kept my mouth shut, and I will have to live with that for the rest of my life. I tried to help him…I did…I…I guess I just didn't try hard enough.

"For those of you who only knew of Casey by reputation, he was better than what you heard. For those of you that knew him well, I know that you will miss him terribly. I know that he is up there in heaven right now, probably telling God to run a fly pattern and probably starting a football team. I just want to say that I love Casey Collins…that losing him is the most painful thing I have ever felt…and that I miss him so much it hurts inside…."

Kevin had kept his act together for most of the eulogy, but as soon as he finished he began to cry, and as the pastor helped him back to his seat there was not a dry eye in the church. After several minutes of silence and prayer, the pastor announced that all would be welcome at the cemetery for the burial service. Then the choir began to sing again as the teammates slowly carried the casket back out of the church. Steve held the weeping Lisa as they followed their son's casket down the long center aisle. They were closely followed by the Burkes as Ethan tried in vein to comfort his weeping daughter.

Virtually every single person that attended the funeral mass also went on to attend the burial service. The line of cars stretched almost a mile as the procession made its way the short mile and a half from the church to the cemetery. More than a dozen police cars were required to move the enormous procession, and it took almost an hour before everyone had reached the small cemetery and found a place to park their cars. The surrounding side streets were jammed with vehicles. Some of those attending had to walk almost a quarter of mile just to reach the cemetery. But it didn't matter. They needed to be there to grieve alongside Casey's friends and family, and they needed to pay their respects.

Because of the rain, the actual interment service was mercifully short, only about fifteen minutes. When the internment finally concluded, and everyone had left the cemetery but the immediate friends and family, Steve went around the small group and handed each of them a single red rose. He then invited everyone there to come back to his home for a small gathering afterwards.

One by one, beginning with Kevin and followed by Esprit, they each approached Casey's casket and laid a single rose on its cover, and then they slowly made their way to their cars. When everyone else had left, Steve and Lisa gently placed the last two remaining roses on the casket. They stood there silently for several minutes and then they too simply walked away.

The Following Months

The lives of everyone involved with Casey's tragic death were forever changed in the months following his funeral. The unintended consequences of their actions and the unseen forces of nature – forces that we sometimes feel, but never truly know, nor understand – endeavored to work their magic on each of the individuals that previously held a place in Casey Collins' inner circle of life. In some cases, those forces were undoubtedly dark and tragic, while in others, the magic manifested itself in a rebirth of sorts for those more fortunate.

In early November a woefully sad and deeply depressed Frank Giordano was tried and convicted of possession and distribution of illegal pharmaceutical drugs. The maximum sentence was eight to twelve years in prison, but because it was his first offense and the State of New Jersey maintained a policy of 'Presumption against Incarceration' for first-time non-violent offenders, he was given five years probation and a fifty-thousand-dollar fine. However, his trainer's license was permanently revoked, and he was also given a lifetime ban from working directly with children in any capacity. Immediately after the funeral he went to Steve and Lisa and begged their forgiveness. Lisa was willing, and in fact she testified as a character witness on his behalf at the trial. Steve on the other hand continued to blame him for his son's death and refused to speak to him.

Jamie Heist, being eighteen years of age at the time of Casey's death, was tried as an adult, and unfortunately she was not a first-time offender. She'd been arrested once before as a juvenile for possession of a small amount of marijuana. She was tried and convicted of possession of narcotics with intent to distribute. She was given six months in the county jail, but the sentence was suspended at the request of Casey's parents. She too was given five years probation, a ten-thousand-dollar fine and three hundred hours of community service. She was also required to spend twenty-eight days in a drug rehabilitation center. While in her first week at the rehab center she was notified by her parents that she had been expelled from school, and she didn't take the news very well. She ran away from the center early the next morning and no one has heard from her since, although she did attempt to call Esprit on two occasions after her escape, but Esprit refused to take her calls.

Coach Callahan was deeply troubled by Casey's death. He knew in his heart that he had been in a position to help Casey, but he hadn't because winning at any cost was more important.

That fact would continue to eat away at him for the rest of his life. He continued coaching, but with a heavy heart and a guilty conscience. But even so, he led the Eagles football team to its eleventh State Championship that December.

However, on the night before the championship game he abruptly announced that he was retiring from coaching following the next day's game. He was allowed by the school board and the athletic director to name his successor, and a week later he named his offensive coordinator, Coach Martin, as his successor to be the new head coach of the Middletown South Screaming Eagles.

Casey's death affected Kevin Hahn in so many ways. The tragic loss of his best friend forced him to mature quickly beyond his years. Gone was the fun-loving free-spirit surfer-boy attitude. It had been replaced by a fierce commitment to live up to the imaginary expectations of his dead best friend. Not long after Casey's death, Kevin became totally engrossed with the notion that is was now up to him to finish what Casey had started and make it to the NFL. He rededicated himself to football in honor of Casey's memory and proceeded to break most of the single-season quarterback records for passing and touchdowns in the State of New Jersey. He also worked diligently in the weight room and added almost fifteen pounds to his slight frame by December. The records and the additional weight he put on forced quite a few division-one colleges to give him a serious look. In the end he accepted a scholarship to Colorado State University. It was the largest division-one school to offer him a full ride, and it was close to some real great mountains where he could snowboard in the off season. He remained in close contact with Esprit, and the two of them talked at least once a day on the phone, and together they kept the memory of Casey alive.

Esprit came to the conclusion shortly after the funeral that the best way to keep her memory of Casey alive was to keep the baby. She briefly considered both an abortion and giving the child up for adoption, but she quickly decided that either choice would be impossible under the circumstances. Ethan and Jordan wholeheartedly supported her decision to keep the baby, but they were more than a little concerned when she informed them that she did not want to return to high school. Esprit told them that she just didn't think she could handle being under the spotlight that would exist at school because of Casey's tragic death and her pregnancy.

Jordan, always the problem-solver, of course came up with an equitable solution. Two weeks after Casey's funeral, Esprit moved halfway across the country to her parents' house in Vail, Colorado, where she finished her senior year with private tutors and a private nurse to monitor her pregnancy. No one at school knew what happened to her accept Kevin, and he promised to take her whereabouts and her pregnancy with him to the grave.

Esprit finished her home schooling by mid-January. She then applied and was accepted to the Yale School of Drama for the following fall semester. And on April 1st of the following year with both her parents at her side, she delivered a very healthy eight-pound-twelve-ounce baby boy who she named Casey Collins Burke.

The publicity surrounding Casey's death didn't hurt Ethan's congressional campaign one bit. In fact, in early November the sympathy vote garnered Ethan an unprecedented thirty-two-point landslide over his opponent. Just after the New Year, with the full support of Arthur and the National Republican Party, Ethan announced his candidacy for the United States Senate. Jordan, since the funeral, had been forced to split her time as doting mother and supportive wife on the campaign trail, but as Esprit's due date drew closer she found herself more in Colorado with Esprit and less on the campaign trail beside her husband, and that was okay with her.

Lisa and Steve's once rock solid marriage was truly put to the test in the months following Casey's death. Steve's drinking increased dramatically, and as it did he and Lisa were pulled further and further apart, both physically and emotionally. Lisa tried to keep it together in the beginning. She repeatedly begged him to seek help for his problem, but he simply refused and continued to drink away his depression. Finally, one day after a particularly nasty episode where Steve had passed out on the ferry home from work, and she was called by the police to come and pick him up at the dock, Lisa just gave up and decided to move on with her life.

She had spent much of her time in those weeks following Casey's death researching teenage steroid abuse. She seriously considered suing the drug manufacturers because she became aware through her research that there were many types of steroids being produced by these companies that had no other practical or medicinal purpose whatsoever other than to illegally increase muscle mass. However, in the end she was dissuaded from this course of action by several prominent, trial lawyers. They informed her that she would be fighting a costly and losing battle that would only get tied up in the courts for years by the highly paid legal teams representing the major drug companies.

Dejected but not defeated, she created a charitable foundation instead whose sole purpose was to travel around the country on speaking engagements with both student athletes and their parents about the dangers of steroid abuse.

Ethan Burke became her biggest supporter, and he assisted her with the initial fundraising. He also sponsored a bill in Congress calling for more restrictive laws on the production of certain types of anabolic steroids and tougher penalties for those companies that broke the law.

By January of the following year, Lisa had set up her foundation and was traveling throughout the country speaking to kids about what had happened to her son. Not long after the foundation began in earnest, she called a despondent Frank

Giordano and asked if he would like to join her on the road, believing that although he had played a major role in the death of her son, he could still become a positive voice and a guiding light to others by speaking candidly about his past experience with steroids.

As Lisa emerged even stronger from her son's death, Steve continued to freefall into the muck and mire of alcoholism. The guilt that he suffered over his son's death and also the state of their troubled relationship just prior to it could only be lessened by anesthetizing himself with a daily bottle of scotch. He began drinking every day, and soon thereafter throughout the day – morning, noon and night.

He went back to work a week after Casey's funeral, but he couldn't focus on his trading and very soon thereafter his position began to suffer. He quickly started losing hundreds of thousands, and then millions of his firm's money, and though his bosses were sympathetic to his recent tragedy, they couldn't allow him to continue to generate such tremendous losses. When they began to confront him about the losses, the pressure became even more unbearable, and his only way out was to drink more. It was the only way he could find to make the pain go away.

By this point Lisa had pretty much written him off and was already out touring the country with her foundation. He was all alone with his misery. One night after an exceptionally bad day where he'd lost over a quarter of a million dollars, he decided that rather than going home to an empty house and drinking alone, he would go to a local Wall Street pub and drink himself into oblivion in the presence of other men just like him. He sat at the bar for eight solid hours drinking shot after shot until he passed out on the dirty wood floor. At the end of the night the crusty Irish bartender simply picked him up and dragged him out the front door and left him passed out cold on the frozen sidewalk.

Two New York City policemen found him around three in the morning lying in a puddle of his own urine, and since it was well below freezing outside they called an ambulance to come pick him up and take him to the psyche ward at Belleview.

The next morning Steve woke up strapped into a hospital gurney, and as his eyes focused on the alien surroundings he recognized someone vaguely familiar standing over him. It was his friend, Dick Morris from work.

Dick shook his hand and said, “Hi, Steve, I’ve been waiting for you to wake up. Welcome to the club!” For the next two hours Morris shared with Steve his own downward spiral into the darkness of alcoholism. Then he spent another hour sharing his experience, strength, and hope since joining Alcoholic’s Anonymous.

While they were talking, Steve remembered the change in Dick, and he respected the hell out of him for it, so he figured he had little left to lose, and he listened with a renewed interest. When Dick finished he said, “Steve, I’m gong to give you this little book and then leave for a while so you can get dressed. Then I am going to come back and take you out to lunch, and then if it’s okay with you, I am going to bring you to a place where you will be among friends.”

Steve, still bewildered by the whole thing, but desperate to do something to help himself, readily agreed. Later on that day Steve went to his first AA meeting with Dick Morris, and when the meeting began he heard the entire group recite a simple little prayer. When he heard that prayer, for the first time in months, he smiled because something dawned on him, and he knew his life was about to change for the better.

Three days later Steve entered an alcohol treatment and rehabilitation center. Twenty-eight days after that, on the scheduled day of his release, as he was signing himself out and saying goodbye to the staff, he heard a small cough, so he turned around and there was Lisa, just standing there waiting for him in the lobby of the hospital.

She was standing there quietly with a dozen red roses in her arms and a beautiful smile on her face. Steve ran to her and gave her the biggest hug of his life. Then they sat down and talked, really talked for a good long while, she about her foundation, and he of his newfound experience, strength and hope.

Steve left the hospital that day knowing that he was indeed an alcoholic and fully aware that unlike his son, he'd been given, by the Grace of God, a second chance. As he and Lisa walked arm and arm out the doors of the hospital to begin a new life together, Steve kissed his wife and then he let go of her hand for just a moment and got down on his knees. He looked directly up to the beautiful sky, so full of sunshine and promise, and he repeated the little prayer that he had heard just over one month before. The simple little prayer that saved his life:

God,
Grant me the serenity
to accept the things I cannot change,
the courage to change the things I can,
and the wisdom to know the difference.

The End

Authors note

This story is a work of fiction. The central characters are all products of my imagination. Any resemblance to an actual living person is merely coincidental, with the exception of the two college football coaches, Pete Carroll and the legendary Joe Paterno, two extraordinary men who represent what is good and pure about the sport of college football. They are the best that college athletics has to offer.

I selected Monmouth County, New Jersey as the backdrop to this story because it is a local I am quite familiar with. All of the scenes and locals are in fact real places, and some of the minor characters are friends of mine in real life. I thank them for their part in my story.

I am proud to say that I am an alumnus of Middletown South High School, Class of 1978. I incorporated the proud Middletown South Football Program as the model for my story for the following reasons: they have a tradition of excellence that goes back almost twenty years and has become the model that all other area high schools try to emulate. But more importantly, I was inspired to write this story as I watched my nephew and his fellow teammates go undefeated and win three straight State Sectional Championships in a row from 2002 to 2004.

To the best of my knowledge there has never been any steroid usage in the Middletown Football Program, and because of their perennial success and popularity, the South football team volunteered to become one of the first schools in the State of New Jersey to approve mandatory random drug testing for their athletes.

The graphic locker room hazing scene was created strictly from my imagination. However, this kind of cruel hazing continues to plague high school sports across the country and is a problem that should be dealt with once and for all.

I had little previous expertise in medicine or in steroid abuse prior to writing this story. My motivation for writing about it was simply to bring about an awareness of the problem at the teenage level. Any errors or inaccuracies regarding the science and medicine should be attributed to my somewhat limited research capabilities, and not to the fine editors of this book.

As to the political views of the characters, I don't believe there is a right or wrong side to be on, but I do believe every citizen has an obligation to get involved and understand how our government really works.

And one final point, I hope this story left you with this one lasting thought – that no one's perfect and perhaps there's a little bit right and a little bit wrong in everyone.

Brian Daneman

www.ingramcontent.com/pod-product-compliance
Lightning Source LLC
Chambersburg PA
CBHW030822310726
48980CB00006B/597/J

* 9 7 8 0 5 7 8 0 0 8 0 9 7 *